S.S.F. Public Library
West Orange
840 West Orange Ave.
South San Francisco, CA 94080

W9-BRU-667

FEB 19

THE WIDOWS

JESS MONTGOMERY
THE WIDOWS

 MINOTAUR BOOKS ⚏ NEW YORK

This is a work of fiction. All of the characters, organizations, and events portrayed
in this novel are either products of the author's imagination or are used fictitiously.

MINOTAUR BOOKS
An imprint of St. Martin's Press

THE WIDOWS. Copyright © 2018 by Sharon Short. All rights reserved.
Printed in the United States of America. For information, address St. Martin's Press,
175 Fifth Avenue, New York, N.Y. 10010.

www.minotaurbooks.com

The Library of Congress Cataloging-in-Publication Data is available upon request.

ISBN 978-1-250-18452-8 (hardcover)
ISBN 978-1-250-18453-5 (ebook)

Our books may be purchased in bulk for promotional, educational, or business use.
Please contact your local bookseller or the Macmillan Corporate and Premium Sales
Department at 1-800-221-7945, extension 5442, or by email at
MacmillanSpecialMarkets@macmillan.com.

First Edition: January 2019

10 9 8 7 6 5 4 3 2 1

To David,
the love of my life,
now and always

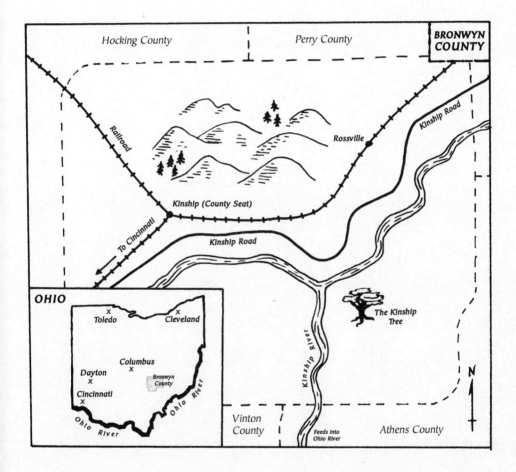

PROLOGUE

September 20, 1924

A hawk soars over Devil's Backbone. Her sharp eyes peer through the softening light of dusk down to the old Rossville Cemetery, closed a decade past, when the dead had filled every apportioned spot.

There: a chipmunk scuttling among the gravestones, some still upright and tended by descendants, some cracked and broken, like scattered teeth.

The red-shouldered hawk spots it, but a thunderstorm is rolling in, great coal-dark clouds churning across the sky from the west. Rain comes sudden, hard. And so she veers east, toward the entry to Ross Mining Company's Mine No. 9, nicknamed the Widowmaker after the 1888 cave-in killed forty-two men.

Six weeks ago, though, the mine was reopened, for deep in the western slope of this Appalachian foothill, in her seams and fissures and walls, rests anthracite coal of the highest grade, coal that will command the best market price. A select portion of the company's coal miners labor to reopen the Widowmaker, building tracks for mule-pulled wagons, and supports for walls and ceilings.

Now the miners trudge out after a nine-hour day. Theirs is a good weary, born of the ache and pull of hard work done well. Since the start of the project they've each received an extra ten cents per day of company scrip—issued instead of good old U.S. cash, and the only tender the company will accept for rent or in its company stores. In a few days, the additional scrip can buy yeast at the company store. In a week, tinned milk. In a few weeks, cheese. Enough that men who labor away in the company's other mines closer to Rossville are envious.

But what the men don't know, what no one knows, is that methane gas—nonodorous, undetectable—is building up near the newly reopened entry, just as it had in 1888.

Now the hawk soars above the entry.

There: a squirrel scuttling among the brush near the man-made mouth into the mountain.

Three men emerge, heading toward the donkeys and wagons that will take them back to Rossville proper. Most of the others, seeing the light, pick up their pace, eager to get home.

Two miners, though, lag so deep in the shaft that they still use their coal-oil lanterns to light their way through the dark, as deep and still as midnight.

"You lollygagging for a purpose?" asks the one farthest along. It is not like his friend to dally. He knows his friend's baby's been sick. He wonders if there's bad news to share that his friend doesn't want the others to hear.

The second man does have a reason, but not about the baby—she's taken a turn for the better. Another subject presses on his heart and mind and he's not sure how to broach it. Still, if he doesn't speak up now, he's not sure he'll ever get the courage. "John says—"

"Don't go tellin' me about John!" The first man waves his hands as if to fend off the very mention of the organizer who'd helped unionize the Mingo Mines up in northeastern Ohio and was now working among the men at Ross Mining. "My woman's got a chopped steak waiting, for my supper, first one in a month of Sundays. I ain't risking decent pay for once."

The second man thinks how his wife and their four-year-old son were delighted by their first tastes of ice cream at the company store just a few days ago. He'd had a taste, too.

But he presses on: "Good for now, but what about a week from now, a year from now? They ain't paying us extra for easy work."

Outside, the squirrel scurries down the slope, away from the mine's entrance, oblivious to the hawk circling above. The squirrel is simply following its instinct to prepare for winter, one acorn at a time, and for a moment the squirrel is lucky.

Lightning strikes near the entrance to the Widowmaker. The strike ignites the methane, and the explosion demolishes the entrance.

The two lollygaggers hear the explosion and the crash and the cries of their comrades farther up the shaft. The two men stop, stare at each other.

Before they can move or decide what to do, Devil's Backbone gives a great shake, as if trying to rid itself of some pest. The support frame over the first man buckles and then crashes.

The second man falls to the ground, clasping his helmet. Rocks, dirt, and splintered wood fall on his hands and back. He sits up, slowly, gingerly. His right arm throbs. It is broken in two places, just above the elbow and again at the wrist.

But he can breathe. He can breathe.

He gulps in great gasps of air, staving off nausea triggered by waves of pain.

He calls for his friend. No answer. Calls again. Silence.

He realizes his lamp is gone. With his shaking left hand, he reaches into the pocket of his bibbed overalls, feels past his cigarette, the one he'd carefully rolled at break time for smoking at the end of the workday. A flick, and the lighter's flame is sufficient to reveal that behind him, too, is a cave-in. He doesn't see the lamp. Likely it was crushed. This tiny flame is his only light, but it is sufficient to reveal that he has about a five-foot circumference around him.

The light burns steady, unwavering. There is no fresh air coming through this new chamber.

For a moment, he considers standing up, leaning against the wall, and smoking his cigarette. No use dying while wishing for tobacco. There is, he reckons, maybe two hours of good air left. It's gonna take longer than that for help to reach him. And by then he'll be suffocating on his own exhaled fumes.

But then—though it is bad luck for a woman to come into a mine— he conjures the image of his wife. Sees her smiling at their son, spooning up ice cream.

He flicks off the lighter. He sits down, breathing shallowly and slowly as possible, trying not to waste precious breath with gasps of pain. He closes his eyes. Somehow the darkness behind his closed eyes—not a shade different from the dark around him—is better. He can just pretend he's sleeping, that his own shallow breaths are hers, sleeping next to him.

On the other side of the rubble, his friend lies still, too, but he's already dead, his legs and spine crushed by fallen rock, his arms splayed forward, his skull split on the floor.

Farther up, near the collapsed mouth of the mine, three other men are also already dead. But the crew leader, nearest the front, sees pinpricks of light in the tumbled entry, like stars. Then he hears one of the men outside, calling that they will go for help.

Outside at the bottom of Devil's Backbone, just as the squirrel reaches the bank of Coal Creek, the hawk finally swoops, talons outstretched, and snatches her prey.

CHAPTER 1

≫

LILY

Six Months Later—March 25, 1925

Lily sweeps the jail cell for the next prisoner, set to arrive in a few hours. There's so much to do on this fine March day. Besides readying this cell, she needs to turn the garden soil, beat the rugs, and clean the sooty glass shade of the hanging coal-oil lamp in the dining room.

Her side stitches—sudden, hard. Lily gasps, forgetting her list of spring-cleaning chores. She steadies herself with the broom and swallows, fighting back a wave of nausea.

Queasiness has found her early this time around. *At twenty-six, carrying a child is harder than when you're young!* That's what Mama would say—if she knew. Lily has yet to share the news of this child with anyone other than Daniel.

"Hey, lady, gimme more coffee afore you keel over!"

Lily starts sweeping again, harder now, so dust and debris skitter past the tidy pile she's made in the empty cell and into the occupied one. The prisoner jumps back, giving Lily grim satisfaction. She wishes Daniel hadn't needed to leave this morning, but duty had called her husband, the sheriff, to fetch another prisoner from the farthest corner of Bronwyn County.

"You trying to ruin my breakfast?"

Usually, prisoners are respectful toward her. But not Harold Johnson. She knows his name because as jail mistress one of her duties is to keep a record of each prisoner who comes through the Bronwyn County jail. Her records are meticulous, to the point of pridefulness.

"I been held too long already. More'n twenty-four hours!"

Less than twelve hours. Every prisoner thinks he's held longer than is rightly fair.

Lily leans her broom by the cell door and expertly flips the straw mattress.

"And I—I need a doctor!" he yells before belching loudly.

Another wave of nausea hits Lily. She swallows hard again and steps toward the large quilt chest in the corner behind her desk, opens the chest, and pulls out a clean sheet, pillow, and blanket for the just-turned straw mattress. He wolf-whistles at her bent-over form and laughs.

Lily slaps the linens back into the chest. Then she steps to the cabinet against the back wall, opens the narrow drawer labeled "J," and pulls out Harold's card. She slams the drawer shut so hard that the cabinet shudders, and then sits down in her chair. She crosses her left leg over her right knee and pulls her skirt up just far enough to reveal the small derringer strapped to her ankle—a gun so compact that it's nicknamed a stocking pistol. A woman's gun, with only a single round, but sufficient, should a prisoner get out of hand. So far, she's never had to use it.

Lily reads from the card the notations made in her own neat, angular handwriting. "Says here, the sheriff brought you in yesterday for public disturbance at the Kinship Inn, where you busted up two of the more elegant chairs in the lobby and left the proprietor with a severely disjointed nose. Hit poor Mr. Williams hard enough to sprain your own wrist!"

Still, the prisoner sure isn't having any trouble wolfing down his biscuits and gravy, using the hand poking out of the sling she'd given him for his sprained wrist the night before. He had not been rude then, for Daniel had stood by watchfully.

Lily puts the card down on the table, picks up a pencil, and taps its point on the card. "Now, you can choose to either act respectably, or I can add harassment to your charges."

With a filthy fingertip of his good hand, Harold taps the silver, eagle-shaped Pinkerton National Detective Agency badge on his tattered lapel.

"See this here? This means you can't treat me like just any prisoner. You hafta show me respect, woman!" He tosses the plate, with his half-eaten breakfast, to the floor. The tin plate skitters, unbroken, toward the bars. "I want a new breakfast! And I wanna see Mr. Ross!"

He doesn't mean her husband, Bronwyn County Sheriff. He means Luther, Daniel's half brother and manager of Ross Mining, over in Rossville. Luther would undoubtedly take up for Harold, even egg him on. The very thought of Luther makes her want to shudder.

But Lily does not move. The door to the jailhouse is open, and from outside come the clucks of chickens in her yard—many housewives in town still keep backyard chickens and gardens, a money-saving effort left over from the Great War—and the sounds from Kinship's main street of foot traffic and horses and the occasional automobile driving by. She allows herself a moment to take in the comforting sounds of an ordinary morning, now well under way. When she speaks, it's so quietly that the prisoner has to lean toward the bars to hear.

"You have no authority. That badge means nothing here."

As sheriff, Daniel was supposed to handle any miners who caused property damage or committed other crimes on Ross Mining land—which encompassed all of Rossville. But the rest of Bronwyn County was also under the sheriff's jurisdiction. With only a part-time deputy, Daniel had grudgingly accepted Luther's decision to bring in hired police agents from the Pinkerton agency, as restlessness grew after the Widowmaker deaths.

Lily has overheard Daniel complain to Martin Weaver, his deputy, that the Pinkertons are desperate men who can't get work elsewhere either because of their own dark pasts or lack of skills or because they are immigrants no one wants to hire outside of mining.

"You know, I been watching you, and not just 'cause you're a pretty thing. You're fixing up that cell, but there's two cots in here. So why not just have your *husband*"—somehow, he turns the word lurid—"toss the new fella in with me? Easier on you. I figure either you got a woman prisoner coming, and that's mighty unlikely, or the prisoner ain't someone you want mixed in with me." He widens his grin, wolflike. "I reckon the sheriff got himself a coal miner."

With that, he spits a foul wad through the bars, into the cell Lily has just cleaned.

For a long moment, Lily stares at the man. He'd pieced together a good bit. For last night, after they'd locked up him up, they'd had a surprise visitor come during suppertime. Another Pinkerton man whom Daniel talked to in the parlor.

When that Pinkerton had gone she asked Daniel, *What does he want with you?*, and he muttered, *Gotta fetch a new prisoner from Rossville.* Usually Daniel just drove to Rossville a few times a week to collect any miners held for violations of the law, but when she said, *Why did a Pinkerton come here? That's never happened before . . .* he'd uncharacteristically snapped, *Enough!* Then Daniel had been quiet through supper with Lily and their two young children, leaving Lily to muse how agitated he had seemed for the past week.

Now Harold lunges to the cell bars, as if he wants to squeeze through them and come for her. "You think mixing me and a dirty-dog coal miner up in one cell would be bad? Well then, you better tell your husband to start coming down harder on those miners. Everyone knows he harbors a soft spot for 'em since the Widowmaker."

Lily keeps her expression placid. She's learned, over the years, that silence invites the guilty and the nervous to talk too much. Sometimes that yields only gibberish. Sometimes it yields vital information.

"It's gonna be *war*." The glint in Harold's eyes turns from lusty to needful. He's world-weary, but she estimates he's younger than her, too young to have served in the Great War. Like too many who romanticize battle, he thinks it would be exciting.

Lily could tell him it would not be. Daniel doesn't speak about his time in the army. But even seven years later, he still occasionally calls out at night from some terror-filled war dream. As a good wife, she'd learned to calm him and then not speak of it in the brightness of morning.

"A real war," Harold says. "And then, rule of law won't matter. Those miners who resist, why, we'll put 'em down like rabid dogs."

Lily returns the prisoner's card to its proper place in the "J" drawer. Then she walks back to Harold's cell door. "Hand me the plate."

Instead, he reaches his good hand through the bars to grab for her. But Lily seizes his wrist before he can touch her breast and yanks him so hard into the bars that one side of his face smashes into the iron. He glares at her through his narrowed, bruised eye, like a walleye fish. He tries to jerk away, but Lily, stronger than her five-foot-three frame suggests, holds tight. He brings his sprained arm around to grasp a bar, but pain stops him.

Still, he gasps: "I'm telling Mr. Ross!"

She twists his wrist. He quiets, except for whimpering.

"Tell *Mr.* Ross anything you like. I'm only defending myself, as is my right," Lily says. "You and your kind will not bring war down upon my county. *Sheriff* Ross will see to that."

For a moment, he is a trapped, wounded animal waiting for its next opportunity to strike back. Lily had seen that, hunting with her daddy. Lily calculates: she will need to jump back and let go of his wrist at the same time. She counts to three and does so.

Harold stumbles backward, falls to the floor. He scrambles over to the tin plate and slings it at her through the bars, missing widely.

"When the sheriff returns, you will clean that up. And you'll scrub the other cell's floor."

He curses her as she lifts the key ring off the peg by the jailhouse door. Quickly, she steps out and then closes and locks the door, sliding the ring over her narrow arm like a bracelet.

Lily gives herself a moment to adjust to the brightness of this early spring morning. She gazes west, over the roof of the old carriage house that now shelters Daniel's automobile and her garden tools, past the outhouse and water well, over to the bell tower of the court building next to their home. Then she walks the few paces from the jail, an L-shaped attachment to the sheriff's residence, and opens the back door. It squeaks loudly behind Lily as she steps into the screened mud-room. Daniel has been promising for weeks now to take a look at that faulty hinge.

In the kitchen, as she thoroughly washes her hands with bar soap under the cold water at the pump sink, she tries to calm herself by refocusing on the tasks at hand: it is nearly time to rouse the children, get them washed up, dressed, and ready for the day. There's laundry; Jolene can tend Micah while Lily uses the wringer washer in the mud-room. Both children can help hang clothes and linens to dry on the line out back. But she'll read to them, too, one of her favorite activities with the children.

Yet as she dries her hands, she's still rattled, not so much from the distasteful encounter with the prisoner. Such occasional bouts are to be expected. She just can't shake his cruel glee at the prospect of a coal miners' uprising and the bloody battles that would surely follow.

Lily slips back out to the mudroom, pulling on an old sweater of Daniel's kept on a peg by the door; it may be spring bright, but the day still holds the chill of winter not quite past. She grabs a basket and eases the back door open to mute the hinge's squeak. She starts the small trek up the slope of their backyard, her focus drawn to slender jonquil stems and buds poking up by the jailhouse's stone foundation. Has her daughter seen them? She'd told six-year-old Jolene last fall that they'd never grow there and immediately regretted it when her little girl's face fell. Jolene had insisted on planting the bulbs anyway. Such faith.

The hens cluck and stir as Lily gathers eggs. A smile finds her lips, even as she fusses back at them, as the morning—before the nastiness with the prisoner—comes back, whole: the floor creaking as Daniel rose before dawn to prepare for his journey to fetch a prisoner. She had reached for him, pulling him to her. His hesitation, concern writ across his brow: *Lily,* he'd said, letting her name fall like a sigh; then *the baby,* and she'd smiled and shaken her head to show she found his concerns sweet but foolish. They had, after all, made love through all but the first of her other pregnancies.

So she'd unbuttoned his pants. He'd blushed. How she managed to make a man like him blush she never could figure, but it pleased her.

They'd made love after all, reconciliation after the previous night's squabble, the past week's uncharacteristic tension. They've never been able to deny each other.

After, he'd smoothed back her hair, kissed her forehead. *I'll be back by lunch,* he'd said, *and I'm hankering for buttermilk pie.*

She'd laughed. She's the one who should have cravings, yet Daniel's been fussing for days for that pie. His favorite. But also his ploy to get her to eat more. Even a queasy stomach can handle buttermilk pie.

Now, still smiling at the memory, Lily glances into her basket. Six eggs. There, in the nesting box, a seventh! Enough for the children's breakfast and Daniel's buttermilk pie.

So Lily gently scoops up the seventh egg. She envisions this afternoon, how Daniel will proclaim this bounty of eggs *a good sign,* part of the lore he'd learned from his own mama. She'll tease him, tell him such things are old wives' nonsense, that likely she'd missed some eggs the morning before. He'll tease her back—*such a modern woman*—and she'll pout playfully until he moans appreciatively at the first bite of pie.

But as she latches the coop door, a man's hand falls heavily on her shoulder, and her daydream dissolves. Lily's right hand reflexively forms a firm fist: thumb outside, knuckles up, as Daniel has taught her. She spins around to see it's Elias.

Lily, relieved at not upsetting the basket of eggs, smiles as she always does at her husband's uncle, an uncle who is more like a father to Daniel. She is about to greet him when Elias says, "Daniel's been found."

Then she sees the daub smeared across the chest of Elias's gray overcoat, the smudge of blood on his cheek, sees the shake in his hand as it falls from her shoulder and returns to the brim of his hat. He pulls the hat up to block the stain on his chest. The hat is not big enough.

"I wanted to be the one to tell you. . . ."

She looks from the spot rising like a blood moon above his hat's brim to Elias's face. In the sudden, stunted silence she hears the men—Martin, Daniel's main deputy, is speaking, and there's a quiver to his voice, and she hears another man grunt a reply—coming around the side of the house, past the jail, up the rise of the yard.

Only then do the stiff planes of Elias's face crack and wrench, as if this is what is too much: that he's failed to be the one to bring her the full news of Daniel's fate.

But he needn't say more. She knows. She knows just what *Daniel's been found* means. . . . Daniel isn't lost; he knows every damned rut and route and turn and stream and hill and holler of the Appalachian Mountains in Bronwyn County, Ohio. He hasn't run off. He isn't ill.

Lily hears a smack, sees that her arms have fallen to her sides, her basket of eggs to the ground. She drops to her knees, tries to scoop the eggs back up. She digs at the goop, clawing so hard that her nails quickly fill with yolk and cold spring dirt.

"Lily, Lily, stop, please. . . ." Elias's voice, as if from a great distance.

Then a loud squeak—the back door that Daniel had promised to fix.

"Mama?" Little Jolene's voice, piping up the rise from the back stoop like an echo of that back door hinge. Somehow as near as if Jolene whispers in her ear.

As Lily turns from the broken eggs, her eyes scrape past the carriage house and jail, her gaze seeming to take forever in its trek down to the back stoop and to their children—Jolene and Micah—standing there, still in nightgowns, no doubt awoken by that damned squeaking door and the men tromping around the front of the house.

Four-year-old Micah leans into his sister. Normally Jolene would push him away, annoyed, but now she pulls him to her. Jolene says again, cracking the word in half: "Ma-ma?"

Daniel's been found. . . .

Lily stands, rubs her hands on her skirt, rushes down the hill to her children, reaching for them even as she runs.

CHAPTER 2

⁂

MARVENA

Marvena wants to comfort the sobbing woman, cowering in a corner of the dark, dank bedroom, but she dares not move. She's pressing down with all of her slender weight on the slash in the dying man's gut, as if she can hold his innards together with just her hands.

"Lloyd, you stay with us now, you hear me?" Blood bubbles up from the miner's wound, around the heels of her hands, seeping into the cuffs of her dress.

Rowena, his wife, weeps loudly.

"Now listen, both a you! Nana will be here soon." Well, at least Marvena hopes she will. She'd sent her little girl off to fetch Rossville's midwife and healer woman. Surely the child had noted the urgency and not gotten distracted by something that caught her fancy—a peculiarly shaped rock, or a spring flower. "Nana will have her herbs; she'll find a way. . . ."

But Lloyd's eyes are already wide ashen pools floating in his coal-blacked face, gazing through Marvena to someplace afar on the other side.

"Goddammit, Lloyd, we need you. The cause needs you!" Marvena cries.

By missing meals to set aside food for his wife and children, the man had made himself so weak he'd stumbled onto his own damned pick-axe. Then, back on the job today after just three days off, he'd spit up blood and bile and careless words like *organization* and *union* and *cause,* only to get beaten and rended anew by two of Luther Ross's hired thugs. They might go by the fancy name of *Pinkertons*—but that's all they were. *Thugs.*

So earlier that morning, Marvena had trekked down from the eastern side of Devil's Backbone, the hill on which their scant, spare cabin nests high above Rossville. She'd brought her younger daughter with her, not daring to leave her alone with only their hound, Shep, and a small pistol for protection, not these days.

Not so long ago, she'd have left Frankie in the care of her big sister, Eula. But shortly after the Widowmaker explosion on the western side of Devil's Backbone this past September, Eula had left home to take a position in the Rossville boardinghouse. And now the fool child had run off from even that.

This morning, Marvena had shaken off her worries about her sixteen-year-old daughter and come down Devil's Backbone with her six-year-old in tow to meet woman-to-woman with the miners' wives. Seeing little Frankie with her serves as a reminder of the burdens the women would face if they, too, were widowed. The support of the miners' wives is key to convincing the men to organize, and Marvena's goal is to rally the women to offer that support, to coach them on how to stretch already thin means. If the miners walk off the job—union or no union—they will be thrown out of their company-owned houses. A few miners and their families, who've run up too much debt at the company store and can't pay rent, already have set up tents made from tarps and quilts and such. Marvena had been in several tent cities, working alongside John—her husband by common law—and seen the wretched conditions, the danger of fire and illness among people huddled together in such a makeshift way.

John had been such a talented organizer that at first it seemed his death would gut the local movement. It had been too heartbreaking—for her and the community—the loss of John and another volunteer trying to rescue the miners deepest in the collapsed tunnels in the Widowmaker explosion September last. But a month later, Marvena and Jurgis Sacovech—John's best friend and right-hand man—took up the cause again, their efforts flagging until Lloyd and Marvena's brother, Tom, took to quietly rallying Rossville miners.

At first, their meetings drew scant numbers to the cave tucked away in the hills near her moonshining still. But since February, with rumors of management reopening the Widowmaker, the meetings had grown—near on twenty last time. They'd had three meetings now, notice spread carefully by word of mouth to trusted allies.

Marvena tries again, her voice an incanting whisper. "The cause, Lloyd . . ." She stops, considers another tactic. "And your wife and children. They—we—all need you."

A touch rustles Marvena's sleeve, and Marvena knows without looking that it's Nana Sacovech, Jurgis's mama and Rossville's unofficial healing woman, drawing on some mysterious combination of local herbs and the lore of her home country of Lithuania. Half the time all that Nana could offer was soothing clucks, but that was better than anything the quack company doctor—usually drunk and whoring at the so-called boardinghouse—ever provided. Marvena knows deep down that Nana isn't going to be able to offer more than soothing now.

Yet Nana's voice is a quavering wisp. "Marvena, please . . . Leave him be."

"You could stitch him up again," Marvena says. "Use more of your herbs, your salve . . ."

"He should never have gone back into the mines," Nana says. "He never shook his fever after infection set in from the wound. I did my best."

Lloyd makes a gurgling sound. His death is imminent. Yet Marvena stares into his eyes. "The cause . . . ," she whispers.

"Let him go in peace," Nana whispers. "Let his wife—"

As if on cue, Rowena's wails crescendo.

Marvena gently eases her hands from Lloyd's gut. She turns and looks into the eyes of the old healer woman. Most things about Nana—her squat build, her apple dumpling face, her white hair so fine and thin that her pink scalp peeks through the strands pulled back for a bun—make her look simple and weak. But there's a steel to her pale blue eyes, harder than the pick end of a miner's axe.

Marvena doesn't have to say anything. Nana nods. She knows what she has to do. Give the man a tincture of her strongest painkiller. She's already reaching into her tote bag when Marvena turns to face Lloyd's wife, to ask if that will be all right.

The dank corners and dark walls of the tiny bedroom twist and rush up to Marvena. The smells of the room—chamber pot, mildew, death—jam her nose like foul snuff. She swallows hard to keep from gagging, as her gaze desperately seeks the one grimy, square window in the bedroom. Rowena, or maybe the wife of the previous miner renting this house from the company, had tacked a curtain trimmed with a spare bit of precious hand-crocheted lace—once white, now a pale gray—over the window, then tied back the curtain with bits of twine.

To let in light.

But though it is a bright late morning, no light comes through. The window is smeared with a patina of coal dust, like everything in Rossville. In the scummy glass, Marvena sees the silhouettes of other miners and neighbors moving restlessly on the porch. Lloyd's bloody undershirt lies on the dresser under the window. Marvena shudders, imagining the man staggering home, his work injuries rended anew by a bloody beating. The grayness and smells of the room press in closer. Marvena bites her lower lip. *God.*

John.

She thinks of him last September, giving her his lopsided grin before rushing down from her cabin on one side of Devil's Backbone to the Widowmaker on the other, intent on rescuing the miners caught in the collapse. She'd chided him—*Why d'you have to rush in?*—and he'd chuckled, *Who'd trust an organizer who wouldn't?* and she'd told him fine, but she'd not hold the venison stew for him, and he'd laughed again and kissed her before heading out the door.

But John and another rescuer never brought the miners out. A second explosion crushed and buried them, too. Seven men, all told, dead. After a bitter month of mourning, fury finally pulled her from sorrow, and she'd taken up the cause again, alongside Jurgis Sacovech.

Marvena gasps, suddenly desperate for air. Lloyd, and near on a hundred more like him, go down, down, down under the earth through tunnels just slightly bigger than their bodies, and into chambers lit only with coal-oil lanterns, and she can't muster the breath she needs in the bedroom of a dying man?

A sob draws Marvena back to the moment. Rowena is staring at Marvena's hands, sticky and slick with Lloyd's blood. She plunges her hands into the bowl of the washstand, Lloyd's blood curdling in the shallow water. She sees blood has tinged the cuffs of her blouse. Later, she will need to scrub that out on her washboard. Now she dries her hands and cuffs on her skirt.

Marvena grabs Rowena and gives her a quick shake. The woman, startled, silences.

"Honey, there'll be time for wailing later," Marvena says. "Not that it'll do any good. Now he needs you to be calm. Nana has something to ease his pain, if'n it's all right by you—"

Rowena jerks free of Marvena's hold. Her face slacks with defeat, deepening the lines that run like claw marks down her cheeks and across her brow. She rubs her eyes, pushes back her hair—hair that is still thick and dark and long. Rowena is, Marvena figures, about ten years younger than her, maybe twenty-five.

"Ease him on, you mean," Rowena says. "And then what. I go back to my folks in West Virginia, they'll take me in, but not all these young 'uns. I reckon I could leave Junior; he'll pass for thirteen; some family'd want his scrip. . . ."

Though she knows Rowena is babbling in desperation, Marvena's throat tightens at the suggestion. "No. No. He's too young; that's just what we're fighting against—"

"Fighting got my man hurt. You and Jurgis and that brother of yourn, keeping stirred up what your man ought never have started, foolish talk of better days."

Marvena inhales sharply, ready as always to defend John, Jurgis, her brother, Tom, herself, and especially the movement—but a deep gasp from Lloyd draws their attention.

Rowena drops her head for a moment, then looks up at Nana and gives a small nod. Nana spoons up some of her mixture to Lloyd's lips.

Marvena goes into the other room, where the children sit on the floor. With them is her younger daughter, Frankie, showing the miner's children her doll, spinning some story or other.

She stops when she sees Marvena, her face lighting up. Marvena gives her a small smile. The oldest of the children—Junior, the one not quite old enough by law to go into the mines—stares at Marvena, his eyes serious under thick eyebrows that are just like his father's. Marvena nods. He sighs, gestures to the other children, and they file after him into the tiny bedroom.

Marvena opens her arms wide, and Frankie runs to her. "Thank you for fetching Nana," she whispers in her daughter's ear before walking out onto the porch.

There she sees the hard faces of the men, the strained faces of their women. Frankie settles down on the front step, heedless of the filthy boots and patched shoes around her. She's playing with her doll again, a whimsical concoction of chestnut face and moss hair and twig body, dressed in a scrap of fabric. A doll that Daniel had made for her. Just like the dolls Daniel used to make for Eula, Marvena's older daughter.

Beautiful, strongheaded, willful sixteen-year-old Eula.

An image of Eula rises, twirling in the dress Marvena had made for the girl's sixteenth birthday last August, the pale blue cotton patterned with tiny red flowers costing a rare pretty penny. Eula, begging to go to a barn dance. Eula, giddy over meeting a boy—a seventeen-year-old miner named Willis Boyle. Eula, sobbing into Marvena's shoulder over her stepfather's, John's, and Willis's deaths in the Widowmaker collapse last September. But then Eula, wrung out of tears, turning bitter, even after Daniel began visiting them again, after all the years apart, coming once a week or so after John's death, trying to get her to smile and laugh as he had when Eula was a little girl and delighted in his visits.

Then the day after Christmas last, Eula left and took up in the Rossville boardinghouse. She still came to visit on Sundays—her bitterness had not extended to cutting off Frankie—until six weeks ago, mid-February.

Daniel promised a week ago that he'd check on Eula at the boardinghouse, come by this afternoon, and tell her what he's learned. Marvena had not gone to check herself because too many Pinks stay there and Marvena is known as the common-law wife of John, the region's best organizer before he died. Marvena hopes Daniel will come up to her cabin today, tell her Eula is fine.

Frankie coughs, drawing Marvena back to the sorrows at hand, and Marvena chides herself for not having bundled the child up better this chilly morning.

But then Frankie starts singing a hymn of comfort: "As I went down to the river to pray, studying about that good old way—"

At the sound of Frankie's voice, a long bright silken thread, the faces of the men and women on the porch ease, soften.

Suddenly a wail rises from inside the cabin. All on the porch lower their heads. The miners who still have on their hard hats take them off.

As the widow's cry fades, a whistle sounds, warning that just ten minutes are left for lunch break. An uneasy hush follows the whistle, and then the miners and the women shuffle off the porch.

Marvena presses her eyes shut, calculates: Lloyd makes the eleventh miner exposed as organizing for a union by Luther's Pinkerton thugs, posing undercover as new miners, since February of 1924, when her husband, John, had started the organizing efforts in Rossville. The first ten had been beaten, then with their families turned out of their company houses, forced to live in tents outside of Rossville but keep mining to work off the scrip they owe the company store.

Will Lloyd's death break the effort? Or galvanize it?

"It's Tom . . . he was taken by a Pink," says Jurgis Sacovech, coming up behind her, his expression drawn with weariness and anger.

Marvena gasps. "Why? When—" She doesn't bother to ask, *By whom?* They don't know the Pinks' names.

"He was grabbed at dinner break, just after noon yesterday. Taken to the holding cell," Jurgis says, referring to the small iron-barred room inside Ross Mining headquarters, a narrow building that also holds the pay office and Luther Ross's office.

Marvena sees her brother, Tom: tall, thin, ruddy face, nose twisted left from some fight or another, his fine, sandy hair. The sight of him, even in her imagination, turns her heart tender. But she pushes her heart back into its own holding cell. "What reason was given for the Pinks taking him?"

"Word is he was caught talking to Lloyd and some other miners," Jurgis mutters.

"I'll talk to Daniel—"

Jurgis snorts. "Your special friendship with the sheriff ain't gonna do you any good. Looks like he's taken his stand—but different than what we'd hoped. I went to the cell early this morning before work. Tom was gone. A Pink took pleasure in telling me that Sheriff Ross had been there even earlier, just after dawn, to transport Tom to the Kinship jailhouse."

"There must be another explanation. I trust Daniel. He don't want no Blair Mountain."

Jurgis shudders at the reference to the bloody standoff between miners and management just four years before in West Virginia. It was legendary and had nearly killed off unionization efforts across America.

"We need to hold off on the next organizing meeting, what with Lloyd—" Jurgis says.

"No! That's all the more reason to meet—"

Another whistle. The five-minute warning.

"You tell Daniel where, yet?" Jurgis asks.

Marvena clenches her teeth. "No." Even Daniel doesn't know about the cave, well hidden behind her moonshining still. But he knows her cabin, of course, makes regular visits there. Knows of her moonshining and looks the other way.

"Well, you need to stop the sheriff coming down here to Rossville till we know for certain where he stands. Especially with Tom gone."

"How else am I to talk with the wives? Prepare them?"

"You're drawing suspicion. Lay low, Marvena."

Another whistle. One minute.

Marvena expects Jurgis to hurry down the dirt road. But he stares at her, resolute.

Finally, she nods. "Fine. But Daniel's coming to see me this afternoon. He'll come out on our side. Make everything right. Mark my words."

Should she tell him now that when she and Tom had seen Daniel last week he'd said he was at least going to talk with an old friend who works in the Bureau of Mines about safety violations, someone he served with in the Great War?

But Jurgis's face softens into another expression. Pity.

So she says nothing as he walks off.

CHAPTER 3

⁂

LILY

Three days after *Daniel's been found,* Lily holds the hands of her children—Micah and Jolene—as they walk from their house, past the county courthouse next door that fills the corner of Main and Court streets, and down to the Kinship Presbyterian church. The trek is not even a block, and yet Lily's stride slows with each laborious step, her heart pounding as if she's run as she had as a child in the woods behind her grandparents' buckwheat farm, down to Coal Creek and the Kinship Tree.

Mama waits for them at the edge of the crowd by the church, a far bigger crowd than Lily had anticipated. She stops short, even as Mama gives her a look: *Come on, young lady.*

Lily looks down at her children. Jolene is trying her best to look brave—a pinch-faced imitation of Mama—but Micah is sniffling. Both stare up at her, startled by so many people pressing in, studying them.

Of course the people of Bronwyn County are curious, fascinated by such tragedy, shocking even in a farming and coal county where tractors overturn and mine walls crumble, crushing or suffocating workers in minutes or hours. But those are expected deaths.

This is different: their sheriff of seven years shot with his own revolver by an escaped prisoner, his body left on Kinship Road near his automobile to be found by Rusty Murphy, one of Ada Gottschalk's farmhands, on the western prong of the hairpin turn by the Gottschalk farm. The prisoner he was transporting long gone. A manhunt is under way, but so far there are no leads.

This is all Lily knows of Daniel's death, all Martin or Elias has told her. No more than what was reported in a small article in the *Kinship Weekly Courier*. It is not enough. She will see this through—burying her husband—and then she will demand to know more, until she is satisfied that she knows all there is to know about his death.

Even now, Lily finds herself scanning the crowd, looking for Rusty or even Ada.

"Go, child." Mama nudges her, using her shoulder, since her arms are full with Caleb Jr., Mama's change-of-life baby. Lily's little brother is the same age as her own son, Micah. But Lily won't be pushed. Micah sniffles. Lily kneels, pulls from her purse the handkerchief Mama insisted she bring to daub her proper tears, which have yet to come for she fears that if she lets her sorrow loosen and run free it will sweep her away. She wipes Micah's nose and kisses the top of Jolene's head.

Even as she forces herself to stride toward the women's door, habit overrules propriety and Lily looks to the men's door; the sight of it triggers a familiar tug of resentment: on Sundays, Daniel always parted from them so easily, smiling and shaking hands with the other men, wives and children separate, unseen, easy to forget.

Suddenly a miner rushes toward her. "Mrs. Ross!" he cries out.

Lily stares at him, startled. She doesn't know this miner, but he gets close enough for his smell—years of coal dust steeped into his clothes, his skin—to sting Lily's eyes and nose, and she tightens her grasp on Micah and Jolene. Respectfully he pulls off his hat, a battered and dusty relic, revealing fine hair like a young man's, but his eyes are ancient, hollowed out. His worn brown coat, frayed at collar and cuffs, hangs shamefully loose on his tall, too-thin frame, like an old woman's shawl.

"I just want to tell you how sorry I am, we all are, and I wanted to ask—" He stops, overtaken by coughing. He pulls from his pocket a handkerchief, stained red and yellow. As he brings his handkerchief to his mouth, a Pinkerton from the crowd grabs him.

It's the Pinkerton man from the other night, the one with the harelip and the jagged scar by the corner of his left eye.

A low buzz snarls through the crowd. Lily's heart beats up into her throat. She'd seen, twice in her youth, how quickly a crowd can turn into a mob.

The Pinkerton pulls back his fine gray wool coat, enough to reveal the grip of a holstered revolver. Lily turns the other way, wanting to run with her children—and Mama and her baby brother, too—back home, but she's blocked by the crowd.

Several other Pinkerton men push toward the miner as the buzz rises, tightens, hovers in fearful balance with sudden stillness.

Then someone shouts, "Goddam Pinks!"

The scornful tag is enough for the Pinkerton to pull out his revolver, for his compatriots to reach for theirs. Most of the crowd shrinks back. Lily draws her children closer, but both Micah and Jolene start crying.

"Enough!" The voice is loud but not shrill.

For just a moment, Lily is bemused—hearing her mama's commanding voice—and then she realizes as the crowd stares that it is her own voice that has risen.

The Pinkerton holsters his revolver and releases the miner, who quickly disappears. Then, as if orchestrated, the crowd shrinks back and a path to the church reappears.

"Go on," Mama hisses at Lily, and gives her a prod, as if she blames Lily for this disturbance. Mama does not like spectacles.

So Lily makes herself walk through the entrance and slowly down the aisle, same aisle she'd hurried down eight years before for their wedding, eager to get to Daniel's side. She slides into the front pew on the women's and children's side. Even as she stares at the cold, pitiless stained-glass window to their right, she feels the probing eyes of the people coming in behind them, people who for this occasion have tried especially hard to wash coal and dirt from skin and clothing. They've been given the day off; even Luther Ross is not so foolish as to insist on labor on this day. And so they've come, in automobiles, on horseback, in mule-drawn wagons.

Soon so many people are packed standing-room-only in the tiny church that their body heat brings forth the smell of their lives from deep within their own flesh; their body heat coaxes from wooden pews and leather Bibles smells of other sinners and mourners who've gathered there time and again. The smells stuff Lily's nose, and she gasps softly.

Her fists clench in her lap as she stares at the cedar box. It's closed. *Good.* At least the undertaker had listened to her insistence on that. She bites her lip, hard, as she recollects: the undertaker had said, *People will want to see.* Mama, Elias, Martin had agreed, muttered about convention and expectations.

But as Lily had taken in the sight of Daniel's body at the undertaker's, as much of it as she'd been allowed to view, she'd thought, *What about my expectations?* She'd expected that he would come back that morning. Now she knows not to hold expectations close anymore.

Even when she'd seen Daniel's body, his death seemed unreal. The decisions she'd been pressed to make seemed like garish details from a foolish nightmare.

But the encounter outside the church has broken that illusion.

Lily unclenches her fists and instead spreads her arms like wings around her children. They quiver with such force that her arms tremble, too. The rest of her is still as stone.

CHAPTER 4

⁂

MARVENA

Marvena stands at her wood-fired cookstove, trying to scoop up the specks of bacon in the drippings she'd saved in a cup, all that's left of the meat that Daniel had brought on his last visit.

She spoons the grease into her cast-iron frypan and, as she waits for it to sizzle, chops potatoes and onions. When the grease pops, she dumps in the vegetables. She slices bread and makes two sandwiches—a lavish two slices of bologna each—and wraps them in wax paper.

As she works, she thinks of the owl that had come to the crab apple tree at dusk the night before. Marvena, outside at the well, had seen it fly from the forest, over the clearing around her cabin, then alight on the tree, right beside her porch. Unnaturally close. It had begun calling. A bad sign. A portent of, perhaps, death.

The memory from the night before now brings to her mind her brother, Tom, taken away. Her daughter Eula, surely still at the boarding-house, turning her heart fallow day by day, night by night. She'd said as much on their last bitter visit just six weeks ago. Daniel had come by as they were arguing, had calmed scared Frankie, offered Eula one of his little rustic dolls dressed in a scrap from the cloth Marvena'd used to make Eula's dress for her sixteenth birthday—before the Widow-maker collapse upended Eula's view of the world and what it offers to women like them. But Eula's fury had boiled over. She'd tossed the doll back at Daniel, run from the cabin. Daniel had stopped Marvena from following her.

Her heart clenches with fury and urgency at both the memory and Eula; she knew she could wait no longer for Daniel to come to her. She'd have to go to him. Ask if he'd truly gone to the boardinghouse to check on Eula. If what Jurgis accused him of was true—had he picked up Tom in Rossville, then taken him to the Kinship jailhouse?

The sandwiches made, Marvena goes to wake Frankie. It takes several nudges and gentle shakes. The child could sleep through anything, even thunderstorms or dynamite booms from the other side of the mountain. It's a trait that Marvena, who'd tossed and turned all night, envies.

"We're going to Kinship today," Marvena says. Frankie swings her feet around off the bed and bounces on the straw mattress, making the wood slats squeal. She's never been to Kinship, only heard of it from Daniel.

"To find Eula?" Frankie's face lights up, just saying her big sister's name, and Marvena can see that it is not the last bitter meeting that composes Frankie's memory of Eula, but happier times. Seeking wood-land berries and greens for supper. Playing fetch with their coon-hound, Shep. Eula patiently teaching Frankie how to braid her hair or lace her shoes when Marvena was just too tired.

"To find Uncle Daniel."

Though spring is nudging its way in, winter yet strokes the cabin door, licks the window, and lurks in the corners of the room. After breakfast, Marvena bundles Frankie in layers and a hat that Eula had left behind. Pulls on her own thin brown wool coat—a worn hand-me-down from Mama, God rest her soul; she'd died of heart trouble when Marvena was eight.

On the front porch, Frankie pets Shep and says what she always does when they leave to hunt greens or mushrooms, rabbit or squirrel: "Be good'n watch our cabin!" Then she feeds Shep the potato peelings.

Eula had found the dog—a mix of coonhound and who knew what—

when he was but a pup, abandoned in the woods, half-starved. It was a miracle a coyote hadn't gotten him. Marvena had protested—they barely got by with four mouths to feed. But Eula begged for the beast: *He'll be a good watchdog!* And so Marvena had given in.

Now Shep gobbles the last of the peelings and stares at her. Marvena sighs, pulls a sandwich out of her pocket, and gives Shep a bologna slice. By the time she's rewrapped the sandwich, Shep's settled down and Frankie has already started running down the rutted lane.

"No, child!" Marvena's voice barks harsher than she means it, so that Frankie stops and stares back with eyes full of hurt, and Shep—who is partial to Frankie—startles to alertness.

"We can't go through Rossville as usual," Marvena says, forcing her voice to softness.

"Why?"

She doesn't want to frighten the child by telling her that Jurgis had warned her away. "Never you mind. I know a back way."

So Marvena and Frankie go round to the back of their scant, spare cabin and climb out of their holler through the woods up the hill, then sidle down unnamed dirt paths, until at last they come alongside Coal Creek, moving slowly between ice-crusted banks. Whipsaw wind slices through thin coats and thinner skins to gleefully tap their bones. Frankie sings them along—hymns, mining songs, ballads. She'd learned most of the music from John. The child never forgets a song.

But then she stops. "Mama?" Frankie says, dancing from foot to foot, her tiny face suddenly desperate under the brim of Eula's old hat. "I have to pee!"

Marvena eyes the slick, narrow path along the steep bank, the dense growth on the rise on the other side. She knows a safer place for Frankie to relieve herself, along the footpath they'll need to take anyway up to Kinship Road. "Hold it for a bit. We're right near the turnoff."

They continue on, silent then, Marvena wedging her body between the steep, slippery bank and Frankie. Then she spots it, the sharp curve up ahead, where Coal Creek joins Kinship River and the waters tumble together toward the great Ohio River. Marvena's heart, beating a steady *thrum* during the miles they've already come, suddenly pounds in her throat at the sight of that curve, at the memory it brings. She grasps Frankie's hand. Then they're around the curve, and there it is—the Kinship Tree.

Frankie gasps when she sees it. She's never seen anything like this before, and Marvena can't help but smile at her reaction. The tree grew from three saplings—sycamore, maple, and beech—fusing and twining over uncounted seasons until their fates bound in one trunk and their boughs shadowed the bank where water pooled, still and dark and deep.

"Go on up a bit and do your business. Mind that you're neat!"

Frankie hurries up the path, well worn from people coming to visit the tree. It's cold, and early, and quiet except for woodland sounds, but Marvena hollers an additional admonishment anyway: "And keep an eye out for people!"

Lovers have marred the Kinship Tree with carvings of their initials. Marvena presses her fingertips to one such set. She'll give Frankie time and then come up the path to the hairpin turn in Kinship Road, and from there they'll take the main road to Kinship. For a moment, though, she allows herself the luxury of turning to rest against the fused trunks, closing her eyes.

The morning after her thirteenth birthday, Marvena slipped away from their small cabin to escape the fight between Tom and Daddy, now out of prison, over Tom's desire to work for Ross Mining. Drifting away down Coal Creek seemed the fastest way out.

She grabbed a dead tree branch from the ground and jumped in. Marvena didn't know how to swim well, but after the initial shock of cold water she drifted easily, arms hooked over her branch, and she reckoned the creek could carry her down to Kinship River and from there to the mighty Ohio.

Then, suddenly, the water churned faster and at last pulled her, tumbling, over rapids, knocking her loose from her branch. She bobbed up at the other end, where the water again ran slow and steady. But deeper. She could not touch the bottom. She saw a figure on the distant bank, staring at her. She screamed and went

*under until someone clenched her around the waist. Gasping, she
saw that it was a boy, holding her so that she was floating. Soon
they were under the shade of a tree whose limbs canopied over a
still pool along the bank.*

*When she could breathe evenly she sat up and took in his fine
shirt, breeches, suspenders. The good leather shoes, now ruined.
He introduced himself—Daniel Ross. The name struck her, hard
as a slap. "Ross? Like Ross Mining? Rossville?" she asked, and he'd
nodded proudly—that was his daddy's company. His town.*

"Mama! Mama!"

Marvena's eyes snap open at Frankie's desperate bleats. She rushes
up the path and finds Frankie, undergarments still down at her knees,
staring at her left foot, which is bleeding through her stockings. Her
shoes are to the side.

Racing to her daughter, Marvena hears an unnatural crunch beneath
her own thinly soled boots. She looks down, spots shards of glass,
mixed with hay, dumped behind the brush.

Marvena leans on a boulder and pulls Frankie to her lap. She studies
the child's foot, sighs at the pieces of glass stuck in the sole. Poor child—
no wonder she's whimpering. But Marvena gives an order—"Sit still,
child!"—and begins easing out the shards.

When she finally gets the glass out, Marvena pulls off her coat and
top and rips the sleeves off her thin blouse, the blouse she'd scrubbed
free of Lloyd's blood on her washboard just days before, and uses it as
a bandage for Frankie's foot. After she finishes, she looks at her
daughter, sees the child's eyes clutching her with need.

Marvena pulls the bologna sandwich out of her coat pocket and
hands it to Frankie. By the time Marvena's hand is back in her pocket,
wrapping around her own sandwich, Frankie has the wax paper off of
hers and has taken the biggest bite she can, filling both cheeks, struggling to chew. Her eyes have already started returning to normal. Marvena lets go of her own sandwich. Frankie will need it on the return
trip.

"Why'd you take off your shoes?"

"You told me to be neat!" Frankie sniffles.

Marvena sighs. As Frankie finishes her sandwich, Marvena goes back through the break in the bushes—black raspberries, a variant of their red cousins, not yet in bloom. She stares down at the mix of hay and shattered glass. She picks up Frankie's shoes, then toes the glass again. Odd. There's no reason for hay to be here. Nor the glass. Someone has dumped them here.

She glances back toward empty Kinship Road. Her face stings suddenly, not from the wind, but as if someone has slapped her, and the smell of the cold spring morning—a heady incense of dampness and earth coming back to life—stuffs her nose and closes her throat. From a distance, a red-shouldered hawk cries. Marvena shivers. The hawk is a sign to be alert, to consider carefully one's situation.

It hits her for the first time that Daniel won't be at his fine Kinship home by himself. There will be his wife, his children.

She returns to Frankie, orders her to put her shoes back on, but Frankie yelps while trying to put her shoe back over her bandaged foot.

Marvena picks up Frankie's shoes. Then she hunkers down. "Come on. Piggyback."

Frankie climbs on, clasps her waist with her legs, her neck with her arms.

Marvena straightens, slowly. "Not that tight."

Frankie loosens her grip. Marvena hooks her arms under Frankie's knees and climbs up the path to Kinship Road, the only paved road outside of Kinship itself in Bronwyn County.

"Mama? Will Uncle Daniel still be mad? Last time we saw him—"

Marvena knows very well what happened the week before when Daniel came to her cabin, the awful fight between Daniel and her brother, Tom, the terrifying moment of doubt that her pleas would not pull Daniel back to himself, that he'd keep hitting Tom until her brother was dead. But she doesn't want to discuss that with her daughter.

"You mustn't call him 'Uncle,'" Marvena says. "Outside our home, he's Sheriff Ross. You can't—just don't—" Marvena's voice wobbles to a stop. She hadn't considered the hazards of a young child's tongue waggling freely.

And yet, when Daniel began visiting her again last fall for the first time in ten years, after the Widowmaker explosion took John, that's exactly what she'd told both daughters to call him.

She opens her mouth to offer further explanation of her relationship with Daniel, but it suddenly seems too complex even for her, let alone for a six-year-old child. And anyway, Frankie sighs and begins to hums softly until she eventually dozes off. In the silence nestled in Frankie's soft breath, with each step toward Kinship, Marvena thinks of her brother, of her elder daughter, and plans what she'll say to Daniel.

CHAPTER 5

≫⋙

LILY

At Kinship Cemetery, as the pastor begins—"Our dear Brother in the Lord, Sheriff Daniel T. Ross, was taken from us to soon"—Lily breathes in the cold air, the scent of the previous night's rain mingling with earth so strongly that she tastes it, metallic and bitter.

Suddenly Lily wishes for her father. Instead of sitting on a hard wooden chair, tottering on a dirt clod, by the empty grave, instead of insisting their children sit in such chairs on either side of her—*It's proper!* Mama had insisted—she wishes she'd opted to do as her father had at burial services for family or friends when she was a child. He'd stood with her by the big cedar tree at the back of the cemetery. There'd been something so comforting about the big, rough trunk against her back, his big, rough hand wrapped around hers.

Now Lily gazes over the hollow grave, past Daniel's coffin on the other edge, to the far corner of the cemetery, past where Daniel will be buried, to the McArthur family section. For Daddy and her brother Roger the only remains here are their names, engraved on *In memory of* markers.

At a tug on her skirt, Lily looks down at Jolene, wide-eyed and trembling. As the pastor rushes through the final prayer in a race with coming rain, Lily pulls Micah into her lap and takes her daughter's hand.

After the service, Lily lets Mama and Lily's best friend, Hildy, take the children, so she can shake hands and nod at condolences, even as she looks, as she had outside the church earlier, for Rusty Murphy, the last man to see Daniel alive. Not spotting him, she looks for his employer, Ada Gottschalk, knowing it's unlikely the reclusive widow would come, but then again, Daniel had been good about checking on her—

Suddenly a man approaches Lily, catching her attention. He is unusually tall, looming in his fine gray wool coat and his carefully brushed black fedora. He, like the Pinkertons, is an outsider with authority, but unlike them he doesn't countenance his pride with a smirk.

Abe Miller. Lily knows him, knows that he works for George Vogel of Vogel's Tonic—the company that makes a medicinal tonic with a small enough percentage of alcohol to make it legal under the Volstead Act. The tonic is sold everywhere, including the general store in Kinship. She, like most housewives, keeps a bottle on hand.

Abe has been part of the warp and weave of her life, a shadow in the background during two key moments early in her life with Daniel. She's also seen him now and again in town, espied him from afar talking with Daniel. Now he is coming toward her, purposefully, and he means to say something to her, and Lily gasps as the notion comes to her, a cold whisper from the back of her mind: *He must know something about Daniel.*

At that moment, Mama steps in front of Lily, holding Caleb on her hip, saying that she and Hildy will go on ahead to the house with Luther, to start preparing for visitors. By the time Mama is finished and Lily can look around again, Abe Miller is gone.

Daniel's uncle Elias lingers with Lily to receive the last of the mourners, and then finally it's just the two of them and a small gathering of men by Daniel's coffin, waiting patiently with shovels.

As Elias takes her by the elbow and walks her back to his automobile, Lily wonders why only men have the honor of seeing the dead through to the final moments, as if women can't bear the sight of burial, as if all that will follow isn't the harder share.

They're a half mile or so down Kinship Road when Lily breaks the silence.

"Thank you for driving me." She shivers. Even with her heavy coat and hat, she's cold, for Elias's Model T is from before the war, an open-carriage model.

"I wouldn't have it otherwise," Elias says. "I can come into town and drive you anytime."

"We'll be getting Daniel's automobile back, though?" Even as she asks the question, Lily realizes that she means to go to Ada's farm to talk to Rusty, to find out what either of them might know about Daniel's last moments.

"Lily, the automobile. The children will see . . ." Elias slides into flat silence.

Bullet holes? Bloodstains? "They've seen worse already—their father's coffin," Lily says. "It was Daniel's automobile, not the county's. Mine, now. I want it back soon."

"When it's repaired," Elias says.

"How long will it take?"

"I don't know. They—they had to order new glass for the driver's side window." He means Lewis Automotive, the only automobile dealer in town. Daniel's Ford is a newer 1924 model, complete with windows that can crank up and down.

"The window was shot out—why didn't you just tell me? All I've been told is that Daniel picked up a prisoner at Rossville, a prisoner who somehow wrested Daniel's revolver from him and shot him. I want to know everything you know." Though long retired as a doctor, Elias serves as the Bronwyn County Coroner as needed in cases of violent or unusual death. In his tenure as sheriff, Daniel had only called upon Elias a few times. He lived on the farm next to Ada Gottschalk.

Lily continues, "I want to know if he was still alive when you—"

She stops at the sudden sound of Elias's sob. She's never known him to cry, even when his wife and daughter died from influenza seven years before. She stares at him with wonder and no small share of envy. Her own grief has hunkered down, deep within, waiting for something—answers to her many questions, perhaps—before it can loosen, rise, disperse.

"A farmhand on Ada Gottschalk's farm heard the shot. Rusty Murphy."

"Martin told me that much."

"Rusty found Daniel's automobile," Elias goes on. "Then he found Daniel."

Lily thinks back to the last moments she shared with Daniel. She'd tried to fall back to sleep after they'd made love. Maybe he'd left their bed earlier than she thought. But the chickens were already stirring, sunlight grazing the top of the hill, when she'd started her domestic ministrations. So she must have arisen around 7:00 a.m., with Daniel leaving perhaps a half hour or an hour before that. Two and a half hours or so for Daniel to go to Rossville, fetch the prisoner, make it most of the way back, get attacked, be found, for the Gottschalk farmhand to go and find Elias, for Elias to come to Daniel, for Elias to then come to her.

Daniel couldn't have lingered, then, in Rossville, with the prisoner. He must have been in a hurry to get back to Kinship. To her.

"Did you talk to Rusty? Ask him what he saw?"

"No, Lily. If anyone did, it was Martin, but I'm not sure what Rusty could tell him. You know he's not too sharp."

Lily nods. She's familiar with Rusty. Every now and then, Daniel hauled him in for drunkenness and disorderly conduct, usually on a Friday night.

Lily shakes her head to clear it, to refocus. They'll be home soon, with no time or privacy for talk at her house, and Lily knows Elias will avoid discussion after that. Like Daniel, he's always been too protective of her. She rushes on to her next question.

"The undertaker wouldn't let me see him fully," she says. "All I know is he was shot. But did he suffer? Linger?"

"He was shot once in the stomach, again in the chest. Close range. No one survives that for more than a few minutes. Not even Daniel."

At this, Lily can't breathe. Then she inhales cold air, drawing it in as deeply as she can, until her chest feels as though it might crack.

She says, "The prisoner, who was he? Someone has to know. . . ."

"A miner. Brought in for roughhousing."

The image of the miner outside of the church, just before the funeral service, flashes before her. He'd wanted to ask her something. What did he think she might know?

"The prisoner's name. I want his name."

"Oh, Lily, I don't know."

"But wouldn't Luther know? Since the prisoner was a miner?"

"Not likely. Luther's men handle the miners who get out of line. Lily, let it be. Martin, Luther's men, others—they'll find him. If he's to be found."

This new notion, Daniel's killer going free, twists Lily's stomach. It is so easy to disappear in these hills.

She considers the situation: by "Luther's men" Elias means the Pinkertons.

They're all too often thugs and thieves, Lily, Daniel had said more than once after busting up disturbances the Pinkertons created at the Kinship Inn, where they stayed. *Why, they saunter about the county as if their company's badges make them better than other men.*

And yet he'd welcomed the harelipped one into their home the night before his death.

Now Lily shudders at the memory of the Pinkerton, how his eyes made her feel filthy, how Daniel, usually protective, so keen on the man's message, hadn't even noticed.

As much as Lily dislikes Luther—he's just as cocky as the men he hires—she vows she will ask him the name of the miner. And the name of the Pinkerton who came to her home. She will, she decides, even go to the Kinship Inn and look for both the Pinkerton man who came to their house and Abe Miller.

She deserves to know the details of Daniel's death. She needs to know them. For she already realizes that the cold fury gripping her heart won't ease, that she won't be able to be a proper mother, to find her way with the new child, with Jolene and Micah, until she does.

"Lily, I want you to know that Daniel was already gone by the time I got to him," Elias is saying. His simple words crackle, shattered glass. "I couldn't save him."

Lily looks over at Elias, looks at his hat, the same hat that hadn't been able to hide Daniel's blood on his coat a few days before. She imagines Elias embracing Daniel, aching to hug life back into him, as she'd once seen Elias try with his own child.

Finally, Lily's heart softens. "I know you did, Elias; I know. I've always trusted you."

Elias looks over at her, with a sad smile. "Not always."

"Not right away," Lily says, offering the correction as comfort. "But ever since you saved my life. Always, since then."

They make the rest of the trip in silence, Elias's gaze intent upon the road and Lily staring past the rolling hills, letting her mind wander back to the day she'd met Daniel.

Lily hesitated as she stared down from her high perch in the Kinship Tree—maybe Mama was right. Maybe she was too old—today was her seventeenth birthday—for such foolishness.

But then she heard her brother, Roger, whooping as he ran up to the tree. Lily grinned. Though he'd bolted first from their gardening tasks at their grandparents' farm, she'd quickly passed him on Kinship Road and made it to the tree first.

She leapt.

The thrilling shock of cool water and then—for just a moment— weightlessness, enjoying the sensation until she could stay under no longer and swam to the surface. Next: a joyous burst of air into her lungs, and then the gentle float downstream.

Roger joined soon enough and round and round they went, laughing and jumping, shucking the notion that they'd become too old for all of this, even as their futures loomed—Roger destined to join Daddy in the family business of McArthur & Son Grocers next year after graduating from high school. Then he'd likely ask Hildy Cooper, Lily's best friend, to marry him.

But Lily chafed at the notion of marrying after high school, feeling no interest in any of the young men Mama deemed suitable. She wanted to set off in the world, find her own way.

One more jump, she thought, before returning to their grandparents' farm. After all, Daddy was trusting them to take care of what needed doing while he went back to town to mind his store. A few days before, Lily'd asked when Mamaw, as they called their grandmother, would be back and why Mama had to be at the Cincinnati hospital if Papaw was there, too, and Mama had hushed her, telling her she asked too many questions—and to just mind Daddy and Roger.

Lily leapt again.

But this time, Lily hit the surface too close to the bank, in the deepest part of the pool. She hit bottom on large, sharp slates. She tried to push off, but the force of her fall had driven her left foot between two rocks. She was caught and she could not pull free, nor could she swim to the surface.

Water filled her mouth. Unbearable pressure mounted in her lungs. Suddenly hands grabbed her wrists and pulled, hard. Hot pain wrenched her left foot, but she was rising, rising, breaking the surface, and there was Roger, pulling her finally to the rocky bank.

The next moments were as much of a bloody, mangled mess as the outer toes of her left foot, shredded flesh from bone. She'd later learn that Roger carried her to the Gottschalk farm, where he and Mr. Hahn Gottschalk got her on a wagon and took her to the Ross farm next door, where a retired doctor and his family lived. Dr. Elias Ross concluded he'd have to amputate the little toe. Infection was already setting in, and they didn't have time to waste getting the town doctor.

The next clear moment brought the realization that she was lying on a dining table. A woman leaned over to Elias, asking, "Who do you want to help? Luther or Daniel?"

Snapping at her, he growled, "Don't ask me to choose! Just fetch one!"

Then another gray stretch of time, and coming around again to see another man. Through her pain, Lily gathered only a hazy

*impression of him: tall, broad, dark-skinned, dark haired—a
sketch of a man. Except for his eyes.*

*Those eyes, dark and sharp, catching her, holding her, and
though she'd never seen this man before, Lily thought,* Oh.
There you are.

*She'd learn his name in the weeks to come. Daniel T. Ross. At
the moment, all she knew was that in the first instant he looked
angry, but then, as he looked at her, fury melted from his gaze
and steady kindness rushed in.*

*As she realized the doctor meant to amputate her toe, Lily
started crying and asked Daniel, "Would you trust him?"*

He'd smiled gently and said, "With my life."

So Lily nodded.

*He pulled off his leather belt and took a flask from his hip
pocket. Screwing off the top, he held the flask to Lily's lips. Lily
swallowed moonshine, her first taste of the illicit stuff brewed
despite local Prohibition. She sputtered instantly and Daniel
gave her a soothing smile. Then he held the strap end of his belt
to her mouth and told her to bite down.*

A jostle in the road brings Lily back to the moment and she realizes
she had been dozing. She opens her eyes, sees that they're rounding the
corner by the courthouse.

"You were moaning," Elias says. "Perhaps Vogel's Tonic would calm
you."

"I'm fine," Lily says.

As Elias eases his Model T off to the side of the road in front of the
sheriff's house, Lily catches the sound of guffaws. There's Luther, on her
front porch, yammering as if he's standing outside a speakeasy and not
a house of mourning for his half brother.

"Rain's coming," Lily says. "You can park in the carriage house."

Elias pulls down the narrow lane on the side of the house, stopping
by the carriage house. Lily gets out of the automobile, not waiting for
her uncle-in-law's assistance. She can feel his worried stare follow her

as she enters the back door to the mudroom. She winces at the sound of the back door—still squeaky. Then she hangs up her coat and hat and enters the kitchen.

For just a moment, unnoticed, she observes Hildy and Mama talking softly with each other. There's a certain cheerfulness to their work, their chatter, as they wash dishes, preparing for the funeral supper, and fuss over the children—Jolene, Micah, Caleb Jr.—gathered at the small table. Hildy is more comfortable with Mama than Lily ever has been.

"Lily," Mama says, noticing her, "you look terrible! You should rest. You should—"

"I'm fine."

Mama lifts an eyebrow. "Callers will come soon to pay their respects, and you should—"

"What I should have done is insist on no callers," Lily says.

"Daniel's loss isn't yours alone," Mama says. "And this house isn't yours alone, either. Soon enough the commissioners will ask you to move on for the next sheriff and his family, and then of course you can move in with me, but until then—"

"Enough!" Hildy cries, shocking both Mama and Lily. "This is not the time for unkindness." Hildy has never defied Mama. She would have made, in many ways, the perfect daughter-in-law, had the Great War not taken Roger.

But then Lily sees the hard hurt in Hildy's eyes. The gaze of a widow, though she'd only been engaged to Roger when he died. Daniel's death has reopened that pain.

As for Mama, after Daddy died last fall trying to help rescue two miners trapped in the Widowmaker, it seemed there'd been no spare space for softness in Mama's heart. During one of their squabbles, Lily accused her of hard-heartedness and Mama said she'd given up on softness, lest it consume her, melt her, and then what good would she be to anyone?

After that, only Hildy could connect with Mama, get her to eat, to move.

The sisterhood of widows. Such a sorrowful sisterhood Lily has joined.

Their silence is broken by the sound of the front door opening and shutting—no doubt Elias, Lily thinks, coming in after securing his automobile.

Lily picks up two of the plates Mama and Hildy have just washed. She starts to leave, to go to the dining room.

"Where are you going, Lily?" Mama asks.

"I thought I'd make up plates for Elias and Luther."

Mama looks bemused. "Elias no doubt wishes to nap before visitors arrive. And I've never known you to spare kindness for Luther."

"I'm just trying to do what's *proper.*" Lily puts one of the plates back on the stack.

"You're supposed to be in mourning for several months, and let others serve you, not—"

Lily walks out of the kitchen as Mama is still going on. In the parlor, she tiptoes quietly past Elias, who's already slumped asleep in the big chair by the fireplace, the chair that Daniel always favored. When she enters the dining room, she's staggered by the sight of the large oak table, heaped with fried chicken and deviled eggs and ham salad and biscuits and pies. A red glass compote dish, large and pedestaled, holds corn relish. Usually, Lily keeps the dish, a wedding gift from Mama and Daddy, on top of the pie safe in the kitchen, filled with her county fair blue ribbons for pies. Apple. Peach.

And buttermilk pie. Daniel's favorite.

Suddenly the bounty and even the red dish seem grotesque. Lily knows that this is ungenerous of her, that she should be grateful for food brought from precious stores of family and friends and neighbors for the funeral supper, for the leftovers that will feed her and the children.

Lily puts a chicken leg, deviled eggs, and corn relish on the plate. She goes out the front door, to which someone—probably Mama—has affixed a black bow.

She finds her brother-in-law, Luther, draped on the porch rail, a gaunt figure in his black coat. The Pinkerton with him—a nervous-looking young man—doffs his hat at Lily. Luther takes a drag off his cigarette. "I suppose you've come to tell me to go around back for smoking? Elias already chided me—"

Lily looks at the standing ashtray on the porch. "Not at all. Daniel never forbade it."

At the mention of Daniel's name, sorrow flits over Luther's face. He's even thinner than usual, and the sallow remnants of a bruise darken his left eye, suggesting a recent fight.

Luther says, "Lily, look, I'm sorry."

But in the next instant Luther's expression contorts back into his usual sneer. "Aww, now, you're bringing me a plate?" Luther stubs out his cigarette and grabs the plate. The Pinkerton—a boy, really—looks at it hungrily. Lily feels a surge of pity for him and wonders what in his young life had driven him to work for the agency, to kowtow to her brother-in-law.

"I want to know the name of the prisoner Daniel went to pick up in Rossville," Lily says. "The prisoner who killed him."

"Course you'd get down to brass tracks," Luther says. He picks up the chicken leg and pulls off a huge bite. "I run the mines. My men handle the miners. I don't know who the prisoner was." He swallows. "Hell, I didn't know Daniel was headed to the holding cell that morning."

Lily clenches her teeth, disappointed that Elias had been right about Luther not knowing the prisoner's identity. "The night before Daniel died, one of your men showed up at our house, to tell Daniel about the pickup. Maybe you at least know who that was?"

Luther shakes his head.

"He had a harelip. Jagged scar by the eye. Pretty distinctive."

A shadow passes over Luther's face. He drops the half-eaten chicken leg onto the plate, pushes it at Lily.

She takes the plate, asking, "What is that man's name?"

"You're describing Harvey Grayson. Like I said, I don't waste my time on details like the comings and goings of miners in and out of the holding cell. That's why I hired the services of the Pinkertons, which I wouldn't have had to do if Daniel had done his job in the first place. But maybe he didn't do it because he himself was half-savage."

The plate shakes in Lily's hands. When Daniel was alive, Luther would not have dared disparage Daniel's mother—a Leni-Lenape Indian woman who had worked for their father, then married him shortly after Luther's mother died. The half brothers were fifteen years apart in age, and Luther had always resented Daniel's mother. She had then died when Daniel was just eleven, and he'd gone to live with his uncle Elias shortly after. Just two years after that, his and Luther's father died. Though Lily had never met her in-laws, she knew Daniel had adored his mother—and hated his father. And that Luther felt just the opposite.

Now Luther grins at Lily's discomfort. "Yeah, half-savage. No wonder Daniel always had a soft spot for inferior humans—"

"Enough! I won't have you speak ill of my husband at our house." Lily's hands now shake so hard she nearly drops the plate. She knows by "inferior" he means those sympathetic to miners—people like her own father. "Nor about other people, in that way."

"Not *your* house." Luther grins and pulls out his cigarette holder. "You're young enough that some new man wouldn't mind having you, after your proper mourning time."

The Pinkerton boy starts to laugh, but Lily shuts him up with a hard look. As she turns to go, Luther says her name with such surprising alarm that she looks again at her brother-in-law.

As he reaches back into his vest for his flask, a genuine look of concern breaks his usual sneer. "Lily, leave the hunt for the prisoner to the men. Let Martin and Harvey sort things out."

Lily nods, but as she goes back in the house she thinks, *Harvey Grayson.* Adds the name to her mental list: *Rusty Murphy. Abe Miller.*

Now she has somewhere to start.

CHAPTER 6

※

MARVENA

Walking up the last rise of Kinship Road, Marvena steels herself against gasping with pleasure at the sudden view that awaits at the crest. Yet her foolish heart pounds and her knees slightly buckle at the sparest flash of memory of a long-ago view of Kinship. Like Frankie, Marvena was six when she first went to Kinship—her only trip before now—walking with her brother, Tom, and their mother on a trip to see their father at the jail. The story is he nearly killed a man who tried to take his moonshining turf, but that makes him sound tougher and more heroic than Marvena imagines her father really was. Time has reshaped her reckoning of him. He's now just a smudge of fury, her mother a thin wobbly line of sorrow.

Fragile scraps of recollection sift through Marvena's mind: a train whistle slicing the frozen night; hot roasted chestnuts bought with a precious penny; the scent and sweet and stickiness of a peppermint someone gave her; a woman in a red wool coat with a dead lynx for a collar, all those eyes peering down at her.

"Mama?" Frankie stirs on Marvena's back as she awakens.

Marvena gently lowers Frankie to the road. For just a moment Marvena savors the relief of being unburdened. She rolls her neck, stretches her arms. "I need you to walk the rest of the way. Can you do that for me?"

Frankie nods, a solemn bobbled promise, and puts a shoe on her good foot, hobbling on the ball of her injured foot. At the top of the rise, Frankie gasps, awe enough for both of them at the town—the proud county seat of Bronwyn County—spread below, a spectacle of church spires and courthouse and train depot and houses.

As they near Court Street, Marvena admonishes Frankie, "Keep your head high. Mind you don't step in puddles." There'd been a brief rain, over quickly, so at least they're not soaked through. "Specially with that cut foot."

"But, Mama, how can I do both?"

Marvena sighs at her daughter's confusion; she reckons that life often demands doing contradictory things in exchange for survival.

As they approach the courthouse, Marvena sees the automobiles and horse-drawn carriages. Just around the corner, people fill the street by Daniel's house and Marvena sees black bunting on his door. *No. No. God, not Daniel, let it be the wife, let it be . . .*

When Daniel last came to see her, he'd shared that his wife was again with child, pride in his expression but concern in his voice. Now Marvena rashly seeks hope in the awful possibility that the wife—Lily—lost the child. That the mourners are for her.

Marvena feels Frankie's small hand in hers, squeezes it, reassuring. Marvena straightens her shoulders, keeps her gaze steady, even at the sight of Luther Ross, that cruel son of a bitch, and two more of his Pinks with their fine felt hats and string ties and pins on their lapels and cocksure attitudes. Marvena wants to grab Luther by his scrawny neck, shake him hard.

"Mama?"

"Hush, child." The admonition is really a reminder to herself: she's here to see Daniel, to ask about Eula. She'd also intended to ask him about his Bureau of Mines friend and Tom, but all that will have to wait with Luther around.

She tries to ignore Luther as she goes up Daniel's porch steps and then reaches for the door knocker, but he grabs Marvena's elbow. "What're you doing here?" She nearly gags at the reek of shine trailing the hiss of his words. Not her shine. She's been careful, with Daniel's help, to keep her business out of Luther's sight. She'd started it up after John died last fall, using the techniques she'd picked up from her daddy. Luther would have taken cruel pleasure in insisting Daniel enforce Prohibition on Marvena.

"You don't belong here!" Luther growls.

The opening door interrupts him, and instantly she knows: it's Lily. Daniel often spoke of Lily, describing with a loving grin something his wife had done or said. As Marvena sees her now, for the first time, it's as if Daniel's words have flown together and created her right there: petite, strong, beautiful Lily Ross. The only woman Daniel had ever loved.

And now here she stands. Pleasingly curvy, yet also a no-nonsense presence—shoulders straight, defiant tilt to her chin. Her dark brunette hair, swept up into a smooth twist, and her black high-necked mourning dress make her smooth, fair skin look like porcelain. Yet a telltale flush to her cheeks, a slight curve to her belly, tell Marvena that Lily is still with child—though if Daniel hadn't told her she'd not have known.

As if of its own will, Marvena's rough hand smooths back the matted strands of gray-brown hair, pulled loose from her bun. She feels suddenly the bow of her back, the scrawniness of her own body, the ruddiness of her skin. Her tongue darts to the empty spot of a bottom incisor.

But then she sees that although Lily's heart-shaped face is unmarred by tear tracks, her blue eyes are dull, darkly circled. A speck of blood on the outside of the other woman's lower lip is a telltale sign that she's been biting into it.

Oh God.

The horrid realization that the black bunting, the people gathered, are absolutely for Daniel binds and gags her.

It's Frankie who saves her by speaking up. "We are here to see Sheriff

Daniel T. Ross, ma'am," each word a careful chirp. Frankie looks up at Marvena proudly: *I didn't say "Uncle Daniel."*

"Sheriff Ross is my husband," Lily says. "I'm afraid that he's dead."

Though she's already pieced this together, Marvena reels back as if Lily has slapped her. Frankie moans but quickly quiets as Marvena squeezes her hand.

At their mournful reactions, the briefest flicker of surprise ripples Lily's carefully still face. *Course*, Marvena thinks, *course she don't know anything about me.*

"Lily, this woman's nothing but trouble," Luther says. "We can take care of her."

Lily ignores Luther. "Perhaps you could tell my husband's deputy your business?"

Marvena glances behind Lily at a sorrowful-looking man. "I'm Martin Weaver, ma'am," he says. She's never met his deputy; Daniel always came to her cabin by himself. So why should she trust this man enough to confide in him?

Marvena blinks back a hot rush of tears. "I'll not be speaking to the likes of him."

A girl, Frankie's size, comes by Lily's side. She clings to Lily's skirts, stares at Frankie. Must be Jolene. Daniel's talked a lot about her and the son, Micah. His hopes for the third child.

"I see," Lily says. "In that case, I'm not sure how I can help you, but—"

Just then, Frankie reaches for Jolene and touches the other girl's chin. Jolene doesn't flinch as Frankie swipes away a bit of jam.

"Frankie! Don't be rude—" Marvena starts as Lily says, "Jolene, I thought I sent you to wash up!" The women look at each other, for a moment simply like-minded mothers. They fall silent as Frankie sticks her jam-covered finger into her mouth and sucks eagerly.

A heavy silence throbs on the Ross porch, strummed by the sounds of Frankie's rhythmic sucking. Luther, barely holding back his seething, gives a look to the Pinks. They tense, lean closer toward Marvena.

Slowly, Marvena starts to turn away from Lily, toward Luther and the Pinks, calculating how she'll keep them in her sight while she and Frankie retreat down the road.

Lily stops her: "You appear to have come a long way. Please come in for a moment."

Luther steps between them. "Lily, that isn't a good idea."

Lily frowns. "Luther, please. This woman has come seeking help—"

"Marvena Whitcomb?" He curls her name nastily. "She's been nothing but trouble for years. Her man was an *organizer.* Trying to turn Daniel against the company our father founded, against me. . . ." Luther is emboldened by his role as revealer and spits over the porch railing with gusto before finishing, "Back in his sowing wild oats days, Daniel's little whore."

Lily's face stills with shock. Marvena feels her child start to tremble and again turns to leave, to protect the few remaining shreds of her dignity.

But she spots the tremor of hurt rippling Lily's brow and is snagged by pity for the woman learning in such a horrific way that Daniel had kept secrets from her. Secrets that extended as far back as childhood.

Though Lily's gone pale, her voice stays firm. "Luther, that's no way to speak of someone who's come for help. This is still my home and I will decide who is welcome here. Now move out of her way, please."

Martin steps around Lily out onto the porch, then takes Luther by the elbow. "Come, now." His voice is half-soothing, half demand. "It's been a long day. Let's have a smoke." He maneuvers Luther down the porch steps.

Lily's voice softens. "I'm sorry about that. Please come in."

Marvena tries to discern if Lily's invitation is in defiance of Luther, out of curiosity about this woman from her dead husband's life, or simple kindness. Whatever the reason, Lily and her little girl turn and enter the house. Marvena starts to follow, but Frankie hesitates at the threshold they're about to cross. Until today, Frankie has never seen any abode finer than their own humble cabin or the tiny miners' houses in Rossville on rutted roads. Here, on a broad street lined with fancy automobiles, the two-story houses boast attic turrets and real pane windows and freshly painted shutters. Why, the porch on which they stand now is bigger than their whole cabin.

Marvena gently nudges Frankie forward. Frankie limps on in, and suddenly Marvena is aware of the oddity of Frankie carrying one of her shoes. In the parlor, Marvena sits just on the edge of a settee. Several women in the parlor stare at them. Marvena pulls Frankie into her lap.

Marvena's gaze settles on the big chair by the fireplace. A man's chair. Imagining Daniel there, she blinks back stinging tears.

An older woman clears her throat. Marvena looks up to see her shooing the other women into the dining room. She also sees Lily in the set of the woman's mouth, the steadiness of her eyes. Her weary look belies that she knows loss inside out.

"Mama," Lily says as she sits in a smaller chair, "where is Uncle Elias? This girl's foot is hurt, and she needs tending."

"Out back. I'll go fetch him."

Mama. Marvena quickly puts it together: Lily's father, Caleb McArthur, had died alongside John, trying to rescue two trapped miners in the Widowmaker last fall. So this was Caleb's widow. Marvena knows all the names of the seven men who died. No doubt, Lily and her mama do, too, but as John's common-law wife, Marvena hadn't taken his last name, so Lily wouldn't have made the connection. Daniel had spoken with obvious sorrow about his lost father-in-law on his visits after John's passing.

Now Frankie slips from her mother's lap and joins Jolene on the big ornately floral-patterned wool rug in front of the fireplace. Frankie stares at a china-faced store-bought doll, but Jolene shows her a doll crafted from bits of wood and metal with a painted-on face. Marvena's heart clenches. Of course he'd made his rustic dolls for Jolene as well. His daughter.

"Do you want to take off your coat?" Lily asks.

"No!" Marvena instantly regrets the snap to her word, but she doesn't want Lily to see her torn blouse. "I'm sorry. I had no idea that Sheriff Ross—" Marvena starts. She suddenly can't catch a full breath, as if an anvil has fallen onto her chest. "I wouldn't come, had I known. I ain't been down to Rossville for a couple of days—word hadn't spread up to me yet. I . . . I didn't know."

"It's all right," Lily says softly.

A steeliness in Lily's eyes belies her soft-spoken manner. Lily has had a few days to adjust to Daniel's death, and now cold anger is battling for the upper hand over pure sorrow. Marvena knows those feelings from having lost John.

Marvena quickly calculates: her last visit to Rossville was three days before. Jurgis's words echo: *Tom was taken by some Pink. He was grabbed at dinner break yesterday, just after noon. . . . Daniel must've come awful early to pick him up.*

Suddenly Marvena's trembling so hard that a strand of hair falls across her face. She pushes it back, her shaking hand nearly poking her eye.

"Sheriff Ross has been helping me with my other daughter. Eula. She's been missing. Since the middle of last month." Marvena calculates. "Near on six weeks. He—he last saw me a little over a week ago, and I told him she was gone, that it might be like her to take off, but not without saying bye to Frankie here. These sisters, they love one another. Anyhow. Daniel said he'd see what he could find out, get back to me, but then—" Marvena stops, unsure how much to explain. "Then, he didn't, an' like I said, I haven't been to Rossville for a few days, because—" Well, she can't say because her friend Jurgis, who has taken over organizing the men with her brother, Tom, warned her away, since Tom was taken prisoner for talking unionization. So she gives a partial truth. "Because my little one's been sick."

Lily looks quickly at their daughters. Marvena looks, too, sees that Frankie and Jolene have become instant friends, the way only very small children can before they become aware of adult strictures. Frankie pulls something from her pocket, whatever the magpie child found alongside the road, and hands it to Jolene.

"She's better now," Marvena says.

Lily looks back at her. "You don't live in Rossville?"

"No. Cabin. Up a ways in the woods on Devil's Backbone."

"Oh. And your daughter—your other daughter, Eula—lives with you?"

"No. In the boardinghouse. Since December," Marvena says, averting her eyes. Both women know what *a woman living in a boardinghouse* means in a coal town. "She's sixteen. Old enough to make her own choices," she adds, willing the tears not to well in her eyes.

After John died last September, she'd put away her tender feelings in a box, where she kept all things too hard to coddle, and focused on the work of unionization, barely able to keep her heart together after losing John, never mind being able to comfort Eula for her loss of a beloved stepfather, as well as her first love, Willis, in the Widowmaker.

Tears prick Marvena's eyes after all. No wonder Eula had wanted to escape from their difficult life. From her. To pack up her tenderness and earn her own way in the world, even if that meant trading on her youth and beauty at the boardinghouse.

"Still, you contacted Daniel to report that she was missing," Lily says softly.

This is far more formal than what really happened. Truth be told, she'd never meant to complain about Eula missing, but when she'd last seen Daniel fear for the child overwhelmed her and she'd flung herself into his arms as she sobbed out her worries.

"Girl has a hard head, and we quarreled aplenty, but she always came once a week or so up to the cabin to see her sister, so when she stopped showing up, I asked the sheriff to check—"

"You didn't go check yourself?"

"I—I had my hands full with my other young 'un." Marvena offers a small—she hoped convincing—smile. Can't admit here of all places that she didn't go to the boardinghouse for fear of running into Pinks who might question her about John and who all he'd turned to the cause. "Anyhow, I asked the sheriff to track down if she'd run off with some fella. He said he'd help, that he'd come back to tell me." Marvena looks at Lily, directly but cautiously. "How—"

"He was shot. By a miner. A prisoner who he went to pick up in Rossville, I'm told. The prisoner hasn't been found. There's a manhunt for him."

Marvena flinches at Lily's raw words. *A prisoner. Tom?* The last time she'd seen Daniel, a little over a week ago, Tom had found her sobbing in Daniel's arms over Eula. The men had fought, saying awful words, Tom accusing Daniel of trying to take advantage of Marvena's sorrow since John's death, of being a coward for not going public with his support of unionization. Of making up his friend in the Bureau of Mines. For a moment, each man had looked angry enough to kill the other. Daniel had taken the first swing, overpowering Tom, until Frankie's cries brought Daniel back to his senses. Could Daniel have truly been so angry at Tom he'd turn on the cause—on her? Could Tom have nursed enough wrath to overtake and kill Daniel?

Marvena wants to find her brother and demand the truth. Yet her heart rends—life demanding contradictory things—for if Tom is Daniel's killer then he must run, never come back, or his life will be forfeit.

"Maybe—" Marvena's voice cracks on the simple word. She clears her throat, starts over. "Maybe Daniel made notes about what he might have learned about Eula's whereabouts?"

Lily's eyebrows lift, as if she is startled by the notion. Well, Daniel fussed every time he visited over reading to Frankie and teaching her her letters and he'd written her through the Great War, so why wouldn't he make notes on his cases?

But then Lily says, "I can check to see if he made note of anything about your daughter."

"Thank you. That's right kind."

Lily hesitates before countering, "You may be able to help me as well. I have no idea who that prisoner from Rossville might have been. If you've heard anything—"

The women's eyes meet. Marvena reads Lily's gaze: *Daniel wouldn't have been shot by a prisoner. He wouldn't have let that happen. . . .*

"None of the *men* want to tell me much," Lily says, emphasizing the word "men," leaning forward as if they might be conspirators. "But surely you can understand how I'd want to know all the details about Daniel's last moments, so if you hear anything about the prisoner's identity—" Lily stops as her mother and a tall, thin man come in from the dining room.

"This is Elias," says Mama. "Dr. Ross. I'm sure you don't mind him tending to your young 'un's foot?"

Marvena looks at Elias. More gaunt than the last time she'd briefly seen him a few years back in Rossville, covering the spare space from his automobile to the main office of Ross Mining in a few long strides, glancing around nervously as if fearful someone would jump him. Of course, she hadn't talked to him then or the other rare times she spotted him in Rossville.

The only time she'd talked to him was when she was fifteen and Daniel was twelve and they were at the Kinship Tree and she comforted Daniel as he cried that he had to run away, that he couldn't take his father's beatings anymore or hear his father call his deceased mother a savage whore because she'd cheated on him. And then he'd confessed that this time in the barn, instead of taking a belt whipping across his back for some misbehavior, he'd struck his father with a pitchfork and then kept hitting him, wanting—yes, wanting, though Marvena said surely he didn't mean it—to kill his father. But Uncle Elias had found them and stopped Daniel, and Daniel then broke free and ran to the Kinship Tree, where he and Marvena were planning to meet anyway. Elias had shown up at the tree. She knew of him—Daniel always talked about his uncle affectionately—but this was their first introduction. Elias had pulled Daniel away from her, said he was taking the boy to live with him and his family in Kinship proper.

Marvena didn't see Daniel again for three years—until Daniel's father died, leaving his small buckwheat farm on Kinship Road to his brother, Elias, his mining operation to his older son, Luther, and nothing to Daniel. Shortly after, Elias retired from doctoring in Kinship and moved his family back to the farm.

That's when she and Daniel resumed meeting at the Kinship Tree, even though by then she herself worked at the Rossville boardinghouse.

Now Marvena thinks: even then they'd had regular meetings. She starts to smile, but then fresh grief overcomes her, and she bites her lip as she watches Elias fold himself down to the floor. He has a tray of swabs and bottles and gauze, items Marvena reckons Lily's mama had gathered because course Lily'd have such fine supplies on hand. Jolene throws her arms around his neck, squeals, "Uncle Elias!," and he hugs her for a moment. He says, "I have to take care of your little friend's foot," and peels Jolene's arms away.

Daniel talked about Elias sometimes, about what a great man he was. But Marvena, though she'd never tell Daniel, did not think so highly of him. Elias had never bothered to tend to the people in Rossville, the men working the mines his own brother established. There was a company doctor, but he was worse than a butcher, so most people relied on their own know-how or luck or looked to one of the older women in Rossville, like Nana Sacovech, for the healing arts. Elias, it seemed, wanted nothing to do with Rossville.

"What is your name, young lady?"

"Frankie."

"Well, Miss Frankie, may I have the honor of inspecting your foot?" Frankie stretches out her leg, allowing Elias to hold her foot.

"This is well bandaged."

"Mama did it," Frankie says.

Elias turns to Marvena. "You did a good job. How did she lacerate it?"

"On glass. On the main road," Frankie says.

"Where, exactly? People will be driving home soon and we don't want their automobile tires harmed. We should get it cleaned up."

"Dunno where 'xactly," Frankie says. "Near a big curve in the big road. I had to pee."

Lily gasps. "By Ada Gottschalk's farm?"

Marvena frowns, spooked by Lily's odd response. "I don't know that name."

That glass—it had seemed suspicious, swept aside, but not just to the edge of the road. Moved to the brush. The dropped jar of another moonshiner? But moonshiners didn't brazenly use Kinship Road.

"This will sting a little," Elias says as he cleans Frankie's foot with rubbing alcohol, and Frankie yelps. Jolene pats her hand and Frankie calms, even when Elias gets out a needle and suturing thread. Frankie squeezes her eyes tight while he makes quick work of sewing together the cut, then bandaging with fresh gauze. Marvena snags up her sleeve, folds it, and puts it in her pocket and is relieved when no one comments.

"You're all set," Elias comments. "Bravest young lady I've met, at least since I had to mend another girl's foot, years ago." He looks at Lily, but she glances away.

Lily says, "It's getting late. I'd drive you and your daughter home, but—"

Marvena's shocked. "You drive?"

Lily nods. "Daniel taught me."

Marvena's eyebrows shoot up. That was more broad-minded than she'd thought him to be. She clears her throat, then says, "He was a good man."

"Since I don't have Daniel's automobile, perhaps you can drive them," Lily says to Elias.

"No!" Marvena doesn't want him to know where she lives. Why should she trust this man who wanted nothing to do with Rossville? He's uncle to both Luther and Daniel, true, but he reminds her mostly of Luther. "We'll walk. Well, I will. I'll carry Frankie."

"Mama, my old shoes are bigger and would fit over Frankie's bandage!" Jolene pipes up.

"What? No!" Marvena protests.

"She's outgrown them," Lily says. "She has another pair."

Of course. Two pairs of shoes, maybe more, for a daughter in a well-off man's house.

"We'll pack you some food, too. Jolene, Mama, fill Daniel's lunch bucket."

Marvena starts to protest again. But the scent of food—good salt ham, fresh-baked bread, green beans, and corn—wafting in from the dining room makes her mouth water. And Frankie is staring at her with begging eyes. Marvena nods.

"I can fetch the bucket later," Lily says, adding, "after I get our automobile back and have some time."

To everyone else in the room, it sounds like Lily means after she's had time to grieve. But Marvena notes the steely look in Lily's eyes, and she realizes the other woman is going to come find her, find where she and Frankie live, as soon as she can. Hope, as fragile as a match flame in a wintry wind, flares in Marvena's heart, flushes her face. Will

Daniel's widow really find news of Eula and go to the effort to bring it to her?

Before her hope sputters out, Marvena leans forward and nearly smiles as Lily does, too. Then Marvena whispers, so only Lily can hear, "When you come to Rossville, find Nana Sacovech. Don't ask for her directly, but look for the sheriff's lunch bucket left out on a porch rail on the main street of miners' houses. She'll send you my way."

CHAPTER 7

⁕

LILY

Lily's first thought upon waking the next morning is, *Marvena. Such an unusual name. Marvena.* It snags at her, taunting.

She rushes to the wardrobe and runs her hands over the sleeves of Daniel's suit jacket, smoothly pressed. She breathes deeply the scent of his Chesterfields and menthol hair tonic still infused in the fabric. Just a few pants and shirts hang in the wardrobe; his socks, undershirts, underwear, and grooming supplies fill a bureau drawer. He was buried in his wedding suit. She'd asked about his revolver and immediately felt foolish as Martin and Elias and the undertaker exchanged looks. Of course Daniel's murderer would have run off with his revolver. She'd told the undertaker to dispose of the suit and underclothes he was wearing when he was killed but had taken back his shoes, hat, and billfold. Perhaps someday Micah would want them.

Now she dips her hands into the pockets of Daniel's suit jacket, testing the seams with her fingertips. She feels only the silk and then disappointment. She wishes for some scrap of evidence—anything—that might tell her more of her late husband's relationship with Marvena, Eula, and little Frankie.

"I brought you some tea," Hildy says from the doorway.

Lily turns to see her best friend staring at her wide-eyed. Only then does she realize that she's clenched Daniel's jacket between her fists, stretching the fabric as if she means to rend it.

"I don't want tea, Hildy. I need coffee. Good, strong boiled coffee."

Last evening—after everyone else had finally left—Mama and Hildy had insisted on staying over and tending to her, nagging her to drink tea infused with Vogel's Tonic.

"Oh!" says Hildy. "I'll take this down. I can make boiled coffee right quick—"

"No!"

Hildy recoils, and Lily is sorry to see the hurt in her sweet face. But she can't bear another day of Mama and Hildy hovering over her, fussing at her that she should rest.

"I'll be down in a moment," Lily says, tamping the harshness in her tone. Will she ever know how to speak naturally again? Or will every word, every moment, forevermore be tinged with hurt and anger?

"At least let me help you get dressed."

Lily takes a deep breath. "I'm fine. Really, I am. It's time for me to do it myself."

"Already? But . . ." Hildy's voice trails off. She stares down at the teacup, clicking against the saucer in her trembling hand.

"It's not going to get easier anytime soon, Hildy," Lily says. "Not until I—" She stops, not ready to say, not even to her best friend, that she can already feel Daniel slipping away from her. Meeting Marvena and learning that Daniel had had a relationship with her made her question her and Daniel's life together. She needs to know the truth of his death—and life.

Mama always thinks she asks too many questions. But she has to keep asking. Because, eventually, she will have to live with his death, but she can't live with the notion of his murder explained as being at the hands of an escaped prisoner. She knows Daniel too well to believe he'd be bested by a prisoner and knows, too, that it's possible the men looking for the prisoner, even Martin, might keep the truth from her. To protect her, not necessarily from harm, but because so many believe women are too sensitive for life's brutal truths. That's only, Lily thinks, because they've not experienced the brutal truths life gives particularly and uniquely to women.

Lily refocuses on Hildy and tries again, softening her voice. "I'd like it if you could come by sometimes to help with the children."

"So you can rest!" Hildy says, brightening.

Lily nods but thinks, *So I can track down Daniel's killer.*

Hildy leaves and Lily finishes dressing, thinking that at least her morning sickness has passed. She's glad she hasn't told Hildy or Mama of her pregnancy. Both would harp at her to rest so much she'd never get them to let her be and she'd never get a chance to start her search.

Downstairs in the kitchen, Mama and Hildy already have biscuits in the oven and the children settled at the table with glasses of milk.

"Mama!" Jolene cries, running to her mother.

Lily hugs her daughter close and then Micah. What will these children remember of their father? What will she tell the new child of the father he—or she—will never meet?

"Don't Mamaw and Aunt Hildy's biscuits smell good? Can we have black raspberry jam?" Jolene asks.

That had been Daniel's favorite.

Seeing the flash of pain across Lily's face, Mama starts, "We have apple butter—" but Lily stops her with a small head shake and moves swiftly to the back porch. She shoves the door open and the loud squeal makes her jump. *Dammit,* Daniel had said—*Oh. Oh.*

Lily steps forward, lets the door slam shut behind her. Another squeal.

She notes the jonquils; one of the buds has just started to open, a yellow dash against the gray stone of the jailhouse. She opens the cellar door and heads down.

Standing before the jar-laden shelves, as if she's come to them in supplication, she wants to remember her first moments down here with Daniel, when he'd built the shelves. And yet all she can think of is how people are forever digging in the earth to put things in, seeds and the dead, or to pull things out, potatoes and coal.

Only two jars of black raspberry jam remain amid the bounty of other canned fruits and vegetables. She picks up one of them and heads back up the cellar stairs only to find Fiona Weaver—the wife of Daniel's top deputy, Martin—stepping out of the jail cell.

Fiona and Lily aren't friends; they tolerate each other because of their husbands' bonds of friendship and work as sheriff and deputy and because they're in the Kinship Woman's Club, a book and good-works club of the town's finest matrons. At the monthly meetings in the parlors of hosting members, Fiona and Lily have often crossed each other over the years—Fiona against women's right to vote, Lily adamantly for. Fiona against unionization, Lily for. Why, Daniel would be startled to hear the vehemence with which she defends it, remind her that as the half brother of a coal company owner and as sheriff he walks a fine line—

Lily gasps, catching herself. The mask of judgment that usually stiffens Fiona's face melts away to pity. It's an expression Lily can't bear. She snaps, "What are you doing here?"

Fiona stops, eyes widening. "Martin asked me to come over and tend to a prisoner he brought in day before yesterday. Martin didn't want you to worry the day of the funeral."

Hope surges in Lily's heart. "The one who . . ."

"No, no. Mr. Marshall again."

"Oh." Just one of the regulars who goes moon-howling wild each paycheck.

Fiona is saying, ". . . he's been discharged, but I thought I'd finish cleaning."

"Don't start measuring for new curtains just yet," Lily says. Fussy, prim Fiona—bringing meals and cleaning out chamber pots?

A flash of hurt, and then Fiona's usual mask returns. "Don't worry; I don't want my husband taking the sheriff's job. He has a perfectly good business!" She means Martin's shoe store in Kinship.

"Course, he'd likely be more careful than to get himself shot—" Fiona stops at her own forward words. "I'm sorry; I didn't mean . . ."

Lily gazes past Fiona, up the rise to the hen house. Last summer, Daniel had come home black eyed. The prisoner—a man who thought he should be free to discipline his wife any way he saw fit—had not only a black eye but also a broken nose. The idea of a prisoner being able to overtake Daniel was almost laughable.

Daniel hadn't gotten "himself shot." Someone had murdered him.

Fiona puts her hand gently on Lily's arm. "Let the men sort it out. It's not our place—"

Lily pulls her arm away. She's supposed to be the quiet, demure widow awaiting news, only the news that's considered proper for her to know? Well, she's done that long enough. "I'm making it my place. Go home and tell Martin that I expect to hear from him by the end of the day. The name, at least, of the prisoner who supposedly killed Daniel." Lily holds out her free hand, palm up. "Give me the keys!"

Fiona returns the ring to Lily.

After breakfast, Lily tells Mama and Hildy that she needs to go on an errand and steps quickly out into the mudroom, putting on her coat and hat before Mama can nag at her about a widow customarily staying at home.

Lily walks briskly past the courthouse and heads toward Kinship's town square, bordered by the train depot and old canal towpath and the opera house on the east and Douglas Grocers—Mama had sold Daddy's business this past winter to a loyal longtime employee, an older bachelor—as well as Kinship Inn and the bank on the west.

Kinship Inn, a three-story brick building with a sweeping front porch and imposing columns, is overrun by Pinkertons. The proprietor is staunchly anti-union and, it's rumored, accepts payments from Luther to house his hired guns. That a speakeasy is hidden in the basement of the building is a poorly kept secret.

There will be talk among her fellow townsfolk—what was the sheriff's widow doing at the inn? Only a day after his burial? But Lily squares her shoulders as she sweeps past the doorman, who stares as he holds the door for her.

Inside, she blinks to adjust to the dim gaslights. At the front desk, Mr. Williams studies her over his wire-rimmed glasses, perched precariously on the tip of his thin nose, which is still swollen and bruised from the beating he'd received at the hands of the prisoner who'd so taunted her just before *Daniel's been found.*

"Mrs. Ross, my condolences," he says. "How may I help you?"

"I'm looking for two men. One is a Pinkerton, Harvey Grayson. He came to see Daniel the night before Daniel's murder. He is the one who told Daniel to come to Rossville to pick up a prisoner. I thought he might know something about this prisoner, something that might shed some light on my husband's death."

Mr. Williams flinches at Lily's bluntness, then offers her a patronizing smile. "Oh, I see. Well, dear, shouldn't Deputy Weaver be the one doing the asking?"

Lily holds his gaze, unblinking. He can either answer the question or try to remove her by force—not a spectacle he'd care to create, she's sure.

The man sighs, flips open a large leather-bound ledger, peruses. Finally, he looks up at Lily over his glasses. "He checked out. Last night."

The day of Daniel's funeral. Yet she had seen him outside the church, pulling away the miner who had cried out to her. "Did you yourself see him leave?"

Mr. Williams shakes his head.

"Any idea where he might have gone?"

"Some of the Pinkerton men stay in company or management housing in Coal Creek. Or it's possible he was reassigned by his company to another town."

Lily considers: If she contacted the Pinkerton Agency, would someone tell her where Harvey had been sent? Unlikely. The organization is known for working outside the law, thus its appeal to men like Luther. And she's a woman with no authority.

"Well, when did he take up lodging here?" Lily asks.

Mr. Williams looks back at the ledger. "Eight weeks ago."

"That's long enough that he surely got mail here."

"He might. I don't study where our patrons' mail comes from, Mrs. Ross."

"Could you see if he left a forwarding address? Or if he has any mail that he didn't pick up?" It is a long shot, but if he'd left behind a letter from a hometown she could track down the sender and find out from that person where Grayson might have disappeared to.

Mr. Williams turns, looks in the numbered slots in the case behind him. Then he looks back at Lily. "No mail left behind. No note with a forwarding address. Now, if that is all—"

"I did say I'm looking for another man. Abe Miller."

At the mention of the name, Mr. Williams trembles enough to send his glasses sliding off even his swollen nose. He doesn't bother to pick them up.

"Mrs. Ross, I—I don't think you want—"

"Oh, but I *do* want. Tell Mr. Miller that Lily Ross came calling."

"I don't think that's wise—"

"Tell him," Lily says. "He'll be unhappy if he finds out I asked you to and you didn't."

Back home, Lily goes straight to the jailhouse, the better to avoid Mama's glare and pestering questions. Lily drapes her coat over her chair, starts the small coal stove for heat, and sits at her desk. There's the card she'd written up on the day of *Daniel's been found,* the card about the Pinkerton who'd been so grotesque, who'd taunted her about bringing in a miner. She stares at the name: Harold Johnson. Martin had left a brief note that he had discharged the man; Mr. Williams did not wish to press charges.

Of course. The Pinkertons represent good business in Kinship.

Pushing the note and card aside, her hand trails to the bottom drawer. Daniel's drawer, where he kept the notebooks she'd filled with his dictation about cases. Once, she'd teased him that he should take his own notes in the field and he'd teased back—*Isn't that partly why I hired you as jail mistress?* It was true, he didn't care for writing, had rarely written her even during the Great War, whereas she'd written him nearly every day.

But Marvena had seemed sure that Daniel would have taken notes about anything he found out about Eula. The notion doesn't fit what Lily knows of Daniel, but then the relationship with Marvena doesn't, either. Might he have kept a separate notebook about cases he didn't want her to know about—cases like Eula? Lily reaches in, pulls out the notebooks. She'd bought a batch of them long ago at the general store, when Daniel first became sheriff in 1918, notebooks with brown parchment covers, and written his name and the dates on the front. There is, she sees, just one notebook she hasn't labeled. She opens it. Nothing is tucked inside, and the pages are all blank, waiting to be filled.

She sets it aside and starts going through the others, desperately fanning through past entries, suddenly possessed of the notion that somewhere in notes about past altercations she might find a clue as to who the escaped prisoner was.

Nothing.

The altercation Fiona had referred to had been with a farmer. Another time, Daniel had been shot at by a drunk in town, but the drunk had missed. There had been no direct threats from anyone in the mining community. Daniel had been a popular sheriff, easily reelected.

Lily realizes they'd all simply come to assume Daniel would be fine, come home each day safe and sound. Though at first she'd been disappointed that Daniel had changed his mind about joining her father in the grocery business after the war, she'd eventually come to not only accept but also love their life, Daniel's standing in the community, and her work as jail mistress.

Staring into the now-empty drawer, Lily catches sight of something shoved to the back, meant to be hidden by all those notebooks. A flat, long box—Lily recognizes it instantly as a See's candy box. Daniel, though, has not bought her a box of chocolates since last Christmas. Was he waiting to give her this, a gift of appeasement for the past week's tension?

Lily pulls the box out. She lifts the lid and inhales the lingering scent of chocolate, but the box doesn't contain candies. Inside, there's a simple hair comb, a few teeth missing. A few blond hairs—lighter than Marvena's, Lily notes—entwine the tines. Two buttons. A needle and thread. A piece of gold foil, from one of the chocolates, carefully folded to preserve the embossed design. A bird's feather. A pretty rock—pink quartz. An old Indian arrowhead.

And a little doll.

It's one of Daniel's funny handmade ones. But this one's dress is from a scrap of material she does not recognize—pale blue cotton, patterned with tiny red flowers. She stares at the doll, at the dress of unknown provenance. It is not Jolene's.

And this is not a collection of a man. Or of an older woman. It's a young woman's collection—a young woman still on the brink of childhood. The kind of collection she would have made just a few years ago.

Eula's?

Had Daniel gone looking for Marvena's daughter as promised and found only this?

She inhales deeply, suddenly unsure of how to breathe properly. Her gaze falls on a wooden chest in the corner, used to store extra sheets and thick blankets for the winter and a few old pairs of pants and shirts; sometimes men are brought in filthy and covered in their own sick.

The chest is deep, with sufficient layers for hiding small items. Notes for cases he'd rather she not know about? She's never suspected such, but then, she'd never anticipated a woman like Marvena was part of Daniel's life. The notion is sufficient to launch Lily from her chair to the chest. She lifts the heavy wooden lid, frantically pulls out blankets, shirts, pants, vigorously shakes each one, loosens nothing but lint, drops the items to the floor.

Disappointment shoves her back to her desk. She grabs up the rustic doll, stares at it as if it might suddenly offer answers to the questions spinning in her head. Where else could she look? She knows every nook of their house.

Oh. The chest in the attic. Where they kept her old wedding suit, his old army uniform. She hasn't looked up there for years, though occasionally Daniel went up to pack away items for her—their Christmas ornaments, the crib, which would need, come to think of it, to be brought down and cleaned up for the baby, a task Daniel would do—no, would have done.

"Lily?"

She whirls around and sees Martin in the doorway of the jailhouse. She quickly drops the box in the drawer, knees the door shut, suddenly protective of the little box. The other man with Martin is Tanner Riley, chief of the Bronwyn County commissioners.

"Please tell me you've found the prisoner who killed my husband."

"Oh, Lily," Martin says. "I'm so sorry, but—"

"A name, then!"

Martin's frown makes his usual baby face look older than his twenty-eight years. "It's Tom Whitcomb. Marvena's brother."

Lily stares at him. Speckles dance over his face, and she blinks hard and inhales slowly, to keep herself centered. Then she says, "How long have you known?"

"I went to Rossville this morning, Lily. Several Pinkertons and miners confirmed it."

So Luther truly hadn't known the prisoner's name yesterday when Marvena showed up. No doubt he'd have thrown the name at both of them.

"And why was Mr. Whitcomb arrested in the first place?"

Martin and Tanner exchange looks: surprise at Lily's cool questioning.

"The Pinkertons we talked to say roughhousing. But Tom has been known to talk organization, even at work. You know how Luther feels about that. Daniel, too. That is—" Martin stumbles over his words. "How he—how he felt."

Oh yes, Lily thinks. She knows well Luther's strong opposition to unions. And on that he and Daniel had been agreed—until last fall. The Widowmaker collapse had shaken Daniel's belief that Luther's anti-union stance was right. He had loved his father-in-law dearly and had mourned his death caused by trying to rescue the trapped miners. Of late, he had talked with her privately about coming out against Luther in support of unionization—of what that would mean to him and how that might impact their family. Many of the shopkeepers in Kinship—including Martin—side with Luther on this matter, for while Luther lives with Elias on the farm, other managers live in Kinship. Then, too, the coal company keeps the railroad busy and the railroad employs many men in town.

"Well then, has anyone talked with Marvena Whitcomb?"

Martin stares at her.

"The suspect's sister? Might she know something of places her brother is likely to hide?"

Again, Martin and Tanner exchange looks.

Tanner clears his throat. "We—we aren't sure where she lives. We asked in Rossville, but none of the miners or their kin would admit to knowing."

Lily gives Martin a hard look. "She mentioned that she'd talked with Daniel about her daughter. That's why she came to this house. She must have felt pretty confident he would help her, to come to his house." *Our house.* "Surely he knew where she lives?"

Martin glances away as his face reddens "Well, yes. But . . . I never went with him to her cabin. Just saw her once, in Rossville."

"I see. Please tell me that at least there's still a manhunt for Tom Whitcomb."

Tanner says, "Now, Lily, there were plenty of resources expended the first days, but by now the prisoner is surely long gone. It's hard to track a man in the hills—"

"No manhunt?" Lily grabs Martin by the arm. He looks at her, startled. "Then have you talked to Rusty Murphy? The farmhand who works for Ada Gottschalk? Surely someone has thought to ask what he observed, what he might know?"

Tanner looks perplexed at the suggestion, but Martin looks back at Lily. "I tried. But the man's run off as well."

A missing prisoner—the supposed killer. A missing Pinkerton—the one who'd come to tell Daniel to pick up Tom. A missing farmhand—the first person to find Daniel.

Lily rubs her forehead, as if that will erase the sudden throbbing in her temples. "Well then. I guess there's only one reason you're here." She clears her throat. "We kept the house in good repair, but I'd like a few days to clean from top to bottom."

Their clothes, of course they can take those. Books, kitchenware. The automobile. She can go to Lewis Automotive today, demand it. Much of the furniture is theirs; perhaps they can store it for a time in the carriage house? Mama will take them in, of course, but she can't

imagine staying with Mama forever and drawing on her precious resources, the proceeds from the sale of the grocery. What had Daniel set
aside in savings? If there's some savings, she could sell the furniture,
maybe start over in Cincinnati in nursing.

Martin smiles gently. "No, Lily, we're not here to boot you out. We're
here to ask if you'd consider being the acting sheriff."

As Lily gasps, Martin smiles gently. "It's not a position, with the demands of my business, that I can fill, and Fiona—" He glances down.
"Well." He looks back up. "She told me about your visit earlier this
morning. So we thought if you were interested—well, we presumed to
bring the paperwork. If we complete it this afternoon, I can take it over
to the judge. And you can be sworn in tomorrow afternoon."

Tomorrow? Lily can't breathe or move, as if the air freezes around
her, and she with it.

Tanner misinterprets her hesitancy. "Now, we know it's a most unusual position for a woman, but with these modern times and all—
well, my little woman just can't stop reminding me of her right to vote
and the power of the women's temperance league!" His chuckle fades
at Lily's stiff silence. He blows his bulbous red nose into a handkerchief
and adds, "It would just be until November, until a special election for
someone to fill Daniel's role through next year, until the 1926 election.
And Martin will stay your deputy—"

"If you'll have me—" Martin says.

"Course she will. And, Lily, we'd still want you to be jail mistress.
So you'd be paid for that, same as always, and a small bonus for the
title of sheriff. But don't worry. The Pinkertons can handle most trouble with miners. They have their own means." Tanner looks pleased at
the thought of those cruel *means.* "You won't even have to transport
prisoners from Rossville's holding cell to the jailhouse!" Tanner grins
as if being sheriff is no real challenge, so of course even a woman could
do it—in title only, of course.

Lily clears her throat. "How nice. Specially since while transporting
a prisoner, my husband was shot."

As Lily turns over in her mind what's being offered, she looks at
Tanner Riley, his thin, barely patient, patronizing smile. So much eas-

ier this way than electing a new sheriff, one who might make it a mission to ask questions and unearth the truth. One who might not support the Pinkertons the way Tanner would like. A bonus: saving money by not paying her as they would a proper male sheriff.

But they are offering her something else. They've underestimated her, as she finds men so often do with women. They're offering her access as sheriff to go places, to ask questions.

"What a kindly offer. I'd be glad to accept," she says.

She waits until they leave, then goes back inside the jailhouse. On the front of the unused notebook, she writes her name. "Lily Ross." Below that, "March 29, 1925." She hesitates just a moment, then adds next to her name: "—Sheriff."

CHAPTER 8

⤳

MARVENA

Even as night falls on Devil's Backbone, Marvena beats a rag rug of scraps gathered and saved over time, tied and braided and sewn together. It's the final chore of the day. She's washed her blouse sleeve and re-stitched it to its bodice. Swept the cabin clean. Scrubbed the cookstove top. Now, she does not care that she's beaten the rug so long against the trunk of the oak tree that dirt no longer gusts free. She could beat this rug into threads, then the tree into a whittled version of itself, and still fury and pain would burn deep within her.

Marvena has beaten the rug for so long that even Shep, snoozing on the top step of the porch, no longer jolts at each thump.

Thump.

For the threatened unionization efforts.

Thump.

For Daniel's death.

Thump.

For Tom, missing.

Thump.

For Eula, still gone.

Thump.

For poor Frankie, inside the cabin, sulking over having to breathe in steam from the kettle and drink more elderberry tea, because yesterday's trek had brought back her rattling cough.

Thump.

For Lily's graciousness in their shameful meeting, and for the doubt gripping Marvena's heart that Daniel's widow will come with news about what she'd found in Daniel's notes about Eula. Still, upon returning the previous day Marvena had quickly sidled into Rossville, left Daniel's lunch pail with Nana, instructed her to put it out on her porch. She'd hurried out a back way without being spotted. If Lily comes to Rossville, she'll see the pail. There's but one long dirt road in town, with just foot and mule paths elsewhere, and Nana and Jurgis's house is one of the first upon entering the town.

Thump.

For her beloved John, sealed forever in Devil's Backbone. Leaving her a lonely widow, too. Leaving her to carry on their work for unionization at Ross Mining.

Thump. Thump. Thump!

For her own heart cracking open with deeper sorrow than befits friendship. For the fear, rising from a vault deep in her heart, that John died knowing better than she did that part of her still yearned for Daniel.

With her next *thump*, a memory loosens: Shep has the same markings as a coonhound they'd had years ago, one Marvena had witnessed being mauled by a black bear. Daddy had run out of the cabin, half-drunk, but clear-minded enough to know eight-year-old Marvena didn't normally scream, so he'd grabbed his shotgun. He shot the bear and then the mauled dog to put it out of its misery, then taught her to shoot, right there, his face taut with fear. He'd made Marvena shoot and shoot and shoot both the dead bear and dog over and over until she couldn't much tell the remains of one from the other. *Sometimes, you've got to do the hard thing no one else wants to do,* he'd told her.

Recollecting the scene feels like a bad sign. Suddenly her arms and hands ache and tremble. She stops beating the rug and it flags in her hands.

Marvena drags the rug with her—not even caring that she's sweeping up the very dirt she'd just thumped out—and sits down on the porch step. Shep moves over toward her, nudges her arm insistently until she scratches his scruff. He sighs happily, settles his head on her lap.

A snap. Marvena startles, sits up. Maybe the snap is just a critter, emboldened by nightfall to creep too close to her cabin? Another snap. No. It's a foot carelessly cracking some stray branch or other felled by the passing harsh winter.

Shep lifts his head, turns his gaze to the darkness.

Marvena attunes to the trespasser's tread. Her hunting knife, freshly sharpened, is in its sheath on her waistband, her pistol strapped to her ankle. Her shotgun is just inside the door.

At the next snap, Marvena stands, pulls her knife from its sheath, just as Jurgis Sacovech steps into the clearing, then jumps back, hands up. "Whoa, Marvena—"

Marvena re-sheaths her knife. "You know to holler out when you get close."

Jurgis looks down, accepting the reprimand. Then he glances back and calls, "Come on!"

Around the corner of the cabin comes Alistair, Tom's son. Marvena grins, happy to see her nephew. Then she notes the boy's coal-darkened face, and her grin slides away.

Course he'd have been taken from school and put in the mines to work off his father's scrip, just as soon as Tom was thrown in the holding cell. In the shock of Lloyd's death, Tom's disappearance, and Daniel's death, Marvena is ashamed to realize she hasn't thought of this.

Alistair's face knots and he fights off tears. Marvena rushes to the boy, hugs him. He curls, quivering, into her embrace. At eleven, he's nearly as tall as she is but still just a child.

Marvena looks up at Jurgis. "But they can't—" The boy is too young, even by non-union standards, to be in the mines.

"Rules don't matter to the likes of Luther," Jurgis says. "Specially now. Reckon you were right—Sheriff Ross was holding Luther in check, at least a little. But Luther's gone and closed the school—repairs, he says."

Years before, Daniel had pressured his half brother into having a simple one-room school in Rossville, free to all, sufficient for teaching the children up to age fourteen.

"Repairs?" Marvena snorts. "That skinflint just don't want to pay the schoolmarm!"

"Without the sheriff . . ." Jurgis gives the boy a pointed gaze. "We need to talk."

Marvena releases Alistair. She looks in his eyes. "Go in the cabin. Tell Frankie I said you can have th'rest of the corn pone."

The boy hesitates at the mention of the dense bread, made from corn-meal, lard, and water, so Marvena adds, "There's sorghum, too."

He lights up at the reference to the sweet yet savory dark syrup made from sorghum cane. Marvena usually nurses a few quart jars through the year, until she can barter again with one of the farmers who follow the time-honored yet tedious process of boiling the cane down to make the syrup, sugar cane being more precious and expensive to come by. But Alistair's hopeful expression at the thought of the sweet reminds her that he really is just a child.

"And you can have all you like," she adds.

Marvena watches as Alistair bounds past Shep and into the cabin. Then she turns back to Jurgis. "I know you're not here just about Alistair."

"Well, that's partly why. But there's several points of concern—"

"Get to it."

Jurgis's jaw tightens. He looks at Marvena defiantly. "First, what the hell were you thinking, going into Kinship?"

"You know of that?"

"Everyone knows of that by now."

"Well, if I'd known about D-daniel . . ." Marvena pauses, hating the quaver in her voice at even saying his name.

"You were supposed to lay low. But instead you go to the sheriff's widow—"

"Goddammit, I didn't know! And I was going to Daniel—" Suddenly Marvena's arms are shaking, as if beating the rugs really had tested them to soreness. "I didn't bring up unionization with Mrs. Ross, if that's what's a-worrying you."

Jurgis lifts his eyebrows and crosses his arms. From the woods around the cabin's clearing, night sounds start to creep closer. "Well, why in God's name did you go, then?"

The truth bursts out of Marvena. "Because of Eula! The damned fool girl's been gone since mid-February."

"I'm sorry, Marvena. There's been talk, that Eula's been *seen,* with Pinks. Getting in their fancy cars. Likely run off with one of them. After all, miners are paid in scrip—no good to her—while Pinks are paid, and pay, in cold, hard cash. She's abandoned us, Marvena. And now we've got bigger things to worry about. Can't you just let this go?"

Marvena's hand moves to her knife after all. She stares, cold, at Jurgis. She wants to run him through for saying that. She won't do it of course—she hasn't made it all the way to thirty-five living hand to mouth, especially as a woman, without learning to carefully gauge every word and action.

"*Let this go*? You mean, let *Eula* go? Let *my daughter* go? Would you?"

Jurgis looks at her directly, now, and she sees in his gaze that yes, yes, he just might. Many men would. Men who think nothing of using a woman, like she'd been used, like Eula had been used, who see it as a point of pride, even as they toss aside the woman like a dirty dishrag for the same fool carnal pleasures.

But not men like Daniel.

Jurgis says, "Eula's probably happier with whoever she ran off with—miner or Pink. Or even by herself. Even if you can suss out her whereabouts, she won't thank you, and no good would come of it. More'n likely, Eula'd get back by betraying all she knows of our efforts."

"All right, then." She wonders at her own voice sounding stilted, distant, as if it's echoing back to her from across a holler. Jurgis nods, as if that settles the matter of Eula. But Marvena is not going to let go of her daughter that easily.

"I told you, few days ago at Lloyd's, it looked like the sheriff took Tom from the holding cell," Jurgis says. "Well, now the talk is that Tom killed him on the way back to Kinship."

Marvena stares hard at her old friend. "I figured that much out when I visited Mrs. Ross. You really believe that?"

Jurgis shakes his head. "Don't matter what I believe. The deputy, Martin Weaver, was in Rossville this morning, with other men, asking questions. Wanting to know how to find you."

Marvena lifts her eyebrows.

"No one gave you up," Jurgis says. "Not this place. Or your still. And I'm telling you, maybe it's time to lay off organizing."

"No! Now's the time to press harder. Tom was more'n likely set up. Why, with Daniel gone, Luther would be free to get a more supportive man into office—"

"Marvena! That's dangerous territory! You can't go accusing the sheriff's brother—"

"We live and breathe dangerous territory," Marvena says. "Now, you take Alistair on back, and you tell the men we'll go on as planned."

"Marvena, you have to take in Alistair, and we have to stop union talk for now."

"No. If we stop now, give in now, when will we get the momentum back?"

Jurgis looks as shocked as if she'd pulled her knife out after all. "Marvena . . . you can see, with Tom gone, they're putting the boy to work in his stead. Today wasn't so bad, but soon enough they'll put Alistair in the narrowest shafts, setting dynamite for new veins."

She presses her fingertips to her forehead. Her hands have gone suddenly cold. She's already lost so much. John. Eula. Daniel. Tom. What will those losses mean if she doesn't take this moment to push the men toward real change?

She sees Alistair's face. Then the weary faces of the men, at the last meeting in the cave near Marvena's still. Some from Ross Mining. Some from other companies in Bronwyn County and beyond. The quest to unionize Ross Mining is quickly growing into a regional movement.

"If I hide Alistair here, the men will know I've lost heart. Then someone will say where I am. The new sheriff and his men will come, looking for Alistair and Tom. And *here* is too close to the cave. Once that's found, where can we meet that's safe?" She pauses for effect. Her gift, the gift of speechifying, has caught up both her and Jurgis. "But if they see Alistair, a mere boy, working the mines, won't that enrage and embolden them? That, with Lloyd's death, may be the tipping point we need. As foolish as it may have been for me to go into Kinship, it was even more so for me to have hidden up here. I can do no good by hiding. So tomorrow, I will go down to the town as I ever have, working among the women, pretending I'm just there to help Nana with doctoring. Tonight, Jurgis, you will take Alistair back home with you. Then gather the men. We will meet in the cave—"

"Tonight! So soon?"

"We can't let the men lose heart. So, yes. Tonight. Spread the word to the men as you can, and have Nana spread it to the women. Just the men we know are fully on our side. We need to meet while Luther's distracted by Daniel's death, and afore the men lose steam. They need to know Daniel . . ." Marvena pauses, but this time, it is to keep her voice from cracking. She clears her throat, goes on. ". . . t'know Daniel was on their side."

Jurgis gives Marvena a long look, and for a moment she fears he's going to revolt. She holds his gaze steady. At last, though, he says, "And will they believe you?"

"Yes. They will. Because it is true."

Jurgis stares at her. Marvena reads in his expression a mix of wonder and dismay at her coldness, but she keeps her gaze steady.

"What about gathering the dynamite?" he asks, his voice nearly a whisper, as if even the squirrels and other small woodland creatures might be Luther's spies. "We haven't even started!"

The plan was to get enough men to walk off that Luther couldn't quickly or easily replace them, so that he'd be forced to let the men decide for themselves if they wanted unionization. And to get the most loyal to sneak dynamite out of company storage—not so much at once that it would be missed, but enough over time that they could use it to defend themselves if necessary or threaten to blow up the Rossville depot and tracks if Luther won't listen.

Up from Rossville rises the sound of the train whistle, the last departure of the night.

Marvena stares down at her feet and at the rug. An idea comes to her. The sticks are small enough to roll up several in a rag rug. And, why, womenfolk love to work on such crafts, so there'd be no suspicion at a gathering of select miners' wives making rugs. What if she could get the women to bring her dynamite, sneak it out in rugs, hide it in her most secretive spots in the woods and cliffs on Devil's Backbone?

Then she thinks of the school, closed for so-called repairs. If asked, she could say the women were making them to sell in Kinship to raise funds. And that would solve another problem—she'd have an excuse to go to Kinship to find Lily if the woman didn't find her as promised.

Marvena plucks up her rug. She looks at Jurgis. "Don't worry. I have a plan."

She heads into her small one-room cabin, with Jurgis behind her. Alistair is sitting at the table with Frankie, trying to get her to eat the corn pone and sorghum that Marvena had said was his.

Marvena puts the rag rug down by the door and swallows the coal-hard lump back down from her throat. How can she do this to Alistair, her own nephew, when just days ago she protested the notion of Lloyd's older boy in the mines? But she hears again her daddy's words from so long ago: *Sometimes, you've got to do the hard thing no one else wants to do.* When she stands up, she looks evenly at the boy. "Alistair, you're going to have to go back with Jurgis."

"No, Mama!" Frankie protests because she is lonely, not because she knows to worry for Alistair's fate. But Alistair, after only one day in the mine, is smart enough to be scared. Marvena sees it in the tight shine to his eyes.

"You be a man, now," Marvena says to her nephew. "Do the hard things you have to do." Then she offers him the only comfort she can, knowing full well it may be a lie. "Everything . . . will come out right. Mark my words."

From the porch, Marvena and Frankie watch as Jurgis and Alistair vanish into the night's chill darkness. An owl's call shakes Marvena back to the moment, and she shudders at the sound—a sign of death. Past . . . or future? Daniel, a believer in signs ever as much as Marvena, would have also frowned at the warning.

Marvena shoos Frankie back into the cabin and sets to making another ministering kettle of hot water. Tonight, they will gather in the cave, and she'll need to take Frankie with her.

CHAPTER 9

※

LILY

Late that night, after the children are in bed, Lily lies wide awake, waiting. She wants to make sure they are asleep before she steps out of the bedroom to go up to the attic, her last hope for finding clues within the house about Eula. If Daniel had done any investigating as Marvena asked, he might have taken notes after all. But he wouldn't have put them where Lily could easily find them. She rarely went up to the attic—that was Daniel's task—and it would be odd to their children to see her climbing the stairs. And these past days have been so upsetting to them, no need to burden them further with odd behavior.

Odd. With Marvena's sudden appearance in her life, on the heels of Daniel's death, her life feels completely odd. At odds, in any case, with the life she thought she'd had: Safe. Secure. A close, honest marriage. But Daniel had kept Marvena from her.

That fact had trotted alongside her all day, like a wolf waiting to lunge at her throat. When she'd gone to ask Hildy to be jail mistress. When she'd told Mama the news of her being acting sheriff and listened to her explode with worry. When she'd walked over to Lewis Automotive and demanded the return of Daniel's automobile. Her automobile. She could drive it, she assured Mr. Lewis, without the replacement of the side window.

She'd instructed Mr. Lewis to let her know when the new door and window were in. Behind the garage, by herself with the automobile, she stared for a long moment at the bullet hole in the driver's side door, the missing window. She'd looked inside, noting that all the glass that surely must have fallen onto the bench seat and floorboard had been cleaned up. Then she'd slowly eased into the driver's seat, trailed her hand over the steering wheel, hand lever, hand brake, and key in the ignition. Had he been sitting here, when he'd been shot? Or had he gotten out of the automobile first, started to give chase?

Now the images of the missing window, the bullet hole in the driver's side door, haunt her as she stares into the dark, yearning to drift off to dreamless sleep.

It occurs to Lily that all the times she's lain awake at night, restless and troubled, have been because of Daniel. When he was away at war. Before that, when they honeymooned in Cincinnati and he went out, against her wishes, for one last fight in the boxing ring. Before that, when she was recovering at the home of Elias and it was, for a few days, Daniel's job to carry her downstairs in the mornings and upstairs at night, and though he refused to look down at her face, she felt his fingers trembling, aching to curl into her body. She'd ached for that, too, though then he was twenty-four to her mere seventeen years of age.

She aches for that now, as she stares across the room at the wardrobe, right by the window. There is enough light—it is a full moon—glinting through the curtains that she sees that she's carelessly left the wardrobe doors open. She looks at the gray lines of Daniel's clothes and realizes she's seeking among them a glint, a glimmer, a movement.

Focus, Lily admonishes herself. She lights the coal-oil lamp on the bed stand, planning to head up to the attic, but she finds herself in front of the wardrobe, shivering, touching the sleeve of one of Daniel's work shirts. She pulls it on over her nightgown. Inhales. His scent is still on his shirt, musky and yeasty and salty and smoky.

In the hallway, she pauses, thinking she hears Jolene moaning. But then it's silent, save the creaks of the house. She slowly opens the door to the attic—that door's hinge, so rarely tested, is silent—and treads carefully up the stairs. In the attic, Lily briefly touches the crib, then steps around the box of ornaments, an old rocker. There, against the back wall, is Daniel's old footlocker.

Lily kneels before it.

On the top is her wedding suit dress, a bit dated but still a lovely olive-green linen. She studies it. She needs something to wear to the swearing-in ceremony tomorrow. She's only put on a few pounds since her marriage, and she's not yet showing with this new child. Surely the jacket will fit and she'll only need to take out a few stitches in the skirt's waistline.

Next she carefully lifts Daniel's army uniform, studying the medals still pinned to the jacket front, the Verdun with the orange ribbon, from France to all U.S. men who'd fought in the Meuse-Argonne, the Victory Medal with the rainbow ribbon and the three metal crossbars: Meuse-Argonne, Ypres-Lys, Defensive Sector. She runs her thumb over the silver Citation Star, precisely pinned in the middle of the ribbon.

Daniel'd earned it trying to save her brother, Roger, and several other men. Roger had fought alongside Daniel, part of the American Expeditionary Forces' Thirty-Seventh Division—tagged "Ohio's Own" because most of the men came from the state—Seventy-Fourth Infantry Brigade, Roger an assistant gunner to Daniel, a machine gunner. But Daniel hadn't been able to save Roger from trying, on his own, to take out a number of German soldiers and, in so doing, drawing the attention of a sniper.

Lily carefully refolds Daniel's uniform and places it beside her dress. Next Lily spots a thin packet of letters from Daniel, sent during the war. She starts to reach for them, but then she sees Daniel's old boxing gloves. She hadn't realized that he'd kept them.

When she and Daniel first moved here, she'd sometimes see him punch a bag he'd hung in the carriage house. Then he'd stop, lift his gloved hands, his left arm only going up far enough to make a corner with his body. She'd pretended not to see the pale, pinched look around his mouth, bitterness at the fraction of mortar shell from the Great War still biting into the muscle of his left shoulder. Those nights he moved slowly as they made love, while she took the lead. They never talked about his lost boxing career, his years fighting for George Vogel.

Lily carefully sets the letters aside and pulls out the gloves. The leather is tight, stiff. She runs her finger over the thick stitching. With sudden, desperate need, she picks apart the knot holding the two gloves together. One glove drops to the floor; the other she holds to her face, pushing her nose into the opening, inhaling slowly, deeply, the scent of leather.

Daniel's hands were large, so there is no need to loosen the laces as she slips on the gloves. She bites into the tan trim, savoring the satisfaction of feeling her teeth sinking into the leather, as she pulls the gloves on the rest of the way. It reminds her of biting into Daniel's belt so long ago to endure the amputation of her little toe and what she'd foolishly thought would be the worst pain of her life.

Daniel never let her put on his boxing gloves. Once, after they'd moved here, while unpacking, she'd playfully started to put them on, but he'd snatched them away.

I told you before, some things aren't meant for women . . . not a woman who's my wife. . . .

It was a rare argument. Startling. Like the one they'd had on what would be Daniel's last night on earth. Perhaps she should feel guilty, pulling on his forbidden boxing gloves, just one day after his burial. But they'd spent their marriage doing things *proper,* and now . . .

She savors having her hands where his had been. The gloves wobble ridiculously on her thin wrists. Lily stands, moving to a clear area in the middle of the attic, and takes a few light swings just to see if the gloves will stay on.

They do, and she throws a harder punch into the air, and then another. The punches come faster. She thrusts her fists forward, first right, then left. Her right jab is faster, more controlled, but her left is stronger. Something takes over; she forgets about her children sleeping, that attic noise might stir them.

A punch at Daniel, for holding back the knowledge of Marvena.

A punch for Eula . . . *his daughter?* The possibility, lurking at the back of her mind ever since Marvena's visit, jabs up from her gut and through her heart.

A punch for Marvena.

He'd hate for Lily to act like this.

Well, she hated *him* for keeping Marvena secret, this whole other relationship, important enough that the other woman brazenly came calling, expecting Daniel's help as her right.

Punch, jab.

Had he thought her so foolish, so simple, that she would have turned cold to him if he'd told her the truth about a past lover and, possibly, child? Or was she foolish and simple to cling to the notion of *past*?

Punch, jab, uppercut.

Let Daniel stop her. Let his spirit come back, show her one of his precious signs.

Daniel's boxing gloves are suddenly too heavy. Lily's arms fall to her sides, shake. But she savors the soreness. A call-and-response between anger and ache.

Was this how Daniel felt when he trained, when he fought?

Then she feels something in the right glove that she must have dislodged with her swings. An edge of the paper teases her fingertips.

She pulls out the pieces and stares at them in her hand. The faded bluehair ribbon is the one she'd given Daniel, all those years before.

Her gaze shifts from the blue ribbon to the paper, a ticket for a boxing match, Daniel Ross versus Frederick Clausen. The ticket is dated August 20, 1917.

Daniel's last fight after their marriage.

His last fight before enlisting in the Armed Expeditionary Forces.

His last fight, at least in a ring.

She stares at the blue ribbon, as if it can transport her back in time.

Lily still limped a week after the emergency surgery, but she held her shoulders straight as she slipped through the barn door, determined to see Daniel once last time before returning to her parents' house in Kinship. To bring him a slice of buttermilk pie.

But once inside the door, Lily stopped.

In the far corner, his back to her, was Daniel. He'd stripped off his shirt and pulled on boxing gloves. Sweat soaked his undershirt as he pummeled again and again a punching bag hung from another hook.

She took in every bit of him with her gaze—the bow of his head as if he worshiped at the swing of the bag, the pull and stretch of his muscles with each wrathful thrum, thrum, thrum *of his fists against the bag. She felt in that beating rhythm his intention to keep going until mind and memory and muscle all melted to mere spoonfuls of sopping grayness.*

In every punch, she felt each moment of her time at the Ross household: the blurry, fitful days after Dr. Elias Ross performed emergency amputation, right there on the dining room table; sorting out details about the people tending her: Sophie, the doctor's wife, who was so much younger than Elias, and Ruth, their ten-year-old daughter, and Miss Mary, the old woman who was their live-in helper; realizing it had been decided for her that she'd recuperate at the Ross farm, because Mama was still in Cincinnati with her parents, and Daddy and Roger were busy renovating the store, and here Elias could keep an eye on her and make sure infection didn't set in. She'd known in general of the Ross family, of course, and that the family had founded Ross Mining and Rossville, and had assumed—naively it now seemed after living here—that such a family must be fine and proper.

From Miss Mary, she learned that the man who'd calmed her at surgery was Daniel, Elias's nephew—and that she recovered in Daniel's old bedroom. Elias and Sophie had taken him in when he was just thirteen because his father, Elias's brother and founder of Ross Mining, was so abusive to him. With Lily here, he slept in the barn, no longer used except for two field horses, where he also was training as a boxer. He'd been a boxer from age eighteen but recently been hurt in the ring. Elias had gone to retrieve him, tried to talk him into studying medicine, but because he was a "savage," Miss Mary said with disdain, he was going back to

boxing. Lily asked why she called him savage—just because of the
boxing?—and Miss Mary said no, Daniel's mother had been a
full-breed Leni-Lenape Indian woman, who had worked for
Daniel's father's first wife. Shortly after that wife—may she rest in
peace! Miss Mary proclaimed—died from breast cancer, Daniel's
father had remarried the Indian woman.

Now, watching Daniel land each punch, Lily did not find him
savage. He was beautiful. She felt her face flare with heat, just as
it had when he'd carried her up and down the stairs as she healed.
As it had the previous night at dinner when she'd looked up to
steal a glance of him at dinner and caught him staring at her.
A tender moment, until it was interrupted by his older, by ten
years, half brother, Luther—who, she learned, had inherited Ross
Mining from their father, while Daniel had been entirely cut out
for years. Luther had cackled with glee that Daniel's "whore"
would be jealous.

Lily knew what "whore" meant. She didn't care. She was
sorrowful when Daniel stood, announced he'd be leaving for good
the next morning, to go back to Cincinnati to resume his boxing
career. And then he'd strode away. Through the dining room
window, she'd watched him mount his horse and ride off.

This morning, she'd tied up her hair with the pretty blue ribbon
that Mrs. Ada Gottschalk had given her on a visit because, the
dear woman said, she knew Lily's own mama was preoccupied.
Lily came down the stairs on her own, using the cane that Dr. Ross
had given her, and was disappointed that Daniel was not at
breakfast.

She'd insisted on cleaning up for the family and then cut a slice
of the buttermilk pie she'd helped make the night before—"Daniel's
favorite pie," Ruth had whispered when they made it, as if this
were the deepest secret about the man—the pie that Daniel had
left without tasting. Lily left her cane in the kitchen and took the
slice of pie out to the barn.

And so it was that she found herself staring at Daniel thrusting *his fists into the bag as if he wasn't aware she was standing there, and for a moment Lily feared she'd made a terrible mistake, the mistake of a young girl's foolish heart.*

But suddenly he stopped. Without looking at her, he spoke. "This is not a sight for girls."

"I'm not a girl!" Lily snapped. "It was my seventeenth birthday the day you met me."

Daniel pulled off his gloves, tied their laces together, and hung them on another hook by his shirt. He turned and looked at her. Held by his gaze, she moved steadily forward.

At a divot in the floor she stumbled, but though he lifted his hand as if wishing to catch her, he did not move toward her. He held her only with his eyes, trusting her to right herself.

Finally, she was before him, handing him the plate. He cut off a bite of pie. She focused on taking in the details of his face—the cauliflowered left ear, the thin slice of scar above his left eyebrow, the hard turn of his lips, the sharp slope of his nose.

He ate a bite, then another and another. She watched his throat move with each swallow.

He finished the pie. "Delicious," he said, with a flash of smile. But then his expression reverted to seriousness. "I'm only back because I had an injury, and my first loss, in the ring. I'm just here to heal and train so I can go fight again in Cincinnati for George Vogel. Do you know who that is?"

"No. And I don't care."

"You should. His name strikes fear into the hearts of many men. He runs a huge operation . . . never mind. I'm leaving tonight to go back to Cincinnati. Lily," he said, turning her name into a sigh. "You're too young for me. As Luther would tell you, I'm not a nice man."

She inhaled, savoring the spice of him. "I don't want a nice man. I want a good man."

It was Daniel's turn to catch his breath. Emboldened, Lily tried to stand on tiptoe. Too soon. She started to fall, and this time he did catch her. The plate shattered on the barn floor. Lily lifted her

mouth to Daniel's, and for one sweet moment he pulled her to
him, his fingers gripping her arms, her own fingers finding the
muscles in his back.

But the door opened and there was Miss Mary, fussing and
yelling for Elias.

Daniel made a fist, kissed his thumb, pressed it gently to
Lily's lips.

"I will be back," he whispered. "When you're old enough."

"How will I know you're all right?"

He grinned. "Just watch for a sign. My mother would say
a hawk, looking at you."

Lily gave him a soft smile. Then, slowly, she knelt to pick up her
blue hair ribbon. Before turning to leave with Miss Mary,
she tucked the ribbon in his right boxing glove.

When Lily comes back to herself, she is on her knees, next to the footlocker. Daniel's gloves are on the floor. The ribbon and ticket are in her fist.

She unclenches her hand and looks for a moment at the items. That he kept the blue ribbon surprises her as uncharacteristic sentimentality. Keeping the ticket, though, surely had to be for another reason. A reminder of some sort? Two years after their initial meeting, they'd met again, when Daniel returned to Kinship for a boxing match. Shortly after that, they'd wed at Mama and Daddy's house, then gone to Cincinnati for their honeymoon, staying at the Sinton Hotel, a gift from Daniel's boxing manager, George Vogel.

They'd argued over a fight scheduled during their honeymoon, Lily not wanting him to go, but Daniel told her *no one crosses George Vogel,* insisting he owed George this one last fight—a rematch with Frederick Clausen, the man who'd bested and injured him two years before—and had stormed off to fulfill the obligation. She'd wept herself to sleep with worry when he didn't come back, but she was too fearful to go into the strange big city by herself to find him. When he came back the next morning, he'd been calm and quiet. He told her nothing of the fight or his activities after it—only that he'd won, had celebrated with George and his cronies, and had enlisted in the American Expeditionary Forces.

He asked her if she would forgive him for their argument, and both relieved that he was back and struck with fear that he would be leaving again for the war, Lily had quickly done so.

Now Lily studies Daniel's uniform. The morning after that fight, he'd told her that once he returned he'd never have anything to do with Vogel again—a promise he hadn't kept.

She tucks the ribbon and ticket into the pocket on Daniel's shirt. Then she puts the boxing gloves back in the footlocker next to the packet of letters. She carefully picks up the letters, her heart thrumming, as if just by touching them she'll turn them to dust. Then she feels a thick booklet that's been slid at the bottom of the packet underneath the letters. She pulls it out—a Kinship Trust Savings & Loan passbook.

Lily sets aside the letters while she studies it. The cover is stiff; the passbook has rarely been opened. There are a few entries after the first one, dated December 1, 1919. Just after Daniel's first election as Bronwyn County Sheriff. It's for $40.00. The next entry, January 3, 1920, is for $42.00. After a few more monthly entries for similar amounts, the pages are blank.

She has to smile, just for a moment—that was Daniel. Good intentions of precise note-taking, then falling aside. But quickly her smile fades. The sheriff's monthly salary is now $165 a month. Back in 1920, it was $150. Lily tracks every bit she spends on the household, food, clothing, and such. She's certain Daniel couldn't save more than 25 percent of his monthly income. Where had this money, in this separate account, come from?

Lily flips back to the front of the passbook, looking for any notations. This time she sees the careful note in Daniel's handwriting in the inside front cover of the passbook: "Payable in full upon my death to Lily Ross," followed by the account number. Lily tucks the passbook in her pocket. Why had he never told about this account?

Lily places Daniel's uniform over his old boxing gloves in the footlocker. She shuts the lid, secures the latch. She picks up the packet of letters. Eventually, she'll reread them all, but not this night. Tonight, reliving the memory of the ribbon is enough.

She takes the letters, the passbook, the ticket and ribbon, and her wedding suit back down to their bedroom. She drapes her suit over a side chair and then puts the smaller items in Daniel's drawer, alongside the chocolate box she'd found in the drawer in the jailhouse. She regards the items for a moment, her magpie collection of newly discovered bits from Daniel's life. They're crowding the familiar remnants, his shave kit and brush.

She picks up the brush, breathes in its fading menthol scent, puts it back, shuts the drawer. Suddenly she is too hot. She goes to the window and opens it just a bit, enough for a cool, thin night breeze to ease her of the desire to claw at her suddenly hot skin.

Then she picks up her notebook and fountain pen from the top of the wardrobe. She sits on the edge of the bed, staring down at what she'd written on the notebook's cover—her name and "—Sheriff."

Mama would say, *Don't count your chickens before they're hatched!*

For a moment, Lily stares at the curtain lifting and falling on the breeze.

Then she sets to work, writing out a timeline of the morning of Daniel's death, notes about Harvey Grayson, Rusty Murphy, Marvena Whitcomb. And a list for after she's sworn in: go to bank before it closes to inquire about the surprising, separate account.

Then, most important, find Marvena.

CHAPTER 10

❧

MARVENA

At nearly midnight, Rossville miners nearly fill Cobbler's Rock. Marvena calculates: there are nearly twice as many as their last meeting, in February, during the brief warm spell.

Now Marvena sits on a small rock on top of a flat, large boulder—makeshift chair on makeshift stage—as Jurgis speaks to the men gathered before him. He's warming the group, preparing them for her, talking about John Rutherford's work, about how Marvena as his widow—in fact if not by law—has taken on the mantle of his call for the past six months.

Marvena knows she should focus on Jurgis, but she's distracted by Frankie, sitting and humming near a small fire. Frankie's near on old enough to be left at home alone and Marvena had almost done so tonight, but a sign of foreboding—that damned owl, still crying near her cabin—made Marvena bring her along. Frankie had put on her new shoes, the hand-me-downs from Jolene, preening. But at least her foot had healed enough that she could walk all the way.

Suddenly tears prick Marvena's eyes. She looks away from the men—she cannot let them see her cry; she cannot let herself cry, lest she crumble. She turns her gaze back to the small fire. It throws large shadows on the cave walls, and to Marvena the shadows seem not to be of those gathered but of those lost.

Damn this sentimentality, hitting her just as she is supposed to rise and speak! Marvena tries to refocus her thoughts, stares at the petroglyphs on the wall curving to her left, stark images of people, animals, and symbols that bore no understanding now, and she wonders what ancient needful rites drove those people to this cave as she and her people are now driven.

The petroglyphs give her strength. And so when Jurgis calls her name, Marvena stands, strides to the edge of the flat rock.

She takes in the smudged and careworn faces of men whose families immigrated not so long ago from Wales and Scotland, Germany and Liechtenstein, Italy and Poland and Lithuania, some of them already miners, some new to the work. Some had been rescued last September, thanks to John's and other volunteers' efforts. Still, seven dead in all, including John and Caleb McArthur, Lily's father. The toll would have been higher without John leading the nonsanctioned rescue. Luther had been willing to authorize only a token rescue.

"Look at us," Marvena says, starting so softly that the men lean forward to hear the low strum of her voice, "here, under the earth, again. We meet in darkness. Why? Because we cannot meet in light. We speak in hushed tones. Why? Because we cannot speak out clear and free. What happens if we say loudly in the bright of day that we have rights? We have mouths to feed and feet to shod? Children to care for?" She stops. Looks at the men. She finds the angriest-looking man in the front row. She stares at him. She knows what he's lost.

Marvena drops her voice as she speaks directly to him. "What happens?"

His words, a strangled cry: "They turn you from your house, and your baby—"

Marvena nods. "That's right. You dared mention unionization to another man, the wrong man, a Pinkerton plant, and next thing you know, you're turned out—not of your house, Ross housing! So you move to the tent city. And then what happened to your baby? Tell us!"

The man speaks so softly that Marvena doesn't hear his words but she says as if she has and is repeating them, "Your baby catches whooping cough, and the drunken company doctor says it's nothing, just croup, and your baby dies." She pauses. Her words echo off the cave walls, through the silence of the men. When the echo fades, she goes on. "You were promised decent wages for decent work, and now you're held to company house, company store, company doctor." She gives each utterance of "company" a loathsome twist. "And if you dare say but we have mouths to feed, feet to shod, families to care for, you're taken even from that but not from your work. Your work only doubles. So what would you do? Other mines are organized. There are organizers who can come in, help us demand unionization, get some guarantees—"

Someone from the back cries out, "You all forget already the strike in Hayden last fall? Folks there were turned out of our company homes, set up camp in tents, and one night—"

He doesn't have to say what happened next at the coal-mining town just north of here, one of ten small mining towns, all separately run, scattered throughout the northern and eastern portions of Bronwyn County, more than fifty throughout southwestern Ohio. Some are unionized, some even peaceably integrated with Negro workers, Mingo being the best example. But here, in Bronwyn County, Rossville is the biggest mining town.

All here know what happened next in Hayden, in the strike for worker safety spurred in part by the Widowmaker explosion. Late one night last November, Pinks drove through, shooting tommy guns into the tent camp. Two women and three children were killed.

"New Straitsville still burns, and nary a thing's changed!" someone else hollers. They mean the mines in that town, when strikers decided to destroy the mines to get back at unrelenting bosses, setting a coal seam afire in 1884. The fire yet burns underground.

"Yeah, an' '94 was a waste," someone else adds. After the Panic of 1893, wages were so slashed in depressive times that miners across the country—in bands of hundreds and even thousands—struck. For a time, it seemed they'd gain the desired wages and safety provisions, but bosses brought in strikebreakers—scabs—and hired gunmen such as the Pinks and sympathetic sheriffs deputized many; in the end the militia-like standoffs, hunger, and desperation turned the struggle against the miners, and United Mine Workers was nearly destroyed.

"An' don't forget Blair Mountain!"

The gathering quiets. For most of these men, 1884 and 1894 and many conflicts between and since are already tales of yore, passed on by fathers and uncles, mothers and aunts.

But the Battle for Blair Mountain, fought just four years before, is fresh to many.

John, Marvena's husband, was a survivor of the battle. Into his unionization talks John had woven the story of how he'd left behind his elderly parents to support strikers at Blair Mountain in Logan County, West Virginia, when it turned into the largest armed uprising since the Civil War, lasting five days with weeks of skirmishes after that.

Even now, Marvena can hear John's voice, low and steady, sharing the facts: In the peak of battle, ten thousand armed coal miners faced a third that many lawmen and strikebreakers. But the benefit of numbers was undone by Sheriff Chafin's men holding the greater advantage of higher ground, better weapons, and coal management–funded private aviators who dropped homemade bombs—and even some government bombs left over from the Great War—on the strikers.

Near on a hundred strikers died, John would say, *just thirty on the other side.* The battle ended when, by order of President Harding, the army intervened. The striking miners scattered, but nearly a thousand were caught and held on murder and conspiracy charges. The battle nearly broke the back of unionization, again plummeting United Mine Worker membership.

Now the men's voices rise, some for unionization at any cost, some still unsure. Jurgis comes to Marvena's side, touches her elbow. She looks at him, smiles. She knows how long to wait, how to hear when the timbre of the voices turns too sharp, a warning that blows will be struck. It's a skill she learned from her parents' fights, knowing just when to scream as loudly as her six-year-old self could to distract them from each other and focus their wrath on her. That seemed better than letting them kill each other.

Out of the corner of her eye, Marvena sees that Frankie has stopped playing with her rocks and is anxiously staring at her mother. Jurgis goes to the child, wraps an arm protectively around her little shoulders.

Marvena looks back at the miners, waits calmly, and then finally barks one word: "Men!"

They settle somewhat, and Marvena says, "Do you not know you must all join together? Helping your brother is helping yourself! Why do you think the Pinks knew they could get away with shooting and killing innocent women and children in the Hayden tent city? Because of fear. Fear! You think you stink of coal, a stink you seek to wash away with company store pumice, but you know what? You really stink of fear and cowardice!"

The men fall into seething silence. *Careful. Push a little more . . . but not too hard.*

Marvena chooses her next words thoughtfully, speaks them softly: "Yet you are not cowards. You go down in the mines every day. You hunt when you can, to add food to your family's table. The men who send you into the mines would crumble if they had to do half of what you have to. Can you see Luther Ross going into the mines he owns?"

A few laugh. Everyone here can agree on one thing: hating Luther Ross.

She waits for the next wave of silence, then goes on. "How many miners are in this region? Thousands! How many boss men? A fraction of that." The men look at one another, a bit of hope sparking. "And all of you are armed. You have shotguns and rifles. Why, the companies themselves have armed you, with dynamite and axes and picks! If you march together, more than the unionization of Ross Mining is at stake. It's better treatment for all. It's said each man must work for his fortune, for bread for his family. But what good is individual work if the system is set against you and for only a few at the top? Now, now is the time to strike, to band together, an army of men fighting for *themselves.*"

Some of the men look at one another, startled. They'd come to hear about the possibility of the United Mine Workers helping Ross Mining unionize, not to be told to become an army.

"You all know Sheriff Daniel T. Ross. You know he was shot dead."

There are murmurings, nods. The men mostly liked him, even though he was Luther's half brother. As far as they knew, Daniel had not committed to being either for or against the cause of unionization. But all in all, he was known as a fair man, and all could agree that it was a shame—and shameful—that he'd been murdered.

"I met with his widow, Lily Ross. And she told me a Pinkerton sent him to Rossville. And you know what I know, that she didn't? I know that Daniel had had enough of our ill treatment! He was planning to go public in his support of our cause. He was going to get help for us! He was planning to report safety violations to a friend, an official, at the Bureau of Mines."

As gasps rise from the men, Marvena thinks back to the fight he and Tom had gotten into. What if that had made Daniel change his mind about looking into Eula? About reporting to this friend, whom he'd never named? Or what if he'd gone to Luther, threatened him with going to the Bureau of Mines unless Luther addressed safety issues?

A terrible notion rises in her mind: What if Luther had opted to stop Daniel forever?

The accusation blurts out before she can think better of it. "I believe Luther found out, and I believe he set up Daniel to be killed before he could help us!"

The men stare at her, dumbfounded at this allegation. She pauses, shocked by her own words, yet thinking it could be true. Still, her stomach curdles at using Daniel's death in this way. At the realization that she's pushing the men past the unionization efforts that Daniel would have sanctioned and toward all-out rebellion.

A man calls out, "Come on now. We all know your own brother Tom was the prisoner the sheriff came to fetch! How do we know you're not just covering for him?"

She blinks hard, keeps her voice even. "Yes, Tom is missing. But I have no need to defend Tom. He is no murderer. Would any here put it past Luther to use Tom as a scapegoat?"

The men mumble agreement with this possibility.

"No matter what's happened to Tom, this fact remains: without Daniel around to temper Luther's cruelty, he'll grind the men of Rossville down even harder. That will encourage other managers, even in unionized mines, to come down harder, too. Maybe even bust up the unions."

The men's muttering grows, and Marvena's voice rises along with the men's wrath: "Who, then, will take up arms and join together for the good of all, when the time comes?"

Later, Marvena eases Frankie down on the straw bed, covers her gently with the quilt so as not to awaken the sleeping child. Frankie mutters, then rolls to her side.

Marvena finds her way by habit to the table, lights a coal-oil lamp. She pours herself a dose of her shine, settles into a chair. The men are galvanized. They'd all agreed: two weeks to grow their numbers. Also: sneak out dynamite and bring it to their women. Marvena will collect it along with rag rugs, then walk out of Rossville with it rolled up in the rugs, and she'll take it to her hiding spots. When they're ready, the men will stop work. Protect themselves from Pinks with their knives and coal picks and axes and hunting rifles. And, if Luther Ross won't listen to them, blow up the train track and the loading yard. A few miners will be hurt or even killed. But this will happen anyway if they stay on the job. At least they'll be fighting for their rights.

Marvena sighs, takes another sip of shine. Her mind whirls. She can't relax. A chill comes over her: something is wrong. And then it strikes her: Usually Shep comes from under the porch, where he sleeps of a night, to greet them. But this night he hadn't, and she was so exhausted that she hadn't realized it until now.

Marvena grabs her shotgun and lamp, steps out the front door. No sign of Shep. Did a black bear get him? A wolf? Her heart tremors with a surprising rush of sorrow.

Then she hears Shep whimpering under the porch.

Marvena hunkers so she can see under the porch. In the lamplight, she sees that one of Shep's ears has been lanced, nearly off, lashes cross his back, and his front right leg twists back in a sickening, unnatural angle. Broken.

No bear or wolf had done this to Shep. The predator was far more dangerous: human.

"Shep," Marvena says softly, reaching under the porch for him. If she can just get him to wiggle forward a little, she can pull him by the scruff out the rest of the way. Fix him up. Save him. He looks at her, eyes wide with pain, and moans. "Come on, boy. Let me help you."

Dammit. She's not going to lose anyone else. Not even a fool coonhound.

CHAPTER 11

※

LILY

"I still think this is the damned foolest thing I've ever heard tell of a woman doing," Mama says the next morning as Lily steps into the kitchen. Mama's round face is so puckered with outrage that her mouth looks like the top of a drawstring purse. "And just two days after—"

Mama stops shy of finishing—*after Daniel's burial.*

But Lily sees, besides the outrage, the lines of worry on Mama's face. Lily goes over and kisses her on the cheek. "Yet you came. Thank you."

"Well, don't take my presence as approval. Though you do look right nice. . . ." Mama's grudging compliment trails off as she looks at Lily's abdomen. A look of suspicion crosses her face, and Lily quickly turns away, toward the table where the children sit.

"Now, you all be good while I'm out—" Lily starts. But then she sees that Jolene is playing with one of the tiny dolls Daniel made. This one has a dress from a bit of white-and-red-checked fabric that Lily recognizes—and something else. A bronze button, with thread tying it to the top of the doll's head, like a hat.

Lily rushes to the table, snatches the doll from Jolene. "Where did you get that?"

"It's one of the dolls that Daddy—"

"I mean the button." It's from Daniel's jacket, the one he'd been wearing when he left the morning of his murder. She always made sure his buttons were secure. "Where did you get it?"

"From that girl. Who came the day . . . that day." Lily's heart turns as she realizes Jolene can't bring herself to directly reference her father's burial just two days ago.

"Am I gonna get a switching?" Jolene's voice trembles. "She said I could have it."

"Did she say where she got it?"

Jolene shakes her head.

Lily forces a smile. "That was nice of her, Jolene. It makes a nice hat. May I borrow it?"

Jolene nods slowly, but her lip trembles. "Mama? Are you going to be all right?"

Lily kneels before Jolene, tucks a stray strand behind her daughter's ear. "I'm going to be fine. Say—would you like to come with me? Hold the Bible while I swear in?"

Jolene's face brightens with joy as this time she nods vigorously. Lily pockets the doll and turns to look at Mama. "Don't hold lunch for me. I have some things I need to take care of."

"Beats all I've ever heard tell of, a woman sheriff," Mama mutters. But then she rushes over and puts her hands to Lily's face. "Don't let a tin star make you do fool things, child."

As Lily looks down at Mama's face, she sees her mother's scowl is a thin mask for all her past losses, for worry about what her tomboy, impetuous daughter will do. No doubt her trip to Kinship Inn has already gotten back to Mama.

Lily doesn't say anything; she won't make reassurances she likely won't keep. But she scoops her mama up in a hug and presses a gentle kiss to the top of her graying head.

"I, Lily Ross, do solemnly swear, that I will support, uphold, and defend the Constitution of the United States, the Constitution of the State of Ohio, and the Charter and laws of Bronwyn County, Ohio; that

I will faithfully, honestly, diligently, and impartially perform and discharge all of the powers and duties incumbent upon me as sheriff in and for the county of Bronwyn, state of Ohio, according to the best of my ability and understanding. So help me God."

After her swearing in, Lily lowers her right hand and takes her left hand from the Bible that Jolene holds while staring up, beaming with pride. Jolene pins a sheriff's star on Lily's lapel.

"Good luck, Sheriff Ross," says the judge.

Just that quick, the ceremony is over. Jolene tucks the Ross family Bible under her arm. Lily takes her daughter's hand and turns in the courtroom to see that a small audience has gathered. Martin and Hildy. There in the back row, Luther and Elias. Word had spread.

Lily thanks Martin for coming and then asks Hildy to walk Jolene back to the house.

"First duty as jail mistress?" Hildy quips.

Lily gives a quick smile but flicks a wary gaze toward her brother-in-law and uncle. Even across the courtroom, Lily sees the glaze to Luther's eyes. After Martin, Hildy, and Jolene leave, Lily hurries past Luther and Elias in the hallway, hoping to escape with a nod.

But Luther's words catch her. "So here's our new pretty little lady sheriff." His voice is sloshy, the sloppiness of a drunk.

"Luther, don't—Lily, please wait—" Elias is saying. Lily stares down the long hallway, tiled in black and white, a checkerboard that makes her momentarily queasy. She puts her hand to her stomach; she'd either not had or not noticed morning sickness in the blur of days since *Daniel's been found,* but now, of all times, it seemed to be returning.

"I'm sorry," Elias says. "I thought—we thought—we should be here for such a momentous occasion since we're family."

After Elias's wife and daughter died in the 1918 influenza epidemic, Luther, a lifelong bachelor, moved from his Rossville house and into the farmhouse, supposedly to temporarily keep an eye on Elias. But it wasn't temporary, and now Elias kept an eye on Luther.

Lily offers Elias a quick smile and pats his arm. Family had always meant everything to Elias, and he'd lost so many—his wife, his daughter. Now his nephew Daniel.

But she looks pointedly at Luther. "Do you know where Harvey Grayson has gone?"

Luther looks confused. "Who?"

"The Pinkerton who showed up here, the night before Daniel died. You told me the man's name is Harvey Grayson."

Luther stares at her blankly and Lily realizes that he doesn't recollect their conversation on the porch. He probably doesn't even recollect his nasty words to and about Marvena.

"I was at the inn yesterday to locate Mr. Grayson," Lily says. Just yesterday? It feels like a lifetime ago. "He left the day of Daniel's funeral. If he was reassigned, surely you received word from the Pinkerton Agency? So you could tell me where he was sent?"

Luther shrugs. "The agency doesn't share where their agents are reassigned. Why should they? I don't care, so long as I have sufficient numbers. One's as good as another."

"Like miners?"

Luther grins again. "Something like that."

"I've also learned that the escaped prisoner is Tom Whitcomb. The brother of Marvena. Did you know that?"

Luther's grin dissolves into a frown. "Of course," he says, blustering. *He didn't know,* Lily thinks. God, did he pay attention to anything except drinking and trying to squeeze every bit of profit out of Ross Mining?

He looks at Elias. "I'll wait for you outside." He staggers down the hallway, whistling.

Lily finally looks back at Elias. "You're driving, I hope?" She really didn't want her first duty as sheriff to be filing a report on Luther having an accident.

"Of course, though it will be hard to convince him. You know how stubborn Luther can be." Elias smiles sadly. "He and Daniel had at least that much in common."

Elias looks at Lily, waiting, she knows, for her to soften. But she keeps her gaze hard.

"Lily," Elias says, "he's hurting, too. Things were hard between him and Daniel, but—"

"Don't!" The single word comes out as a snap.

As Lily watches Elias walk away, she suddenly longs to catch up, to apologize, but she doesn't want to confront Luther again. So she waits, giving herself a moment to simply breathe.

Minutes later, Lily steps out of the courthouse. She notes that Luther and Elias are nowhere in sight and is just observing that the spring day has turned blustery when two men rush up to her.

"Mrs. Ross! Mrs. Ross!" one calls. The other one, right behind him, holds up a camera; a loud pop and a flash of light and for a moment Lily can't see.

When her eyes clear, the man who called her name is grinning, pencil poised to notepad.

"So, Mrs. Ross, how does it feel to be the first lady sheriff in all of Ohio? It's a novelty position, but does this take some of the sting out of your husband's death?"

Lily glances behind the men, calculating; other people on the steps and walking in front of the courthouse have stopped to stare at this spectacle.

"Darby Turner," the man says, "with the *Cincinnati Enquirer.*"

Odd, Lily thinks. She doesn't see anyone from the *Kinship Weekly Courier,* which had carried the news of Daniel's death on its front page. Possibly other papers in the state had carried it as a news item, farther in. She hadn't thought her appointment especially newsworthy, although she knew it would be duly reported locally.

"Really something, a lady sheriff!" Darby is saying. "We did some digging and it seems the first was in Texas, about seven years back, similar situation—the sheriff died in office, and his wife, who'd been his office deputy, filled in as sheriff. Just until the next election, of course."

Lily gives a tight smile. "Was her husband shot by an escaping prisoner, too?"

The man recoils. "No. Stroke."

"Mmm. Still hard on the poor widow and the man's children, I'm sure. And this other lady sheriff, until she—*of course*—gave up her role at the next election, was she a novelty?"

The reporter frowns. "I don't know."

"You weren't here, as far as I know, covering my husband's death. So, novelty though I might be, why come all this way? And how did you know so quickly?"

Mr. Turner grins. "We received a tip. Now for my question. Is it safe to say you plan to carry on the role in the same way that your husband did?"

"I couldn't possibly dream of filling my husband's shoes," she says, forcing a demure smile to her lips. "I'm sure Commissioner Riley and Deputy Weaver will guide me, though."

Lily starts to enter the bank but stops short upon spotting the playbill poster in the bank window: "One Week Only! May 1–8, Kinship Opera House, Carson's Troupe, Five Vaudeville Acts: Miss Hennypen's Violin, Maestro Bo's Magic Show, Master Gill (All the Way from London!) the Elocutionist Recites Shakespeare, William and Guthrie's Amazing Dancing Mule, PLUS the newest Clara Bow comedy-romance, *Kiss Me Again!*"

Lily puts her hand to the pane as she studies the line drawings, rendered in thick black lines, of the violinist, the magician, the mule, and the photo of Miss Bow's enchanting pout.

The playbill reminds her of another from nine years ago. Lily leans into her hand on the glass. The image of Daniel's poster conjures itself with dizzying force.

Lily had been on a rare trip with Mama to Roer's Department & Dry Goods Store. While Mama coveted the new lace-up shoes on display, Lily lingered in front of Kinship Trust Savings & Loan, staring at a poster ad for three weeks from the day at the Kinship Opera House, "The Middleweight Fight of the New Century for the Greater Appalachian Region," with a photo of Daniel Ross, wearing just black shoes, socks, shorts, and boxing gloves, legs, fists, arms in a fighter's stance, leaning toward his imaginary opponent with a cocksure grin.

For the past two years, she'd cursed Daniel Ross for unearthing desires she'd never known before, making her miserable for the want of delicious, terrifying things, leading her to dare dream he wanted those things, too. Then leaving. Telling her there'd be a sign of him—of all things, a hawk looking at her. She'd not seen that or any other sign of him, and she'd stopped believing in signs. But dreams of him had not stopped, and that made her confused and angry.

Yet the sight of him, even in a grainy publicity photo, dissolved her anger like sugar on the tongue. She remembered that last moment in the barn.

He was beautiful.

He was everything she wanted in life.

The sudden knowing of how much she'd missed him broke loose, spilled over her, washed down her back, between her breasts, over her arms, though her groin, soaked her flesh.

When Mama called her name, she was leaning into the wall, forehead against the poster. Mama had given her a little shake, then clucked: *Boxing brings out men's savagery.* Yet, as Lily followed Mama into the dry goods store, she had sworn to herself she'd find a way to go to that boxing match, to see Daniel again, to confront him. . . .

A man accidentally jostles Lily—another Pinkerton. He stares at Lily, then at the sheriff's star on her lapel, and then looks back at her with a sneer before continuing to the street.

Out of the corner of her eye, Lily spots him joining several other new Pinkerton men walking down the road from the train station, a cocky swagger to their steps, their coats pulled back to reveal their weapons. A shopkeeper—Mr. Douglas, who'd bought out her daddy's business—steps back from sweeping to let them pass.

A woman with a pram crosses the street, away from the lurid gaze of one of them.

Another question to jot in her notebook: *Why is Luther bringing in more Pinkertons?*

She squares her shoulders, walks tall, and enters the bank.

Inside, after Lily has requested the manager, she sits in a leather chair in the waiting area. She's never had reason to be in the bank—Daniel took care of all of their finances—and so she gazes at the polished woodwork, the black-and-white-marbled floor.

A side door opens; Mr. Chandler, the bank manager, emerges. "Mrs. Ross," he says.

Lily follows him into his office. After they've settled in chairs, Mr. Chandler looks solemnly across his desk at Lily. "Mrs. Ross, we thought highly of your husband. We are all sorrowful at his loss. As the estate is settled, I'm sure his holdings will transfer to you."

"I'm here to ask about a second account, separate from his primary account," Lily says.

Mr. Chandler's eyebrows lift. He steeples his fingertips together. "I see," he says, and Lily takes his sudden reddening as indication that he's well aware Daniel did have a separate account. She unclasps her pocketbook and pulls out the second savings and loan passbook.

"I found this. It's out of date. I'm hopeful that you can tell me the full balance?" Lily pushes the passbook to him.

"Sheriff Ross did keep a secondary account. He set it up to pass in its entirety to you in case anything happened to him. If you'll wait a moment, I can look up the exact amount for you, but I think you'll find on the question of finances that you needn't worry." The banker gives her a sympathetic look. "Daniel wanted you to be taken care of. He'd be surprised you've become acting sheriff."

Surprised? He'd be furious.

After Mr. Chandler steps out of his office, sudden fear pinches Lily's throat, unbidden thoughts creeping forth: What if Daniel had changed his mind about this account going to her? What if he was one of those husbands who kept a secret account for a mistress? There was Marvena, but she wants to believe—needs to believe—that whatever had been between them was over long before Lily was part of Daniel's life. And Marvena certainly didn't have the visage or dress of a well-kept mistress.

Lily feels a moment of satisfaction at the thought, then shame at judging Marvena so superficially, and then shame comes full circle to fear. Her stomach is contorting by the time Mr. Chandler reenters the office and sits down behind his desk. He slides a piece of paper toward her. "It will take a few days to create a ledger for you of all the deposits and withdrawals over the years, but here is the balance as of today."

Lily has to fight to keep from gasping as she stares at the figure. Just over six times what Daniel made in a year.

$12,520.68.

Abe Miller is standing on Lily's front porch when she returns to her house. He leans against the porch post, casually flicking ashes into the standing ashtray.

So. He has received word at Kinship Inn that she'd come looking for him.

There are no scars on his smooth skin, no grime under his nails, no flecks on his perfectly pressed suit, and yet Lily sees in the directness of his gaze, the precision of his stance, even in how he holds his cigarette so steadily as its ash grows too long, that this man's goal is simple, calculated: efficient, passionless survival.

"I've heard you came calling for me," Abe says.

"You came to Daniel's burial," Lily says. She clenches her hands into fists to keep them from shaking. "You tried to speak to me at the cemetery."

Abe smiles, but there's nothing to it, not even bemusement. It's merely a reflex at her devotion to propriety, even in the most unusual circumstances. "I've come to offer condolences on Mr. and Mrs. Vogel's behalf."

"Thank you. Please tell the Vogels I appreciate that."

"Certainly. Now then, I'm here as well because we've received news of your appointment in Daniel's stead as sheriff. So in addition, I offer congratulations on Mr. Vogel's behalf. We were, ah, very beholden to your late husband. As he was to us."

Lily's face flames as the sum echoes in her head: *$12,520.68 . . .*

After Daniel had returned from the war, he'd taken her again to the Sinton Hotel in Cincinnati, a second honeymoon, this time a gift from him, not George Vogel. They had a wonderful time. But one morning, Lily had awoken to find her husband gone from their bed.

Daniel could no longer fight due to shrapnel that had torn through his shoulder—his heroics in the Great War had been reported in not only the *Kinship Weekly Courier* but in the Cincinnati and Columbus papers as well. Only one person could get Daniel to leave her side.

George Vogel.

She'd dressed in the garnet V-necked dress she'd worn the night before and searched the hotel until she found them in the bar: Daniel. George Vogel. Abe Miller. Goons tried to turn her away, but George waved them off and her in, his gaze leering. This was the second time she'd met George and Abe. Suddenly she felt exposed rather than elegant in her dress.

As she'd taken a seat next to Daniel, George told her that Daniel had just agreed to work for him. And when she'd looked back at Daniel in horror, he'd simply stated that George had heard of their stay at the Sinton, asked him to work in his business in Cincinnati, but that he'd declined the offer. Instead, he'd follow up on another tidbit of interesting news from George—that Bronwyn County Sheriff Tate was planning to retire. Daniel would run for sheriff. He'd win, given that he was a war hero.

Lily started to protest—*But what about Daddy's grocery?*—until Daniel put his hand firmly on hers. And she had read in his expression: *My love. Trust me. Trust me.*

And she had.

Now she thinks about how Daniel rarely pursued moonshiners. He always told her that Prohibition would have to end sooner or later—it was too expensive and dangerous to enforce. Not only that, but also he had his hands plenty full with law enforcement that would make a real difference in people's lives—stopping domestic abuse. Preventing deadly feuds over incidents that might seem petty to anyone else but mattered a great deal to the people involved.

Though as a suffragette Lily had been for Prohibition, she understood Daniel's reasoning that Prohibition laws were often unfair and ineffective and would no doubt eventually be repealed. Even before Prohibition was the rule of the entire country and functioning in states county by county, it seemed only to increase thirst by curiosity.

It's a surprise to no one that Vogel's Tonic is about 10 percent alcohol, and what if, rather than go to the expense of producing most of it following the Volstead Act rules that governed the manufacture of "medicinal" alcohol, Vogel had a good supply of cheap, unregulated hooch? How much would that be worth to Vogel over the years?

$12,520.68?

She'd never thought that Daniel might be taking money to look the other way for George Vogel's company using illegal alcohol from the county's moonshiners—a much cheaper way to produce Vogel's Tonic than following the regulations. Another shock, like learning of Marvena, about Daniel's life, after his death.

Abe draws on his cigarette until it is barely a spark between thumb and forefinger. Then he ignores the ashtray and flicks it into the budding peony bush on the other side of the porch rail. "Of course, Mr. Vogel is quite concerned that nothing interferes with his business."

Lily shudders, as if a skeletal hand taps her bones. *Of course.* George Vogel would have his own private protection, even more fearsome than the Pinkertons. During the war, Lily had scoured the newspaper and watched newsreels at the Kinship Opera House, eager for clues about what was happening on the front beyond the sparse details in Daniel's letters. Often the news cited Mr. Vogel for donating generously to the war effort from his Vogel's Tonic fortune, a true patriot. Just behind those words, though, was a hint of the vast power that he wielded; Vogel and a few other men, it was clear, were the true men of power behind Cincinnati's elected officials, the men who ran the city with a reach that extended beyond the city and the state of Ohio. In every image of Mr. Vogel, Lily saw the same coldness to his eyes, the same bemused smirk he'd worn the first time she'd met him and Abe.

Lily shudders, pushing aside for now the memory of that first meeting. Instead, she thinks about how twice in the past five years George had been in the news in connection with mobster-style killings and attempts by the U.S. Justice Department to prosecute him, but the charges had all been dropped abruptly and—Lily guesses, looking across at Abe now—that wasn't because Vogel was a clever attorney. How many Abe Millers does he employ? How many other professionals?

"Is the reporter Darby Turner on his payroll?"

"Why do you ask?"

"He was waiting for me after I was sworn in. Asking if I'd fill Daniel's shoes."

"I do believe Mr. Darby has been known to—what's the term?—freelance. But back to my point. If something does come up that might affect Mr. Vogel's business, just ask for me at the Kinship Inn. As you've learned, they always know where to find me."

Abe starts to doff his hat but instead steps forward, and taps the sheriff's star pinned on her lapel. Taps twice. Grins. This time, with warning. "But mind you don't wander off too far, down strange alleyways, looking for answers. Daniel isn't here to rescue you now."

With that, Abe steps off the porch.

Lily sees a delivery of bottled milk by the front door. Who'd washed the empty bottles and set them out? Mama? Hildy? Or Jolene? She shudders at Abe being here, so close to her family. Lily picks up the crate to carry it in and pushes her thoughts onto her next step. Going to see Marvena.

CHAPTER 12

※

MARVENA

Marvena and Frankie arrive at Nana's house just as she is serving noon dinner, two round pans of corn pone and a thin broth of root vegetables and a beef bone. Somehow, it will have to be enough for the three of them plus six other women and a host of children. These women are the wives of men Marvena trusts, plus Rowena, the widow of Lloyd, the miner who died as she watched on, the same morning that Daniel was murdered.

After lunch, Frankie runs off with the children to the scrap of yard behind the house. Nana shoos Marvena out the back door with the bone from the soup. There's marrow aplenty for it to be reused, but Nana insists that Marvena give it to Shep. It will help him heal, she says.

Now Marvena stands just outside the back door, smoking a pipe—a rare treat—and watches Shep gnawing away at the bone. Then her attention turns to the backyard swirl of children, caught up in a game of baseball using a hedge apple as a ball and a large tree limb as a bat. Marvena's heart pangs. Alistair should be among the children. The children should be at school. But Luther's closed the school, and Alistair is in the mines.

Frankie distracts Marvena from her mournful thoughts by hitting the hedge apple ball on her first try and running as fast as her legs can pump to a rock designated as second base.

Marvena smiles, glad to see Frankie carefree for a few moments. The poor child had wailed piteously about Shep. Marvena had cleaned the poor dog's wounds and put a splint around his broken paw. He'd been able to limp three-legged down the hill. As soon as Nana saw Shep, she added her own healing poultices to his wounds.

Marvena knows that mixed up in some of Frankie's tears for the dog were ones for her daddy and Daniel, for Eula, for Tom. Then she thinks, as Frankie runs next to third base, about how Frankie is so isolated up in the cabin; she's getting on close to old enough to go to school, though she couldn't go to the Rossville school without a father in the mines, if Luther ever reopens it, and Kinship is too far away for a daily trek.

Already so much is changing without Daniel. Along with her worries about organizing the men, and her nephew, Alistair, in the mines, and the school closing, Marvena is worried, too, about her small moonshining business. Daniel had protected her only source of income—mostly barter, but better than scraping off hunting and foraging—since John's death, even setting up a special deal with George Vogel's business meaning that she didn't have to sell a goodly percentage of her product to him at low cost, like other moonshiners in the county. Vogel could legally produce his "medicinal tonic" under the Volstead Act, if he produced the alcohol at a sanctioned manufacturing site. But his site was only a front. It was a lot cheaper, and quicker, for him to just buy up illegal moonshine, with Daniel's protection. Likely he did so in other counties, with other sheriffs under his thumb. Marvena had never figured out why Daniel would agree to such a deal. All she knew was that he'd made an exemption for her. But with Daniel gone . . . well. Whoever becomes the next sheriff—and that man will surely fall into Vogel's pocket, too—won't have reason to protect her.

She taps out her pipe, puts it back in her pocket, and goes back in, meaning to help with cleanup, but Nana and the other women have made quick work of the task and are waiting for her in the front room, gathered in a circle, sitting on a hodgepodge of chairs pulled from the few rooms of the abode. In the middle of them is a big pile of tattered clothes and linens.

Then Marvena spots Nana's rocking chair, empty, saved for her. Place of honor. In the next chair is Rowena, staring down at her hands in her lap. She'd barely spoken a word since Marvena had come to find her in the tent city, on the eastern edge of Rossville.

As Marvena strides to the rocking chair and sits, she hardens her expression. These women mustn't see any sorrow or pity in her face.

"I know you're wondering why I've asked you to come here, to bring these clothing items," she says. "Well, it's because I trust you. And I trust your men." She reaches over and puts her hand on Rowena's arm. "Your son."

Rowena looks at her and offers a thin smile. "Junior's working the chute."

The chute. God. That's one of the more dangerous spots outside of the mines.

"It means we get to stay here, where we know people." Rowena's voice rises defensively. "We have more than if'n we went back to West Virginia, even if Ma and Pa would take us in—"

"It's all right, Rowena. We're all doing the best we can and we all want better conditions. So we're going to take action. What I need for us to do is to make rag rugs from these scraps."

The women exchange puzzled looks. Rowena asks, "How does a rag rug help?"

Marvena gives a small headshake. It's perhaps cruel, but she wants to see how these women react when the Pinks come. She'd spotted one who'd been on the porch with Luther earlier, when she and Jolene walked through town. He'd given her a long look, then hurried off. She guesses that sooner or later that Pink or another will come to Nana's door.

"I will explain that later," Marvena says. "But first—I want you all to do this. Trust me."

There's a long stretch of silence. Then Rowena reaches down, grabs a man's shirt. Rowena's chin trembles as she looks at it. One of Lloyd's, Marvena realizes. Course she'd have taken his clothes with her to make into other garments or hang on to for her boys. Nothing can be wasted. Rowena pulls her scissors from her pocket and begins cutting strips. Silently, the other women follow suit.

The strips pile up quickly. Marvena picks up three, knots them at the top, starts braiding. Eventually, the women will have long, thin braided ropes, and then they'll start coiling the braids together into circles and sew the edges to hold the coils together.

Yellow over red. Blue over yellow. Red over blue. Repeat, repeat. The women quickly get restless, not knowing why they've been called together for this task. The children's whoops from outside filter in through an open window.

One woman sighs. "They sound so happy. Probl'y think it's a lark, being out of school."

Another woman gives a short, bitter laugh. "'Closed until further notice.' Mr. Ross thinks he can get away with that, with Sheriff Ross gone. The need for repairs is just an excuse! The schoolhouse roof's been leaking all winter."

"Ours too!" says the first. Several laugh, bitter acknowledgment of similar straits.

The second woman shakes her head. "We din't know how much the sheriff done for us until he was gone. Holding back his brother—"

"Half brother, I heard. Sheriff's mama was an Injun—"

"Well now, there's nothin' wrong with that! My daddy was half Cherokee—"

"No one was saying anything was wrong with th'sheriff, Addy Mae! I reckon we can all agree he kept his brother—*half* brother—under control. Least held him back a bit—"

Nana looks across the circle at Marvena, her gaze showing irritation with the women's gossipy tone. But Marvena just smiles. *Let them list their grievances. Confirm for themselves why it's worth the risks to fight for unionization.*

"Prices at the store've doubled in just the few days since the sheriff's been gone—"

"We had enough scrip set aside to get a nice side of ham, but now—"

"And rent may go up, too, I heard—"

"Well, soon enough, we'll all have to whore ourselves out at that boardinghouse!"

The women fall back into uncomfortable silence, cutting their eyes from Marvena. They know that she worked there once, that Eula had worked there until leaving town.

"Like I said, we all do the best we can," Marvena says. Yellow strand over blue.

There's a sudden rap on the door. All the women look up from their braids, share nervous glances. Marvena looks at Nana. "Whoever it is," Marvena says, "welcome them in."

Nana opens the door to a Pink, the one Marvena had noted earlier. Nana steps back. "Well, hello, sir, don't just stand there; come on in!"

He brushes past Nana, glares around the room. "What is going on here?"

Marvena stands up, looks around quickly. All of the women look startled and terrified. *Good. None of them, then, are betrayers, trading news of unionization talk for extra scrip or lighter loads for their men.* "We're making rag rugs. That is all."

The man looks around, confused. "Rag rugs?"

"That's right," Rowena says. "For Marvena. Because—"

She falters, but another woman, the one who'd referenced the boardinghouse, says, "Because we get together and combine what we have. Make things we can use—"

"We're going to sell them. In Kinship." Marvena says. "Fundraiser, for the school roof."

Nana says, "I reckon the fancy Kinship ladies will pay top dollar!"

"Won't Mr. Ross be pleased!" says someone else.

"Enough!" he snaps, and the women fall silent. Go back to their cutting and braiding. After a moment, he shakes his head and points at Marvena. "We're keeping an eye on you."

He leaves. As soon as Nana shuts the door, someone says quietly, "Marvena, what is going on? I know you don't believe Mr. Ross will take money for roof repair."

"Let's just wait a spell," Marvena says. "Keep braiding."

Yellow over red. Blue over yellow. Red over blue. Repeat, repeat.

Marvena gets to the end of her cord and then says, "You all saw my hound's condition."

The women stare. It's a shame but not a surprise—a dog attacked by a wild creature.

"His wounds weren't bite marks. He'd been lashed by a knife," Marvena says softly.

The women gasp and exchange horror-struck looks.

"I reckon someone either got word to the Pinks that we were meeting, and told them where to find me, or someone who'd been part of our movement changed his mind, scared off by Sheriff Ross's death. Either way, it was supposed to frighten me," Marvena says. "I don't think word got to the wrong ears yet about our meeting spot, or someone would have come after us there, but it's dangerous. I want you to talk to your men, tell them to spread the word, but right carefully, about what happened to poor Shep.

"And tell them we need to speed up preparations. No more meetings for now. In a few days I'm going to come back, and collect up the rugs you'll finish up. Your men will pass you dynamite. Two sticks each. You'll roll them into the rugs. Bring them here. We need just enough for a threat if Luther Ross won't let the men talk unionization. The last thing he wants is for his business to be destroyed. I'll take it and put it somewhere safe."

One of the women looks skeptical. "Now, how are you gonna know where that is?"

Marvena smiles, thinking of her still and her hiding spots for her jars. "I'll know. Anyone wants out, that's fine, no judgment. Just leave now."

For a moment, the women look at the braids they've been making. The children's voices waft through the small house. None of the women make a move to leave.

Then one of them chuckles. "Well now, how 'bout that. Who's going to look in a bag of rolled-up rag rugs?"

"Now, don't get all high-and-mighty!" Nana snaps. "I say it's a fool plan. Dangerous."

Marvena holds her breath. If Nana tells them it's not going to work, that Marvena's likely to get caught, they'll stop.

But in the next moment Nana shakes her head. "But I reckon it's the best plan we've got. Well, get on back to work now. I'll make tea."

After the women leave, Marvena and Nana stand out on the front porch. Marvena looks at Daniel's lunch pail, sitting to the side of the top step.

She reaches for it, but Nana stills her hand, asks softly, "What are you doing, child?"

"Daniel's wife ain't going to come here with his notes—if he even made any, or visited at the boardinghouse. I need to go ask after Eula myself."

Nana lifts an eyebrow. "Marvena, you know Jurgis wants you to lay low. It's dangerous enough that you're here, with all the Pinks around. You need to stop fussing after Eula—"

Marvena jerks her arm away from Nana. "Wouldn't you go after your own child, try to find out anything you could?"

"Yes, but—oh, Marvena." Nana looks down.

"Nana, tell me! What is it?"

Nana's chin quivers. "Eula," she whispers. "She came to me, for bitter herbs."

Marvena swallows hard. She knows this means the girl had a child she wanted to lose.

"I—I gave them to her, told her what to do. But then . . . a week later she comes back to me, says it didn't work. She wants more." Nana looks down. Marvena has to lean forward to hear the rest of what she has to say. "I tell her no, too much will hurt her, and if what I gave her didn't take care of . . . of the baby, she must be further along than she thinks. But then when I saw her again, outside the store, and I asked her how she was doing, she just smiled and said she was fine. That she'd worked everything out. She looked so happy, I thought maybe the herbs had worked after all. Later, I thought that she had told the father and they'd run off together."

Marvena lets go of Nana, staggers back. "Oh, Nana, why didn't you tell me?"

Nana shakes her head. "What would you have done? Gone to the boardinghouse, raised a ruckus, and you already have too much notice here; that's why that Pink came by—" Tears start rolling down the old woman's face. "I just keep telling myself Eula is fine, fine, run off with someone, maybe even someone she loves."

Nana picks the lunch pail up off the porch floor.

"I'll take care of Shep," Nana says. "You watch out for you and Frankie. Then come back in a few days for those rag rugs. I'll watch for Lily Ross. She'll stand out, in this town. If I sense we can trust her, I'll send her your way. You'll see. She'll find news of Eula in Daniel's notes to set all our hearts at ease."

CHAPTER 13

꙳

LILY

Lily slows as she passes first her grandparents' old farm and then Elias's farm on Kinship Road. Beside her on the bench seat is a basket of baked goods for Marvena and Eula—muffins and biscuits, left from the funeral supper buffet but still fresh—and Daniel's shotgun, a Winchester Model 12 he'd kept over the mantel. After Abe Miller left, she'd gone back in the house and retrieved the shotgun. The stocking gun doesn't seem sufficient for her new role. Until she can get a revolver, the shotgun will have to do.

There are twists and turns aplenty on Kinship Road but only one hairpin turn on the road, just past Elias's farm. The turn, which parallels the sharp bend in Coal Creek where the Kinship Tree grows, forces Lily to come to a near stop. Brush and berry bushes and other trees hide the Kinship Tree from view, but for just a moment Lily sees herself, running down the road from her grandparents' house and turning off onto the footpath leading to the twined tree.

After the bend, Lily pulls off just west of the footpath. A fist forms in her stomach, punches up through her heart and into her throat. Here is where *Daniel's been found.* Where he was murdered.

She's meant to go straight to Rossville, to find Marvena, but Lily sets the hand brake. She presses the palms of her hands to her cheeks, suddenly too warm even in the chilly weather. She imagines Marvena and Frankie, walking down this side of the road so as to face the flow of traffic. She remembers Frankie saying she'd cut her foot on broken glass at the hairpin.

Lily gazes across the road at the field, where a few cows gathered under a lone burr oak tree for shelter from the misting rain. She forces herself to imagine each moment as it supposedly unfolded: Daniel slowing by necessity on the hairpin, somehow the prisoner getting Daniel's gun, forcing him to stop. The prisoner getting out of the automobile. Daniel jumping out—but would he do that, unarmed? Perhaps he thought he could run the prisoner down. But the escaping prisoner shot at least four times—once shattering the window glass, once hitting the door. Two more hitting Daniel, in his stomach and in his chest. With which of the four shots? It shouldn't matter, and yet it does. Lily's eyes sting as she realizes she'll never know this detail unless she talks to the murderer, makes him confess.

She blinks hard, forcing her thoughts back to Frankie cutting her foot on the remaining glass, sloppily swept off the road. What mother, Lily wonders, would have her daughter cross from the roadside offering the privacy of trees in order to relieve herself by an open field on the other side?

Lily gets out with her shotgun, strides to the open field. She kneels looking for glass, sifting through pebbles and weeds along the fence and in the road's edge.

There is no glass.

She crosses back to Daniel's—her—automobile, goes around it to the footpath that leads to the Kinship Tree. It's tempting to let her mind wander down that path, to the happier times of jumping in the pool with Roger, but she focuses on her search. Just a few steps down the path, she finds a trampled spot where one might easily take care of privy needs. She also finds the pile of glass that a child, with urgent need to relieve herself, might overlook.

It makes even less sense that someone would have swept the glass from the other side of the road to here than Marvena having her child pee on the other side of the road.

She calculates: two hours from Daniel leaving her side to being shot on the way back from Rossville, is possible but tight.

Yet what the evidence of the glass and logic tells her is that it's more likely that Daniel never made it to Rossville. That he'd been waylaid at this spot, so perfect for an ambush, on the way to Rossville, that his automobile and his body had been moved to make it appear he'd been shot on the way back to Kinship.

Back at her automobile, Lily studies the driver's door—the missing glass, the bullet hole. Her hand trembles as she reaches to the bullet hole, puts her finger to it. There is an angle, as if the shot had come from a high position.

Lily turns slowly, looks back across the road, to the open pasture and the cows. If he was shot going this direction, toward Rossville, he would have been attacked from the pasture side or the road because of the shots in the driver's side door. Surely, as sharp and experienced as Daniel was, he'd have seen the attacker, or attackers, coming.

A story rises unbidden from memory, of Daniel telling her of Roger's death from a German sniper. It was the only story he'd shared in detail from the Great War, the only one that visibly moved him. Daniel told her the sniper had shot several times, unsure in the dark if the first round had met its mark.

It was pre-dawn when Daniel had last left her side. It would have been barely light by the time Daniel was at this hairpin on his way to Rossville.

Lily stares at the burr oak in the pasture, the tree by which the cows huddle. She climbs the tree with her gaze, stopping when she spots a limb hanging half-split. Not lightning; there have been no recent violent storms. The weight, then, of a man.

Lily gets back in her automobile, releases the brake, starts again to Rossville, but as she comes out of the hairpin she sees the dirt lane to the Gottschalk farmhouse. Lily knows she must confront the widow Gottschalk, ask her what she knows, demand to speak to the farmhand, Rusty Murphy, who had found Daniel.

But first, she must get to Marvena, find out whether in fact Frankie had cut her foot on the wooded side of the road. Find out more about Marvena's relationship with Daniel and about the missing Eula.

The rain has stopped by the time Lily reaches Rossville.

This is only her second time coming to the mining town. She only vaguely remembers coming with her parents once, as a child, on a Memorial Day when Daddy decided they must visit the graves of his parents.

Daddy rarely talked about his childhood in the town. His mother had died from some unnamed, untreated illness, and shortly after that his father had died from a fall off a mine shaft elevator. Daddy, at seven, made his way to Kinship hidden in the back of a mule-drawn wagon, then hiding in the alley by the grocer's. The elderly grocer and his wife, who couldn't have children, caught him digging in the trash and took him in, giving him their last name of McArthur.

At the crest of Devil's Backbone Mountain, dense green forest alongside the twisty road abruptly give way to the hollow below, wherein lies Rossville: land ground out and refilled for the industry of pulling coal from the surrounding hills, their old names long forgotten, now just Mine No. 1 and Mine No. 2 and on through Mine No. 5. Near ridgetop on each is the opening to the mine, square, reinforced with wood beams. Coal freighted out by man and mule goes into tipples at the mine shafts at ridgetop and then is sent rattling down enclosed chutes that spine down hills flayed of timber, down to open tops of coal cars on the tracks.

Dust rises constantly from the coal house and open train cars, then settles over the town, a gritty sigh. The tarry smell of coal—chuting raw from down the mountains, burning in ovens for cooking and heating, moving through town in railroad cars—infuses every nook of Rossville.

Lily slows to study one of the boys at the bottom of a chute. She guesses him to be eleven, though she knows Luther would tell her he's the requisite age of sixteen but small for his age, and who could argue? For many mining families, certifications of birth are rare; and the more who work from a family, the better off the whole household. He stands up on a ladder watching the coal spill into the top of a coal car. It's his job to gauge when the car is full enough, to push up the lever, to stop the spill of coal. A man stands watching the boy, rings a bell to signal the train pulling down the track to bring the next coal car for filling. The boy goes up on his toe tips each time to reach the lever. If he falls, the coal will swiftly bury him.

It strikes Lily that the rare times Daddy referenced Rossville it was with a guilt-stricken turn to his voice; that Daddy had insisted last September that he help with the rescue efforts at the Widowmaker because he had escaped Rossville so young and so easily.

Lily drives slowly past the mining operation and the rail yard and depot, noting on either side of the road the company houses: meager boxes with only tweaks of gable or roofline to distinguish one from another, nested tight together, crouching over the lean road.

Marvena had told her to look for Daniel's pail out on a porch rail. She drives up one side, turns, drives down the other. She doesn't see the pail. Lily stops, gets out, carrying her shotgun low and partially covered by her skirts. Maybe by walking, she'll spot it.

At one house, Lily hears a ballad being sung by the woman as she shakes out rag rugs on her front porch step. The ballad, in circulation for a few years now, is familiar to Lily:

> *"Down, down in yonder valley*
> *Where flowers fade and bloom*
> *Lies our own Pearl Bryant*
> *A-mouldering in her tomb."*

On goes "Pearl Bryant," the true story of Pearl, murdered by a jealous lover, the theme consistent, though flourishes vary from singer to singer.

Lily shudders, realizing that Daniel's murder is likely to make its way into a ballad. She doesn't want the chorus to be that he was shot by a prisoner who got away.

She approaches the porch, but the woman goes inside, slams her rickety front door as hard as it will allow. Lily tightens her grip on her shotgun. Will anyone even be willing to help her find Marvena Whitcomb?

A door squeaks across the street. Lily whirls. There on the porch stands a squat older woman. She looks up and down the road, clearly afraid of something, and gestures to Lily to come up on the porch.

Lily looks around, sees no one on the street. The old woman is a good six inches shorter than even Lily's five-foot-three, and her face is soft and round. But there is a sharpness to her gaze, a grimness to her smile. And she's holding something behind her back.

Warily, Lily tightens her grip on her shotgun as she approaches the house.

The woman brings a lunch pail from behind her back, just long enough for Lily to get a glimpse of it, and of *D.T.R.* scratched under the rim. Daniel's pail.

Lily looks up at the woman as she puts the pail behind her back. Softly, Lily says, "That pail is—was—my husband's. I loaned it to Marvena Whitcomb. Is she here?"

The older woman stares at the star on Lily's lapel.

"Lily Ross?" An accent—not quite German, maybe Polish—thickens her words.

Lily nods.

"Ah. Interesting." The woman taps the tin star but, unlike Abe, with fascination.

Lily can't help but smile a little. "It was a surprise. So is Marvena Whitcomb here, or—"

The woman moves her hand from the star to Lily's face, and her expression changes to concern. "You are wearying yourself, child. Come in for just a little, have tea."

"That's very kind of you, but perhaps you could just tell me who you are and—"

"I am Nana Sacovech. I tell you how to find Marvena. First, though, tea."

"But—"

"Mrs. Ross."

Lily looks back at Nana.

"You're more stubborn than even Daniel was, may he rest in peace," Nana says, shaking her head. "Life is hard. Have tea."

CHAPTER 14

⫸Y

MARVENA

On the trek back from town, Marvena and Frankie search out poke-weed and fiddlehead fern for a salad. Frankie says she's hankering for beets, too, for supper. It's a mite early to harvest, but Marvena lets Frankie pull a small bunch of beets from the garden. Then, after settling Frankie down to rest, Marvena parboils the beets. While they cook, Marvena centers her new rag rug in front of the potbelly stove. She admires the rug, heart swelling a little for what it represents and because it's right pretty. In a few days, she'll go back to Rossville, collect the other women's rag rugs, each rolled tightly around a stick or two of dynamite, then boldly walk out of the town and take the dynamite to her favorite hiding places.

When Marvena comes out on the porch to peel the cooked beets, she hears an automobile coming up her thin, rutted lane. Daniel's. She knows that sound as surely as birdsong. She sets down her pail of beets. As the automobile comes into view, her hands automatically rise to tuck back strands of her hair.

Then she shakes her head at her own foolishness. Of course it'll be the deputy, Martin.

When the automobile stops on a flat grassy patch in front of her cabin, Marvena stares at the driver's side door with the bullet hole, the space where the window should be.

Marvena carefully keeps surprise from her expression and takes an accounting of the other woman as she emerges from the automobile: her sturdy stance with fine squared shoulders, her bow mouth, her blue eyes—brighter today than when they'd first met, but still sorrowful. Even in a thick coat, Lily Ross is a petite, shapely beauty. A woman meant for finer things, lovelier places. And yet she seems perfectly relaxed, holding Daniel's shotgun in one hand and a basket in another.

Course Daniel had wanted her.

Marvena gives her head another bitter shake, ashamed to think Daniel so shallow. He'd seen more in Lily than surface niceties.

Lily takes a few steps toward Marvena and starts to greet her, but Marvena spots the star pinned on Lily's lapel. "Why're you wearing Daniel's badge . . . ?"

"I'm not. He was buried with his. This is mine. Temporary appointment, courtesy of commissioners, until the election."

"The commissioners have gone and made a *woman* sheriff?" Hell, as John's widow and by her own grit she'd had to work hard to be accepted as a leader. And somehow, this fancy Kinship woman gets *appointed*? "Well, don't that beat all."

For a moment, Lily looks bemused. But then her expression hardens. "Not just any woman. The sheriff's widow."

Marvena flinches at Lily's raw statement.

Lily goes on. "I reckon I'm a figurehead only—to their way of thinking. They're counting on a woman not asking too many questions."

"Yet here you are. Say your piece, then. If'n you found something in Daniel's notes about Eula, you'd best be telling me."

"He didn't leave behind any notes."

Marvena clenches her fists. "Then why're you here, a-pestering me?"

"Word is that your brother, Tom, was the prisoner Daniel was sent to collect. That Tom somehow wrestled free, and killed Daniel, and made his escape into the woods. There was a manhunt for him, but it's been called off. Of course, manhunt or no, if he shows his face again it's likely whoever finds him won't wait to ask questions before they start shooting."

For a long moment, the two women stare at each other. Then Marvena flings her arms wide. "Well, feel free to look in my cabin and around my property. He ain't here, but you don't have to take my word for it."

"I believe you. But I've learned a few things you need to know. And I have a few questions, too. I can ask you, or ask around in Rossville." Lily's hand trembles on the shotgun.

Damn. Maybe the woman doesn't know how to handle a gun after all. Last thing she needs is for the sheriff's widow—the new sheriff!—to accidentally shoot her damned foot off on her property. "Before you go poking into every hill and holler, asking fool questions you mayn't want the answer to, you might ought figure out how to handle a shotgun."

Lily stills so suddenly that Marvena catches her breath. In the next instant Lily sets down her basket, lifts the shotgun, fires. A squirrel falls from the tree. "Do you like burgoo stew?" she asks with a grin.

Marvena grins back. *Well then.* "Daniel learn you that?" She eyes the cabin door, worried Frankie will have been awakened by the gunfire.

"My daddy. He grew up here in Rossville. Used to go hunting with *his* daddy."

"Yeah?"

"He was orphaned early—his mother died of some illness; his father was killed in a mining accident in Rossville. Daddy was taken in by the McArthurs in Kinship—they never had children—and he took their name, inherited their store."

"Lucky man!" Marvena snaps her words, as cleanly as spring peas.

Lily turns red, suddenly overtaken with emotion. Marvena regrets her comments. Of course Lily's daddy wasn't lucky—dying alongside John in the Widowmaker this past fall.

A moment ticks by, accounted for only by a new wind stirring the crabapple blossoms' sweetness, and in that spare slice of time Marvena's heart turns a mite tender, spiting her desire to count Lily soft and spoiled.

Maybe she is. But she's also trying to find her way. Just like Marvena had, after John.

A little more gently, Marvena says, "Well, did your daddy learn you how to clean a critter once't you've killed it?"

Lily looks so stricken that Marvena nearly laughs, and then her almost chuckle folds into a sigh. "No use standing there like a fool trying to catch your death of cold. Get the damned squirrel and come on in."

Marvena lays the squirrel out on the small table by the potbelly stove. Damned if Lily hadn't hit it perfectly square in the head; not a bit of meat will be wasted. With some root vegetables, the squirrel meat will cook up into a thick, savory stew—a welcome break from another meal of soup beans, dried pinto beans she'd bartered for, cooked with onion and bacon fat and water. She hates to admit it, but the biscuits Lily's brought will also be a welcome break from corn pone. With the salad of beets and greens, she and Frankie will eat like royalty this night. Frankie is still napping, and Marvena is for once thankful at how deeply the child can sleep.

Marvena points at the spot just under the squirrel's tail. "Start there." She hands Lily her knife; Lily's hand trembles as she take it. "If'n you're going to throw up, go outside." The woman is, after all, standing on her new rag rug.

"I can do this! I used to work with Elias, tending patients during the flu outbreak. I've dealt with worse than this—"

"Well, things that don't normally rile you up can turn you inside out when you're in the family way—" Marvena stops, wishes she could grab back the words as soon as she's said them.

Lily's head snaps up. "Daniel told you?"

It's best, thinks Marvena, to skirt the direct answer—*yes*. "Women learn to see. Just go sit down. I'll make you some tea. Chamomile."

Lily shakes her head but moves to one of the two chairs by the table. "Why do so many women think tea solves everything? You and Mama. And Nana Sacovech."

"So you met her." Marvena slices from under the squirrel's tail to the top of its hind legs. She pulls the legs free of the skin. "I can give you something stronger, if you'd rather?"

"You mean shine?"

Marvena gives Lily's sheriff's star a pointed look. "Course not. I mean Vogel's Tonic. But in my own jars."

"Just call it what it is. I'm not going to drag you in for it. I know Daniel mostly looked the other way about shine unless folks got too out of hand." Lily looks down, reddening.

Huh. Does Lily know that Daniel was George Vogel's enforcer for this region, for getting moonshine cheap so he could resell it as watered-down "tonic," while claiming it was made square with laws that allowed for pharmaceutical manufacturing of alcohol? Did Lily know that Vogel would no doubt test her, expect her to follow the same rules of loyalty—and exact a deadly price if she doesn't? No. She reckons not.

Marvena gets two tin cups, pours shine into each, brings them to the table. "Sip it slow."

But Lily takes a full drink. "Smooth," she says.

Marvena lifts her eyebrows. "So, what did Nana have to say?" Hopefully, nothing about the movement. Just because Lily's father had been for unionization doesn't mean Lily is. She's clearly a woman willing to go against the opinions of the men in her life.

"Not much. She didn't tell me how to find you right away. I think she wanted to be sure that she wanted me to find you. We talked awhile, mostly about weather and gardens and such. I told her about my grandpa working here."

"Don't think that'll make folks here accept you any easier. They'll be suspicious of a woman with a badge. You know why women don't go into mines, don't you?"

"The lore goes beyond just mining towns. Yes. It's bad luck."

"Well, some folks are going to see you the same way, poking around in men's work."

Lily studies Marvena's face, searching, and Marvena hardens her look before her expression reveals she might know more about this than ordinary. *Good God, but Daniel's woman is nosey. The men who appointed her might have underestimated her.*

The notion almost makes Marvena smile, but she bites her lip as Lily goes on. "Anyway, Nana proclaimed me too weary looking, made me drink tea. Chamomile." Lily lifts an eyebrow and takes another sip of the shine.

Marvena chuckles. *Dammit.* She does not want to like Daniel's Lily.

"Even with Nana's help, it's not easy to find me," Marvena says.

"But you can be found," Lily says softly. "Even by people you'd rather not find you. I met your dog, Shep. Nana told me he'd been attacked while you were away from your cabin."

Marvena looks down at her cup. She has no reason to fully trust Lily, not yet. "Frankie and me went mushroom hunting near dusk. Stayed out too long. Came back after dark."

"I see. So to go trekking about mushroom hunting, Frankie's foot must have healed fast? From that broken glass on Kinship Road?"

Marvena frowns, unsure why Lily has suddenly turned the conversation in this direction. "It's on the mend, right nice."

"Good. That's good. Tell me—why did you pick that spot for Frankie?"

"Why's it matter?"

"There are a lot of spots to stop, if you need privacy, on Kinship Road."

"We didn't walk the whole way on the main road," Marvena says slowly. "It's not the most direct way from our cabin. We came down some paths I know, then along Coal Creek, and then Frankie needed to relieve herself. But it's too steep on the bank, and so I made her wait till we got to the path from the creek bend up to the main road. See, there's this unusual tree—"

"The Kinship Tree," Lily says. "I know it. And the path."

"Then you know we had to come up the path to the road to come to Kinship."

Lily nods. "That makes sense. On the way to here, I stopped where Frankie said she cut her foot. There was still glass down that path. On the side opposite the pasture."

Marvena knows she should understand the import of Lily's statement, but it eludes her.

"You saw that the driver's side glass was shot out of Daniel's automobile?"

Marvena swallows hard, keeps her eyes steady on Lily. She nods, urging Lily on.

"The glass was on the side of the road *to* Rossville. If he was shot on the way back *from* Rossville, wouldn't the glass have been swept off to the pasture side of the road?"

It takes a moment before Marvena gasps. She'd spent little time in automobiles. She'd not made the connection Lily had.

Lily reaches in her dress pocket and pulls out a tiny, rustic doll—one of Daniel's creations. Marvena doesn't recognize it as one of the many he'd made her daughters, but she recognizes the button tied like a hat on the top of its head. A button from Daniel's overcoat.

Lily touches the button. "My little girl told me yours gave this button to her when you came to my house the day of Daniel's funeral."

"Mama?" Frankie has finally awoken and comes out from behind the quilt, rubbing her eyes. "Am I gonna have to give back the shoes?"

Marvena starts to command Frankie back to bed, but Lily speaks up first: "Of course not, honey. I was just telling your mama how nice it was for you to give my little girl this button."

Frankie hobbles over, eager. "Is she here? Can I play with her?"

"She's back at our house. Can you tell me where you found this?"

"Where I cut my foot. I saw it, thought it was a play-pretty..." Frankie looks at her mama. "Am I in trouble?"

"No, honey."

"So can I go outside? I wanna pick some flowers. For a bouquet."

Marvena says, "Go on. Stay where we can keep an eye on you."

Frankie hurries outside and begins picking flowers along the edge of the woods, the yellow blooms of ragwort and spring cress. For a long time the women sit silently, sipping their cups of shine, staring out the window at the child.

Finally, Lily says flatly, "I kept his buttons sewed on tight."

Marvena is bewildered. "All right. You're a good wife. I don't see—"

Suddenly Lily grasps Marvena's wrists with both of her hands. Marvena fights the urge to try to pull away, sensing Lily's grip will only tighten. Instead, Marvena goes still, stares back into Lily's eyes, feels finger bones dancing up her spine as Lily says, "Here's what I imagine: Daniel had to be taken by surprise, no doubt. Otherwise he'd have fought back and his attacker would have been killed instead, or at least so sorely wounded that he'd not get far in these hills. Then there's the fact the driver's side window was shattered and there's a bullet hole in the driver's side door. Two shots, before a third and fourth hit him in the stomach and chest, which means he was out of the automobile, facing toward the shooter.

"I haven't figured out why Daniel stopped in the first place, but he did. Maybe the hay I saw mixed in with the glass has something to do with it, a bale fallen from a wagon. In any case, he gets out. Senses danger. Turns back to reach in his automobile for his revolver. His button catches on the door handle. He's in a hurry so he pays it no mind, yet it slows him just enough so that when he turns it's too late to spot his shooter. There's a tree in the pasture by where he was shot, and a broken limb up in the tree. There were no windstorms the morning Daniel was shot. So I'm guessing that someone, from up in that tree, shot at him. Then, after Daniel died, took Daniel's revolver to make it look like he'd been bested, and then ran away."

Lily abruptly releases Marvena's wrists. For a long moment, the women sit quietly together, stewing in the possibility that Daniel had been set up. The notion riles Marvena, yet she's relieved to think Tom hadn't killed Daniel.

At last Marvena says, "Tom was taken from work, put in the holding cell the night before Daniel died."

Lily nods. "So Martin Weaver has told me. Tom is the prisoner we think Daniel went to pick up on the morning he was killed. A Pinkerton—I've learned his name is Harvey Grayson—came the night before to tell Daniel to come to Rossville to fetch a prisoner. At least, that's what Daniel told me he said. Do you know Grayson?"

Marvena smirks. "I don't know the Pinks by name. You doubt what Daniel told you? The reason to come to Rossville?"

"It was unusual—the visit and the rush to collect a prisoner from the holding cell. What would be so special about Tom as a prisoner?"

Marvena's heart clenches as she recognizes the cleverness of the plan: kill Daniel and set up a miner they already had in custody. Not just any miner. A miner whose sister is the widow of an organizer, who's known by many to have taken up the cause.

With what had happened to poor Shep, she's already reckoned it's possible there's a turncoat in the cause, that Luther and his men know of her efforts, know that Daniel's heart had finally turned. Removing Daniel, as she'd theorized at the last gathering in the cave, would make it easier to suppress unionization efforts. Maybe Luther and his supporters think Lily easily manageable, think that Marvena would be broken by losing her brother and Daniel.

And likely she *had* lost Tom. Once they'd made it look like he escaped, it would be easy enough to kill him. To dump his body in Coal Creek or bury it in a remote spot in the woods.

Marvena looks at Lily. At the house, she'd seemed to dislike Luther. But Marvena is still not sure whether to trust her. Had Daniel told her he was going to come out for unionization? Did the loss of her father to a failed rescue effort ensure her empathy or embitter her?

Carefully, Marvena states what Lily could easily learn from anyone. "Tom was known to talk unionization. Daniel was known to be opposed. On the side of Luther."

"But ever since my daddy and the other men died, Daniel talked about the possibility of switching his view. And I believe Daniel was about ready to come out publicly for it, too. Luther said you were the widow of a miner, an organizer," Lily says. "Is that another reason Daniel turned pro-union?"

Marvena nods.

"I see. Has your husband been gone long—or was he one of the men lost in the Widowmaker last fall?"

Lily's tone has turned tremulous and Marvena realizes that Lily is probing the nature and depth of her relationship with Daniel.

"In the Widowmaker." *God. The woman doesn't know her father died alongside John. Daniel would not have filled her in on this detail.* "My husband was John Rutherford."

141

Lily takes a shaky breath. "I recognize that name. He's the other rescuer who—So your husband and my father died together?"

Marvena nods. "Like Luther said, me and Daniel were friends since he was a boy. We met by happenstance. We saw one another off 'n' on . . . till he met you. For the past ten years, we didn't have more than nodding acquaintance. Then after the Widowmaker . . . Daniel came to tell me the news about John. He—told me about your father, too. Daniel checked on me and Eula and Frankie after that, but there was nothing more than friendship between us."

Well. Nothing more from Daniel. As Marvena has come to realize since Daniel's death, his visits after John's passing had stirred in her the old feelings, But there's no use telling Lily that.

"Thank you," Lily says quietly. After a moment, she adds, "If John was a unionizer, and Tom was wanted for stirring up unionization, are you involved, too?"

Marvena pulls her hands away, looks down. The woman is sharp. But Marvena doesn't want to trust her with full disclosure of her role. Not on a second meeting. Trust is hard for Marvena. She'd learned how to gingerly approach trusting again through John. But then he'd died, and Eula had taken off to consort with Pinks, and now Jurgis thinks she should forget about Eula.

By the time Marvena looks back up at Lily, to try to decide how much more to share, Lily has stood up and walked over to her coat hanging on a peg. She gets out a small box from a deep pocket. She returns to the table and sets it before Marvena.

Marvena stares at the box, with gold foil lettering she can't read and the image of a delicately coiffed woman putting a candy in her mouth. *Another gift of food?*

"I promised I'd look for any notes Daniel may have made about Eula," Lily says. "I looked, though he wasn't one for taking detailed notes. I was the one who wrote up the files for our prisoners and Daniel's cases. He barely wrote me during the Great War—"

Marvena startles at that. She'd received many a letter from Daniel at the general post office in Rossville during the war. Not that she could read them—she'd never learned. And she'd never told Daniel that. But she'd kept all the letters.

Lily smiles. "It's all right; some men are just terrible about things like writing," she says, misinterpreting Marvena's reaction. "Daniel was always . . . taciturn. Anyway. I did find this box in his drawer at the jailhouse. I think you should open it. See if the contents are familiar."

With a trembling hand, Marvena lifts the lid. A faint sweet scent rises from the box.

She stares at the hair comb, with Eula's blond hair entwining the tines. She spots a spare button from the dress Marvena had made for the child's birthday with fabric Daniel had given her. Foil, from one of the chocolates. Feather. Rock. Arrowhead, carved from rock. One of the many tiny dolls, like Daniel used to make for Eula when she was little, like he'd made for Frankie. And of course Jolene. She didn't realize Eula had saved some of the dolls.

Marvena looks up at Lily, sees that she's gazing at the quilt that hangs over the sleeping area of the cabin. Her gaze is laser focused on a patch, made from the same material as both Eula's Christmas dress and the doll's—pale blue cotton, patterned with red flowers. Nothing went to waste in Marvena's cabin.

Marvena reaches for her cup, mouth aching for shine. But her throat is suddenly so tight she won't be able to swallow.

"Eula's?" Lily asks.

Marvena nods.

"Where would Daniel have gotten it? The boardinghouse?"

Marvena nods again. "When I told him she hadn't been seen, he likely went there first."

"When was this?"

"About a week and a half ago."

"Was this the last time you saw him?"

"Yes. He was supposed to come by with news of anything he found out . . ."—she pauses, mentally counts back—"five days ago."

"The day he was killed," Lily says softly.

Marvena holds Lily's gaze with her own. "Yes."

Lily stands. "I'll go by the boardinghouse, but it will have to be tomorrow. It's getting dark and I need to get home."

Marvena nods. "Thank you." She puts the lid on the box, pushes it toward Lily.

Lily shakes her head. "You keep it." She stands, gets her coat, opens the door. They hear Frankie singing as she plays along the wood's edge. "She has such a pretty voice," Lily says.

"Like her daddy," Marvena says. "John was always humming some tune or other. . . ."

Lily's stance stiffens. She says, "Frankie and Eula . . . they're full sisters?"

Marvena considers how to answer—tell her an easy lie of *yes*? But as Marvena studies the woman, she softens, reckons that Lily has shown herself to be tough, coming here, and that she's earned hearing the truth. "What Luther said was true. Daniel and I were friends from childhood. Then, lovers. He left for his boxing career with George Vogel—anything to get away from these hills and hollers. His father was hard on him. He didn't much like living on the farm with Elias and his family, either.

"He left when he was eighteen. By the time he came back a few years later, I was already working at the boardinghouse. By the time he came back the second time, I'd had Eula."

"When was this?"

"Let's see—Eula was six by then. Daniel had lost his first fight, been injured. Came back to his uncle Elias's to recover, retrain. Anyway, I'd moved back here—this was our grandpappy's cabin first, then our daddy's, and then Tom moved to Rossville to work for Ross Mining. I took up my daddy's business to eke out a living for me and Eula. Truth be told, I don't rightly know who Eula's father was. Anyways, by the time I saw Daniel again, I'd already met John. And Frankie is definitely John's."

For a moment, Marvena sees him, sitting on her porch, making another doll, when she and Eula came home one night, after a rare afternoon away at a taffy pull. Daniel gave the doll to seven-year-old Eula with his usual fanfare, and then Marvena had sent the child inside. She had news for Daniel, news she thought he'd find hard to bear—she'd met John Rutherford, a man who'd never married, had no children of his own, a man with sadness carved around eyes and mouth, and arms too lean. He'd taken a fancy to her, watched over Eula.

Daniel had been happy for her. More than that, relieved. He had, he said, met the woman he would someday marry—Lily McArthur—when she was old enough. In the meantime, he was going back to Cincinnati, to fight again for George Vogel. He just, he said, wanted her to know.

And then Daniel had asked, Would John Rutherford be kind to Marvena? To Eula?

John—nearly old enough to be her father. Yet she felt her heart ease at the thought of him. Not the passion she'd felt with Daniel. Something steadier. And she'd nodded.

Daniel had pulled her to him then, given Marvena the lightest of kisses on her forehead. She knew then that they would never make love again. He released her, then walked out her door—not for the last time. But for the last time as her lover.

Now Marvena looks at Lily, watches Lily take in this bit of news, her face clearing as she places it in her own life's timeline.

And in that spare moment, Marvena is tempted to confess all to Lily about the movement, the meetings, to beg her for help.

But then Lily's shoulders stiffen again, and the moment is gone. Marvena thinks, *Wait. Wait'n see if she really does go to the boardinghouse, come back with news about Eula, or at least a report of whether or not Daniel really did go there, and what happened if he did.*

Then, without turning, Lily says again, nearly a whisper, "Thank you." She plucks her coat from the door and leaves, shutting the door gently behind her.

Marvena watches through the window, as she has so often of late, the sheriff drive away.

Later, after Frankie is to bed, Marvena sits at the table, shotgun across her lap. On the table are her coal-oil lamp, and a blue Ball canning jar serving as a vase for Frankie's bouquet picked earlier, and beside that the box of Eula's that Lily had found in Daniel's jailhouse drawer.

Marvena reaches a hand out to pet Shep's head and then remembers that the dog is not here. Even as a pang squeezes her heart, she shakes her head at her fool self. Daniel dead, Tom missing, Eula gone, Alistair in the mines, Luther cracking down harder than ever. And she's missing a damned dog? But she is. She hopes Shep is safe with Nana and Jurgis. She wishes she could feel safe again here, wishes she could be sure she can keep Frankie safe.

The flame of her lamp flickers shadows over the small white box. She'd let Frankie look in the box, too, felt the hurt of the disappointment in Frankie's face that so little was in it.

But maybe they'd missed something? Something that could give a clue as to Eula's whereabouts? Now Marvena slowly pulls the box toward her. One more look through. She places each item in a careful row on the table.

Marvena stares into the now empty box. To the proprietress, this would all be trash. So why keep it? Give it to Daniel?

Something glints. Marvena blinks—damn her overly soft emotions for the girl, getting the best of her! But no—there's the glint again. In the corner of the box. Marvena pokes her fingertip in and feels the hard stone. Carefully, she plucks it out.

It's a tiny diamond chip, fallen out of some piece of jewelry.

None of the girls at the boardinghouse could afford to buy these pretties. But then, neither could any miner. Only a wealthy man could, men from Kinship.

Or a Pinkerton, as Jurgis had warned her.

CHAPTER 15

⤜

LILY

It's late afternoon when Lily eases her automobile slowly down the rough rutted lane from Marvena's, then back into Rossville. She stops in front of the boardinghouse and considers going in as she'd promised Marvena, but by the time she does that she'll have to either drive at night—something she's never done—or give up on stopping in on Mrs. Ada Gottschalk. She's uncomfortable with either notion.

Twilight has fallen by the time Lily drives up Mrs. Gottschalk's lane. As she pulls her automobile to a stop in front of the farmhouse, she sees someone—Ada, no doubt, for the widow lives alone—peering out of the front window at her.

Lily starts to pick up her shotgun but then thinks better of it. She doesn't want to scare the woman away. Not when she hasn't spoken to Lily since the Great War, and with good reason. Lily goes up the steps to the porch and knocks on the door.

Mrs. Gottschalk gave me this mess of green beans when I stopped by to check on her. . . .

Lily gasps at the memory of Daniel coming into their kitchen after a day of rounds. He made a point to regularly check on widows, the elderly, and other folks he thought vulnerable.

"Mrs. Gottschalk?" Lily calls. "It's me, Lily Ross. I know you've heard about Daniel. He—he always spoke highly of you."

Or . . . *Mrs. Gottschalk sent these black raspberries. Come with me to check on her next time—your families used to be such great friends; she gave you that blue ribbon—you do remember the ribbon. . . .* Then, seeing Lily's face flame at his teasing and mistaking it for belated modesty over her forward teenage behavior, he'd lean in for a kiss.

But then, as now, it was shame burning her face. Daniel kept Marvena from her, but she'd kept secrets from him, too, secrets that would have made him ashamed of her.

"Please, Mrs. Gottschalk. I've been told your farmhand Rusty found Daniel. I know you thought highly of Daniel, too. I just have a few questions."

A few moments pass. And suddenly Lily is dizzy. She presses her eyes shut just for a second to regain her balance.

"I'll come back tomorrow then. I—I'm guessing you haven't heard, but I'm the sheriff now. And I need to talk with you about Daniel's death."

Just before sunrise the next morning, Lily rises, turns on the gaslight, and attends to her toiletry needs. At the bureau she picks up Daniel's brush, breathing in the slightly lavender scent of the Brilliantine pomade he used to style his hair, always neatly parted on the left.

She thinks of her visit with Marvena. Though it is possible that Eula is Daniel's daughter, Lily finds comfort in learning that Frankie is not, in hearing Marvena's admission that she and Daniel ceased being lovers when Marvena met John, before she and Daniel met.

Yet it's only partial solace. It will be hard enough to live without Daniel. But it is an added burden to realize he hadn't trusted her to know about Marvena and Eula. Had she seemed so weak to him? He'd kept much from her, about his boxing career, his time in the Great War—that she understood—but she wants to believe she'd have also understood about his relationship with Marvena. It hurts to think that she must have seemed too weak to understand.

Lily opens Daniel's drawer, hurriedly puts away the brush, shutting the drawer so hard that the bureau mirror rattles her image. She dresses and hastily pins up her hair, ignoring messy bumps and loose strands. Then she eases down the steps, mindful of her sleeping family.

In the kitchen, the woodbin under the stove is empty. Lily steps outside to gather an armful of wood from the back stoop, planning to make a quick batch of biscuits. Then she will take the children to Mama's, go back to Mrs. Gottschalk's, then to the Rossville boarding-house as she'd promised Marvena. But before her hand touches the first stick of kindling, she freezes, still as Lot's wife looking back.

In the tender rise of this morning on the last day of March she gazes upon her chickens, heads and bodies wrenched asunder, strewn in dew-slicked grass.

She stands for a long time, silent, then finally goes inside to get the large canning kettle for the bodies and a smaller pan for the heads. The clanging of the pots stirs the children. They're downstairs on the back stoop before she can finish cleaning up the slaughter.

Micah screams. Lily wants to go to her children, but her hands are covered in blood, feathers sticking to her fingers and palms—as if she's been tarred and feathered. The imagery brings a rush of coppery bitterness up to her mouth.

Lily looks at Jolene, who has already drawn Micah to her. "Go to Hildy! Tell her to find Deputy Weaver."

She's just finishing cleaning up the chickens when Martin comes into the yard. "Oh God, Lily. Who would do this?"

Whoever hurt poor Shep? Maybe someone in Rossville hadn't liked seeing her there. Pinkertons? Miners who don't yet trust her? Someone attempting to scare her, to goad her into swallowing the escaped-prisoner tale whole, like spoiled pudding.

Lily doesn't say this to Martin. She isn't sure if she should trust him, her husband's best friend. At one time this would have cracked her heart. But now her heart's gone cold and hard. He would, after all, have been the one most likely to order the windshield glass swept aside. And he hadn't told her that it had been on the side of the road heading *to* Rossville, not from it.

As she washes her hands at the pump, she says, "Take the chicken bodies to Rossville. Give them to anyone who wants them. They're still fresh enough to fry up. Tell them this is a gift. From Lily. The sheriff. Toss the heads. Or give them to anyone wanting fishing bait."

"Lily, are you sure—"

"It's best this way. Burying them out back will only draw foxes or worse."

Then she goes back into the house. Visiting the widow Gottschalk and the boardinghouse will have to wait another day. Today, her children need her.

That night Lily sits on the edge of the children's bed, Micah on her lap, rocking back and forth, and she can just hear Mama say she's coddling the boy, but he's been in and out of hysteria all day over the chickens. Lily cherished them for their eggs, but Micah had loved them most of all for their silliness, their clucks and head bobs. Hiccups pepper his half sleep, remnants of his earlier relentless sobs. Jolene sleeps quietly on her side of the bed, her silence as eerie as her brother's wailing. She clutches one of the many dolls Daniel fashioned for her.

Now Micah's smaller breaths settle, begin to match hers on an inhale or exhale, a sign that Lily can safely place him down beside his sister. Lily lays her boy down, pulls the quilt over both children, then goes downstairs to the front parlor.

Hildy, who insisted after word spread to her of the chickens that she will spend a few days with Lily, dozes on the couch, her knitting slack in her hands.

Lily sits down in her chair, places her shotgun across her lap.

Just after midnight, Lily jolts awake.

Hildy is still sound asleep, but Lily hears something outside the house. She follows the sound to the kitchen, sees through the window the shape of a man by the jailhouse, locking the door. He picks up a coal-oil lantern, then steps away.

Quickly and quietly, Lily steps out onto the back stoop, raises her shotgun. The man turns, startles, nearly drops his lantern and his ring of keys.

It's Martin. He's the only one, other than her, who has a key to the jailhouse.

"What are you doing, Martin?"

"Lily . . . I didn't want to disturb you, after what you've been through."

"I'm the sheriff. It's my job to be disturbed."

"Could you lower the shotgun?"

"Maybe. Answer my question." She doesn't lower the weapon.

"A man was found hiding in a barn outside of town. The Hilliards' farm. The man wouldn't answer questions, so old man Hilliard held him at gunpoint, sent the son to get me."

She lifts an eyebrow but finally lowers the shotgun.

Martin sighs. "Lily, it's going to take a while for people to accept you as sheriff."

"Uh-huh. So he's in jail for sleeping in someone's barn loft?"

"Loitering. Stealing food from the Hilliards' cellar. Lily, it's Tom Whitcomb. He refuses to talk, but it's clear he's been hiding out for days."

"Move aside."

"Lily."

"Either open the door, or move aside so I can do it."

Martin's hands shake so that it takes a few tries to manage the lock before he can pull open the door. He presses open the heavy door, steps in. Lily follows him.

In Martin's flickering light, she sees that three cells are empty. In the cell nearest the door, a man lies on the cot, his back to her. Lily walks to the iron-barred cell. The jail is cold. The man doesn't yet have a blanket or pillow for the straw mattress. She notes, too, that Tom has taken off his boots and put them in the corner opposite the mattress, toe by toe and heel by heel, perpendicular to the wall; something about this exacting neatness with such sparse possessions makes her doubt that that this is a man who has the spontaneity—even if Daniel had made it to the Rossville holding cell to fetch him—to kill in the heat of a moment.

Perhaps it is the cool air finally stirring through the jailhouse that rouses him, or perhaps she makes some sound while studying this man who she's supposed to believe is Daniel's killer. In any case, Tom moves, groans, sits up, turns, stares at Lily.

The only expression he musters is an expectant lifting of his brows, a feat given his welted face—lip split, nose swollen double, right ear pulverized into a cauliflower mass. He gives her shotgun a pointed look.

"If'n you're going to shoot me dead, do it right quick." Tom's voice wheezes through his swollen lips. "I'd rather die fast than by being slowly worn out, wondering about your aim."

Well. His quick tongue confirms that he must be Marvena's brother. Tom sighs. "Let me talk to Daniel."

Lily glances at Martin, who looks stricken. "This is the most he's said since I got to the Hilliards' farm. I reckon he doesn't know—"

Lily looks back at Tom. "Daniel was murdered a week ago."

In spite of welts and bruises, Tom's face registers shock. "What? Daniel's dead?"

Sorrow suddenly overcomes Tom's expression of shock, and it's enough to make Lily's heart clench. *God, has it really been just a week since Daniel's death?*

"A Pinkerton man came to our house eight days ago. Daniel said it was to tell him to fetch a prisoner in Rossville. Supposedly, the prisoner killed him during transport, then went on the lam. Talk is, that prisoner is you."

Tom looks at Martin. "No, no, I never—"

"*She's* the sheriff," Martin says. "Tell her."

Now shock overtakes sorrow on Tom's face and Lily allows herself a grim smile. "A lot can happen in six days. It's surely long enough for you to be long gone from Bronwyn County. The state, even! Yet here you are. Why?"

"'Cause I never killed him, I didn't even know, I—" Tom's voice grinds as he drops his head to his hands.

"Just tell us, plain and simple then, how you got out of the Rossville holding cell and what you were doing hiding in the Hilliards' barn."

Tom looks up, stares over her shoulder at Martin. "Not with him here."

"Go, Martin," Lily says.

"Now, Lily, look here—"

"I'm not going to shoot him. Just go."

She waits a moment after hearing the door click behind her. Then she studies Tom, sees the shock and sorrow and fear swirling his countenance. Judges the emotions to be genuine. And she sees something else in his face. Hunger.

Well. In all her years as jail mistress for Daniel, she'd never known a starving prisoner to give clear answers. Maybe a good meal is a better motivator than the business end of a shotgun.

She starts toward the jailhouse door, saying, "I'll be right back."

Lily opens the food slot and slides in the plate. Tom grabs it and crams a whole biscuit into his mouth. A large chunk crumbles into his beard. He claws the crumbs out and sucks them from his filthy fingers, while eyeing the cup of coffee she holds.

"Slow down," she says. "You'll sicken yourself, gobbling so fast on an empty stomach."

He takes a few smaller bites of biscuit, and only then does Lily pass the cup of coffee to him. She's glad to get rid of the cup. The smell of the coffee roils her stomach. She's as sensitive with this pregnancy as she was with her first, the child she'd miscarried shortly after Daniel went to serve in the army. The sudden thought makes her pause, but then she shakes away the worry. She sits slowly as a cramp stitches up her right side, and puts her shotgun across her lap. Finally, Lily studies her prisoner.

She could start by again demanding to know where he's been the past six days, but she guesses that even the satisfaction of a good meal isn't going to be enough to get him to readily fess up whatever he might know. Another tactic occurs to her.

Lily clears her throat. "I've been talking with your sister."

Tom looks surprised. "How do you know Marvena?"

Of course this man would know that Daniel had kept the knowledge of Marvena from her all of these years. "She came to our house three days ago, the day of Daniel's funeral. She said her daughter was missing, that Daniel promised to help her find the girl."

"Fool woman, risking everything over that little whore!" Tom mutters.

Lily startles. "Eula's your niece!"

"Oh yeah. I'm right tore up over her."

"Yesterday, I went to see Marvena. She claims she didn't know when she came to our house that Daniel had died or that you'd been taken prisoner. She also told me that after she got back from our house she'd gone mushroom hunting with Frankie and when they returned she found her dog beaten. Then last night after I visited her, someone killed all of our chickens. Decapitated them. Left their heads and bodies in our yard. My children saw that this morning."

Tom goes pale.

"Someone's gone to an awful lot of trouble to rattle Marvena and me. And, if I'm to believe you and Marvena, to set you up as Daniel's killer. Why you in particular?"

"I've been known to run my mouth about unionizing. That don't go over too good with either Mr. Ross or the Pinks."

"I'm guessing that you're not the only miner that's true of."

"Well, there's also the matter of me not liking Daniel coming around Marvena after her husband died last fall." Tom gives her a hard look.

"Dammit, do you want me to think you're guilty? Shoot you dead after all?"

"If you was gonna do it, you would have."

Lily allows herself a hard smile. "Maybe I like the thought of you frying in Old Sparky."

Tom looks stricken at the nickname for the electric chair at the state penitentiary. Lily goes on. "I'll fetch Deputy Weaver. Let him know you fessed up to killing my husband."

Tom yelps, "I never done it! If I had've, like you said, I'd have been long gone by now!"

"So tell me where you've been?"

Tom sighs. "All I know is I was pulled off work days ago—"

"What day?"

Tom shakes his head. "I don't rightly know. What is today?"

"April 1."

Tom stares off, seems to be calculating. Then he looks back at Lily. "The twenty-fourth."

Lily's heart pounds. The night that Harvey Grayson, the Pinkerton, had come to the house about a prisoner for Daniel to fetch. She forces her voice to remain even. "Go on."

Tom shrugs. "Not much to tell. Sometime in the night, one of the Pinks came and got me. Put a blindfold over my face, and took me somewhere. I was kept for a few days, and then I got away, and hid out until old man Hilliard found me."

"Who pulled you off work? Took you out of the Rossville holding cell?"

"Pinks don't exactly introduce themselves all proper like," Tom says. "I don't know."

"Does the name Harvey Grayson sound familiar?"

Tom shakes his head and slurps more coffee. Frustration wells in Lily's heart. "Did he have a harelip?"

Tom nods.

Grayson.

"But I didn't get a look at whoever pulled me from the cell," Tom says. "I was asleep, and they set upon me afore I was fully awake. It was dark when I got away from where I was held, and I didn't memorize faces. I just ran."

"But you didn't keep running. You could have been long gone by now," Lily says. "Not the action of a man guilty of shooting the sheriff."

Tom stares at her, hope widening his eyes and expression. "So you believe me?"

She does, or at least she wants to. Still, doubt nettles Lily. What if she's figured wrong about Daniel being shot on his way to Rossville? What if the glass and hay and button had just been swept all the way across the road, for some reason, even if that was more inconvenient?

"It would help if I had an idea why someone would want to kill Daniel and set you in particular up to take the fall."

Suddenly Tom stares down into his now empty coffee mug. "I've told you all I know."

Lily shakes her head. "You haven't. And it's not going to matter if I believe that you didn't kill Daniel. In the end, if it's just your word, well—"

"I'm fuel for Old Sparky?" Tom scoffs bitterly.

Lily regrets her earlier taunt about the electric chair. "Why do you think you were set up? Why is someone trying to rattle Marvena and me? Do you think Daniel's death has anything to do with Eula? With him looking into it?"

Tom shakes his head.

"What then?"

Tom drops his head to his hands. "I don't know whether to trust you."

"At least tell me why you didn't keep running. Most men would have—guilty or not."

"With me gone, my boy'll be in the mines. He—he's just eleven."

The image of the boy she'd seen at the Rossville chute flashes before her, softens her at last. "What's your boy's name?"

"Alistair." His voice breaks on the syllables. One hand roves to his bashed eye. She sees that he's afraid of having said so much. If she pushes him too hard, he's not going to tell her anything more. A break might do them good, and yet she wants to win his trust.

It occurs to her that she still has the garden to put in. Seasons past, Daniel had done the tilling. A pang curdles her abdomen. She doesn't feel up to the gardening task. She picks up her shotgun. "I could use some help. And I reckon we could both use some fresh air."

A few hours later, Lily sits out by the patch garden in one kitchen chair, her feet propped up on another, watching Tom turning the heavy earth with a spade, Jolene breaking up clumps with the hoe. Lily started out helping, but Tom insisted that she should rest, so finally she'd had Jolene bring the two chairs up to the top of the yard, by the garden.

Micah, sitting to the left of Lily on an old tablecloth she's spread out over the ground, merrily bangs a wooden spoon against the bottom of a saucepan, though every now and then he looks to the empty coop and wails. She picks him up and hugs him until he settles. She's bundled him up in extra shirts. The shotgun is by her right side.

Lily hears footsteps coming up behind her—Martin's tread. "Everything all right, Lily?"

"Why wouldn't it be? It's a beautiful day, and Tom here is putting in my garden for me. Good for me. Fresh air for him."

"The prisoner ought not be out of jail. What would Daniel think?"

"Daniel would say I'm a better shot than he ever was."

Martin clears his throat again, a nervous tic. "Luther came by my house this morning and said he'd tracked down Harvey Grayson, just like you asked. He's visiting his wife down in Kentucky, but he sent a telegram confirming that he released Tom to Daniel on the morning of the twenty-fifth. He's willing to testify to that in court."

Lily looks out at Tom, standing in her garden. He's stopped moving, leans into the spade as if it's a cane. His body quivers. Jolene drops her hoe and stares at Lily.

Martin reaches into his vest pocket, pulls out the telegram, holds it out to Lily. She takes it, reads it quickly, and tucks it into her skirt pocket. "Luther came to you?"

Martin cocks an eyebrow. "He said you two weren't getting on very well."

"That's not what happened!" Tom yells. "This is a setup, if ever—"

He stops as Jolene starts crying and runs to Lily.

"Go inside," Lily tells Jolene. "Take Micah."

After the back door squeals and slams shut, Lily looks back at Martin. "By rights, Luther should have come to me. Plus, a telegram is not sufficient. Mr. Whitcomb here has given me a different testimony. Before I can make an arrest and ask the judge to file formal charges, I need Harvey Grayson to come in for questioning. In person."

"He's in Kentucky, Luther says. With his wife."

The image of Grayson leering at her, the night he came to their house to bring word to Daniel to fetch a prisoner, rises up tauntingly. Lily shudders, pitying his wife—if it's true he has one. "He got there, I'm assuming, by train. He can come back here by train."

"That will take days."

"He has another day to get here, to make his accusation, before I release Tom."

"What? Lily!"

"By law I can only hold a suspect for questioning for forty-eight hours. Unless the suspect confesses. Which he hasn't."

Lily rises. She's light-headed, but she forces herself to stand steadily. "Procedures, Martin. You must know that Judge Whitaker is a stickler for procedure. He's not a fan of Pinkerton men. Though my brother-in-law is, I also know he doesn't take kindly to coming up on the wrong side of the judge. Especially Friday nights."

Martin frowns.

Maybe she's gone too far, referencing the technically illegal Friday-night poker games at the speakeasy in the Kinship Inn basement that everyone—including Daniel—turned a blind eye to. As a woman, she's not supposed to know of them. Of course, there's much of life she's not supposed to know about but does, and she's not in the mood for pretense.

After she locks Tom back in his cell, Lily comes out of the jailhouse for fresh air and finds Martin waiting for her.

"Now Lily, listen here," Martin says. "Why would you want to let go the man Harvey Grayson swears he turned over to Daniel?"

"All right, let's say Grayson turned Tom Whitcomb over to Daniel. Let's say somehow that skinny, undernourished miner bested my husband. That he got Daniel's revolver. Wouldn't he shoot Daniel from within the automobile, immediately?"

Martin nods. "Sure, but—"

"But the window was shot out. The door was shot into. So for some reason, Tom runs *around* the automobile, starts shooting as Daniel gets out. Misses with the first two shots—for there'd be no reason to waste bullets if the first shots hit Daniel—and somehow Daniel still doesn't best him. Then Tom shoots him, and runs off with Daniel's revolver."

Martin blanches at the scenario Lily's just painted, but she goes on. "Suppose all that is true. Daniel's revolver had a seven-round magazine. Three bullets left. He kept it fully loaded when he went out on his rounds. Where's the revolver? Tom wouldn't have thrown it away. He'd have kept it for protection. If he was a cold-blooded killer, wouldn't he have used it to kill Farmer Meyer, rather than be easily overcome?"

Lily waits for Martin to take in what she's said. Long moments pass. And then comprehension widens Martin's eyes.

She nods, grimly, seeing that at last Martin understands. She says, "Tell Luther I want to talk with Harvey Grayson myself. I want to know exactly what he said to Daniel the night he came here. I want him to look me in the eyes and tell me exactly what time he handed Tom over to my husband on the morning of the twenty-fifth. Or I won't hold Tom a moment longer than I have to. And I'll consider Grayson the one on the lam—and a suspect."

That night, after dinner, Lily fills a tray with corn bread, buttermilk, and a bowl of thick beef stew. She brings Jolene with her to the jail and hands the tray and lantern to Jolene. Lily works the lock and key and then, after opening the door, pockets them and unburdens Jolene.

"Jolene, you wait right here by the door," Lily says. After the chickens, she's afraid to send her daughter at night on even the short walk from the jailhouse to the kitchen door.

"But Mama, I want to say good night to Mr. Whitcomb," she says.

"After I've talked with him, sweet pea," Lily says.

Jolene's face folds up in a pout, but she waits. Lily puts the lantern on the desk, moves to the cell. She slides the tray through to Tom. He takes the tray and Lily notices that his hands, despite the day's labors, are now steady.

Tom scoops up a heaping bite of stew, moans appreciatively, closes his eyes as he savors it. Lily pulls her chair over to his cell, gets the lantern from the desk, puts it by her chair. She doesn't want Jolene to hear their conversation echoing across the jail cell. She sits. Waits.

After he's finished about half the bowl, Tom says, "You going to sit here all night watching me eat?" He nods toward the door. "Your little one is bound to be tired."

"You too," Lily says. "You worked hard. Thanks for turning the garden for me."

Tom picks up the corn bread, sops up thick broth remaining in the bowl. "I'm grateful for you standing up for me today, but once that Pink's here, no one else will believe me."

"Then tell me why you think you were set up. Why someone else wanted to kill Daniel."

"Two birds, one stone. I'm wanted for unionizing," Tom says. "With your husband."

Lily gasps at this revelation. She knows that Daniel was planning to speak up as being pro-union, but an editorial in the local newspaper is far less serious than actually helping miners organize. That would have been overstepping the boundaries of his role as sheriff.

But then, Daniel had certainly done that on the matter of Prohibition.

And on the matter of Marvena.

Daniel as an activist for the unions would anger many people who were anti-union. Luther, of course. But other management, who worked for Luther. Kinship shopkeepers, who liked to stay in the good graces of management and the Pinkertons, who weren't bound to shop in the company store. Even owners and managers of other mining companies in other counties nearby. A sheriff actively working on behalf of unionization was dangerous.

Lily recollects reading about the Battle for Blair Mountain. News of the bloody West Virginia fight had made even small newspapers like the *Kinship Weekly Courier*. Then the memory of a different prisoner in this very cell—the Pinkerton they'd held for roughhousing, the one who'd taunted her on the morning of Daniel's murder, just minutes before Elias came to her with the news *Daniel's been found*—came back to her. He'd been hoping for a fight, for a war. She had warned him that Sheriff Ross would not stand for that in Bronwyn County.

Now she is Sheriff Ross.

Lily walks up to Tom's cell. "I know that Daniel told Marvena about my father, Caleb McArthur, dying alongside John Rutherford, trying to save those poor trapped miners last fall. So I'm sure you're aware of who my daddy was. Please. If Daniel's sympathies had anything to do with his murder, please for his sake—for the sake of my daddy, for all the other men who died that day, for your son's sake—please tell me what you know."

He hesitates. Lily waits silently, barely daring to breathe in the fragile moment while Tom decides whether or not to tell her what's on his mind. Finally, he looks up at her. "Daniel found out that Luther was planning to reopen the Widowmaker again soon, from the eastern side of the hill. There's been talk, leaked from some in management who are against it but too afraid to stand up to Luther. Under the old, closed Rossville Cemetery."

Lily inhales sharply, steps back, leans against the desk.

"No one knew 'cept me and Marvena," Tom says, "but Daniel promised he would contact someone for us. A war buddy, who works at the Bureau of Mines. Daniel didn't give a name."

Lily frowns. Daniel hadn't talked about any friends made during the Great War. Then again, he hadn't talked about the war much at all. There's so much she didn't know about her husband's life until his death.

Tom goes on. "Would you know who—"

"Mama?" Jolene's weary voice pipes from the doorway.

"Tend your little one," Tom says. "Then I will tell you what happened after I was taken."

Lily's heart folds on itself for a moment. She doesn't dare speak, for fear the quivering need in her voice will make him change his mind. So Lily nods, stands, then heads to the door.

But just as she steps over the threshold and reaches to take Jolene's hand, pain slices through her abdomen. *The baby.* Blood and life suddenly rush from her, and as Lily sinks to the ground, calling for Jolene, loss overcomes her.

CHAPTER 16

※

MARVENA

Three days after her meeting with the women, Marvena is back in Rossville to collect the dynamite and sneak it out, rolled up in the rag rugs. She and Frankie had crept down Devil's Backbone early that morning hours before dawn, taking winding ways Marvena knew from childhood but hadn't been on in years. She'd hated taking Frankie out in the cold and dark again, but she can't risk leaving her alone in the cabin.

Now, just over the ridge above Rossville, Marvena spots the back of the boardinghouse below. The glint of the tiny diamond in Eula's box flickers in her mind's eye. It has been winking at her ever since she discovered it, three nights before.

Shivering, Marvena thinks, *Focus on the mission!* But then she thinks, *Eula.*

Daniel hadn't come back with news. Lily had delivered the box he'd found of Eula's and had promised to find out more, but she'd never come back, either. What a fool she'd been to think that the wife of a man who'd kept someone like Marvena a secret all these years would want to help her. The only reason Lily'd come to visit was to satisfy her curiosity.

Now Marvena kneels down and looks at Frankie. "Can you get to Nana and Jurgis's house from here? On your own?"

Frankie nods.

"See that alley? Right there, between the schoolhouse and company store?" Marvena whispers to Frankie. "Cut through there, then on down to Nana's. I'll be there right quick. I just—I just have an errand."

Marvena watches Frankie dutifully cut through the alley. Then she treks down the hill, holding her nose and fighting back a gag at the rotting trash heap at the back of the house. She walks around to the front of the house. The door hangs half-open on loose, rusty hinges.

Once she is inside, it takes a moment for Marvena to adjust to the dimness of the tiny foyer, to see the long, narrow corridor extending before her, a suffocating tunnel. She inhales the weary odors of cabbage and tobacco and body odor, new sources but same old smells, and they threaten to loosen a rush of dark, unwelcome memories.

Go, go on back out. . . . But Marvena walks down the hallway and through a door into a large dining room, filled with wooden tables and chairs. She steps in quickly. Light filters in from the scummy windows and there are a few coal-oil lamps burning on some of the tables.

At first Marvena is alone, but a moment later a tall, thin blond woman, in a grimy cotton dress and apron, comes out of the kitchen, holding an armful of tin plates. She sets the stack clattering onto a table, regards Marvena with a bemused smile.

"We're not hiring, honey," the woman says, "and you're a bit long in the tooth anyway."

"I'm looking for Joanne Moyer."

The woman lifts her eyebrows at Marvena's firm tone. "That's me. And who are you?"

"Marvena Whitcomb. Eula's mama."

"She's been gone over a month now. Sorry, honey." Joanne shrugs. "Girls like that come and go all the time."

This, finally, is too much. Marvena leaps, shoving Joanne against the wall, pinning her shoulders. "I want to know—"

Joanne struggles to break free. "Crazy woman! I don't recognize you, but I've heard of you. Guess your young 'un ain't far from the tree . . . so don't think I won't call Mr. Luther!"

In one swift movement, Marvena pulls her knife from its sheath tucked just under her skirt's waistband. She puts the blade to Joanne's throat. "An' don't think I won't slice you if'n you don't tell me what you know of her."

"I . . . I don't know much . . . she just run off with a miner."

"Is that what you told the sheriff?"

Joanne's eyes widen. "I—I never talked to the sheriff."

Now Marvena smiles, coldly. "I know he came by here. Asking on my behalf after Eula. And that he left with something of Eula's."

"He did?"

"Are you denying he was here?"

"All right. He came by. Like I told the sheriff, I don't know much. She went out a few nights with another boarder here. A kid from Germany. Or maybe Liechtenstein. Anyway, the next morning, they'd neither one come back."

"A miner?" And yet she'd fallen in love with a miner. With John. And so had Eula. Maybe in spite of losing her sweetheart Willis last fall, she'd fallen in love again. "What was his name?"

"I don't know. Not like people here check in and out on a hotel register."

"I want to see Eula's room."

"It's not her room no more. Look, after she came back, like I told the sheriff, I gave away her clothes to the other girls."

"*Gave?*"

"Fine—sold! You know how it works. Look, you want the money I got from them—"

"No! I want to know where my daughter is!" Marvena's voice rings around the room.

"I told you, Eula took up with this miner. They left. Neither ever came back."

Marvena releases Joanne, steps back, but doesn't sheath her knife. Joanne stays with her back against the wall, as if Marvena's gaze has pinned her there.

Timidly, Joanne says, "You said the sheriff had something of Eula's from here?"

With a sinking feeling, Marvena realizes that she shouldn't have revealed that. "It's just a small chocolate box with a few notions." Marvena thinks of the feather and rock and comb. The tiny diamond, stuck in the corner, winks at her again. "Didn't you give it to him?"

Joanne shakes her head. "Like I told him, like I'm telling you, I got rid of all of Eula's things. She didn't have much. He insisted on searching and I sent him on up, even though the room was still empty, then. There was no point in stopping him. He was determined. Scary."

"When did he come by?"

Joanne thinks for a moment, then says, "Musta been about a week before he died." She shakes her head. "I was right sorry about that. He was a good man."

Marvena considers. Daniel must have come here right after seeing her the last time. After she sobbed about Eula being missing. After his fight with Tom. She could imagine how he looked to Joanne, his eyes still bright with fury. Unstoppable.

"And after he searched the room?"

"He came charging down the stairs, even angrier than before. Didn't look at me. Just rushed out. He wasn't carrying anything, though he could have tucked something inside his coat. Like that box. But I cleaned that room myself. Swept, turned the mattress. Nothing in there but a bed, empty dresser, washbowl, and pot. I couldn't figure out why he'd be so angry."

"Did he say where he was going?"

"No. And the mood he was in—I wasn't about to ask him."

Marvena stares at her for a long moment. But there is no duplicity in Joanne's face.

"Has anyone else come by asking about Eula?" Marvena asks. She doesn't want to mention Lily by name, to reveal they've met at her cabin.

Joanne shakes her head.

Marvena sheaths her knife. "I'm leaving. You will not tell anyone else I've been here."

Joanne's hand flies to her throat, strokes it. "What makes you so sure about that?"

Marvena grins. "You really want to tell Luther Ross—your *boss*—that you've been talking with the likes of me?"

A bit later, at Jurgis and Nana's house, Nana says, "It's all here—except Rowena's."

Nana, Jurgis, and Marvena are in the back room, looking at the five rag rugs, tightly rolled, each containing two sticks of dynamite. Ten sticks. They'd hoped for a dozen.

"Forget Rowena's," Jurgis says. "It's too dangerous for you to go into the tent city—"

"Isn't it worse still to deny the gift of the risk Rowena and her boy have likely taken?"

"You don't know that he did pull the dynamite—"

"I'm certain he did," Marvena says. "His father died at the hand of a Pink."

"I'll go with her," Nana says.

Jurgis looks at his mother. "What? No, Mama. It's too dangerous."

But Nana smiles up at him, reaches up, pats his cheek. "Now Son, who's going to question an old healer woman going to the tent city to do her healing arts, with her two assistants?" She turns her sunny smile to Marvena and Frankie. "Besides, it's been a while since I've taken herbs for poultice, teas, and such."

Jurgis sighs. He's not going to talk his mama out of this. The morning bell sounds—ten-minute warning for work to commence. The plan is for Marvena and Frankie to leave while the men are at work and the Pinks are near the work sites.

Marvena kneels down. "Help me gather this up, Frankie," she says.

Carefully, they secure the rolled rugs with twine, and then they put the bundled rugs in Marvena's large tote bag.

Marvena cups Frankie's petite face with her hands. "Now listen, if something happens, if we're stopped, you don't know anything about this, all right?"

Wide-eyed, Frankie nods.

"Promise me!"

"I promise, Mama."

Marvena looks up at Nana. "You too."

"Marvena, you can't take all the blame—"

"Yes, I can," Marvena says.

They walk down Kinship Road, nearly out of Rossville and up the rise to the tent city.

An hour and a half later, Marvena and Frankie are in the hills of Devil's Backbone to place the dynamite in two of Marvena's hiding spots, safer even than the meeting cave near her still. They made it to the tent city with no problem, and Nana went about her way delivering various herbs to people she knew could use them. Marvena quickly added Rowena's promised sticks and rag rug and went on with Jolene.

They hike up and down steep slopes, winding new paths between and around buckeye and silver maple trees, Frankie delighting in the fuchsia blooms of low-growing redbud trees, grace notes against the soft green of the forest, but it's time the child learned more practical lessons of the land, and Marvena points out the pawpaw trees, which in the autumn will bear large green-skinned oval fruits. Later as they work their way through thickets of black chokeberry bushes, Marvena gives pointers on finding the tangy berries they'll bear in the fall.

All this makes Frankie hungry now, though, for Marvena catches her pulling up morels, about to shove them in her mouth.

"Stop!" Marvena grabs her daughter's hand and studies the morels, the lumpy caps with deep waves. "Look at these carefully, Frankie. False morels. The real mushrooms have longer caps with more even ridges, and if we cut them lengthwise, they'd be hollow inside. The false ones are poisonous and can kill you!"

Frankie's eyes widen as Marvena tosses the morels to the ground. "But it's hard to tell the false from the true ones!"

The comment strikes Marvena. Eula had once said the same thing, as Marvena taught her mushroom hunting. For a moment, Frankie's face blurs, and Marvena sees Eula as a child. She clears her throat. "Yes. We'll look for morels after we're done with our work. Seek out some tulip poplars. That's where fiddlehead fern often likes to grow, and if we find morels growing there they should be fine—but we'll take them home and cut them open to find out. Here, take this now."

Marvena reaches in her pocket and pulls out a wax paper packet of deer jerky—a precious gift from one of the miners' wives in the tent city—and allots a strip of the tough, salt-cured dried meat to each of them.

They eat their sparse meal as they continue until finally, top of Devil's Backbone, they come to a remote clifftop, jaggedly craning out like a headless neck.

They work quickly, unfurling half the rag rug bundles and hiding the dynamite in a deep crevice in a formation, tall as a man and wide as a cabin, of large rocks and boulders, tumbled so long ago that moss greens the gray stones.

She bids Frankie to roll up the now empty rugs and put them back in her sack, and then she treks to the tip of the cliff. Marvena loops a rope around a sturdy oak at the top of the cliff and belays the other end of the rope around her waist, then rappels a few feet down to the most secure hiding space her father ever showed her, an ancient pine growing out of the cliff face of bedrock. The tree is one among many, but it stands out to her for the peculiar twist and turn of its limbs, like arthritic fingers. She tucks the last parcel of dynamite into a crevice behind the pine. She starts to climb back up to the top, back to Jolene, but the cry of a distant red shouldered hawk catches her attention. She turns, looks out across the expanse between this cliff and the next, spots the bird circling high above.

Then she looks below, to the hills covered with pine and budding-out trees. It's the start of April, and soon the hills will be lush with tree blossoms, heavy with sweet scent. She'd loved to take Eula out to enjoy these woods, teach her about paths and trees and mushrooms and pawpaws and berries and wild herbs, as she is doing with Frankie. Had Eula trekked these paths that Marvena long taught her, side by side with a boy she loved? Could that explanation, so simple and easy to believe, really be true? She wants to believe it so much—

"Mama?"

Marvena's heart double flips at the sound of her daughter's voice. "Eula?" she whispers.

Then the voice calls again for her.

It is Frankie, calling for her. Marvena turns her gaze from the valley and begins climbing to the daughter, who is present.

CHAPTER 17

꙳

LILY

A day later, Lily stirs to momentary wakefulness. She vaguely remembers being brought here, to the house she grew up in, then Elias coming to check on her, Mama insisting that Lily and her children stay so Mama can tend her back to health.

Now a coal-oil lamp burns dimly on a corner table. Someone has left a blue Ball canning jar filled with a small bouquet of yellow jonquils.

Lily shifts in the bed, testing for soreness. The stickiness on the thick wad of cloth between her legs tells her that she is still bleeding, but not as badly as earlier.

Lily slips back into sleep, dreaming: she's in a boxing ring, dressed in just her slip, Daniel's boxing gloves fused to her wrists. People cheer, but she can't see them or her opponent, yet she keeps swinging and punching, unable to stop, and after a while she can't move her fingers because she no longer has any, Daniel's boxing gloves having replaced her hands.

Lily. A voice from outside the dream. Arms pull her close, rock her in ancient, soothing rhythm. Lily relaxes into the embrace, hears heartbeat thrumming, smells lilac and talc. *Mama.*

Sometime later, Lily opens her eyes, meets her mama's gaze soft with sorrow. "Mama," Lily says. "This is more than I can bear." She longs to weep, but her tears remain stubbornly locked in her heart.

Mama kisses the top of Lily's head, keeps rocking her, says, "No, child. This is just more than you should have to bear."

Two more days and nights of sleeping, longer awake times filled with Mama insisting she eat broth and bread, cleaning her, changing her dressings, inspecting each cloth for blood and clots, muttering with provisional hope as the blood lessens. Sometimes Hildy comes to help.

Lily lets them tend to her without struggle or embarrassment. It's what women do—tend to the bodies of their loved ones in life and in death—she'd helped tend Mama birthing Caleb Jr. after all, and what's more, they've had to tend to her thusly before.

Her dreams shift to that bright, sunny August day on her seventeenth birthday when she was weary at the prospect of another day spent canning in Mamaw Neely's kitchen.

She dreams of running down Kinship Road after her young, strong, thoughtless, beautiful brother, seventeen and laughing and alive and blissfully unaware he'll die so young. She dreams the thrilling shock of cool water after jumping from the Kinship Tree, the deep plunge to the muddy bottom, the push up from the slick rock to the surface, the joyous burst of air into her lungs, the gentle float downstream.

In her dream, it's just her and Roger on a hot, itching, overly bright August day, alive and whole, jumping in cool water over and over, laughing in their endless careless, carefree cycle.

It's day, this awakening. She reaches down, tentatively, between her legs. No padding. She's clean, wearing a soft pink nightgown. Too big, one of Mama's. Lily gets up, stiff but moving of her own accord. She pulls back the quilt to eye the sheet. No bloodstains.

She brings the quilt back up to her chin, troubled by her dream of her and Roger at the Kinship Tree, seemingly better than the nightmare of being in a boxing ring with Daniel's gloves for her hands. Considered together, the dreams seemed to imply that her life had been better, safer, before meeting Daniel. Lily stares around the room, her heart pounding as she blinks back tears. This had been her room, when she'd lived here with Mama and Daddy. She closes her eyes, not to sleep again, but to remember.

On Lily's nineteenth birthday, August 2, 1917, just a week before Daniel's Kinship boxing match advertised on the playbill, Daniel had shocked everyone by coming to Mama and Daddy's house. He pulled from his pocket the blue ribbon Lily had'd given him, held it out across both palms as if he were offering the world's most precious bolt of silk. With her hand, she closed his over the ribbon, and Mama pointedly harrumphed, while Daddy fought off a grin.

After days of chaperoned visits, Daddy had mercy on them and drove them out to the Gottschalks' farm. Daniel and Lily had barely been able to keep a proper distance between them as they walked toward the black raspberry bushes along Kinship Road.

That night was the boxing match. Lily told Daniel how she looked forward to attending, and Daniel recoiled, telling her the boxing ring was no place for a woman—not women like Lily, anyway. When she protested, he'd said he'd been miserable, waiting for her to be old enough to properly woo, and here she was, acting like a child. And with that, he'd walked away.

Later that night, Lily went to bed early after supper. She slipped under her covers still dressed and counted to one thousand, and then she got out of bed, opened a dresser drawer, and dug out the few coins she'd saved from gifts and odd jobs. She opened the window, wiggled through, dropping into the bushes below. Then she ran, still hobbling a bit after the loss of her toe two years before, toward the center of town.

Lily bought her ticket and made her way to the standing-room-only area in front of the stage. She'd never felt such a press of bodies. The smell of sweat and perfume and alcohol roiled with body heat. Her pulse thrummed in her ears. She gasped with relief when she got to the front, then gasped again when Daniel came out. His bare torso was already slick with sweat from warming up.

The crowd rhythmically chanted his name—"Dan-iel, Dan-iel, Dan-iel"—and Lily's heart clanged against her chest wall.

The other boxer rushed in, overeager, wanting to best his opponent in his own hometown. Daniel threw a swift right punch into the other man's jaw. Blood and a tooth spewed from the man's mouth. The man swung at Daniel, who easily avoided the punch.

And then Lily felt a tug in her heart, like a ribbon linking them, and Daniel's eyes turned to her. Connected. Flashed. Angry.

Her gaze replied: Daniel Ross, if you want me to be your wife, you must not, you will not, ever keep me out of any part of your life, ever again.

The other boxer swung, clocked Daniel in the jaw. The crowd booed. Daniel threw a left uppercut that knocked the other boxer back but not out.

And then a man grabbed Lily. He pulled her hair with one hand, her arm with another, and Lily screamed, but no one noticed, or if they did, no one cared. In moments he had her out in the alley, pinned against the brick wall.

Lily had tried to kick him, but he was far too big for her. She caught a glimpse of two men she knew, men who often came into her father's store, screamed one's name. They paused, stared down the alley as she screamed for their help, but they went on. In the next instant the man who had grabbed her had a knife to her throat.

He pushed his face close to hers, and his foul breath turned her stomach, "No one's a-coming to save you, so it'll go better if—"

But suddenly there was Daniel. His arm went around the man's neck, pulled him away from Lily. The man dropped the knife in shock. Lily sank to the filthy ground.

Daniel was still in only his boxing shorts and shoes. His upper lip was starting to swell.

The man flailed. Daniel tightened his chokehold. The man groaned, stilled.

"I'm going to kill you," Daniel had said flatly.

The man wet himself, the dark stain spreading down his shabby trouser leg. He started pleading. Lily stared up at Daniel, shocked. She saw that he meant it.

"Daniel, no, we can get Sheriff Tate, or . . ."

Daniel looked at her evenly. "We'll save the county the expense of jailing him, and other girls"—even with all that had happened, his emphasis on that word cut her—"from being hurt, at least by this son of a bitch. So, mister, I'm going to kill you."

But in the next moment a large, round man in an expensive suit came out the back door of the opera house, followed by an unusually tall, gaunt man in a fine gray coat.

"Oh, we can't have that," said the stout man. He was smoking a cigar. The smell, mixing with the alley's smell of urine—feline, canine, human—made Lily gag. "I could get you off of murder charges, but it might cost more than you're currently worth to me. Now, who is this fine young woman you rushed out to rescue?"

"My fiancée," Daniel said. "Lily McArthur."

"Oh, I see." The stout man appraised her, like he was assessing a horse or an automobile. He was so ridiculously round that he should look amusing, but even in the dim alley Lily saw the cold lines around his mouth, the uncompromising hardness of his eyes.

Meanwhile, the tall, gaunt man looked bored as he pulled back his coat, put his hand on a revolver. An automobile pulled up to the end of the alley. Lily's attacker moaned anew.

"Lily, this is George Vogel," Daniel said.

George Vogel. The man Daniel had said two years before was his manager. The man he had said she should fear.

"Luckily for both of you," George said, "Daniel quickly knocked out his opponent, the match declared over, before he ran out to find you."

Luckily for both of you . . . there was a knife edge to the words. Lily started trembling.

Two thick, large men in suits got out of the waiting automobile.

Suddenly George was impatiently bored. "Abe, take care of this."

Abe, the tall, gaunt man, stepped forward. Daniel shoved Lily's attacker to Abe, who pressed his gun to the man's back and marched the now-sobbing man toward the automobile.

Daniel came to Lily then, pulled her to him. She pressed her face to his chest, finally allowing herself to cry. When finally she could cry no more, she looked up at Daniel. Just the two of them remained in the alley.

"What . . . what will happen to him?"

"Jail, like you said. I'm sure just jail."

But Lily sensed that Daniel, no longer angry with her, was sparing her. Suddenly she recollected reading a story once in the Kinship Weekly Courier—a murdered body found on the bank of the Ohio River, whatever means the killer had used to try to weight the body undone by the current. But the story also claimed there were no suspects. She wondered if her attacker would be dead within the hour, his body driven down to the Ohio River for dumping.

She pressed her face back to Daniel's chest, breathing in the deep yeasty smell of his sweat, taking comfort in the tickle of his hair on her face.

"Goddam, Lily," Daniel said. "You've got to listen to me, trust me. I can't lose you."

Lily reopens her eyes. Now they are dry. And her heart is back to a steady *thrum*. He hadn't lost her. But she's lost him. And their child. She can't go back to being the frightened girl in the alley. She must find out who killed Daniel and why. Bring the killer to justice.

Lily is brushing her hair when Mama comes in. Mama looks weary, her face filled with lines that eddy and flow from eyes to cheeks to jowls and back round again to mouth. A thin gray strand has pulled from her usually neat bun, and her hand trembles as she tucks it back behind her ear. Of course Mama is worn-out, from tending to her.

Mama puts her hands on her hips and frowns at Lily. "Child, are you trying to rip out your hair with that brush? And I'm not sure you should be sitting up already—"

"What is today, Mama?"

"April 4."

Lily calculates. Two days. "I'm ready. Mama, the woman who came to see me the day of Daniel's burial—Marvena Whitcomb—it was her brother in jail the night I . . . that night." Lily drops the brush to her lap. "Mama, I need you to check for me. The prisoner who was there that night—Tom Whitcomb—is he all right? Is he still there?"

Mama stares, not trying to hide her shock at Lily thinking of this prisoner at all.

"He was about to tell me something important about Daniel," Lily says.

Mama crosses the room and takes the brush from Lily. As she brushes Lily's hair, Mama explains, "Jolene fetched Hildy, and Hildy came for me. We sent a neighbor for Elias, and he moved you and the children here. When I went back to get fresh clothes for you, I noticed the jailhouse door was open. I looked inside; no one was in there, Lily. He must be long gone."

"Dammit! Get Martin for me! I need to know why—when—"

"Lily! Right now, you need to rest. You can talk with Martin later." Mama's voice is pulled too thin, a thread about to snap. "Better yet, leave these things to Martin, to the men. . . ."

"I'm not sure I can trust Martin. I'm not sure who to trust, besides you and Hildy."

"If that's the case, then you're best off letting this go."

"Let Daniel's killer go?"

"If that will keep you safe. Your children safe. It's what Daniel would want."

Mama puts the brush back on the end table. It's a relief, feeling her hair smoothed. Mama sits on the edge of the bed and lifts a tress of Lily's hair. "You've always had such lovely hair."

"Thank you for taking care of me," Lily says.

"I haven't brushed your hair since you were a child—"

"I mean—"

Mama puts her fingertip to Lily's lips. Mama doesn't like to talk directly about such things. "I need to tell you something, about me and your daddy," Mama says. "I didn't want your father to go to Rossville last September, to help with the rescue. We fought about it." Mama shakes her head. "Last words out of my mouth to the man was that he owed it to his family to take care of us. He walked out, with me shrieking at him."

And just a moment before, she'd been noting how Mama doesn't like to talk about difficult things. Maybe she's wrong to see Mama as simple and fussy. Mama'd lost a son. As a widow, she'd had to stiffen her spine to take care of your child.

"All I'm saying, child, is what goes on between a man and a woman can't be all sweetness, and if Caleb is looking down at me from the heavens, I've got to believe he's remembering more than my quarrelsome ways." Mama smiles. Her eyes are bright, but she, too, holds back her tears. "If Daniel didn't tell you everything, well, isn't that the way of things sometimes? Even if a man and a woman love each other dearly?"

Lily looks down. She'd never told Daniel about her first pregnancy. She'd always thought she would, when he was back from the war. But so often he'd carried hurt in his eyes, even when he grinned, and she didn't want to add to it. Maybe he saw hurt in her eyes, too, from things that happened while he was away at war. Maybe that's why he hadn't told her about Marvena and Eula. Maybe he, too, always thought he would.

"What I'm trying to say is that whatever you may find out now that he's gone, Daniel was a good man," Mama says. "I know I was gruff with him sometimes . . . worried about you marrying a man so worldly, but after a while I loved him, too, saw how good he was to my daughter. What a good father he was. But he's gone and you have to take care of you and Jolene and Micah. You don't have to keep the role of sheriff, especially after this. No one will blame you if you walk away. You and Jolene can have this room. Micah can share with Caleb. You'd be a help to me, you know." Mama's lips quiver as she tries to smile. "You always were."

Lily knows this is only part of the truth. When she'd lived at home, she'd helped, but she'd also chafed and rebelled, making Mama fret and speechify about what-will-people-think and knowing one's place in a community.

Lily suddenly clasps Mama's hands. "Mama, I need your help. Please go tell Martin that he must fetch Ada Gottschalk for me. That I need to talk with her—for Daniel's sake."

Mama looks shocked. Her hands quiver in Lily's grasp. "Ada? But why? Why?"

"Her farmhand was the first one who found Daniel. But the farm-hand has disappeared. I want to know if there's anything she can tell me. Anything that can help me figure out exactly what happened the morning Daniel died."

"Lily, please, let Martin do the questioning—"

Lily stares evenly into Mama's eyes. "Mama, inside me now there's a thin vein of hate. For everything. And it's growing, and it'll keep growing if I don't settle on the truth of what happened. Please. Maybe Mrs. Gottschalk can help me find a bit of that truth."

"If Martin refuses?"

Lily clenches her jaw. "I am not asking. I am ordering, as sheriff."

Mama's face sags with the fullness of her fear.

"I'll be careful," Lily says.

"That would be a welcome surprise."

Lily smiles. Mama—however worried she is about her—is still Mama.

Mama sighs. "I'll go talk to Martin."

As Mama leaves the room, Lily sinks back into her bed. She's pushed aside, time and again, a memory even more painful than that of being attacked in the alley, in fact her most painful memory until *Daniel's been found.*

On a fall day in 1918, Lily stepped out of the Kinship Opera House, now a makeshift hospital for flu patients, where she worked as a nurse alongside Elias. She leaned against the placard in front of the opera house—a hand-lettered sign that read: "Closed for Entertainment Until Further Notice, by Request of Mayor—" and gulped in great breaths of air, a relief from the smell of sick, dying, dead, on the cots inside. She had just witnessed another child die, a six-year-old boy.

Lily gazed across the town square. Many shops were shuttered; others displayed hand-lettered signs in their windows—"War Bonds Sold Here!" Or: "No Pro-Germans; Loyal Americans Only." Or: "Krauts not welcome here!" Across the square, at her father's shop, McArthur & Son Grocers, signs plastered the windows and exterior promoting war bonds and "Use Cornmeal; Save Wheat for Our Troops and Allies!"

Lily's father had refused to put up anti-German signs, and that had cost him business. Just two weeks ago, a band of men came to the store and pulled everything that had the whiff of Germany: jars of kraut, bratwurst and blutwurst, spicy mustard, dark rye bread, packages of apricot Linzer cookies, foods he'd been bringing in from importers in Cincinnati for years, just for his loyal German customers. The men piled it all in the street in front of his shop, set the pile afire, a crowd gathering to whoop with glee.

When several of the men came back—this time to buy canned vegetables and cigarettes—he did not turn them away but looked them in the eye as he slowly counted back change. Even offered one of the men's little daughters a peppermint dot.

Why would you serve them so? Lily had demanded at supper that night. She was at home with her parents while Daniel and Roger were away serving in the Armed Expeditionary Forces. Because they're humans, too, Daddy had said. Wrongheaded and scared, but humans.

Now Lily roused herself from resting. Surely she could take a few minutes to go to the post office to check, as she did almost every day, if there was a letter from Daniel or Roger. There hadn't been, for weeks. But suddenly she didn't want to do that. She wanted her daddy. She wanted him to wrap his strong arms around her, tell her that Daniel and Roger would come back, that the grocery sign would be amended to "McArthur & Sons Grocers" when they joined the business after the war. After breakfast that morning, she'd realized she was pregnant with her and Daniel's first child.

A reserve of energy, born of need, propelled Lily from the sign, across Canal Street.

Lily was in the middle of the street when the horses came thundering toward her. She jumped out of the way, barely missed being run over. Her father ran out of the store, grabbed her from the edge of the sidewalk.

The horses were pulling a cart, and on the cart were two men and a woman—Ada Gottschalk—weeping and screaming. The men laughed at her distress, held her back as she tried to scramble to the edge of the cart. As she begged, "Please, please," her voice carried her thick German accent on just that one word. She and her husband were immigrants, coming to this land in their early twenties, optimistic about building a better life.

Sickness thickened in the pit of Lily's stomach as she stared. Tied to the back of another horse was Ada's husband, Hahn Gottschalk. He'd been stripped of his shirt—chest, back, arms, and face slathered with hot coal tar from the waist up, dusted with chicken feathers. His wrists were bound to the harness, his ankles lashed to the stirrups. His eyes were closed. But they fluttered open and he saw his wife piteously wailing. The men who had brought them hollered, "We brought this filthy German to you, Caleb McArthur, so you'd make him buy war bonds!"

Hahn struggled, but his wrists and ankles were bound too tightly. He opened his mouth to speak, and the men watched, grinning, eager to hear whatever he had to say so they could mock it or use it as an excuse for further brutality.

No sound came out.

"Lily, go fetch Sheriff Tate," Lily's father said softly.

Lily shook her head. "No, Daddy, let's just go inside the store."

But her father let go of her, stepped forward. Lily grabbed his arm. "No Daddy, no! Come inside; let them be; it's not our trouble. . . ."

Daddy shook her arm free and turned and stared back at her. For a moment, Lily could hear nothing, could see nothing except her father's eyes filled with shame, could feel nothing except the terror of realizing that his shame was not because of men who would treat another so brutally but because of her plea. Her cowardice.

Then he stepped forward and said, "You will let this man and his wife go."

"He's not bought war bonds! He's not a patriot!"

"We are, we are, we're just having trouble; he borrowed for a new plow; surely you can understand!" Ada cried. "Lily, please, remember how we helped you when you were hurt? Jumping from that tree? We took you to Dr. Ross's farm . . . please tell them we're good people—" One of the men slapped Ada to silence her.

"You will let this man and his wife go," her father thundered again.

"What are you gonna do 'bout it?"

Lily looked up, saw one of the men standing before her father, shotgun pointed at his belly. Her father stood, cross armed, resolute. "You really want to shoot me here? In front of all of these people? That's what you'll have to do before you do more harm to these good people."

The man glared at Daddy, spit at his feet, then walked back to the cart.

"Unlash the German then," the man said. The one holding Ada let go of her. He jumped down and started untying Hahn as Ada crawled down from the wagon.

"Some of you watching, come help me get our friend and neighbor to the opera house!" Lily's father called. He turned, looked at Lily.

She wanted to look away, her face burning with shame, but her father's gaze held her. "You," he said. Lily waited, knowing the rage she deserved. But then a sorrowful smile broke his face. "You go ready a cot and bandages for Mr. Gottschalk."

A week later, Hahn was able to go home with Ada. That after-
noon, Lily miscarried her and Daniel's first baby.

Later that morning, Elias takes Lily's pulse, nods with satisfaction, and then presses her abdomen gently. "Tender?" he asks.

Lily shakes her head. "Not too bad."

Elias sinks into the rocking chair by Lily's bedside. "I think you are well enough to go home in a few days."

Lily frowns. She is restless and eager to get back to pursuing the details of Daniel's murder. "I feel well. How about tomorrow."

Elias's brow furrows with concern. Finally, he sighs. "Fine."

Lily gives him a soft smile. "Thank you for taking care of me," Lily says. Though Elias is long retired and Kinship has a doctor, Mama has insisted that Elias is the best and he has not hesitated to drive in from the Ross family farm.

"Your mother gets most of the credit."

"Her, and her sassafras tea," Lily says.

That draws a chuckle from Elias, though Lily knows that each spring he gladly accepts a canning jar of the dark red tea. Puts "pep in his step," he always tells Mama, making her smile.

Lily allows herself two small luxuries, first the joy of seeing Elias, for a moment, not drawn with sorrow. All that he's done for her spins through her mind: amputating her toe to save her leg, holding her secret of the first lost baby from Daniel.

Then there's the relief of tension finally breaking between them, of the return to companionable silence they long ago earned, through the long months of tending influenza patients sometimes back to health, often through the final moments before their passing, long hours in the makeshift hospital in the Kinship Opera House or in their homes if they couldn't bring the patients in, with Lily acting as Elias's second in command. They'd shared the task of telling folks that their loved one had passed. She'd been with Elias when his wife and daughter both succumbed to the flu.

Through all of that, they'd learned how to not only be comfortably silent together but also read each other's silence, whether the quietness of despair or of hope. That had been wrenched from them since Elias came to tell her *Daniel's been found,* yet tried to shelter her from details of his death, since Elias had tried to defend Luther's behavior at her swearing in.

Now Elias stands and pats Lily on the arm. "You should take it slowly. Let Martin handle the investigation into Daniel's death—"

Lily looks away and pulls her arm from Elias. Their companionable silence is again snapped in two, punctuated by the shutting of the door as Elias leaves. Lily clenches her fists. Why can't those she loves the most understand her need to find out what happened to Daniel?

That afternoon, Mama comes back with yet another cup of tea.

Lily smiles—*Mama and her tea!*—until Mama says, "You have a visitor. Ada Gottschalk. As soon as I told Martin your request, he left to get her. And he's back already."

So soon? Lily's stomach suddenly burns.

"Can't Martin ask her what she knows?" Mama asks.

Lily shakes her head. "I want to talk with her alone. I just need a minute to get ready."

"Take your time. Drink your tea," Mama says, then leaves the room.

But Lily ignores the tea. She gets out of bed, slowly covers herself in a robe, then walks to the rocker.

A few minutes later, Ada Gottschalk stands in the doorway. In shape and size, she's the same petite, dimple-faced woman with the neat gray bun pinned to the top of her head that Lily recollects from the times she came over to Lily's grandparents' farm, to visit with Mamaw Neely, the same woman who has always been in the background of her earliest memories.

Lily forces herself not to look away from Mrs. Gottschalk's gaze, turned from a warm blue to a hard gray. She's aged more than the past seven years can account for. Lines crevice her brow, crackle her cheeks, making her round face seem hard and gaunt.

Lily clears her throat. "Please come in."

Mrs. Gottschalk enters, sits on a chair near Lily.

"Thank you for coming to see me." Lily hates the quiver in her voice.

"I didn't realize that I had a choice," Mrs. Gottschalk says flatly.

"Oh! I—I hope Deputy Weaver was kind."

"Please. I came because I feel badly that I did not attend Daniel's funeral. It is hard for me, as you might imagine, to be out in large gatherings. And—and because I should have come to the door when you came by in the first place. I do not like to think that I am cowardly."

These words, from Widow Gottschalk, are too much. Lily looks down. "I—I always meant to come see you. To apologize—"

"That is not necessary now." Mrs. Gottschalk clips each word. "What do you want?"

Lily looks back up and clears her throat. "I heard that your farmhand found Daniel. But that Rusty is missing."

Mrs. Gottschalk shrugs. "I wouldn't say 'missing.' Just 'gone.' He may well be back. He's been known to take off on foolish binges. Though he's far too old for such nonsense."

True. There are several cards on Rusty in the jailhouse files.

"In any case, I have a new farmhand now," Mrs. Gottschalk says. "So if you pick up Rusty on a binge, tell him not to come back."

"I wanted to know what Rusty told you about finding Daniel."

Mrs. Gottschalk lifts one eyebrow. "I've told Deputy Weaver what I know."

"Which is?"

"Are you asking me as sheriff, or as Daniel's wife?"

Lily sits up straighter, finally directly meets Mrs. Gottschalk's eyes. "Both."

Mrs. Gottschalk swallows. "Rusty told me the week before Daniel's death that he'd planned to move some of the hay from the barn out to the fields. He did so that morning and I reckon that's when he found . . ." She shakes her head before she goes on. "Anyway, after Rusty got Daniel up to the house, I tried to tend to him before Dr. Ross could come, but his wounds . . ." Mrs. Gottschalk pulls a handkerchief from her purse, dabs at her eyes under her spectacles.

"Did he . . . did Daniel say anything?" Lily's words are a harsh whisper.

Mrs. Gottschalk's face finally softens. "I'm sorry. He was already gone."

Lily glances away, stares at the blue Ball jar vase. The flowers are gone now. She hadn't noticed until this moment.

She looks back at Mrs. Gottschalk. "Rusty didn't mention anyone else on the road?" She thinks of the broken limb of the tree, across from where Daniel had died. "Or nearby?"

Mrs. Gottschalk shakes her head.

"Nothing unusual? Out of place?"

"No. He moved the hay. Realized a bale had fallen off. He went back for it, and that's when he found him." Mrs. Gottschalk dabs her eyes again. "I want you to know I didn't just come because you're sheriff—a ridiculous job for a woman." She gives Lily an appraising look, and Lily's face reddens, as she feels herself to be again the fearful young woman of seven years before. "I came because your husband was a good man. Your father, too. And I want to tell you something. After what happened to him, Hahn wasn't the same. He spent foolishly, borrowed even more foolishly to keep our farm going in difficult times. But Daniel came out to our house. On official business of the sheriff's office. Hahn was behind in payments, owed for farm supplies. Daniel was supposed to serve an eviction notice.

"Instead, he gave me money enough, and then some, to pay off the note on our farm, so I could own it free and clear." At last, Mrs. Gottschalk allows a smile, but Lily knows it is not for her. It is for the memory of Daniel. "I reckon he didn't tell you this."

Lily swallows hard. No, he hadn't. So much he hadn't told her. Trying to protect her. Would he have ever told her, in time?

"Well, he'd want me to have my pride," Mrs. Gottschalk says. "I don't rightly know where he got the money. I didn't ask."

That huge balance in Daniel's second account . . . Another secret he'd kept from her.

"I'm glad he did that," Lily says.

"Daniel said it was the least he could do, considering Hahn brought you to Elias's farm after your accident, into his life," Mrs. Gottschalk says. She gives Lily a curious look. "You know, I always thought you were a brave child." For a moment, Lily considers telling her about the attack in the alleyway. It had broken her courage. But she hadn't even told Hildy or Mama about that. Only Daniel, and George Vogel and Abe Miller, knew.

Lily looks away and Mrs. Gottschalk sighs. "Anyway. I think that's why he always checked on us. And on me, after Hahn died. Two years ago."

"I'm so sorry." Lily looks back at Mrs. Gottschalk. "I've always, always been sorry—"

Mrs. Gottschalk holds up her hand. "I'm telling you this because our families have been friends going back a long ways. And because you've taken your late husband's job as sheriff."

Lily nods. "For now. At least until—" She stops. She cannot tell this woman, of all women, of her deep need for justice and vengeance.

But perhaps Mrs. Gottschalk sees it in Lily's face, for at last she gives her a tender smile, one truly meant for her. "What I'm saying is, Daniel had his own way of doing things. But everything he did was for his community, from my way of looking at it." The smile snaps away, and Mrs. Gottschalk lifts her eyebrows. "You have big shoes to fill, Sheriff Ross, and I don't mean because you're a woman—though plenty will try to use that against you."

She stands, goes to the door, stops. Looks back at Lily. "Here's why I really came—to tell you this: If you ever have need, let me know and I will try to help. As a member of this community. Because that's what Daniel would have wanted."

After Mrs. Gottschalk leaves, Lily picks up the cup of tea, sniffs it. Chamomile. It's grown cold. But she takes a sip anyway. She has to get strong for what lies ahead.

CHAPTER 18

⤜

MARVENA

On this cool, misty morning, Marvena studies her small patch garden behind the cabin—a mess of carrots and green onions have been pulled, too early. Second time this week. She'd hung a quilt to air out on the line between porch and oak tree, too, and it had gone missing.

Now she feels a presence in the woods nearby—a feeling she'd learned to cultivate from hunting even small creatures—and the skin on the back of her neck prickles. This is no opossum or rabbit or squirrel. And black bears and deer didn't neatly pull vegetables or snag quilts.

Human.

She points her shotgun at the thicket where small broken twigs are telltale signs of some creature coming forth from the woodland to her cabin.

"Come on out now; show yourself!" Marvena calls. "Or I can just start shooting."

The air tightens around her. She cocks the shotgun. Puts her index finger to the trigger.

"Wait." The voice, broken and gravelly, comes from the thicket. Tom tumbles forward, wrapped in the quilt, and collapses.

Marvena rushes to him, falls to her knees beside him. She pushes back the quilt, takes in the welts and fading bruises on his face. He's healing from a beating, but his eyes are shiny and wild and his skin is hot and dry, though he's shivering. No, he's tremoring. He smells of vomit.

"Oh God, what—" Marvena can't find the words.

"Martin . . . Martin let me go . . . told me to run . . . but I couldn't. . . . Alistair . . ."

Marvena scans the yard. "Hush now; let's get to the cabin."

Marvena's back aches. For a full day she's sat in a kitchen chair pulled alongside the bed in her small cabin, where Tom rests and heals. After helping Tom into her cabin, she and Frankie had taken turns tending to him or keeping watch outside and listening for unnatural sounds.

Now Tom looks up at her. "Hey, baby sister." His voice is hoarse. "We oughta talk."

"Not now. When you're stronger."

"I'm strong enough," he says. "I've put some things together. The day before Daniel was killed, I was pulled from work to the holding cell by one of the Pinks. Then, middle of the night, I was grabbed from my sleep and someone blindfolded me. I thought to fight, but then I thought . . . Alistair. And I thought of all we've done to organize. I thought, if I fought, I might be making it worse for everyone. So I let myself be led out to an automobile. We drove for a time, and then he had me get out. Took the blindfold off of me, and I see I'm at some hunter's cabin."

"Were there any signs as to whose?"

"Nah. Looked like it hadn't been used in years. There were two more fellas—I don't know if they were Pinks, or just hired in for this, keeping a watch on me. This went on for days. Then one night I heard them talking about how they only had to hold me a few more days. They had a good laugh, talking about how they'd get to rough me up to make me look like I'd been on the lam, then drag me in to the sheriff. After the fight he and I had, I was scared."

"How did you get away?"

Tom offers a wobbly grin. Now he's got more teeth missing than accounted for. "Mighta been your shine that saved me. The two Pinks got to drinkin' more than usual that night. I reckon they were bored, or maybe the lightning that night was stronger than usual. Anyway, one fell asleep, and I asked the other to let me go take a piss. He was unsteady, so I grabbed a fallen tree limb and knocked him out. I ran off, and hid out here and there, and then got to a barn."

"Oh, Tom, why didn't you keep running? You could've been outta these hills by now—"

"And leave Alistair?" Tom reaches, puts his hand on Marvena's arm. His hand is cold. "Leave you? Frankie? The cause?"

Marvena puts her hands on his, rubs to get warmth in his hands. Just like when they were little and winter nights nipped through cracks—now sealed with tar—in the cabin. "Go on."

"Well, I got sloppy. Hungry. Caught in the farmer's cellar, taking a ham. And then I was hauled into the jail—and that's where I learned about Daniel's death. Being wanted for it. And I met the new sheriff—Daniel's widow! But you know that. You went to see her. She told me."

Tom gives Marvena a long, hard look, and she reads in his gaze exactly what Jurgis had already told her—she'd overstepped her bounds. Marvena rubs her eyes. Weary.

"Yes, I went to Kinship, to see Daniel, try 'n' find out what happened to Eula, and that's how I learned about Daniel. And don't give me lectures about—"

"Marvena, Eula's been gone a long time, and we know she was taking up with Pinks—"

"No!" Marvena says. "I—I shouldn'a but I went to the boardinghouse, and Joanne told me Eula took off with a new young miner."

"What? You believe that?" Tom asks, but the effort costs him. He is racked by a deep, rattling cough. "Eula wouldn't waste her time with a poor miner. She was only after money."

The tiny diamond flashes before Marvena's eyes. Mayhap he's right, but she won't stand for more mean talk about Eula. She jerks her arm from Tom.

He sighs. "Marvena, I reckon I've said some terrible things. But I've never liked seeing you hurt, and you've been hurt enough."

"There's no escaping hurt. It always finds you somehow, so you might as well face it."

"But there's no need running after it, and I fear that's what you're doing with Eula. Like you did with Daniel."

"You've talked too much. Rest, and I'll bring you some good sassafras tea." God, she is starting to sound like Nana. *Vile thugs beat you near to dying. Is way of world. Have tea.*

Marvena goes to the cookstove to start Tom's tea, all the while remembering that hard afternoon, one week before Daniel was murdered. The last time she saw Daniel.

She was out front of her cabin splitting wood—though it was a Sunday, there was no time to rest—when she heard Daniel calling her name. She stopped her labors, turned; for a moment, caught in that wide devil-may-care grin of his, Marvena felt as though they were gazing at each other a lifetime ago.

Eula. The child's name whispered across her heart and mind, and she ran to him as she once had. He caught her as she tumbled into him, slowly wrapped his arms around her.

Daniel asked what had her panicked. She told him about Eula being gone for nigh on three weeks, how it wasn't like her to not visit Frankie each week, how Tom said there was gossip that Eula had been seen consorting with Pinks, trading on her relationship with Daniel.

At that, Daniel had inhaled, as hard as if he'd been suckerpunched, and said he'd find whomever Eula had run off with and kill the bastard. Tingles had spider-danced over her scalp and brow as she watched the blood drain from his face, his brow pull tight.

Marvena started shaking. Daniel took off his topcoat, draped it around her shoulders as she said, "I just . . . just can't believe what people are saying. That she took off with a Pink."

"Did Tom say which Pinkerton? I'm going to find the son of a bitch, and so help me God, if I have to kill him to get Eula back—"

"Daniel! You don't even rightly know if'n she's your daughter!"

"Doesn't matter. I've loved her all along like she is."

At that, Marvena dropped to her knees, sobbing, and Daniel knelt before her, pulled her into his arms, rocking like that for long moments.

But then Frankie, Tom, and Alistair had come back from gathering greens, and Tom had accused Daniel of playing with Marvena's emotions, of not really meaning to come out in support of unionization or follow up on his promise to call his old army friend at the Bureau of Mines. Tom even went so far as to suggest he was using the promises as an excuse to fool around with Marvena now that John was out of the way.

At that, Daniel's wrath and skill as a boxer came out in full force, his left jab tossing Tom to the ground, pounding Tom's face as Marvena and Alistair shrieked for him to stop. It wasn't until Frankie wailed that he finally did, looking up, eyes glazed, as if he were seeing another time and place.

Fear and bile rose to Marvena's mouth, and she had to swallow hard to keep from vomiting, for even as Daniel let his fists drop, and stood, and stepped away from Tom, Marvena could see the terror in Tom's eyes—terror that had nothing to do with the damage of a swift punch. Without Frankie's voice calling Daniel back to himself, Daniel would not have stopped.

And yet Daniel had scooped weeping Frankie up in a gentle hug, comforted her until she calmed, told her he was sorry she'd seen that, but that her uncle would be all right. And then he had lowered Frankie to the ground and walked over to Marvena.

He stared in her eyes for a long moment. Whispered: "Trust me."

The last two words he'd ever speak to her.

Tom sighs, bringing Marvena back to the moment as he sips the sassafras tea; Marvena's dosed it with her shine. He takes another long drink, then says, "I think we can trust her."

For a moment, Marvena's heart lifts and she thinks he means Eula, but then Tom adds, "I told her Daniel was working with me on unionizing. I thought she'd know if'n he'd made the call for us, or meant to."

He means Lily. Marvena tightens her jaw as she asks, "Did you ask her?"

Tom shakes his head. "I didn't get the chance."

"Just as well. I don't know that we can trust her."

"She was willing to listen to me. She stood up for me. Luther's bringing in some Pink who told Daniel to go fetch a prisoner—me—who claims he handed me over to Daniel. But she doesn't seem to believe it."

Frankie's earlier confusion over distinguishing false morel mushrooms from the true comes to mind, and Marvena shakes her head. *No.* She had trusted Lily to follow up on seeing what she could learn about whether or not Daniel had gone to the boardinghouse—and Lily hadn't done so. She hadn't been back into Rossville or up to visit, which with Tom here is also just as well, but still, what this neglect suggests to Marvena is that Lily hadn't really cared about helping her find Eula. She'd just wanted verification that Daniel had been true to her.

But Marvena doesn't want to go into this much detail with Tom. She can't bear to see his hard expression about Eula, or his doubt of Daniel.

Still, her hesitation gives Tom a chance to spin his own interpretation of why Marvena doubts Lily. "You still in love with him?" Tom asks.

The piercing words sting, so sharp her skin feels like it might peel itself free of her. Marvena starts to protest, but the truth is, though she'd loved John, there was a part of her, a part she'd hidden away from herself until now, that hadn't entirely let go of Daniel.

"Marv—I'm sorry—" Tom starts.

She waves a hand at him, a hushing gesture. "You shouldn't have told her about working with him," Marvena says. She looks back at Tom, eyes hard. "What if Luther and the Pinks were behind Daniel's death? God, what if Daniel, like a fool, trusted Luther, threatened him with a call to his old friend at the Bureau of Mines? Now Lily's going to keep digging."

"Then she could be our ally! In Daniel's place."

In spite of his weakness, Marvena swats the top of her brother's head. "Are you a damned fool? She don't scare easy, but that just means she doesn't know—or is just willful enough to ignore—how much she *oughta* be scared."

Marvena clenches her fists, puts her head to them. She's already wondering what she'd set in motion, telling Daniel the talk about the Pinks and Eula. It's more'n likely that, sure, Lily would have started questioning the escaped-prisoner cover story all on her own. But by showing up, Frankie's foot cut, Marvena had set in motion Lily questioning sooner rather than later, sent her to the countryside to find that glass, to start putting things together.

No, she hadn't known, hadn't intentionally done so, but now, dammit, she feels responsible for Lily. For Daniel's children.

"All right," said Tom. "She oughta be scared, sure. But maybe that's all the more reason she needs us, and if she needs us, we should trust her—"

"No! She came and talked to me, promised she'd follow up at the boardinghouse about Eula, but I went there, and Lily never did check up on Eula."

Tom's eyebrows go up and he starts to speak, but Marvena goes on. "No, no, don't you give me any sass about Eula and letting go of worrying about her! If Lily had really wanted to help me, if she was really interested in helping—"

"Marvena."

She starts to shush her brother again but sees such deep sorrow in his face that she clamps her mouth shut.

"Marvena, Lily hasn't been back to Rossville or here because she lost her baby. I saw it happen." Tom's eyes fill, and he closes them quickly.

The very air around Marvena seems to stiffen. Lily's baby. Daniel's baby. Suddenly she aches for Lily. And for this part of Daniel, gone.

"You said when I found you that Martin had let you go?"

Tom opens his eyes. "He came after Lily had been taken to her mama's, from what I could figure from overhearing. He got the keys, unlocked the cell door, and told me to run."

"Why?"

Tom presses his eyes shut. "Said he didn't know what would happen, now that Lily was so sick. Said he'd be acting sheriff for a bit, but he didn't know if he could hold off Luther or the commissioners or all the folks wanting a resolution, right quick, for Daniel's murder."

Tom shakes his head and looks up at Marvena. "God, the man started crying. A grown man. Said he didn't want my blood on his hands. Said he couldn't stand it if Daniel was up in heaven and saw him be a coward about me. That he wouldn't want me killed, not in cold blood, not as an excuse. And he said if I ever got found and told anybody, he'd just lie, say some buddies of mine somehow set me free."

"Oh God, Tom. I know you love Alistair, me, and Frankie, and I know you care about the community, but you should have listened to him. Gotten out of the county! Out of the state!"

"I shouldn'a come here. I just wanted to wait, get stronger, strong enough to grab Alistair and run . . . I dunno where I'd have gone, or worked, but . . ." Tom's voice trails off.

Marvena pats his hand. "It's all right."

In spite of his protestations about Martin crying, Tom tears up. "I want to see Alistair," Tom gasps, with a half sob. "I can't go back to work, and they'll just keep working him. We're going to have to leave for good, but for where? None of the mines 'round here will have me."

Even if he wasn't on the lam, a miner who left a company owing scrip, with no papers to show he could be hired free and clear, wouldn't find work.

It would be better for Alistair, for all of them, if Tom could just heal up enough to leave, at least heal up enough to hide somewhere other than here.

But Marvena offers comfort. "We'll get Alistair to you when it's time. You can leave together. I've got a little put aside and you can have it to go out west, maybe. Start over there, somehow. For now, you need to rest up."

She stands, about go to the stove to make more tea.

But her cabin shakes suddenly as a blast rumbles and echoes up the hill.

She stumbles to the ground, to her knees beside the straw bed. Marvena and her brother clutch each other, wide-eyed. Their eyes say to each other, *Alistair.* He's small enough; he'll be laying the lines of blast in the narrowest crevices to make new, big openings.

With Daniel out of the way, it's started early. Dynamiting under Kinship Cemetery for a new opening in the Widowmaker mine.

CHAPTER 19

≫≫

LILY

The next morning, April 5, Lily returns home. By mid-morning, she is restless.

She goes out to the jailhouse, and her eyes immediately drop to the threshold. It's been scrubbed clean. And the jonquils. The blooms should by fully open, sunny faces turned to the sky. But the earth is trampled where they had been; only a few straggly leaves remain. The key ring shakes in Lily's hand, but she takes a long breath and opens the door.

There are no prisoners. There is a note on the desk from Martin that states there had been an overnight hold for disorderly conduct. Nothing about Tom. Hildy has already cleaned the chamber pots and turned the straw mattresses; she must have scrubbed the threshold as well. The jailhouse is spotless.

From the desk drawer, Lily pulls out her notebook. She pushes aside her emotions, makes herself summarize the moments before her miscarriage, reconstruct her and Tom's conversation. Then she reviews her notes from her visit with Marvena. Her discovery of the candy box with Eula's items. Her discovery of Daniel's second bank account and, inside his boxing gloves, the ticket from his last official fight and her blue ribbon.

Lily locks up the jailhouse and goes inside. She finds her sheriff's badge among the blue ribbons for pies, returned to the red compote dish on top of the pie safe, and she pins the star on. In the parlor, Jolene is reading to Micah. She waits for Jolene to finish the story, then tells them to come with her to their mamaw's.

"Are you sick again?" Jolene asks.

"No, honey," Lily says. "I just have . . . errands to do."

After leaving the children with Mama—Lily hurries away before Mama can press for details—she walks first to the *Kinship Weekly Courier* and surprises the editor, Mr. Lindermann, with a request: What can he learn about the fight between Daniel Ross and Frederick Clausen on August 20, 1917?

It will take a while, Mr. Lindermann says, but he'll see if he can contact someone at the *Cincinnati Enquirer* to look up any articles about the old fight.

"Official request?" he asks, eyeing her badge.

"Personal curiosity."

When she steps out of the newspaper office, a truck filled with lumber rumbles by, too fast. She coughs from the dust it raises.

A woman on the sidewalk near her gives her a foul look and eyes her badge. "Those trucks have been making a mess of the road! Why, my boy almost got run over the other day! Isn't there something you can do about it?"

Lily gives her a long look, confused.

"Well, I have heard you've been laid up," the woman says. "So you mayn't have heard about the extra trucks. The extra train runs. Making everything dirty." The woman shakes her head. "It's been in the newspaper." She points at the building behind Lily. "Ross Mining is reopening Mine Number Nine." She uses the official name of the Widowmaker.

Lily staggers back. "What? But after the collapse—"

"New opening. West side of Devil's Backbone. Under the old cemetery. Well, my husband tells me it's the price of progress, that Ross

Mining is why Kinship Road was built in the first place and graveled. Still—" she sighs, and brushes at her shoulder. "If you could get your brother-in-law to have his trucks slow down, it would be awful nice."

The woman hurries on and Lily walks toward Martin's shoe repair shop. She jolts into a man, and says, "Excuse me," but her thoughts are elsewhere. Daniel would have fought Luther reopening the Widowmaker, every bit of the way, even if he had remained against unionization.

The bell over Martin's shop door dings as Lily enters. By the time the sound's faded and she's exhaled the smell of leather and glue and dye, Martin has stepped from the back of the shop and up to the counter.

He looks concerned. "Heard you'd left your mother's. Are you sure you're ready—"

"I'm fine." Not entirely true—she still feels sore and her heart thrums with this added sorrow, but she won't discuss intimate matters with Martin. "I'm back on the job. And I want to know how Tom Whitcomb came to be released from the jail."

Martin clasps the shoe and rag he's holding extratight. "I don't know. The next morning, after you were taken to your mother's, I came to the jailhouse to check on him. The door was open, and so was his cell. The keys were just outside the door."

Lily studies Martin's face, suddenly florid. He's lying to her. He's never, she realizes suddenly, been good at deception.

But he goes on. "Luther thinks that some of Tom's friends got word that you were sheriff and were just lying in wait to overtake you, get the keys, get him out."

"So I lose a baby, and that makes it easy for Tom's friends to release him, is that it?"

"No, no one's saying that. But I didn't know; if we'd've known, then—" He stares down at the shoe he's holding, gives it a wipe.

"Then you wouldn't have asked me to be sheriff? Figured the strain would be too much?"

Martin looks up at her. His eyes are bright. "Oh, Lily, I'm so sorry."

Lily stiffens her heart. "I'm guessing I should expect a visit, asking me for the star?"

"No . . . no. I don't think so."

"Well, do not expect me to voluntarily turn it in. I was bound to lose this baby from the beginning." As she says the cruel words, Lily knows they're true, knows that Daniel sensed it, too: that that was why he'd been reluctant to make love with her. Knows that's why she couldn't bring herself to share the news of the child with Hildy or Mama. "What now of Tom?"

"There's a new manhunt for him."

"He says he didn't kill Daniel."

Martin shrugs. "A man will say most anything, I reckon, to keep from sitting in Old Sparky. Doesn't matter what he says. If he's found, he'll be accused. Plenty will come forward saying they saw Harvey Grayson hand Tom over to Daniel at the holding cell in Rossville."

"And what about Grayson? Before I—" Lily stops, reconsiders how to phrase this. Calculates how long it's been since she lost her baby. Four days. At once, that seems like forever ago yet also just a moment ago. "A week ago, you told me that Grayson was on his way here to bear witness that Daniel took Tom from the holding cell."

Martin shakes his head. "He never showed up."

Lily lifts her eyebrows. "Any word as to why?"

Martin looks down. "I did ask Luther about that. He says the Pinkerton company reassigns their men all the time and he doesn't have control over that."

Convenient. Grayson goes missing again, now that Tom escapes once more.

Lily starts to leave, but Martin calls, "Wait!" She turns around and watches him reach under the counter. He brings up a revolver, sets it down on the countertop. "For you," he says.

Lily walks over, eyes the firearm, picks it up. It's a Colt .45 revolver, much like Daniel's.

"You need a proper gun," Martin says. "Your stocking gun won't do and you're right scary with a shotgun."

Lily looks up at her husband's best friend, sees just the shadow of a smile playing in the corners of his mouth. God, she wants to trust him.

"I've gone ahead and ordered a new Colt for you from the Remington Arms Company. Until then, this is an old one of mine," Martin says. "I've cleaned it. Oiled it." From under the counter he pulls out a box of .45 Colt lead bullets.

"Thank you, Martin." Lily tells herself to just leave it at this, but she must know. "Martin, the driver's side window was shot out of Daniel's automobile. Did you oversee the cleanup?"

Martin gives her a long look before saying, "No. I—I didn't think about going out there, where Daniel was shot. I hope Tom's long gone. I think believing anything else is—"

Lily reads the word in his expression: *dangerous.*

She wishes that she knew if it is offered as protection or warning.

That night, she reads and rereads Daniel's few letters from the war, looking for any reference to the buddy Tom said Daniel had planned to contact, to help somehow with organizing. Maybe, as an investigator in the Bureau of Mines, he could also put at least a temporary halt to reopening the Widowmaker, at least until the new opening's safety is assured.

The letters don't specifically mention friends, just offer assurances that he's fine and of his love, details about weather and rations. Only one comes close, the letter about poor Roger:

> *My dearest Lily,*
> *By the time you receive this, you'll have likely received the news of Roger. Whatever you're told, I want you to know he died bravely, trying to save another soldier who'd made the mistake of coming out of a trench at nightfall, maybe thinking he'd heard a Kraut. Our ammo man, a fine soldier, tried to stop Roger, but he was too strong for us. I think he did get the other soldier back to his trench, before a sniper took him. Lily, the fighting here is fearsome. Only the thought of your sweet face keeps me brave. I live for your smile.*
> *Yours always, Daniel.*

The letters, which at the time seemed so intimate, now seem a smokescreen. She knew so little about his childhood, his boxing career, the war. Why hadn't she pressed him more? Well, men didn't talk much about the war after they came home. But the other areas . . . she could have. And yet she knows why: she'd felt, from the moment they'd met, as if she *did* know him.

That was why she fell in love with him so easily, so fast. With him, she'd felt at home. More herself than she'd ever been. She knew—from his glances, his touch—that he'd felt the same with her. There was no need to talk about it, and surely there'd be time. . . .

But they'd been fools. They'd each seen how fragile is life. They'd just wished to ignore that, to get lost in the ease of being with each other.

Now Lily chafes in her own skin, itchy, irritable. Because of Marvena. And Eula. The lost child. But mostly because she's come to fear she never really knew Daniel. As if their time together were only a dream. A foolish girl's fancy.

The next morning, not even a wisp of cloud frosts the tops of the hills around Kinship. Warmth stirs the day, like a languid hand troubling a cool, still spot tucked along a creek bank.

After breakfast, Lily stands on the back stoop, considering what to do, given that she's not supposed to work on the garden yet or drive. Well, she can check the garden. The back door squeals as she opens it. That hinge Daniel was going to fix. She goes to the carriage house, finds a can of oil, douses the hinges, tests the door. Silence.

After she puts away the can, she stops in the yard and catches herself staring up at the cloudless sky. She realizes that she is looking for a hawk—one of Daniel's beloved signs. He'd told her, before he left for the war, that if she spotted one looking at her that would be a sign that he was fine. She'd teased him once, a few months after his return, that she never did get his sign. And he'd teased back that she just wasn't a believer in signs, so how could they find her?

True, yet here she was, looking for that very sign, when clearly Daniel was not fine.

Lily drops her head to her hands, inhales slowly, forcing her mind to clear, until at last it comes to her—not a sign, but an idea for a way to be able to get around as sheriff and continue looking for clues to Daniel's murder.

Lily takes Micah back down to Mama, and then with Jolene in tow she stops at Hildy's house and asks her to come back to the carriage house. She opens the doors, looks at the automobile, and then back at Hildy and Jolene.

"Where are we going?" Jolene asks.

Lily smiles. "You'll see!"

"Oh no, I thought Elias gave you strict orders not to drive," Hildy protests. "Not for another few weeks."

Lily keeps her smile fixed. She's not going to wait that long to seek out Marvena again, to return to Rossville. She's lost four days with the miscarriage.

"No. He said I shouldn't go anywhere *alone*," Lily says.

She drives them out of town, up Grassy Hollow, just off of Kinship Road. It's gravel, not smooth like the main road, but also not as steep, and less trafficked.

When she gets to the top of a rise, she presses her foot down on the clutch while slowly lifting the throttle lever, steering to a wide spot on the right side of the road. She pulls the hand brake into neutral, then presses the brake pedal. When the automobile idles to a stop, she reaches to the dashboard and turns off the coil box switch. The engine shuts off, and Lily puts the hand brake lever all the way back to set the parking brake.

"Are we picking black raspberries?" Jolene's voice squeaks at the prospect.

"Too early yet for that. We'll go to the place near the Gottschalks' farm when it's time," Lily says. For a moment, she sees Ada in her old bedroom at Mama's, telling her to let her know if she needs anything, sees Hahn in the middle of Kinship, in front of her daddy's grocery. "Today Hildy is going to learn to drive!"

Hildy gasps. "What? No! I have no reason to drive."

"Of course you do. You're jail mistress now."

"The furthest I go is from the jailhouse to the outhouse. That doesn't require driving."

In the backseat, Jolene giggles.

Lily says, "I may need you to go somewhere for me."

"I'm not fetchin' prisoners!"

Lily raises her eyebrows. "What if I deputize you?"

"You can't do that!"

"Course I can. And I'll teach you to shoot."

"I'll refuse!" Hildy says.

Lily puts on a mock frown. "Then I'll have to fire you."

As soon as she says it, Lily regrets teasing too hard, for Hildy's face crumples in dismay, just like when Lily would tease her in their childhood. "But I like being jail mistress."

Lily pats her friend's arm, amends: "I'm not going to fire you, Hildy. But I do want you to learn to drive. It will be good for you. It'll be fun! And it's easy."

Hildy looks doubtful.

"You can do it, Aunt Hildy!" Jolene says. "Daddy taught Mama."

"That's right; *Daniel* taught you!" Hildy wails.

Lily's heart pangs. Yes, he had. She gives her head a shake, to stay in the moment. "And I want Jolene to see that not only can a woman drive, but she can teach someone else to drive."

Hildy drops her head to her hands.

Lily turns off the engine, shows Hildy all the steps for driving, and restarts the Model T. But by the time Hildy is in the driver's seat, the engine is rattling like a rat with its tail in a trap.

"Now what?" Hildy cries.

Lily, who's slid over to the passenger side, points to the coil box switch.

Hand quivering, Hildy turns the switch.

"Now pull the spark lever up some more—no, no, the one there, on the left. The right one's the throttle—slowly, that's it."

Hildy does so, and the engine smooths out. She slumps back in the seat.

Jolene claps. "Aunt Hildy did it!"

Lily says, "See, that wasn't so difficult after all."

The women fall silent, listening to the hum of the Model T's engine.

Then Jolene giggles. Within moments, they're all laughing, great raucous belly-busting bursts of laughter, laughing until they're gasping and tears are running down their faces.

When they stop for breath, Lily nudges Hildy. "Now you know how to start the automobile, don't you want to know how to drive it?"

Hildy looks at Lily and grins.

Lily commands until finally it all falls together in Hildy's mind and she pulls out on Kinship Road, high gear, tops twenty-five miles an hour, wind blowing over the top of the windshield, and she whoops, and Jolene hollers, "Wheeeeee!" and Lily looks behind to see that Jolene's hands are thrown high up in the air as if she can catch the wind, and that sorrow, for the moment, is gone from her sweet little face.

And then Lily hears another voice of laughter. Her own. Guilt at the notion of ever feeling joy again pinches her. But with the next breath, for just a moment she lets go of guilt and anger and sorrow and fear and whoops, too, joyous, carefree.

The next morning, Lily takes Hildy with her to Rossville. Lily trusts Hildy, as much as she does Mama, but there are details she doesn't want to share in earshot of Mama because they'll scare her. She fills Hildy in, though, on everything she's sorted out so far and that she's written in her notebook: her belief that Daniel was ambushed and shot on the way to Rossville, that Marvena had asked Daniel to find out about Eula's whereabouts, the box of Eula's that Daniel got from the boardinghouse, Tom's insistence that he was not taken from the Rossville holding cell on the morning of Daniel's murder but earlier that day by a Pinkerton, and her frustrations that two men are missing whom she'd very much like to interview: Rusty Murphy, the farmhand who found Daniel's body, and Harvey Grayson, the Pinkerton who'd come to their house to tell Daniel about collecting a miner—Tom—from the Rossville holding cell and who was willing to bear witness that Daniel had indeed done so but who is no longer coming to town with Tom's second disappearance. Hildy gasps with surprise upon hearing Lily share Tom's claim that Daniel had not only planned to come out for unionization but had also contacted a friend at the Bureau of Mines, and shares Lily's frustration at not knowing the name of that friend. Finally, Lily even tells her about the extra account Daniel had, about Abe Miller, who worked for George Vogel, Daniel's former boxing promoter, warning her not to get in the way of George's business, and the realization that the money in the account was likely for Daniel looking the other way as sheriff as George took moonshine from the county for his "Vogel's Tonic" pharmaceutical business.

Through it all, Hildy listens patiently, nodding. The only thing Lily holds back is that though she is relieved Daniel was faithful in the conventional sense, deep down she holds a keening hurt that he'd never told her about Marvena. But then, it doesn't need to be said aloud for Hildy to understand this.

"What does this all mean?" Hildy asks quietly as they near Rossville. "For figuring out who killed Daniel and why, if it wasn't really Tom?"

"I don't know," Lily says. "Yet."

At the Widowmaker, just outside of Rossville, they watch from afar as dynamite blasts out underneath the side of the hill with the cemetery where her paternal grandparents are buried. Lily contemplates: the mountains hold the trees up firm and strong; now men use the felled trees to build the supports and shafts inside mines to hold the mountains up firm and strong.

Lily makes Hildy drive up to Marvena's cabin, Hildy yelping at every bump even as Lily coaches her on the twists and turns. At the cabin, Lily and Hildy look around carefully, even peering in windows, but they don't spot either Marvena or Frankie.

Down in Rossville, Nana says she hasn't seen Marvena recently. The old lady tries to be casual, but Lily can tell that she's troubled. When she asks about the reopening of the Widowmaker, Nana says, "All I can do is pray for Jurgis, for all the men. God save us all." She shakes her head and looks away for a moment. Her eyes are bright with barely masked fear when she turns back to Lily and Hildy. *Life is hard. Have tea?*

Back in Kinship, after Hildy goes home, Lily finds Magistrate Whitaker, ask about laws about desecrating burial sites. She even mentions that her father's parents are buried there. He merely lifts his eyebrows, grunts, "I'll be sure to look into it," doffs his hat, turns away.

That night, in a foul mood from the unsatisfactory answer, Lily puts the children to bed early. Lily looks over the past weeks' issues of the *Kinship Weekly Courier*. There's a small article about her appointment as sheriff, five pages in. She tries to focus on reading the next installments of "The Curious Case of the Whistling Pigeon," a serialized crime story about a Canadian Mounty, his beloved Lenore, a stolen emerald, and a spooky mansion. Six weeks after the serial started, poor Lenore still needs rescuing.

Lily jumps. She's nodded off, and now someone is knocking at her door.

It's Martin. He looks grim in the doorway. She gestures for him to come in and he sits on the edge of the settee, after Lily returns to her chair.

"Lily, I've gotten a tip," he says, "about a still, close in to Rossville."

Lily studies Martin, trying to see what she might read in his face. Daniel rarely talked about busting up stills or turning moonshiners over to revenuers. It is a polite pretense in Bronwyn County that whiskey is not a problem here. But occasionally he'd tell her that he'd been to a still and let the moonshiner go, *just for now.*

She gives Martin a long look. "How did you get this tip?"

"Someone left a note at my home today," Martin says.

Lily lifts an eyebrow. "A note. For you."

"Folks are still getting used to you. And you're still healing after your—your loss." Martin blushes at the reference to Lily's miscarriage. "I can go myself, take a few other men. But I wanted to tell you first."

Lily inhales sharply. "Do you really expect I'll say, 'Why sure, go on without me'?"

Martin shakes his head. "No, but what if it's a setup of some kind?"

"More like a test," Lily says. "That note wouldn't have been postmarked or telegrammed from Cincinnati, would it?"

Martin frowns his confusion. "Cincinnati? No, it was handwritten."

"Do you have it with you?"

He nods, pulls out the note from his jacket pocket, and hands it to

Lily. She unfolds it; it's in neat handwriting on Kinship Inn stationery, not signed of course. Yet she guesses: *Abe Miller.* The note states: "Please check up on Coal Creek Rise, about .8 mile up, then 30 degrees northeast into the woods for illegal distilling activity." *Please check up Coal Creek Rise, about .8 mile up, then 30 degrees northeast into the woods for illegal distilling activity.*

Lily looks at Martin. "Coal Creek Rise?"

"A path up from the creek and near the workers' cabins," Martin says.

The lane that leads to Marvena's cabin. Lily never knew it had a name.

She recalls the moonshine Marvena had had her sip during her one visit. "Is this Marvena's operation we're busting?"

Martin looks away as his face flushes. "I don't know anything about that."

"Of course you do," Lily says. He'd kept from her the knowledge of Marvena—not that she expected her husband's best friend to tell her of such—but he'd also more than likely held back the truth of how Tom escaped the jailhouse. *What else?* she wonders.

Lily picks up her shotgun and revolver. "All right. I'll have Hildy stay with the children. Then we'll round up a few men to go with us and see whatever it is we're supposed to find."

CHAPTER 20

꙳

MARVENA

The stiff night smells like the promise of coming rain, though its scent is doused by the strong odor of corn mash fermenting with yeast. Afar off a coyote howls, then a bit later a screech owl, and in between shivers and sighs of smaller night creatures. Marvena is at ease in the embrace of the young night; the moon is rising, nearly full, its bottom curve appearing to be snagged by the tops of trees. She works alongside the few men—mostly distant Whitcomb cousins—in her employ. The men's voices are a garble of talk and laughter; Marvena doesn't bother to sift out distinct words or to tell them to quiet.

The cave, too, is where her daddy and his before him stowed supplies and tools, in the deep, dark cool, for their operation. Tom, mending well enough to make the trek up the ridge from the cabin, is in there now with Frankie.

Marvena gauges, just from the scent, that this run is about halfway through distillation. She tends the low fire, mostly embers, under the first large copper kettle. A copper tube coils out of the kettle's lid into another container, and from there another tube coils to a third container, and then, through a spout at the bottom, liquid slowly drips into a canning jar, just like the ones she uses for preserving fruits and vegetables.

One man tends the jar. Another guards the edge of the clearing.

Marvena is about to return her focus to the process when she hears a sharp trill.

"Woo-hoo." A woman's voice.

The guard startles, looks up.

Lily steps into the clearing. She's far too relaxed, her hands behind her back. *Setup.*

Before Marvena can say or do anything, the guard steps forward. "Well, look a here. You lost, little lady?"

"Fool!" Marvena cries. "Don't let her—"

The guard starts to lift his shotgun, but Lily whips out her revolver and shoots just above his shoulder.

"Goddam, who the hell are you?" the guard shouts. "Temperance League bitch!"

"Shut up, Arlie," Marvena says. "That there's the sheriff. Lily, let's talk—"

The man by the canning jar reaches for his revolver.

"I wouldn't do that if I were you," Marvena says. "She ain't just a lucky shot. She can take out Arlie and you before you remember which is the shooting end of your gun."

Marvena looks back at Lily. "Lily, let's talk. Woman-to-woman, like you said once. You don't have t'do this."

"I'm sorry. But I do. I suspect the tip-off came from Abe Miller."

"Who?"

"He works directly for George Vogel. As . . . an enforcer, I guess you'd say. I can't ignore that and expect to be left in peace."

"Well, how'n the hell did this Abe fella know where—"

Lily cocks an eyebrow, ticks her gaze from man to man.

Of course. Some money and a fear of Vogel would be enough to buy betrayal. But why would Vogel, a world away in the fancy city of Cincinnati, care about Marvena's little operation?

As if reading her thoughts, Lily says, "Marvena, you need to understand. I've only met George Vogel two times. But I have no doubt that he is a man who demands absolute, full loyalty. He is . . . uncompromising. I'm being tested."

Marvena shudders, understanding. Though she's never understood why, Marvena knows that George had been the only man with a hold on Daniel. Now that Lily is sheriff, George has a hold on her, too. Not only does she have her children to protect, but she also won't want to do anything to upset the balance of power in the county, leastways not until she figures out what happened to Daniel. Marvena can't blame her.

Four men step out of the woods.

Marvena glances around, calculating. Somehow, Lily organized them to come up around the camp. She swallows hard. *All right.* So long as Tom and Frankie stayed in the cave. So long as the cave remained undiscovered.

But then Martin steps forward. He has Frankie, holding the trembling child by an arm.

No sign of Tom, though.

A few hours later, in the county jailhouse in Kinship, Marvena stares through the bars of the cell at the plate Lily is offering. She wants to tell her to go to hell, but she's so hungry that her stomach feels as though it is cutting itself in two.

"Hey, she don't want it, I'll take an extra supper!" says Arlie in the next cell.

Marvena wants to tell him to shut up, but she presses her lips tightly together. There's no point, anyhow. They'd already betrayed the whole operation to Lily.

Marvena snatches the plate through the food slot, carries it back to the cot, sits. She eats a bite of good salted ham. She has to keep herself from moaning with pleasure and relief. Next she takes a bite of apples, fried up with brown sugar and butter and cinnamon. Fancy, rich food. Marvena hates to admit it, but Lily's a good cook. She clears the plate quickly.

"There's more if you'd like—" Lily starts.

"I'll take seconds!"

"Hush up, Arlie!" both Marvena and Lily call.

A bit of a smile, despite her weariness, plays across Marvena's lips. But she carries her plate back to the slot. Lily takes it. She crosses her arms, waits for Lily to go away, but Lily just stands there, looking at her with that sorrowful expression.

"I didn't have a choice," Lily says.

"You apologize to everyone you lock up?" Marvena asks.

"No, but—"

"Then stop doing me favors. If'n you want to do something for me, bring me Frankie!"

Lily puts the plate on her desk, leans on the edge. "She's been fed. She's sleeping."

"Uh-huh. And what happens tomorrow?"

Lily shakes her head. "I'm not sure. We've never had a situation like this."

Marvena grabs the cell bars. "So help me God, if'n you drag her off to the orphanage . . ."

Lily looks horrified. "No, she can stay here!"

"Raised up fine? So's by the time I'm out—"

Hurt turns inside out on Lily's face, but Marvena tells herself that she wouldn't take back the words if she could.

"Hello?"

Both women jump at the deep male voice, then stare as a tall man strides into the jail cell. In the light of the coal-oil lantern he carries, his face darts in and out of shadow.

He looks at Lily. "Well done."

Lily stands. From the sudden tension in her shoulders, the closing of her expression, Marvena thinks Lily is afraid of this man. She starts to speak, but the man holds up a hand to silence her. Then he crosses to the cell.

"Mr. Miller!" Lily sounds startled.

Marvena thinks, *Ah. Abe Miller.* Daniel had told her about him.

Lily continues, "I'm not releasing Marvena—"

Marvena starts to protest, then realizes that Lily is trying to protect her from this man.

He ignores Lily, looks at Marvena. She feels as though, under his gaze, she's being taken apart, bit by bit. Marvena forces herself to match his cold stare.

"So you're Marvena Whitcomb. Daniel put forth a great deal of effort to shelter you, but with him gone, your protection is over."

Lily steps forward. "Whatever deal he had for Marvena, I'm willing—"

She stops as the man snaps his eyes to her. "We're still sorting out what our arrangements with you will be. We thought you proved yourself quite able tonight."

"Dammit, when I get outta here—"

Marvena's words wither to a stop when he looks back at her. Even in the half-light, the coldness of Abe Miller's eyes is unmistakable. "You will be released tomorrow," he says.

"You don't have the authority—" Lily starts.

"Arrangements have been made," says Abe. "However, Miss Whitcomb must now follow the agreement the other producers have with Mr. Vogel, or give up production altogether."

Marvena turns over his fancy words until they become something she understands. The meaning hits her, and she gasps. "But I don't know what the agreement will require of me."

Abe shrugs. "It doesn't matter. The terms will be explained later. Choose."

"Mr. Miller, please, she has a young daughter to care for—"

Abe looks at Lily. "That is not any of my or Mr. Vogel's business, though we're aware of her situation. The girl of course can go home tomorrow, when you release her—"

"I haven't agreed to that. Charges have to be filed."

"It's been taken care of." He looks at Lily and Marvena realizes, as Lily flinches, that she's afraid of this Miller. Of Vogel. Enough to cede her authority to theirs, just as Daniel had.

Miller looks back at Marvena and it's all she can do to keep from shrinking back at his thin smile, too. "Now then, Marvena, what's your choice?"

Marvena calculates: give a portion of her meager income to Vogel and his operation? It's not just that she doesn't want to lose money; she doesn't want to be beholden to him. Nothing made Daniel look afraid except when he mentioned George Vogel. This representative can't be any better.

And once she is in his hooks, will she be free to spend time on organizing the men for unionization? Or would Vogel just want more and more from her?

Through gritted teeth, she says, "Why, sir, I've seen the error of my ways, and I'm giving up the sin of moonshining for good."

"Very well." Abe turns to Lily. "Tomorrow morning, and not before, this woman and her daughter are free to leave. As is—" He looks around the jailhouse. "Which one of you is Arlie?"

Arlie says quietly, "Here, sir." *The fool. So he's the turncoat.*

"Ah, as is Arlie over there. The rest of Marvena's men . . . well, they were not so willing to cooperate when asked, so indeed they will need to be sent on to face their charges—"

Marvena says, "Come on now; let them go—"

"Miss Whitcomb, you should be counting your blessings," Abe says. "If you produce again, I will know, and there will be no second chance for you."

"Why would George Vogel possibly care?" Lily says. "One small still! And Daniel—"

Abe allows another flicker of smile. "I'm surprised you'd care so much for Daniel's friend. In any case, you do not have the relationship with George Vogel that Daniel did."

"And what, exactly, was that? What hold did George have over my husband? I can't believe Daniel was motivated simply by the payments he received from George."

Marvena recoils at Lily's words, wants to holler at her, *What are you playing with? Stop!* She's afraid of making their situation with this Abe—and George Vogel—even worse.

But Lily is going on, inflamed by Abe's thin smile. "Oh yes," she says, "I've figured it out—that Daniel got separate payments from George. . . ."

Her voice withers to a stop. Marvena notes the look on Lily's face as the other woman figures out, finally, that she's pressing too hard.

"If Daniel didn't tell you of the hold Mr. Vogel had over him, it is not my place to decide whether or not you should know it."

"But Mr. Vogel doesn't have a hold over me—" Lily starts.

"Doesn't he?" Abe snaps the words like a whip.

"Well, you said . . . if ever I needed help . . ." Lily falters at Abe's look.

Abe says, "Choose the use of your favor wisely, Sheriff Ross."

Marvena wants to scream at her, *Use the favor to get back my business!* But then she sees in the sorrowful look flickering in the shadows on the other woman's face: *I'm sorry. I'm sorry.*

The next morning, outside the jailhouse, Lily says, "Please, at least let me drive you?"

Marvena shakes her head. Her men have already been transported to the state prison, pending trial—except Arlie. Lily had given him a head start the night before, after Abe Miller left. Marvena had hollered at him that he'd better never show his face around here again as he'd scurried out. Now she'll have to go back to living hand to mouth on hunting and gardening. She doesn't like the notion of asking the very men she's pushing to strike to help her out.

"Thanks for the offer of a ride," Marvena says, "but I'm ready to stretch my legs a mite."

"I couldn't ask Miller to help you. Not until I find out what happened to Daniel."

"Then what? You unleash the wrath of Vogel on whoever had a hand in Daniel's death?"

She'd meant the words as a sneer, to show that she didn't believe Lily was tough enough to do so. But Lily's suddenly hard gaze startles Marvena—yes, that is exactly what Lily plans.

From inside the house, the women hear the voices of their three children all singing together: "Too-ra-loo-ra-loo-ral, Too-ra-loo-ra-li, Too-ra-loo-ra-loo-rah, That's an Irish lullaby." Frankie's voice rings the strongest, and Marvena knows that she'd have been the one who convinced the other two to make a chorus with her.

"I lost the baby," Lily says flatly. "I haven't had a chance to ask after Eula."

"I've been myself," Marvena says. "The proprietress tells me that Eula ran off with a new miner who took a fancy to her. She didn't know his name."

Lily gives Marvena a long look. "You believe that?"

Marvena shrugs. "I want to." She looks down. "I'm sorry about your baby."

"Thank you. Deep down, I knew from the outset that something was wrong, but I didn't want to admit it to myself. There are lots of things, I'm finding, that are like that. Anyhow, I reckon some of Tom's friends were watching for an opportune moment to overtake me and get the keys and set Tom free. So while I was laid up, that's what happened. So I've been *told*."

Her snap on the last word makes her look back at Lily. Marvena reads in Lily's expression that she doesn't believe what she's been told. A sense of unease overcomes her. *I want to,* she'd just said, about believing the simple explanation for Eula's disappearance.

"Have you seen Tom?" Lily asks.

"No," Marvena says, knowing that Lily won't believe her. "I'm sure his friends made sure he got a long way from Bronwyn County. That'd be the smart thing."

"Tom also told me that Daniel was going to do more than come out for unionization. That he was going to contact a friend at the Bureau of Mines to inspect Ross Mining."

Marvena looks down, not wanting Lily to read her expression as she'd just read Lily's.

"Tom said Daniel referred to this friend as someone from the war. But Daniel almost never talked about the war with me. So I don't know who that might be. I've read and reread all of Daniel's letters from the war, looking for the name of this friend. I haven't found anything."

Letters. Could the name be in the letters he'd sent her? Marvena doesn't know many who can read. Maybe one of the children who'd been with their mamas at Nana's house the other day? She'll have to think carefully about who to trust, to ask. Should she ask Lily? But no. If Lily's willing to let Vogel stamp out her little business, would she be willing to betray anything she learns about the unionization cause if it might help her avenge Daniel's death?

"I don't know what Tom was talking about," Marvena says.

"I'll come by in a few days, in case you recollect—"

"There's no need for that."

Lily walks down the rise of yard, from the jailhouse to her back kitchen door, opens it, goes inside. A moment later, she steps out with Frankie, gently holding the girl's hand. Marvena's heart grabs at the sight of her littlest daughter.

Frankie runs to Marvena, flings herself at her mama, suddenly sobbing.

"It's all right," Marvena says, catching the child up in her arms. "I'm all right. I'm here."

Then she carries Frankie past Daniel and Lily's house, out to Court Street, and begins the trek, again, back to her cabin.

CHAPTER 21

꙳

LILY

The next day, a man, who introduces himself as LeRoy Sanderson, the new farmhand for Ada Gottschalk since Rusty's disappearance, comes to Lily's house with bad news.

"It ain't a pretty sight," LeRoy says.

"Show us," Lily says.

"The smell is kinda fierce, too—"

"Go!"

"I'm jus' sayin', you bein' a lady an' all. Maybe you'd better leave this to the men."

"Either share the news, or I'll arrest you for harassment!" Lily snaps.

She isn't sure that is a real charge, but it is enough to get him to drawl, "Well, I was down t'the creek fishing, and then I saw something, rollin' up agin the bank. Mrs. Gottschalk said I'd better come right quick to report it."

Lily's stomach turns, but she simply nods and then sends Jolene, with a basket of fritters they'd just finished frying up, down to Mama's with Micah. Then she rounds up Martin and some other men and follows LeRoy back to Ada's farm.

By the time they gather behind Ada's farmhouse, LeRoy's again dithering about the propriety of a woman seeing what he's found.

Lily is impatient to get to the site and the body before full dark sets in. She puts her hand to her revolver. "Do you want me to bring you in for interfering with an investigation, or lead us to the bank where you supposedly found this body?"

Ada Gottschalk, standing behind them on the back stoop of her farmhouse, clears her throat impatiently. "Mr. Sanderson, lead the sheriff and her men on down. She can handle it."

Lily looks back at Ada to give her a smile of thanks, but the woman has already turned to go back in, to tend to the bread Lily can smell baking in the oven just inside the kitchen door.

He turns, and she and Martin and two men they have deputized follow him to a line of trees just on the other side of Ada's newly turned vegetable garden. A soft spring rain has started. Lily shivers in her coat, pulls her hat down more tightly on her head.

They all smell the body before they get to the bank. Martin puts his sleeve to his nose. Lily makes it a few more steps before pulling out a handkerchief from her pocket. One of the deputized men veers off the path, vomits.

They're all quiet the rest of the way down the path to the bank. Here large rocks edge between earth and creek. Lily looks at the body. Female. Facedown. The dress is faded, but Lily can see it is mainly blue. Snagged in an eddy of broken branches and rocks. Lily steps forward.

Oh God. Lily silently prays, *Not Eula*—though Eula is the only girl she knows of who is missing in Bronwyn County. She does not want to deliver bad news to any mother, but she shudders at the thought of going to Marvena to utter the words: *Eula's been found.*

"Lily, you don't have to—"

"Yes, I do, Martin," she says. "Help me pull her in. Roll her over."

Within minutes they have the body out of the water, up on the path. There's little intact of her face; what's left of her is bloated, skin peeling back from muscle and bone. She could have been in the water just weeks, or longer if she'd frozen after she'd first fallen in.

"I need your pocketknife," Lily says. Her voice sounds so distant, wooden.

Martin tosses his knife on the ground next to Lily. Then he jumps up, runs a few steps before stopping to retch. Lily holds her breath, swallows back bile. She slices off a piece of cloth from the girl's hem, stares at the swatch in her hand. She recognizes the same red-flowered blue cloth as that of the tiny dress on the doll she'd found in Daniel's drawer. As the cloth patching the quilt in Marvena's cabin.

Lily figures the girl's body had snagged underwater in rocks and branches, rather than going downstream to the mighty Ohio River, and that a winter colder than usual made the water icy enough to preserve the body for a time. But the rush of water in the spring thaw had carried the body down, where it snagged again in the eddy by the Gottschalks' farm. At the hairpin turn.

Lily looks over the girl's body. She doesn't see any bullet wounds or stab marks, but those could have been obliterated by decomposition. There is, though, a thick indentation in the waxy yellow flesh of her neck. The indentation is about the thickness of a rope. Had someone tried to hang her or strangle her? Or was there another explanation?

Lily walks over to the men who've gathered with Martin. They're all staring at her, silent.

"We need to fetch Elias," she says. She pauses, her voice catching. The last time he'd have been called as county coroner would have been after Daniel was found. Lily clears her throat, goes on. "The girl's body will need to be examined before she's transported to the Kinship funeral home, and prepared for a proper burial."

Then she looks at Martin. "You and I—" Lily stops, looks at the bit of cloth in her hand. "We're going to go tell the poor girl's mother."

Yet she knows she will not need to say anything. Marvena will read the terrible news writ into her face.

CHAPTER 22

※

MARVENA

A loud snap startles Marvena awake from a fretful dream.

It takes her a moment to adjust to the dark of her cabin. Frankie stirs on the straw mattress next to her, and Marvena sits up, touches the child's forehead, checking for warmth, suddenly terrified that her foot—though nearly healed by now—has set up with an infection that Marvena somehow missed. But Frankie feels cool to the touch.

Marvena wants to find the source of the snap. Tom? Surely he'd not be fool enough to come out of the cave now. He'd gone deep, deep down a narrow, dangerous tunnel when he'd heard Lily and her men, then stayed hidden.

She'd gone to him, dark of night, as soon as she was back. He had raged, wanted to rush down the mountain, find whoever had betrayed her, find Luther and kill him, grab Alistair.

She'd slapped her brother then, just to get him to hush, told him not to be a fool. He'd be dead before he could get near Luther, and what good would that do poor Alistair?

She told Tom to bide his time, that the men were set now not just in Rossville but throughout the region to rise up.

Now Marvena sits up, slides to the foot of the bed, picks up her shotgun. She gets her knife, too, sheathed in its leather cover, and tucks it in her skirt's waistband.

Shotgun at the ready, she goes out the front door onto the porch. She almost laughs when she sees the source of the loud snap, the nearly full moon revealing that a dead branch on the sycamore tree had fallen to the ground.

There's a soft chill to the air, yet Marvena sits down on the porch swing and sets her shotgun aside, wrapping her arms around her chest. She rubs her arms for warmth. She doesn't want to go back in the cabin, fearful she'll wake Frankie, who'd barely stopped weeping since they'd left Lily's this second time. The child wept for her cousin Alistair. She wept, missing Jolene and even Micah. She wept for her Uncle Tom and the man she'd known as Uncle Daniel. She wept, wanting her big sister, Eula, back.

Marvena rocks slightly in the swing, resting the back of her head against the heavy chain. Might be that she'll doze out here, a blessedly dreamless sleep. She can't quite recollect, but she senses she'd been dreaming of Eula. Or of a barn dance, of her and Daniel as partners—a ridiculous dream. She and Daniel had never danced like that.

Still, her heart is racing, and though she tries to tell herself it's the snapped branch that's worried her to restlessness, she feels a tightening in the air. She's staring down the lane, waiting, watching for a sign—a sound, a movement, a stirring.

For a long spell, it's just her, the porch swing, the moon. "In the stillness of the midnight," Frankie singing the refrain from her favorite hymn, "Precious Memories," comes to her.

Then she hears the automobile. The sheriff's.

Marvena holds the shotgun steady, even after the automobile stops, even after Lily gets out of the driver's side, and Martin gets out of the passenger's side. Neither of them raise weapons. They start to the porch, but then Lily turns, mutters something to Martin, and he stops, leaning into the vehicle's open door.

He stares at the ground, but Lily walks to her, eyes on her steadily.

Marvena's hands sink down with the shotgun. She hears it clatter to the porch as if from a great distance, as if the sound of it is already a memory or perhaps another dream. Marvena trembles. *Oh God, oh God, let this be a dream.* But she knows the truth before Lily steps on the first porch step. She sees it in the woman's walk, in her eyes, not pity, worse than pity. Sorrow.

Then Lily is in front of her, and she holds out her hand, fingers closed over her palm. Marvena wants to look away, but something pulls her gaze down to Lily's hand.

Lily opens her fingers, and Marvena sees the filthy calico cloth, tiny red flowers on pale blue cotton, same cloth she'd used to make Eula's sixteenth birthday dress, same cloth that offered scraps to patch old quilt curtains and make a tiny dress for one of Daniel's whimsical dolls, the one Lily had found in his drawer in the jailhouse. Lily starts to speak, but the scrap of cloth signifies the bitter truth: *Eula's been found.*

Marvena stumbles forward, as if something horrid has shoved her from behind, knocking the wind from her lungs. Lily catches her, dropping the cloth, and some part of Marvena wants to twist away from the other woman, but she has no strength for it. All of her will is caught by the wretchedness twisting her heart and lodging in her throat, and she slumps silently in Lily's arms.

CHAPTER 23

꧁

LILY

Two days later, Lily glances over at Mama, rewrapping her dried apple stack cake.

"You're going to worry that poor cake down to crumbs," Lily says. She's putting jars of food—canned peaches, pickles, jams—in a wood crate. She hesitates, suddenly wanting to keep the last jar of black raspberry jam for her children.

"That poor woman, losing a child, it's the worst—" Mama stops, puts a hand to Lily's face, and Lily sees in Mama's eyes what she said while Lily was recovering after the miscarriage—*Take care of yourself, child.* Now Lily put the black raspberry jam back in the box, reminding herself to be generous with Marvena and Frankie. She can pick more black raspberries later in the summer.

They hear the front door open, a somber deep male voice.

"Elias is here," Lily says. She puts the jar in the crate, closes the lid, picks up the box.

"Should you be lifting—"

"I'll be fine, Mama," Lily says.

They go to the parlor, where Elias is kneeling to greet Jolene, Micah,

229

and Caleb Jr., all gathered around him excitedly. Like Daniel, he always had a soft spot for children, and always thought to bring them some treat or another. This time it's butterscotch buttons. He'd been so good with his own daughter, and Lily suddenly misses Sophie and Ruth. How would Elias's life be different if they'd survived the influenza outbreak years ago? They'd both died within days of each other shortly after the horrific scene with Hahn and Ada Gottschalk. For one, it was likely Luther wouldn't be living with him.

Elias scrambles up. "Good morning, Lily. Here, let me get that crate for you." He hurries to her, takes the crate.

Though it's only nine o'clock on a Wednesday morning, Elias looks weary. As county coroner, Elias had examined the remains of the girl's body, reporting to Lily that she'd suffered a broken neck, likely from a fall into the creek upstream, hopefully dying immediately.

When Lily informed Elias that the boardinghouse proprietress had told Marvena that Eula had run off with a young miner, Elias suggested that Eula fell to her death as it appeared and the young lover had panicked and run away. Maybe, Lily had said. But doubts gnawed at her later as she wrote out the facts of Eula's death and Elias's theory in her notebook, adding her concern that the young miner seemed too easy an answer for Eula's death.

"I'm not sure how receptive Miss Whitcomb will be to our comfort," Elias says now. Lily and he had visited Marvena after Elias completed his examination of Eula's body, to tell her the assessment that the girl had likely fallen. Elias had asked to pay for the coffin and burial, and Marvena had refused his offer of a burial at Kinship Cemetery—the nearest cemetery to Rossville, with the old one closed, snarling that she didn't need *charity* and that she could pay for it herself. The conversation moved on to a church service—but she'd held firm against that, though she was willing for Lily to attend the burial.

"She's part of our community," Mama says. "So we have to try."

Then Mama presses down on her hat with one hand, hugs the waxed-paperwrapped cake to her ample belly with the other. "Well then. Let's get a move on."

———

Marvena eyes the gifts of food warily, and Lily knows she's thinking, *Charity.*

Lily says, "Mama's dried-apple stack cake is very good."

Marvena turns cold, cinder eyes to Lily. "I'd reckon so," she says.

Lily suddenly realizes that their presence means Marvena feels she must lock away her sorrow. Lily looks at Elias, kneeling again, this time with Jolene and Frankie.

"How's that foot of yours?" he's asking Frankie.

"Oh, lots better!" Frankie says.

Elias places a hand gently on Frankie's shoulder. "I've brought you something." He reaches in his pocket, pulls out another butterscotch button.

"Thank you," Frankie says, unwrapping it eagerly. She sucks on the candy so hard that her cheeks dimple, her lips poking out. Her eyes grow wide at the taste.

As Elias drives through Rossville, the few people—women mostly, very young children, a few elderly men—watch his passing automobile, wary at its unfamiliarity. Several women, though, solemnly wave at Marvena. The able-bodied men, of course, are at work. Elias, Lily, and Marvena sit in the front seat, staring rigidly forward.

In the back, though, Nana Sacovech and Mama jabber over the tops of Jolene and Frankie's heads, like old magpies who've known each other for a lifetime. Between them, Frankie and Jolene sit quietly, Jolene holding her friend's hand.

Just outside of Rossville, instead of going straight on Devil's Backbone Road, Elias takes the left fork. "Shortcut," he says.

Lily wonders if he knows this route will take them past the new entrance being blown in the side of the Widowmaker under the old Rossville Cemetery, wonders just how much Luther talks at home about his business plans.

When they get to the hill, Mama and Nana Sacovech fall silent. All of them—except Elias, who keeps his eyes rigidly on the rutted road—stare at the side of the hill, a great maw blasted out of its side, wood slat frame holding the opening firm.

An explosion inside the hill shudders the road, their automobile. The men working outside don't pause; they've gotten used to the boom and shake of constructing a new tunnel.

"Your nephew has 'em working fast." Marvena's tone twists bitterly.

"Two of my brothers are buried up there," Nana says, pointing up to the closed cemetery, its hilltop crowned with headstones jutting up like thorns. A cross-barred gate blocks the road to the cemetery. "And my grandfather and grandmother."

"The cemetery is no longer used," Elias says.

Lily startles at the matter-of-fact statement, harsh for Elias.

"Don't keep us from wanting to visit the dead," Nana says, crossing herself.

"How will the graves keep from poking through?" Jolene asks. Lily glances back and sees the fear widening her daughter's eyes.

"It will be fine, honey," Elias says, back to his usual soothing way. "Your Uncle Luther has had tunnels like these built before. He knows what he's doing."

Lily turns forward, tries to catch Marvena's gaze, wanting to find some way to offer comfort, but Marvena stares out the side, looking away from all of them.

At Eula's graveside service, Lily at first sits in the back with Mama, the children, Elias, and Hildy, plus the pastor's wife and two stern-looking women, their expressions clearly showing they've been pressed into service from the church in Kinship. Only Marvena, Frankie, and Nana sit in the front. Gazing at the empty wooden chairs, Lily wishes more people from Rossville were there, but it is a workday and Luther certainly isn't going to stop work for Eula's funeral.

Pastor Filmore's familiar words drift on the breeze: "We cannot understand the mystery of God's ways, or why a young woman is taken from us so soon, only hold fast in our faith in our Lord and Savior Jesus Christ, knowing he shall rise again in the Second Coming to judge the quick and the dead. . . ."

It seems to Lily that this life holds enough judging as it is. She moves up to the front, by Marvena, ignoring the stares and gasps of the pastor's wife and her friends. But inside she smiles at Mama's slight, approving nod and is pleased when Jolene moves up to sit by Frankie.

When the pastor is finally done, Frankie stands and leads the closing hymn she'd selected, "Precious Memories." Soon the other voices fall aside to the haunting beauty of Frankie's voice and words of the refrain: "Precious memories, how they linger, how they ever flood my soul—"

After the service, Lily carries sleeping Micah over to Daniel's grave, still unmarked. It will be months before the headstone is in and placed. Lily sees it in her mind's eye: *Daniel T. Ross, Beloved Sheriff, Husband, and Father, Jan. 15, 1893–March 25, 1925*. Daniel, the sign maker, would have approved of the crisp lettering.

Lily hears her name, feels a touch on her arm. She turns to face Marvena.

"I'm so sorry for this loss. Eula should not have died so young," Lily says.

"None should die so young, but in the mines men and boys do all the time. To the likes of Luther Ross they're part of a machine, not worth as much as mules. This isn't going to stop me organizing the men in Rossville. What I need to know is this—will you, as sheriff, oppose or stay out of the way of a public forum at the Kinship Opera House?"

Lily glances at Daniel's blank headstone. What would Daniel have her do? She waits, breathless, for an answer to come to mind, even for one of his ever-promised signs. Finally, she exhales, looks at Marvena. "I will have to deputize at least a dozen men who are sympathetic—or at least not trigger-happy on the subject. Luther will bring in more reinforcements. We'll need our men to make sure they don't get too far out of control."

"I'm willing to wait a week—but no longer. Does that give you the time you need?"

Lily nods.

Marvena starts to walk away, but then Lily calls to her. The other woman turns back, stares at her with cold, cinder eyes, silent, waiting.

"I'm—" Lily swallows hard, not sure if she can say what she's thinking. But she takes a deep breath and forces the words out: "You told me that you didn't know if Daniel was Eula's father. But I'm guessing—I'm hoping—that he loved her like a father."

Marvena's eyes flash with sorrow, and she looks away. "He did," she says softly.

Of course he did. Love for the man her husband was floods her heart. *Of course.*

Finally, when all has been bitterly wrung from them, Marvena and Lily step apart.

Marvena returns her gaze to Lily. "The other day you offered to drive me and Frankie back to our cabin. If you could do that today—just you—I have something to show you."

Lily nods. Elias can take everyone else back into Kinship.

CHAPTER 24

≫⧽

MARVENA

This boom—deeper, distant—rattles Marvena's cabin, shudders from floorboards up through her legs and spine. The tea in her and Lily's cups sloshes but not over the tops of the cups. Marvena knows not to fill them all the way when there's dynamiting.

Lily stares out the window at Frankie on the front porch with her Daniel dolls. Playing, so Marvena told Lily, though the child was really on the lookout for her uncle, in case Tom was fool enough to come to the cabin. She'd gone to the cave to tell him about Eula, but he was gone. Had he left the county after all? She hopes so. Yet she couldn't imagine him leaving without Alistair, any more than she could imagine Eula running off without saying good-bye to Frankie.

Boom. This time Lily says, "Doesn't that scare her?"

"You get used to it, after a time," Marvena says. "Sound you have to worry 'bout is the alarm. Though by the time that goes off, it's usually too late to help those in need."

Lily looks from the window to Marvena, then down to her cup. She inhales the steam. "Not even a dollop of shine?"

"I've shunned my evil ways, Sheriff."

235

Lily lifts an eyebrow at the sharp sarcasm and takes a sip.

"Sassafras," Marvena says. "Builds your blood. Useful after—"

"Marvena. I know you didn't want me to come up here to talk about women's troubles."

Marvena studies her, considering. Now is the moment—finally fully trust her or not. She slips behind the quilt curtain. She kneels, pulls the lockbox out from under the bed, opens the box. For a moment she lets her hand rest on the letters from Daniel.

Then she picks up just the candy box. Back at the table, Marvena's hand trembles as she pushes the box across the table to Lily. "When you didn't come back after your first visit here, I went to see Joanne Moyer at the boardinghouse. She told me that Daniel had asked after Eula, and that she'd told him that Eula had taken off with some young miner, a new boy who hadn't stayed long. That he insisted on searching Eula's old room, and that he rushed out, upset and angry after searching. I reckon he found this. Don't seem like much. But studied the box, inside and out, for a right long time, and found something it would be easy for you to miss, if you just took a quick look."

Marvena opens the box. The scent of chocolate—sweet, bitter—drifts up. She points to the scrap of cloth. "Go ahead. Take a look."

Lily unfolds the cloth and sees a tiny diamond. She looks up at Marvena, questioning.

"After you came with the news of finding . . ."—Marvena pauses, swallows hard.—"of finding her, I got out this box back out. Sifted through." Marvena looks at the box, the pitiful remnants of Eula's everyday life. She shakes her head to as if that could remove the memory of that awful night, comforting Frankie for hours after Lily left and then sitting by herself at the table and staring into this box by the coal-oil lamp, staring at the few small items that were all she had left of Eula. And then, in the light, catching the glint of the tiny diamond stuck in the corner of the box, realizing that the jewel must have fallen from an earring or perhaps a necklace?

"Oh my. No miner could afford—" Lily says, voicing the conclusion that Marvena had come to. "Did Daniel know? That Eula was seeing more than miners?"

Marvena keeps her eyes steady on Lily. "Tom told him he suspected as much. Daniel said he was going to find out who the Pink was. That he'd break him with his bare hands."

"Do you think Daniel would have believed Joanne? About Eula taking up with a miner?"

Marvena lifts an eyebrow. "I wanted to believe her, so I've told myself Daniel would have, too. But what do you think your husband would have believed?"

"He'd have thought that this Joanne was lying. Covering up. What if word got around that Daniel didn't believe Eula simply ran off with a miner? What if one of the Pinks hurt her? And heard that Daniel was digging for the truth?"

"Nana did tell me that Eula came to her, asking for bitter herbs, for something that would make her cramp enough—"

"Eula was pregnant? When did you learn this?"

"A few days after your first visit here. I was visiting with Nana and some other women in Rossville, and Nana told me."

"So Eula lost the child—" Lily looks away for a moment.

Marvena puts her hand on Lily's arm. "I'm sorry; this is a hard—"

Lily looks back at her. "I'm sure you're telling me this for a reason. Anything you know about Eula might help me figure out what really happened."

"Well, Nana also told me that when she saw Eula next and asked after her, Eula just laughed. Said, oh, the herbs didn't work, but that was all right. She'd found a better solution. As if there are so many choices for a single, pregnant girl!"

"Maybe she did get the miner to run off with her. Maybe they had fallen in love but had a quarrel, he went too far—"

But Marvena is already shaking her head. "I know Eula. Truth be told, I can't believe she'd have a change of heart like that. Daniel must have found this box in Eula's old room. Left in a huff, or so says the boardinghouse proprietress. Maybe he found something else, too."

"If he found something else, it wasn't in our house. I looked everywhere, trying to find any notes he might have made about Eula. Maybe he saw the diamond? Or just didn't believe Eula would run off in love with an unnamed miner who'd only been in town a few days?"

Lily stares at the tiny jewel, taps her finger on the table, thinking.

After a spell of silence, Marvena says quietly, "There's no Pink that would just run off with her. And I know Eula—leastways, how she was after Willis Boyle died last fall in the Widowmaker. It seems her tender heart died with him. The Eula who went to work at the boardinghouse . . ." Marvena pauses, suddenly feeling too strangled to easily talk. She swallows hard, forces herself to go on. "What if Eula thought the father had means, tried to blackmail the Pink? Some of them, after all, have wives elsewhere. So what would a Pink do in that situation? I've calculated it out, and last time Eula was seen was during that brief warm spell in early February, when the ice along the creek bank would have been breaking up."

Lily looks up at her and Marvena is relieved to see that she understands, that there's no need to say aloud the hurtful conclusion: that the man would have killed Eula and dumped her body in the creek, taking advantage of the warm spell.

Lily starts to speak, stops.

"Say your piece. I can take it, whatever it is," Marvena says.

"There was a mark along Eula's neck."

Marvena swallows. She hadn't seen her daughter's body. Lily had insisted that it was not necessary, that she needed to remember Eula as she had been when alive.

"Go on."

"Elias said it could well have been a thick vine or tree root that caught Eula, held her body," Lily says. "But roots like that don't break easily. I used to jump from the Kinship Tree when I was younger, and one time, I got so tangled up, and my foot caught under a stone, that I would have drowned if my brother Roger hadn't pulled me free. It rended my outer toe. Roger and some neighbors next to my grandparents took me to the Ross farm. Elias took care of me, and that's where I met Daniel—" Lily stops, bites her lip. "Anyway. It's easier to imagine that something was tied around her neck, something heavy."

"Like an anvil. Or a pickaxe. There's plenty of things like that around," Marvena says. She hates the quiver in her voice.

Lily nods gently. "Yes. And over time, the rope could work free in the currents as the ice thawed and the water started moving freely again."

Marvena picks up her cup. The liquid sloshes as her hand shakes. She wishes that liquid were some of her shine. She holds the cup with both hands, like a child, and takes a long sip. "Well, anyway," she says at last. "Likely, that's what a Pink in that situation would do. Easier than paying blackmail to a girl like Eula. Or taking care of a child."

"Martin told me that Luther says Harvey Grayson is married," Lily says. "Supposedly he's now in Kentucky visiting his wife. What if on the night he came to our house, he told Daniel that he knew someone in Rossville had news of Eula—instead of simply 'there's a prisoner to fetch'? Grayson had to know Daniel would come after him if he figured out he'd been taking up with Eula. . . . Daniel wouldn't even have to know Eula was pregnant. Or that Eula had been harmed." Suddenly Lily looks feverish. "Did Daniel ever tell you about the time that he forbade me from going to his boxing match?"

Marvena frowns. "He din't tell me every little thing about you. What does that—"

But Lily doesn't seem to have heard the question. "I went anyway."

Of course. Marvena feels a smile taunt the corners of her mouth, in spite of the mind-numbing sorrow of recent days. Of this day.

"And I was attacked. Pulled out into the alleyway. Daniel got there in time, pulled the attacker from me," Lily says. She shudders, as if seeing the memory all over again. "His face . . . he would have killed him."

It takes Marvena a moment to realize that Lily means Daniel would have killed Lily's attacker. "But, he din't?"

"No. I think only because Mr. Vogel and Mr. Miller and their men came along. They took my attacker away. I never knew his name." Lily stares at Marvena. "If Daniel was threatening to tear up a Pink for sleeping with Eula when she was willing . . . what would he have done if he'd found out someone had hurt Eula? He wouldn't have hesitated to hurt him. Even kill him. I'm sure that's not a side of him that only I've seen. In fact, I'm sure he went to great effort to hide that from me. To hide a lot of things from me."

For a long moment, the two women's eyes lock. Marvena says, "Lily I've told you, he was loyal to you—"

Marvena stops, feeling herself about to break down.

But it's Lily who cracks first. The words wrench from her. "Goddammit, Marvena, I know he was loyal. Maybe too loyal, to people like George Vogel. Can loyalty have a dark side? Yes. But I know he was also loyal to his children, including Eula."

Tears start coursing down Marvena's face. Had he died pursuing that loyalty? Seeking justice for Eula?

"And I know he was loyal to me as his wife. And to you as his best friend—"

"Oh, Lily—"

"No, it's true. You were his best friend." Suddenly Lily is sobbing, and seeing her face crumple with anguish is more than Marvena can bear.

Marvena and Lily grasp each other, let their tears come unreservedly, in racking relief, first tears since *Daniel's been found* and *Eula's been found*. Since they found each other.

After they finally let go of each other, the cabin suddenly feels too confining. Marvena goes and opens the front door, gasps in great gulps of sweet country air—the stench of Rossville doesn't climb up Devil's Backbone except on the windiest of days.

"Mama?"

In a voice pulled too thin, Marvena says, "I'm fine, Frankie. Jus' play with your dolls. . . ."

Would Daniel have been set up to be murdered to keep him from finding Eula? With a bonus that without him it would be easier to suppress the miners?

Marvena comes back in the cabin, leans in the doorway. "We'll never know who Eula was sleeping with, but likely that's her killer. And possibly Daniel's, too."

Lily rubs her eyes. "We have to find out. For Eula's sake. For Daniel's. Oh God, Marvena, if we don't find out . . . if there's no justice . . ."

Boom. Fainter. Deeper.

"Justice? You know who's setting those charges in the mines . . . running out hopefully afore the flame runs up the fuse to th' dynamite?"

"No."

"Alistair. He's the smallest, can get to the deepest, tightest places. Tom was telling you the truth. Daniel, last time we saw him, he was going to call an old army buddy who works in the Bureau of Mines, who might could help our cause."

"Daniel never shared a name of his army friend with me. After Tom told me Daniel was planning to contact an army friend, I read and re-read the few letters Daniel sent to me during the war. But the only man Daniel names as a war buddy is my own brother."

Marvena drops her head to her hands. This all seems too much to bear—Eula's death, Daniel's, the thought the two might be related, the fragility of the movement, the danger of the Widowmaker reopening. Lily puts a hand on her shoulder, and Marvena doesn't shake it free as she would have a few weeks before. She finds herself wanting to comfort Lily in turn, but instead she stands so suddenly that Lily's hand falls from her shoulder and slaps on the table. Marvena moves woodenly to the quilt, pulls it aside, and goes behind it for a minute. When she comes back out she's holding a handful of letters, bound in a faded red ribbon. She puts the packet before Lily.

"He wrote me, too," Marvena says.

Lily looks at the letters, touches the bundle, pulls her finger back as if stung. She looks up at Marvena, clearly struggling to keep her expression placid. But hurt stirs her face as she says, "Well then, maybe he told you all about his buddy."

"Maybe," Marvena says. *God, woman,* she thinks, *don't make me say it.*

Lily's eyes widen as understanding comes to her. "Oh . . ."

"He never knew I—"

Boom. Deeper, but even yet bone rattling.

Lily is stone-cold still. Then she unties the red ribbon, picks up a letter, slides it out of its envelope, begins reading, her voice flat. "'My dearest Marvena . . .'"

CHAPTER 25

※

LILY

Lily has tried twice in two days to reach Ben Russo at the Bureau of Mines via telegram. Now she steps out of the telegram office, disappointed that there's no reply. In the bright day, she blinks hard. Then she walks down the street to the Bronwyn County Courthouse, ignoring the people, the storefronts, the life around her.

The letters from Daniel to Marvena swim in her head. Not love letters. Yet in some ways more deeply hurtful. To Lily he'd sent romantic niceties, sexual teases. Glib reassurances that he was perfectly secure. Mundane complaints about the weather, food or lack of it, sleeping conditions. Descriptions of Paris, of small villages.

But to Marvena he'd confided his heart, his fears, his sorrow, even his hurt over Roger's death. How much he missed her and Eula. How much he missed his beloved Lily. How he hoped to survive, have children, have a life free of fighting and hatred.

Lily considers: Daniel had been physically true to her. Shouldn't she be grateful? That kind of faithfulness is more than most women get. And no doubt Daniel thought he was simply protecting her, as he'd always wanted to, from the moment they'd met.

But for truly opening his heart, Daniel had turned to Marvena. She was where he'd found solace, courage, reassurance. Lily was the love of Daniel's life. But Marvena . . . She was the friend of his life.

Lily had seen it in Marvena's face, whenever she glanced up from reading, Marvena taking in Daniel's words in for the first time, so wrapped up that she nearly missed the significance when Lily read: "'Since losing Roger, I try not to get to know the fellas too well here. Don't know how long they'll last. But I'm stuck with a new assistant gunner, fella from Cleveland, won't shut up. Ben Russo. All sorts of stories to tell about his family, his girl, his job at the Bureau of Mines, how he can't wait to get back to it. He says he can get me in, but I tell him me and Roger, we're going to go back, help Pops with the grocery. . . .'"

Pops. That's what Daniel had called Lily's father. As Lily gasped, thinking of her brother, of those innocent plans to run the grocery after the war, Marvena had asked, frowning, "Why did you stop?"

And Lily pointed out that Ben Russo was the name they'd been looking for. The only other soldier Daniel cited by name, except Roger and the commander of their unit.

Ben Russo, at the Bureau of Mines.

Once they found the name, though, Lily kept reading the letters. She didn't need to check with Marvena to confirm she wanted to hear the rest. When she'd finished, she'd looked up and seen the sad slope to Marvena's shoulders, her head in her hands. Lily had left the letters on the table and gone quietly from the cabin.

And now she was trying to find the truth about the death of her husband, a man she was no longer sure she'd really known in life.

A hard jolt against her shoulder makes Lily come back to herself. She's walked far past the courthouse and just run into a man.

"Ma'am? Are you all right?"

Lily looks at an older gentleman staring at her in alarm. She sees both of their hats on the sidewalk, realizes she ran into him hard enough that she knocked them both off.

"Oh yes, I'm sorry."

The man picks up his hat and puts it back on and hands Lily her hat, all the while giving the star on her jacket a pointed look. She knows what he's thinking—that this job is too stressful for a woman. Lily puts her hat back on and walks to the courthouse. Inside, she walks straight to the small office of the mayor.

Mr. Wickler, the mayor's secretary, jumps up. "Do you have an appointment?"

"No," Lily says. "But I want to see the mayor."

The secretary pulls open a date book, makes a show of clucking as he turns pages.

Lily slaps her hands onto his desk, leans forward. "Now."

An hour and a half later, Lily slowly walks up Court Street to her house. Mayor Kline isn't sympathetic to the miners—he would, he says, simply have her suppress any talk of unionization meetings at the opera house. Still, Lily is able to convince Kline that suppression will only lead to more violence. The date is set for Marvena to hold an open rally in two weeks.

Lily thinks about what she needs to do next to ensure the safety of her town and county. Likely, men from surrounding mining towns will also attend. The town will be crowded. She'll have to deputize townsmen who are sympathetic or at least neutral, giving them authority to arrest Pinks or miners if either get out of hand. She should meet with the commissioners soon, perhaps even that night, for the same purpose on a county level.

She is rattled from her thoughts by the sight of Abe Miller again awaiting her on her front porch. He's leaning against the porch rail, smoking.

As soon as Lily is within earshot, Abe says, "I have something from Mr. Vogel. Your answer, he says, to the query you had the local newspaperman make to the Cincinnati paper."

"I didn't—"

"Darby Turner. You spoke with him after your installment as sheriff." Abe pulls an envelope out of his vest pocket, hands it to Lily.

Lily stares at the envelope, relieved to have an excuse to break her gaze with Abe, now remembering who this reporter Darby is. He'd asked her on the courthouse steps, after she was sworn in, if she'd be sheriff in the same way Daniel had been. "But how would Mr. Vogel know . . . ?"

"He's connected to everyone, Mrs. Ross. Everyone. In any case, that's not my concern. I am, in this case, just the messenger."

Lily gives him a sharp look. "Very well." She starts to go into her house.

But Abe grabs her arm. "Oh, delivering the envelope is not the message. The message is for after you've read the contents of the envelope."

Lily pulls her arm, but there's no easing from Abe's hold.

Two men, chatting amiably, walk past Lily's house. They quiet when they see Abe, hurry on, heads down.

"Oh, it won't take you long," Abe says. "What's more, I've checked, and your children—darling Jolene, little Micah—have left for a stroll on this beautiful day with your dear friend Hildy. No doubt to see your mama. And that sweet little brother of yours . . . Caleb Junior, if I'm not mistaken?" Abe smiles thinly, showing just the tips of his teeth.

Lily clenches her jaw and then says, "I prefer to read sitting down."

Abe lifts his eyebrows. "Are you inviting me in?"

Now Lily smiles. "Not at all. I have a perfectly fine porch swing. I'm surprised you haven't taken advantage of it, seeing how often you visit my porch."

Abe lifts his eyebrows and, after a moment, releases Lily's arm.

She sits in the porch swing and then turns over the envelope, embossed with Vogel's law firm's name. Her hand shake as she opens it, sliding her fingernail under the seal; she gets a small paper cut on her index finger, puts the tip to her lips before the blood can drip to her skirt.

There is no letter. Two news clippings fall out.

Lily reads the articles. They're brief. Yellowed. Dated 1917.

Both are by Darby Turner. One, from the front of the sporting section, summarizes the knockout fight of Daniel's last boxing match before he left for France, the fight with Frederick Clausen, the man named on the ticket she'd found in Daniel's glove, along with her ribbon.

The other article, dated a week later, is buried deep in the last page of the news section—between one advertisement for facial cream and another for soap flakes. It states that a pugilist named Frederick Clausen had been found dead in an alleyway after a match with Daniel T. Ross. It was not believed that Clausen had died from injuries sustained in the match, as many had seen him leave the venue on his own volition, but rather from another fight with an unknown man. Clausen, a shoe repairman by day, left behind a widow, three sons, and two daughters.

Images of Daniel flash through her mind, like slides shuffling through a stereograph viewer: Daniel before his hometown fight in Kinship against Clausen, who'd beaten him once. The look of wrathful determination not to be bested again. In the ring, that same look, so amplified that it distorted his face. Later, in the alley, Daniel ready to murder the man who'd attacked her. Daniel, on their first honeymoon in Cincinnati, going despite her protestations for the final showdown with Clausen. And the next morning, his face a tight mask, saying his enlistment in the army was his duty—but what else had he said? She pulls the words forth: *It's a clean break, Lily. When I'm back, we'll make a fresh start, far from here. . . .*

Yet after the war, on their second honeymoon to Cincinnati, she'd found Daniel with George Vogel in the barroom at the Sinton. Suddenly ready to abandon their plan to take on her father's grocery business. Suddenly keen, at Vogel's behest, to become Bronwyn County Sheriff. To take kickbacks for protecting Vogel's illicit purchases of moonshine to repackage as Vogel's Tonic.

Now Lily puts together these snatches of memory, of information, and wonders: *What if Daniel was capable of killing, not in the context of war or an encounter as a lawman, but simply out of personal rage? What if he'd encountered Clausen in the alleyway and Clausen taunted him and they'd fought again, this time not with referees to intervene if things went too far, and Daniel had beaten Clausen to death in that alleyway?*

Oh God. She quickly tries to conjure an image of the Daniel she knew, the Daniel she loved, who had been so tender with her, so gentle with their children, so concerned about the weaker members of their community, widows such as Ada Gottschalk . . .

Lily looks back at Abe, still leaning on her porch rail. He's finished his cigarette.

"All right. I've read them. Your message?"

"I've received word that a certain young miner, a Franz Hinkle, has been identified as the last person seen with Eula Whitcomb."

The diamond fallen from some piece of jewelry . . . A gift a young miner could not afford.

A smile strains Abe's mouth for just a moment at Lily's double take. "He only speaks German, but he's confessed his guilt of the girl's murder to a fellow miner. He's being held at your brother-in-law's office. I believe having found him will make Miss Marvena Whitcomb—ah, what was her word?—*beholden* enough to Mr. Vogel to become a part of his operation.

"As part of this new partnership, we will also make sure that her dear brother Tom's obligations to Luther are settled. His son will thus be free to live with Miss Marvena. While you're at Luther's office to collect the prisoner, you'll also forestall any problems between Luther's men and the miners. Mr. Vogel would be most distressed to learn of any, ah, disturbances that might impede business. We are quite used to our transport drivers coming in and out of the county without fear of gunfire."

"I'm not Daniel. Mr. Vogel does not have a hold on me."

"You stepped into Daniel's shoes. Now you walk in them. As distressing as those articles were to you, imagine if some enterprising reporter would—perhaps interested in learning more about the rare novelty of a female sheriff—investigate your deceased husband? Find witnesses from the alley that night? Wrote an exposé of a war hero and sheriff as a cold-blooded murderer? Why, sensational news like that wouldn't be just in local papers. It would be national news."

He shakes his head, then goes on. "How shameful such revelations would be to Jolene and Micah, Mama, and Caleb Junior. No matter where you went."

For a moment Lily can't breathe. Then she gasps in a gulp of air. She says, "Mr. Vogel's only concern is that I continue to protect his interests, as Daniel did?"

"Did he?" Abe bites off each word.

The full import of the simple question grips her. The image of her assailant in the alleyway all those years ago, being pulled away, flashes before her. That was because Vogel didn't want Daniel upset that his beloved was being assaulted—not because Vogel wanted vengeance on her behalf. What would he do if he thought Daniel had betrayed his trust?

She takes a shaky breath. "Surely Mr. Vogel has plenty of sources for his tonic. Haven't we been through enough here? Can't he just let us be? I don't understand—"

"No. You clearly don't. Let me explain the issues at hand. One: A single bottle of Vogel's Tonic is three percent alcohol, well within regulation. One pint of moonshine is sufficient for thirty bottles of tonic. Five percent of the moonshine we use is from this region. You've surely purchased Vogel's Tonic, know what you pay. So consider the profit margin we're enjoying."

Lily considers: A bottle of Vogel's Tonic from the general store is ninety cents. Likely the moonshiners make less than that per pint. And, of course, Vogel then doesn't have to go to the expense of manufacturing alcohol legally under the strict regulations of the Volstead Act.

"Two: the matter of being assured of the sheriff's cooperation for legal considerations."

"I have no proof that Mr. Vogel is acquiring illegally made alcohol," Lily says slowly. "And my word wouldn't hold against Mr. Vogel's even if I were foolish enough to try."

The notion of her publicly accusing Vogel—and having anything other than the wrath of the man as a result—is so ridiculous that a thin smile traces her lips.

Abe lifts his eyebrows. "Well, Mr. Vogel will be glad to know that you are a quite logical thinker. And finally here's the third issue: your husband offered his loyalty to Mr. Vogel—"

Lily waves the newspaper clippings. "Under duress!"

"But it was offered. And accepted. Mr. Vogel does not take lightly breaches of loyalty. Aside from legal or financial costs, it is, let us be clear, a matter of pride. And by stepping into Daniel's shoes, you've also accepted the constraints that loyalty necessitates. So." Abe regards the tip of his cigarette, as if assessing how much is left. "So, tomorrow you will go to Rossville. Arrest the boy Franz. Stop any disturbances between Marvena and Luther."

"If I can't?"

"Eventually Mr. Vogel will be forced to intervene."

"In that case, whose side will he come down on?"

Abe takes his time lighting another cigarette. He inhales, then flicks a smile along with his ashes. "Mr. Vogel is always on the side of his own business."

Ada Gottschalk pins a pillowcase to the clothesline, reaches down, grabs another.

Lily wonders if the woman has heard anything she's said, the whole story tumbling out as Ada put up the wash: That there's a miner being held as Eula's killer. That he's from Liechtenstein and speaks only German. That perhaps he knows something about Daniel, too. That Lily is supposed to go to Luther's office in Rossville and arrest him. That not only does Lily want Mrs. Gottschalk to translate for her, but also she's the only one she trusts to do so honestly.

Ada puts up the next pillowcase. Lily glances at the laundry basket. It's still half-full. Lily puts her bag, which contains her notebook, into which she's tucked the clipping from Abe, onto the back porch and starts hanging pillowcases alongside Ada.

They work quietly until finally Ada puts her hands to her hips and gives Lily a long, appraising look. "Why are you doing this?"

"You have a lot of laundry. And I want to know the truth."

"All right. But why?"

"Justice," Lily says, but her face burns, as if the truth is trying to reveal itself. Lily wants more than justice. What if she was wrong? What if Harvey Greyson had nothing to do with Eula or Daniel's death? What if Marvena was wrong and Eula really did fall in love with this boy, but he balked, and this boy really is Eula's killer, and Daniel found out?

Suddenly she's unsure of what to believe except that she will find out what happened to Daniel. To Eula. And Lily wants vengeance. Recklessly, fully, no matter what it takes.

"I understand your reluctance, perhaps even fear that this could turn dangerous, but—"

"When isn't life dangerous?" She glances at Lily's left foot. "You should know that."

"Oh . . . thank you, thank you for coming—"

Ada sighs. "I'm not doing this for you." She waves at the now nearly empty basket. "Finish up. And give me a moment to get my hat."

A narrow one-story building, just yards from the chute, serves as headquarters for Ross Mining. The building has just three rooms—the pay office where the men collect their scrip, a holding cell, and at the back Luther's office. In that small room, dim despite a bright day and a large window, for its glass is smeared and gray, Lily sits in a chair across from Luther at his desk. On one teetering stack of papers on the desk sits a coal-oil lamp, its meager light not flickering beyond the messy desktop to the corner where stands one sullen Pinkerton, or over to the unlit coal stove, by which stands another. The chilly office smells of burnt oil and coal dust and alcohol. It seems to Lily that Luther has, whether he realizes it or not, made of his dominion a cavern as dismal and suffocating as any chamber in a coal mine.

Yet now Luther grins imperiously, as if gazing down from a throne. He leans back in his chair, clasps his hands, lifts them, puts them behind his head. Lily keeps her eyes on his, though she'd rather look at the sweat stains of his armpits.

"Now, let me get this right, Lily," he says. "You want me to just let this *killer* go free?"

Lily looks at the boy, maybe seventeen, his left eye bruised and swollen shut, his right eye wide. He rubs the fissures where his wrists had been bound. There's no fear of him running; in addition to the other two Pinks, one stands behind the boy's chair, another at the door.

Joanne Moyer, the boardinghouse manager, sits on the edge of a chair near the window, fanning herself. Ever since being introduced to Lily, she's stared at her with a bemused smile.

Mrs. Gottschalk sits on the edge of another chair, leaning toward the boy—Franz Hinkle—who is still talking to her quietly in German. She nods, pats his hand, comforting.

"You heard her translation," Lily says. She looks up from her notebook, in which she's been writing down the boy's statement. "This boy is no killer."

All the bewildered boy knew was that just after his arriving in Rossville the pretty young woman at the boardinghouse had asked him, using the few words of German she'd picked up, to go for a walk with her and he'd said yes. He'd escorted her as far as the old Rossville Cemetery and then an automobile pulled up. She willingly got into it and left him standing alone.

His description of the automobile was useless; Model Ts all look similar, black with small variations in styling from year to year.

After that, he said through Ada, he walked back to Rossville and the boardinghouse, and there waiting for him in the room he shared with three other men was an envelope with an extra bill of scrip waiting for him.

The next night, the girl, Eula, wanted him to walk with her again. He almost said no but then remembered the envelope. It was like that, every few nights, until one day she was gone. He was taken to work at another mining company. And then he'd been picked up and returned to Ross Mining day before last, until last night he was picked up by Luther's men at dinner at the boardinghouse and tossed in the small holding cell.

"Why should I trust that she's translating accurately?" Luther asks. Ada's presence and her ability and willingness to translate had taken him by surprise.

"She has no stake in doing otherwise," Lily says. "And as we can see, the boy can't speak much other than German. Yet I'm supposed to believe he confessed to Eula's murder last night to a miner named—what did you say his name is, Miss Moyer?"

A frown ruffles Joanne's placid brow for just a moment, and then she smiles again. "Eldon McDermott."

"Eldon McDermott," Lily repeats. "Now, that sounds like a man who knows German!" At Lily's sarcasm, the frown reclaims Joanne's brow. "And where is Eldon now? Luther, can you tell me that?"

"How the hell would I know? I don't keep track of every man's where-abouts."

"I believe I heard someone say this morning that Mr. McDermott had cleared out his room," Joanne says.

"How convenient," Lily says.

"Don't matter," Joanne says. "I recollect this boy leaving those nights with poor Eula."

"Oh, you do? Marvena showed me a box that Daniel found in Eula's room," Lily says. "A Mrs. See's candy box. I can imagine this poor boy scraping together the money for the candy, barely. But there was a tiny diamond stuck in the box. Could this boy afford jewelry that held even a tiny diamond? I don't think so."

Luther looks at Joanne. "Daniel found a box in Eula's room?"

Joanne looks at Luther, eyes wide. "I—I don't know what she's talking about. . . ."

Lily says to Ada. "Ask the boy if he ever gave any jewels to Eula."

Ada looks at the boy, asks. The young boy's voice rises, saying something in German that Lily can't understand, but she gets the essence of it—he's afraid. Ada shushes him, says something comforting. Then she looks at Lily. "He says he never gave the girl any gifts."

Lily looks at Luther. "There you have it. And he can't have given the girl jewelry, in any case. How would he buy it? It's not like diamond jewelry is sold for scrip at the company store."

Luther sighs. "Well. I was hoping to avoid embarrassing Joanne here, but—" He opens a drawer and pulls out a necklace. He lays the neck-lace on the desk, and Lily stares at it, unable to keep shock from her expression. This is an elaborate piece with diamonds and sapphires.

"This was found in the boy's pocket when my men picked him up," Luther says triumphantly. "I put it in my drawer for safekeeping. He must have taken it from Eula. Perhaps the necklace is why he killed her."

"To sell later? That makes no sense. Where would Eula have gotten it, other than from a man with real money?"

"Tell her, honey," Luther says with a snide turn to his voice. The other men snicker, except the boy, who remains bewildered.

"It was mine," Joanne says. Her voice is tiny, and she looks shamed. More than that—shaken.

Lily looks from Joanne to Luther, back to Joanne. *Oh. All right. They'd been carrying on an affair, and Luther had given her this necklace. But why should Joanne,* Lily thinks, *given her occupation, be shamed at an assignation with Luther? Polite society might want to pretend it is shocking, but it is definitely not surprising.*

"Eula stole it from me," Joanne says. She looks at Lily, defiantly this time. "That's right. I found her rooting around in my room, and later I discovered my necklace was missing. I—I told Luther about it."

"Did you tell Daniel when he came to ask you about Eula? Is that why, as you told Marvena, he left in a huff?"

Luther slams his hands against the desk. "Enough!"

The room goes still.

Luther says to Lily, "Why isn't this good enough for you? You have Eula's killer. Congratulations. Your first case as sheriff, solved."

"No. I have a patsy that you drummed up to take the fall for the Pinkerton that Eula was seeing." Lily looks at the man guarding the door. He looks down, away. Lily turns her gaze back to Luther. "Maybe I should ask this man. Haul in every single man who works for you, until I get a name out of someone. The name of the Pinkerton who was sleeping with Eula—she wouldn't have wasted her time with a miner—a boy!—who couldn't give her what she wanted."

Lily shoots Joanne a sharp look. "You of all people in this room can understand Eula. So tell me, Joanne, was it Harvey Grayson she was seeing, the Pink who came to tell Daniel about the imaginary prisoner who got away? You mentioned once that Grayson's married."

"There was a prisoner!" Luther says.

"Right. Tom Whitcomb. How convenient."

"They found my necklace on this miner!" Joanne snaps. But she's not looking at Lily. She's glaring at Luther. *How odd,* Lily thinks. "And the boy confessed last night."

"To his friend—a miner who has conveniently disappeared, just like

Harvey Grayson has." Lily turns to Luther. "I've been here over half an hour, and it's never occurred to you to ask how I knew to come for Franz here, how I received word?"

Luther shrugs.

Lily gives her brother-in-law a thin smile. "Abe Miller told me last night that I would come here today and collect a Mr. Franz Hinkle."

At the mention of Abe Miller's name, Luther pales. He swallows, rubs his face. "Well, if he said, then there's no question . . ."

Lily shakes her head, looks back at the Pink standing by the door. "This boy is going to walk out of here. You will walk with him to the edge of town. You will put him on a horse, and tell him to go as far as he can, and get out of this county. Out of Ohio."

The Pink looks at Luther. When Luther says nothing, the man says, "Boss?"

Luther ignores him. He's staring at Lily with concern. "You can't go up against Abe Miller. You don't understand—"

"Oh, but I do. What Abe Miller wants, what George Vogel really wants, is to avoid a confrontation between your men and the miners, so that his operations aren't disturbed. But we can achieve that without sacrificing an innocent man. What neither Mr. Miller nor Mr. Vogel knows is that Daniel must have found the box while searching Eula's room. And in that box Marvena discovered a stray diamond that must have come from jewelry. Expensive jewelry that clearly a simple miner couldn't have bought for Eula. But not from this jewelry. There is no missing diamond in this necklace."

For a moment, all eyes turn to the pristine piece sparkling on Luther's desk.

Lily goes on. "I know that Abe Miller already found someone to rat out Marvena's, ah, business. It would not be hard for him to set up a plan to find someone to take the fall for Eula's murder, someone who can't defend himself. I'm guessing he thinks if Marvena believes her daughter has been avenged, then she'll be more likely to fall in line and not stir up trouble. But I'm not willing to accept such an easy answer. I think Eula was consorting with Harvey Grayson, that she got in trouble with him, and that he killed her because he was married and didn't want trouble. I think Daniel was on to the truth, and that Harvey Grayson set my husband up to be killed before Daniel could come after him." Her voice is starting to shake, but she forces herself to go on. "Somehow, I will prove this—and find out who helped Harvey!"

Everyone in Luther's office is silent, still. Even the boy stops blubbering. Outside, through the window, the sound of another boom resonates across the town.

Luther looks at Joanne. "You can go now."

"But Luther—"

"Go!"

Joanne hurries from the room and gives Lily a look: *What have you done?*

Then Luther looks at Ada. "Tell the poor son of a bitch what's going on."

Ada talks to the boy, and as he understands he begins to cry again, this time in relief.

"Boss—" the Pink starts.

Luther cuts his man off. "You're going to do what Lily—the *sheriff*—just ordered. Exactly as she said it. And then if it's all right with her, take this woman back to her house."

Lily looks at Ada. "I will be glad to take you—"

Ada smiles. "Oh, please, no fuss over me." She looks at the German boy, says something more, and he nods eagerly. Ada looks back at Lily. "He will take me a bit of the way down Kinship Road before getting on his way. I'll walk the rest. It will be good to stretch my bones."

A few minutes later, only Luther and Lily are left in his office.

"Tell me where Harvey Grayson is. I want him for questioning."

Luther sighs. "I already told you, I don't know where the Pinkerton company reassigned him. I doubt they would tell you. Or if he even is with the company anymore. And you don't have hard evidence. Look, sure, there was talk about Harvey Grayson sniffing around the girl. I warned him off. Knew Daniel would be angry, but . . ." Luther shrugs. "A man wants what he wants, and the girl was a whore, anyway."

Lily stares at Luther. "Dammit, Daniel was your brother! And I know that Eula might have been your own niece."

Luther grins coldly. "Half brother. Half niece, if that."

And there it all is, in that word "half." All that Luther hated about Daniel over the years.

Luther shakes his head, opens a drawer, pulls out a flask, slams the drawer shut. "You'd better be careful. You just had me let the boy go, and if Miller wanted him arrested for the murder of Eula that's not too bright."

"Oh, it's quite brilliant," Lily says.

Luther frowns.

"Because the only reason Abe wanted that was to appease Marvena. He and George Vogel have some notion that if she thought you'd found poor Eula's killer, brought him to justice, she'd be grateful enough to simmer down on riling up the men for unionization. Mr. Vogel doesn't want the county stirred with trouble; it's bad for his business. But as far as Marvena will know, because this is what I will tell her, you just let Eula's killer go because you'd rather have another miner working for you than justice for that poor girl's murder."

"What? No, you . . ." Luther groans. "Are you trying to get us both killed?"

"No. Because there's another way to appease Marvena, to keep a battle from erupting so Mr. Vogel is satisfied."

Luther takes a sip and then a long drink from his flask.

"Allow for talk of unionization," Lily says. "I've already ensured that Marvena can hold a talk about the merits of unionization. And I've already decided to come out in support."

"You think it's that easy? The men signed on knowing it's a non-union shop."

"Yellow dog contracts," she says. His eyebrows lift with surprise at her knowing the term—contracts under which even talk of unionizing means the men will lose their jobs, their company homes, their pay, which is in company scrip, and somehow be expected to pay back the company store with American dollars, not scrip.

"You think you understand, but you don't! The coal we're finding here of late has higher sulfur. That makes it less desirable, but I found some old records about Mine Number Nine—"

"The Widowmaker," Lily says.

"Call it that if you want, but there's a rich vein of anthracite under that hill." He gestures at a stack of old maps and papers on his desk. "It's why we tried before—"

"And seven men died because of it. Including my father—"

Suddenly Luther pounds his fist on the desk, making the papers jump. "I know that, Lily! I know that!"

Luther wearily rubs his hands over his face. "I'm trying, Lily, to find veins of better coal. I'm having the men use stronger supports this time—"

"All for more money for yourself, for your company?"

"Where do you think these men will find work if Ross Mining goes out of business, huh? I've already got Wessex Corporation breathing down my neck to buy me out. They've already done that with several companies in the area. Sure, many of their holdings have unions, but they also are having trouble turning profits. How does going out of business help anyone? If we can turn a better profit, I can increase pay, lower prices in the store, bring in a better doctor—"

"Oh, Luther, do you really believe you'll do all that? Or will you—" Lily starts to continue *just want more,* but she is struck by an unusual expression on Luther's face: sincerity. From his point of view, he's trying to do the right thing by reopening the Widowmaker.

"We can agree a new boom is something we all want. But what about safety?"

"My managers tell me that the accident last fall was a fluke with the lightning, that two lollygagged at the back, and that the miners did a shoddy job building the supports—"

"Because you rushed! It was in the newspaper; the reopening took only a few weeks."

"Yes. They needed to hurry! I don't want to have to sell to Wessex. My father trusted me with the family business. But I won't go broke keeping it in the Ross family name!"

"If there's another accident, you'll end up with another Blair Mountain, union or not."

At the reference, Luther draws back, pales. Then he takes a deep breath, shakes his head. "That didn't turn out very well for the miners, though, did it? And I won't let it come to that. I can always hire in more men to keep control—"

"Doesn't that keep adding up? Why not give your workers some control over their lives?"

"And where would that stop? Besides, these men are uneducated." He shrugs, dismissing the men who work for him as if they aren't fully human. "They're like children. Half of them don't even speak English—you just saw that! These men don't know enough to make decisions to take care of themselves. They need firm management—"

The alarm sounds, stopping him cold.

Lily and Luther stare at each other, their quarrel muted by the sickening shrieking sound, linked for a moment by mutual dread.

CHAPTER 26

≫

LILY AND MARVENA

LILY

The collapse is at the Widowmaker, about five hundred yards into the new tunnel.

By late afternoon, hundreds gather—families, miners, volunteers from Kinship and other mining communities. Luther is there, two of his Pinks beside him at all times. Other Pinkerton men are mixed among the people, watching, waiting.

Coal-oil lanterns are set up, hung from makeshift poles, in case the effort has to go past dusk. By full nightfall it will be too dangerous for the rescuers to go in.

Kinship Cemetery on the side of the hill had caved into the mine shaft's opening. Water from the ground had filled the entry to the tunnel. It is cooling rapidly, and the people mutter among themselves about that morning's red sky—a sign of evening storms. More water on the top of the hill would be disastrous.

While Jurgis organized the rescue, Lily worked alongside Nana and Marvena and Hildy, who came by carriage with neighbors when they got word; she tended to the injured, bringing food to the rescuers, comforting the scared and bereaved.

Lily now stands next to Martin, waiting along with everyone else for the last—at least for tonight—rescue team to come out. Men have entered in rowboats, ropes attached to the boats to pull them back. Two tugs would mean for the men with the rope to pull them out quickly—another collapse imminent. So far they've pulled from the tunnel sixteen men and boys, six dead, the rest with varying degrees of injury and shock. According to the day's work docket from Luther's foreman, two men are still unaccounted for.

They've also hauled out six caskets that fell through; there are reports of many more, farther down into the tunnel. Some headstones as well.

That morning, Lily had watched out for Elias, thinking surely he'd come.

All she can think of is Daddy and how he, along with Marvena's husband and several other men, had not been pulled out. There was a marker for Daddy at Kinship Cemetery but nothing to bury. She wonders if Marvena has a marker somewhere for her husband or if he's memorialized only in memory.

Her only moment of rest is in this moment, staring at the top of the hill, bashed in like a skull, its crown of thorny headstones destroyed. It is as Jolene feared. A child had foreseen it.

The crowd stirs as the rescue reaches the mouth of the tunnel, then cheers as a miner staggers forward out of the boat, arms around the necks of his rescuers. But the crowd hushes again as the other two rescuers pull the canoe forward and lift another man out—a dead-man lift. From somewhere in the crowd, a keening rises. Someone knows the dead man is her loved one.

Martin looks at Lily. "We have to tell them to go home. The search is over."

"But, Martin, they need to help each other, and the bodies—"

Martin grabs her arm, pulls her to him, his weary eyes desperate as he stares at her. "Lily, you have to call this done for tonight. Or let Jurgis or me do it. If we let Luther do it . . ."

Lily looks at the angry faces, feels the tension stirring, tightening. Martin is right.

She goes to the canoe at the front of the crowd, stands on it to gain a little height. "Now the search is over, you all need to go back to your homes!" she hollers. At first no one seems to hear her, so she hollers again.

"Now that the search is over . . ." The crowd quiets. Her voice staggers to a stop. She gazes across the weary, dirty faces. Oh God, how can she dismiss them like this? "Tomorrow—"

Another shriek tears across the night, a man's voice.

Tom emerges from the crowd. "No, no, no!" He's sobbing. "My boy is still in there!"

MARVENA

Marvena runs to Tom, throws her arms around him, trying to press him back into the crowd as two Pinkerton men charge forward on Luther's command.

"No! My boy—"

The men are upon Marvena and Tom, trying to pull them apart.

"Stop!" Lily barks. "Luther, stop your men, or by God, I'll turn this crowd on you! You're outnumbered, and this is not the time."

"You wouldn't dare—" Luther starts, but then even he sees the murderous glint in the people's eyes, their weariness and despair making them restless.

"Unhand them," he says. "Do it!"

The Pinkerton men step back. Tom falls to his knees, still sobbing, and Lily realizes he's been melted into the crowd this whole time, watching to see if Alistair is brought out.

Marvena says, "Alistair was working at the front of the crew."

Lily looks at Luther. "Why is Alistair Whitcomb not on the docket?"

Luther shrugs. "I'm not sure. I'll have to look into that. Meantime, Tom Whitcomb is a wanted man—wanted for your husband's murder."

Marvena looks at Lily. Surely after all they've been through, Lily will protect Tom.

Relief floods Marvena's heart as Lily turns to Martin and says, "I'm holding you responsible for Tom's safety. He's in your custody. Can you do that? While I go find Alistair?"

Martin says, "Yes, Lily, but I should be the one going in. . . . I can't let you—"

"Because it's bad luck for a woman to enter a mine? I think we're past worrying about bad luck. Look, Alistair is about my size. If he is caught in some narrow passage, I can get him out." She looks around at the weary men who've been working to rescue their living and dead. She calls out, "I need someone to row me in. And a flashlight and helmet—"

Martin grabs her arm. "Lily, think about this. Daniel would—"

"Don't talk to me of Daniel! I know exactly what he'd do in this situation," Lily says.

Marvena releases Tom and steps forward. She takes Lily by the shoulders and looks directly in her eyes. "Daniel would find him, yes. But why do you think it has to be you alone to save him? We will do this together."

LILY

Lily thinks of John Rutherford and then her own father. Of Daddy's look of disappointment and shame when Lily would not get help for the poor Gottschalks. And now of a young boy in there and the possibility, if he still lived, of dying alone. She cannot live with herself if she doesn't try.

"Fine," Lily says to Marvena. "Together."

"For God's sake," Martin says. "You could both die. Let me, let some of the men—"

"No. They're bone weary, apt to make fool judgments," Lily says. "We're small enough to find our way through narrow passages to Alistair—if he's to be found."

"That's just it, Lily; if he's not, or even if he is, you're risking—"

"Look at this crowd, Martin. If I don't try, if the boy is lost without any attempt to find him, these men and women will not be reasoned with. It will be the final spark for anger that's been waiting to explode, worse than Blair Mountain."

Martin looks down, shaking his head. "All right. But I don't think Daniel would like it."

"Martin?"

He looks up at her.

"If something happens to us, tell my mama to take in Frankie, just like she'll take in Micah and Jolene."

Ten minutes later, Lily sits at the front of the boat, holding her flashlight up to help Marvena see where to paddle around the floating caskets. Some are intact. Some have busted open, so bones float by.

The men at the front of the tunnel had been crushed under collapsed rocks and earth. At the back, where the water had quickly filled in—one of the foremen reckoned that the last blast had loosed an underground stream—the living had clung to caskets or stray wooden beams.

Lily and Marvena stop, sit in the canoe for unending minutes. It is nearly as dark as night, with moonlight and torchlight from the opening barely reaching this far. Pieces of the wood frame block them from entering farther. Lily stares beyond the light beam into the darkness. Alistair has to be beyond the fallen frame; otherwise, wouldn't the other rescuers have found him?

She and Marvena call Alistair's name. Listen, straining for something. Anything.

The only response, after the echoes of their cries fade, is the lap of water against the canoe. Nothing more.

"Lily! We have to turn around."

Lily ignores Marvena.

"If Alistair's dead, there's no use. . . ."

Lily waits for long moments, then nods, and Marvena dips in an oar to turn them. But then there's a moaning. Lily grabs Marvena's arm, but Marvena has already frozen. Lily looks back into the darkness beyond the timber. She listens.

She waits. Nothing. Then another moan. "Alistair! Alistair, is that you?"

Silence laps by. Then a faint whistle. *Smart boy,* Lily thinks. Whistling takes less air from the lungs than calling. Lily sets down her flashlight, takes off her helmet, and starts unbuttoning her dress. It will be easier to swim that way. "Keep whistling, Alistair!" she calls.

"I am going to swim under the wood," Lily says. "Then I want you to use the end of the oar to reach the helmet to me, through the slats. Put the flashlight in it, and use the strap. Got it?"

Marvena stares at her. "He's my nephew. I should go."

"You a good swimmer?"

Marvena's silence tells Lily all she needs to know. Lily pulls off her shoes, stockings. She's down to her underpants and slip. She stares into the water. Easier than leaping off the Kinship Tree into the creek with Roger.

Then she looks back at Marvena. "If you have to, you pull that rope twice. You don't wait for me and Alistair."

"Oh God, Lily."

"You hear me? You pull that rope and you get out of here, and you go help Mama with our children." Then Lily looks away from Marvena, back into the darkness. "Alistair?" she calls.

A whistle, weaker this time.

Lily stares down into the murky water. She moves to the edge, lets her feet over. The water is cold. She'll have to go in fast, all at once, to keep from tipping over the canoe.

She somersaults forward and, holding her breath, swims between the fallen joists. She pushes up, panicking that there is no air, but if Alistair could whistle there has to be air.

Yet in her mind, she's back at the Kinship Tree, held under until she was pulled up by Roger. *I don't have enough breath to make it back,* she thinks, and then she sees Daniel gazing at her, eyes locked to hers, just as he had that day.

And this flits across her mind: *Thank God. Thank God.* She'd met Daniel, after all.

In the next instant she makes it above water, gasping, some of the foul water getting in her mouth. She spits it out as best she can. Then she makes out Alistair. His arms are hooked over a beam, death grip. His forehead is gashed open. Lily swims over to him, and though his eyes are open, staring, Lily isn't sure the boy sees her.

"You have to come with me," Lily says.

He gazes at her. Through her.

"You father sent me. He'd want you to let go, put your arms around my neck."

A thudding boom shakes the planks and earth around them. In the distance, Lily hears Marvena scream, "No!" The water starts to rise, slowly, but Lily knows it will come faster. Somewhere near them, another support has collapsed.

"Alistair, listen to me," Lily starts.

"Mama?"

Oh God. In his fear and delirium, the boy thinks he's dying, that his long-gone mama has somehow come back to take him on to the other side.

"That's right, son. Put your arms around me. Trust me."

Alistair closes his eyes, lifts his arms from the beam. Lily catches him, his sparse frame barely pushing her back. She forces them both down and under the water. She first shoves him under the beam, then has to let go of him so he can float through. She comes up on the other side gasping for air.

In the canoe, Marvena is screaming. Outside, they must have heard the echo of the boom and decided to pull in the canoe. Marvena is moving farther and farther away.

Lily dives, reaching, searching, finally grabs Alistair's arm and pulls him up. She hooks one arm under his armpits. She treads water, forces herself onward to Marvena.

MARVENA

The canoe is pulling forward. Marvena looks back at Lily and Alistair.

"No!" Marvena screams again, but they can't hear her outside of the cave.

She reaches for her knife, sheathed under her waistband. She could cut the rope, paddle back to Lily and Alistair, haul them in, paddle out. But her arms are already quivering. She doesn't have the strength to go quickly enough. Before the mine would fall down around them.

Marvena leans over the front of the canoe, gives the rope three quick tugs. It's not a signal they've agreed to, but she knows Jurgis is on the other end and she trusts him to be clever enough to understand that she wants him and the other men to stop pulling.

The rope goes slack. Marvena turns around, paddles back to Lily and Alistair.

She tries to pull in Alistair while Lily pushes, but he's gone to dead-weight. He is barely breathing. The boy is too cold; he's been in the water too long. Lily treads water, holding herself and Alistair with their heads just above the water, but Marvena can tell Lily is weakening. And, she calculates, they'll turn over the canoe trying to get both of them in.

"Listen," Marvena says. "They was pulling the canoe back, but I tugged three times. That wasn't one of the signals, but Jurgis had the sense to stop pulling. I'm going to tug twice, then come to the back of the canoe and grab your arm. Can you hold him up with just one arm?"

Lily nods. Marvena tugs the rope twice, then scrambles to the back of the canoe, hooks her heels under the seat, leans out, stretches her hand to Lily. The canoe moves forward. Lily gives another burst of effort and grabs Marvena's forearm, who grasps hers in turn.

"All you have to do is hang on," Marvena says.

And so Lily does. Moments pass as they inch forward.

"Oh God!" Lily cries. "He's stopped breathing! Marvena—"

"Just keep looking at me, Lily."

Finally, the canoe grates on earth. Marvena gets out and grabs Alistair's legs, while Lily holds his head and torso to her chest. They emerge, carrying the boy between them.

Marvena sees Tom sink to his knees, staring at them. The crowd, even Luther and the Pinks, is silent. Nana pulls on Tom's arm. He staggers to his feet, then forward.

Lily and Marvena gently transfer Alistair to Tom's arms. Tom takes his son, curls his face to the boy's chest. He's silent, and then he drops to his knees, still holding Alistair. He lowers the boy to the ground, grabs his shoulders, shakes them, wails.

LILY

Someone puts a large blanket around Lily's shoulders. Shivering, she remembers she's barely clothed. She covers herself with the blanket like a cloak, then stares up. *Martin.*

"My God, Lily, what you've just done—" he starts.

Not enough. If she could have pushed herself harder, gotten to Alistair faster, not hesitated, not remembered the being caught under the water by the Kinship Tree years before.

But then Alistair gasps. He coughs up water, bile.

Nana moves to Tom. "Turn him to his side; let the water drain. Thump his back."

Tom does as Nana asks. Alistair gasps again, then opens his eyes and stares up at his father. Lily starts to tug off her blanket. "Here. He needs this."

"Someone's gotten him another one," Marvena says.

Lily looks up as Luther looms over her.

"Now that that's done," he says, "you need to arrest Tom Whitcomb, Sheriff Ross."

Lily takes the cup from Martin, sips again, then says, "No. There was never a warrant out for his arrest, and I've questioned him to my satisfaction."

Luther frowns. "Goddam, Lily, he's wanted for killing your husband!"

"You didn't even know Harvey Grayson had thrown him in your holding cell."

"Everyone in Rossville knows Tom didn't like Daniel coming around his old lover—"

"Luther. For God's sake," Martin says. He grabs Luther by the shoulders, shakes him roughly. "Let this go for tonight. Don't you think—"

Lily reaches for Martin, wanting to pull him back. She starts to beg him to stop, to not rile any of the Pinks, give them an excuse. But before she can speak, before Martin can even finish his sentence, Luther breaks free, shoves him away. Martin starts to lunge toward Luther.

Gunfire.

Lily drops to the ground, covering her head. The crowd shrieks.

Another shot.

Martin collapses next to Lily. She crawls to him, sees that he's been shot in the neck. Lily pulls off the blanket he'd just brought her, presses it to his neck, trying to stem the blood spurting from him. For just a moment he stares into her eyes, his own widening, and though it's hopeless, she looks up and screams for help into the brawl that's exploded around her. When she looks back at him again, his eyes remain wide yet lifeless. Someone—she looks up; it's Jurgis—grabs Lily and pulls her away from Martin.

Then, nearly as quickly as it exploded, the fight ends. Luther and his men, vastly outnumbered for now, flee to their automobiles, drive up Kinship Road out of Rossville.

MARVENA

"We should follow them!" someone shouts. A cry rallies through the crowd.

Marvena grabs Luther's bullhorn from the ground, then jumps up on a cart.

"Enough," Marvena says through the bullhorn. The crowd settles, just a little. "We would only be asking for more death tonight, on our side as well. We must stay calm, organize ourselves, take advantage of having the town in our control."

Darkness has fallen, but several folks have lit torches. Marvena spots Lily, still on the ground beside Martin. She's covered him up with the blanket, and Jurgis has taken off his jacket and draped it around Lily's shoulders. She barely seems to notice that or Marvena staring at her, willing her up on the cart beside her. But then Jurgis gently pats her shoulder, points to Marvena. Lily shakes her head as if to clear it, moves to the cart, and climbs up.

Once beside Marvena, Lily stares at her, eyes glazed. Marvena holds the bullhorn aside, mutters to Lily, "You have to command them. Tell them to tend to the injured."

Lily takes the bullhorn, but her weary arm slacks. Marvena takes the horn back, holds it up to Lily's mouth, and puts her arm around Lily. The woman is quivering. Marvena tightens her grasp around Lily's shoulders, gives her a little nudge with her hip.

"Tonight," Lily starts, "we need to tend to the injured. Where is Nana? . . . Ah, there. You and Marvena head up seeing to the wounded. We need a place to tend them."

Joanne Moyer steps forward. "Use the boardinghouse. Plenty of room in the dining hall." In the flickering light of torches, she looks up at Lily and Marvena with new esteem.

"You heard her; start moving the injured there," Lily says. "And if Miss Moyer doesn't mind, the dead, too."

Joanne nods and for a moment Marvena thinks Lily is going to rally, but then her eyes alight on Martin and Lily moans, looks at Marvena. "I've got to get Martin back to town, to the undertaker, talk to his wife."

The crowd stills. Someone hollers, "We gonna let her go back to Kinship? Why, she might help raise more against us!"

Lily stares into the crowd. What can she say to them? How can she help them?

And then a memory, from just before *Daniel's been found,* comes to her.

When she was jail mistress and there was a foul-mouthed Pinkerton in the cell and all she thought she had to worry about was making sure that he and the new prisoner, a miner, were in separate cells. How the Pink had lusted for war. How she had said to him, *You and your kind will not bring war down upon my county. Sheriff Ross will see to that.*

Well, now that was her. She was Sheriff Ross. And she would, somehow, make good upon that promise.

So she says, strong and clear, "Hold me here if you like. But you know it is only right that Martin is returned to his wife. He was here, helping rescue, and he died. Please, let me take him home. Then I can help you."

Someone near the front cries out, "What say you, Marvena?"

The crowd stills, watching Marvena, awaiting her word. Silence stretches amid the crowd, more so between Lily and Marvena. Lily looks at Marvena: *Trust me.*

Then Lily gives the bullhorn back to Marvena. *I trust you.*

Marvena takes it, her eyes all the while on Lily's. Then she turns to the crowd. "I was in there with her," Marvena says. "She saved Alistair when anyone else would have given up. When I was about to give up. How much more do you need to know? We can trust her. I trust her, leastways. So do as she says, an' she'll need two men who aren't hotheads to go with her."

Jurgis and another man step forward, volunteering.

Marvena lowers the bullhorn, says quietly, "You drive, and take the sheriff's automobile. Maybe the sign will make Luther's men think twice about shooting, just so's not to have the sheriff's blood on their hands." Lily frowns, and Marvena goes on. "Don't tell me you wouldn't put it past Luther to have his men lying in wait? Have our men keep watch, shotguns out the sides. Do what you must, but get back here in one piece. If you don't, some fool hothead will think you've tricked us and go off after you, bring the fight to Kinship."

LILY

Lily starts down off the cart and startles when she sees Joanne Moyer waiting for her. The woman is holding in one hand Lily's sopping dress and shoes; she must have retrieved them from the canoe. Over her other arm is a dry dress; she holds with that hand a pair of women's boots by the laces.

Joanne nods at the dry dress and boots. "These are mine, and they'll be big on you. But I reckon they'll be better than a jacket that's too big on you!"

Twenty minutes later, Lily restrains her desire to drive as swiftly as possible up and down the rises and around the tilting curves of Kinship Road. A spring rainstorm has arrived. But she has found her second wind. Steadfastly, she watches for ruts, rocks, drop-offs, other automobiles, as her headlights scoop out darkness. This is her first time ever driving at night. She takes the ruts and curves slowly, mindful of Jurgis in the back with Martin's body. Jurgis also keeps his shotgun pointed out the driver's side. Beside her, another man—a miner from another town, whose name she hasn't yet learned—stares out the passenger side, his shotgun also at the ready.

But only slashes of rain and the beady eyes of one wary fox interrupt their passage.

In Kinship, they take Martin directly to the undertaker at the Kinship funeral home. Jurgis and the miner follow Lily to Martin's house, hanging back on the porch as Lily knocks on the front door. At first

Fiona stares at her in the doorway with her usual look of displeasure at seeing Lily, and then her expression changes to shock.

"I'm sorry, Fiona. There was a confrontation. Martin was caught in the gunfire."

Fiona gasps, puts her hand to her mouth. "Oh God. He's just hurt, isn't he, just hurt?"

"I'm so sorry," Lily says. "He's—he's dead."

Fiona gasps again, stumbling forward.

Lily catches the woman and hugs her. "I'm sorry. I'm so, so sorry."

After Lily fetches a neighbor to come sit with Fiona and her son, she walks home, forcing herself to move quickly, though it feels as though she's dragging herself again through a rank stew of muck and filthy water. Back at her house, Jurgis and the other miner wait in the parlor, while she hurries upstairs to change clothes. In her bedroom, Lily gasps as she looks in the bureau mirror. Some of Martin's blood is smeared on her cheek. *God.* No wonder Fiona had stared at her so, just as she'd stared at Daniel's blood on Elias's shirt. . . .

Tears start to prick her eyes, but Lily shakes them away.

CHAPTER 27

⁂

MARVENA
AND LILY

MARVENA

Three days later, Ben Russo sits in Luther's chair in the Ross Mining office, across from Marvena and Lily. He looks exhausted, lines etched more deeply around his mouth and eyes than they were two days before, when he arrived in Bronwyn County, several inspectors from the Bureau of Mines with him. He had, as it turned out, been away to his mother's funeral—thus the delay in responding to Lily's telegrams.

Now Ben's weariness doesn't keep him from being sharp. "What do you want Luther to do? Crawl through Rossville to every home and beg for an apology?"

Even though she thinks, *Yes,* Marvena looks down at her hands to hide her bemused smile. She can see why Daniel had counted him a friend during the war.

"That'd be a sight a lot of folks here would pay to see—if they had any money besides scrip, that is," Tom says. He's standing behind Marvena. He spits into the coal stove behind him, currently unlit, although the mid-April afternoon is cool and blustery, bloated with the promise of rain.

Though the small office is chilly, Marvena is thankful that coal is not burning in the stove. She's worried about Lily, who looks feverish. Sweat dots her brow and upper lip.

"My brother has good reason to be bitter," Marvena says. "Days of talks, and all Luther will say is that he'll reduce what the men owe in scrip and look into better safety equipment?"

Lily says, "She's right. The men and their families need more than that. The Widowmaker permanently closed. The dead from Rossville Cemetery reburied, with dignity, at Ross Mining's expense. The dead from the recent collapse also properly reburied."

Marvena shudders; for the past three days, volunteers had labored to make wooden caskets, to bury the dead in a makeshift graveyard just outside of the tent city.

Now Marvena slaps her hands against the desk. "That's just a bit of what we want. We want to be free to talk about organizing. And agreement for better pay, shorter hours, boys under the age of sixteen kept out of the mines—"

But Ben is shaking his head. Marvena guesses what he's going to say; they've been over this turf several times in the past days. Ben and his men have been going back and forth between Rossville and Elias's farm, where Luther and his men have holed up. In Kinship, a trainload of Pinks have shown up and taken over the Kinship Inn. Some keep watch, shotguns at the ready, from roofs. The miners of Rossville have rallied under Marvena's leadership—and more arrive each day from nearby towns in the region, striking at their own mines, ready to join in the brewing fight. Ready to take it to Kinship.

Everyone, it seems, is eager for a fight. Once it starts, many will die. It's frighteningly easy to envision how a fight here could quickly become bigger and more deadly than the Battle for Blair Mountain.

"Luther Ross will never agree to all of that," Ben says. "With all due respect, Miss Whitcomb, you and your brother need to convince your men to accept what's been offered."

Marvena leans forward, glaring at Ben. "And why in the hell should we do that? I've got three-hundred-plus men out there with pickaxes and dynamite and shotguns, and more men coming every day from other towns. The Mine Workers of America is well organized enough to send more in from out of state, if'n that's needed. Mr. Ross and his Pinks are outnumbered."

"Because you're only outnumbering his men for now. My management wants this resolved fast. I've already heard that the governor is not happy with this situation. He's ready to deploy the Ohio National Guard. If there's more bloodshed, to even go all the way up to the president, and ask for an army detachment to be sent in." Ben grinds his cigarette into an ashtray on Luther's desk. "And if that happens, your men will be outnumbered, ten to one."

Marvena studies Ben; this is not, she sees by his sorrowful expression, an empty threat.

"Marvena," Lily is saying, "Mr. Russo has a point. I don't know how long my men can keep Luther's at bay."

"You're asking me to go to the miners out there, and tell them they've lost friends and loved ones, watched Luther send in men and boys to die in a mine he knew was unsafe, and all they're gonna get is a *promise* of looking into better safety equipment?"

"I've done all I can," Ben says quietly. "I only came when I heard what happened to Daniel. In honor of him. I think he would have contacted me, if he'd had time."

Ben has told them that he never heard from Daniel, who'd promised Marvena and Tom he'd contact Ben only a week before he was killed. Time enough—but perhaps he'd had a reason not to telegram or write to Ben immediately.

"Maybe you can talk with Luther again," Lily says, "help him see that in the long run—"

Tom snorts. "There is no making that son of a bitch *see*. He's already figured out what this fella here just said, and he's waiting us out. Well"—he spits into the cold coal stove again—"if we can't have some decent pay and more than promises about safety, I'd rather die, lots of men would, above the ground fighting than sending our boys in—" His voice breaks off. Alistair is recovering, slowly, but the losses and near losses have shaken everyone.

"Maybe," Ben says, "we should all take a break for a while, cool off."

Marvena stands. "Your bosses ain't the only ones running out of patience." She thinks of the dynamite, hidden away, and decides it's time to go fetch it from its hiding places. They have all of the rest, too, but they'll need every bit if they are going into a full-scale war.

With that, she and Tom leave.

LILY

Lily stares into her lap while listening to the door opening, then shutting, as she is left alone with Ben. She shivers, though heat seems to blister her from within.

"Are you all right, ma'am?"

Lily looks up. "There's no chance they're going to get more from Luther, is there?"

Ben shakes his head. "No. You seem to be friendly with Miss Whitcomb and her brother. Is there any way that you can convince them?"

"They've already lost so much! How can I, how can anyone, tell them now—"

"Mrs. Ross, your community is going to be torn apart if you don't find a way."

Lily drops her head to her hands. "Daniel would have known what to do."

After a moment, Ben says quietly, "Oh, I don't know. Daniel was a good man, sure. But he didn't walk on water."

Lily looks up at Ben. In the day since he's arrived, this is the first time they've been alone. It's also the first time he's shown a sense of humor—something Daniel would have appreciated. But the humor belies something deeper, a core to him, solid, like Daniel's. Yet with a soothing calmness that Daniel didn't have. "Was he? A good man?" Lily gasps at her own thoughts and questions. They seem, even after everything, a betrayal of her husband.

Ben's eyes flick toward the door. "I know he was friends with Marvena; he mentioned her once or twice, but you—"

Lily sighs. That's not what she means. Her stomach turns at the thought of the clippings George had sent by way of Abe, at the thought

of Daniel beating Frederick Clausen to death in some stinking alleyway, leaving the man's wife a widow.

Ben is still trying to comfort her as if he understands the source of
her doubts. "It was you he talked about whenever he could. Shared your
letters with whoever would listen." His smile turns impish. "Well, not
everything in the letters. Every now and then, he'd grin and read silently to himself."

Lily reddens. "I'm sure you got such letters."

"Oh, I received letters from my fiancée, at first." He shrugs. "She
wasn't willing to wait."

"I'm sorry. I hope since then you've met a nice lady—"

"No, and don't be sorry for me. My work keeps me busy and I don't
mind a bachelor's life." He leans forward, turning serious. "I wasn't trying to embarrass you, Mrs. Ross. I'm just saying that Daniel loved you.
Just you. And clearly you loved him. That's why he kept some compromises hidden from you." He shrugs. "It's pretty hard to get through life
without making compromises. Someone is going to have to here,
or—" He stops, shakes his head.

Lily stands, paces to the small, dirty office window and gazes out
at the people milling about outside. Suddenly Ben stands, crosses to
her. He puts his hand to her forehead.

"You're feverish. Are you sure you're all right to continue negotia-
tions?"

Lily nods as he lowers his hand, but then he brushes just his fingertips along Lily's jawline and chin. He lets his fingertips linger against
her face. A tremor threads from his touch across her face, down her
neck, through her body. More heat rises within her, and not from fever. For just a moment the air stills between them. All she has to do is
lean forward just a little. A tiny part of her longs to.

Instead, Lily takes his hand in hers, gently pushes it down and away.

Ben puts his hands in his pockets, steps back, looks down. "I'm sorry,
Mrs. Ross." He goes back to the desk, sits down.

"I'm . . . going to rest for a bit at Nana's," Lily says.

But Ben's already looking away, jotting in his notebook.

Lily changes her mind on the way to Nana's and turns up the main road in Rossville, toward the tent city. As weary and feverish as she is, Lily gives a thin smile at the memory of how shocked she'd been to see Rossville emerge over the rise of Devil's Backbone when she'd first driven here to seek out Marvena.

Now she's walking these Rossville streets—again to seek out Marvena—and the only thing shocking about them is their relative stillness. The mine openings on top of the surrounding ridges are abandoned of workers and mules. So too is the chute at the bottom. Lily shudders, remembering how fearful she'd been about the boy working the chute, how she'd worried he might fall in. It had seemed such an overdramatic fear at the time. She's always known life is fragile. Now she's seen firsthand how it is even more precarious here.

The street rises between boardinghouse and company store—its door hangs open, but its shelves have been cleared—then at the top Lily again finds herself gasping at the sight that emerges. Below is the tent city, spread across a meadow between two hills. From what Lily has heard talking to residents, the tent city had been just a dozen or so families a few weeks before, but since the newest disaster in the Widowmaker the tent city has grown to include miners who've walked out on strike from their own jobs—or simply walked out from non-union companies—to come here, to join forces with the Ross Mining workers. Some lodge in the miners' houses; Nana and Jurgis's is bursting full. But many come here. Word has spread of the fresh disaster and Lily calculates that the tent city below holds twice again as many workers as employed by Ross Mining.

Lily walks down Kinship Road and into the city, and soon she's in the midst of the campsites, surrounded by children running and playing, by men talking in small groups, by women cooking over fires or washing clothes in pots. Sharing and helping, as women always must. The noise and earthy smell of people living in close quarters is overwhelming. And yet it's a community, one tense with anticipation, excitement, and fear. Is this what it felt like for Daniel and her brother and Ben on the front? Lily wonders.

"Sheriff!"

Lily turns at the sound of a man calling to her. She sees that he and his compatriots are trying to tend to another man whose leg is bleeding.

Lily walks over. "What happened?"

"I was coming here on the main road," the man gasps. "Stupid me! Got shot in the leg!"

The man who called to her says, "He'll be fine. Barely scraped his flesh. But you should know about this. He wasn't shot by a Pink." He nudges the shot man, who moans. "Tell her."

"Looked to be one of the fancy shopkeepers from your town," he grunts.

"I don't just serve the town," Lily says. "I serve the county."

She gets the man's name and a description of the shopkeeper who'd shot him and promises herself she'll make a note of both in her notebook. For now, it's at Nana's. She walks on. So already ordinary men from Kinship were arming up. This was growing, a momentum of its own. Soon the fight would be inevitable. . . .

"Now listen up, you can talk all tough if you want, but you're not gonna go fighting in the battle! If'n things get bad, if something happens to me, you're the man of the family, and you have to take the others, lead 'em on over the hills! Sun rises where?"

Lily stops, struck by the fear and stridence of a young woman's voice, coming from just inside the makeshift tent by which she's stopped.

"East, ma'am." The voice of a boy, trying to sound like a man, pipes out of the tent.

A boy. The man of the family. Was his father one of the miners who'd died days before?

"That's right. So follow the sun east. If'n we get separated, don't wait for me. Get to West Virginia. Get to your mamaw and papaw—"

A child runs out of the tent and right into Lily and falls onto her bottom. It's a little girl, who stares up at Lily, suddenly fearful, lip quivering.

"Oh, honey, you're all right," Lily says, scooping the child up.

A woman pops out of the tent. "What did I tell you about running from bees? Why, my swat'll be worse than their sting—"

The woman stops, seeing Lily holding her child. Then she sees Lily's badge. "Oh. I'm sorry, ma'am. Did my little 'un run into you—"

"I'm fine," Lily says. "She didn't hurt me." She hands the child over to the mother. "I'm looking for Marvena. Do you know her, or know where I could find—"

"Oh, course I know her. She came around several times, got my man caught up in big dreams, thinking he could—" The woman stops, stares down.

"I'm sorry. Is he one of the men we lost in the explosion?"

The woman looks surprised at the use of the word "we," but it seems to soothe her. She smiles briefly. "No. He died afore that. Beaten by a Pink." The woman cocks an eyebrow. "Died, I reckon, same day as your husband. I was right sorry to hear about Sheriff Daniel."

Lily wipes her brow with the back of her hand. She's sweating. "Thank you. What was your husband's name?"

The woman straightens her back, tightens her expression as if trying to keep any soft emotion locked up. "Lloyd. Lloyd Zimmer."

"And what is your name?"

"Rowena."

"Well, Rowena, I'm sorry for your loss, too. I'm sure Lloyd was a good man."

For a moment, the two women look at each other. A moment is enough for them to acknowledge each other's loss. What it is to be widows.

Then they hear rustling behind them and look to see a boy standing in the entry of the Zimmers' makeshift home, and several smaller children behind him.

Lily looks at the boy. "Are you the one your mama calls the man of the family?"

He nods. "Yes, ma'am. And I am, too. I worked the chute!"

For a moment, Lily is struck still. This is the boy she'd seen on that first trip to Rossville. Then she says, "Well, you need to listen to your mama." She taps the star on her bodice. "I'm telling you, and you need to listen to me, you are not to fight. Do as your mama says."

He nods again. "Yes, ma'am."

Lily looks back at Rowena. "I don't want a battle, or for your family to have to run. I'm looking for Marvena to try to prevent it. Can you please tell me where she might be?"

Rowena says, "Likely, up the hill over yonder. That's where she put her stash."

"Stash?" Lily frowns. Does the woman mean shine?

"Dynamite. I reckon she's about ready to put her final plan in motion."

"Which is?"

"Why, blow up the Widowmaker for good, if'n Mr. Ross won't talk unionization."

Lily watches the woman and her children go back into their tent, and then she hurries away, in the direction that Rowena had pointed.

But then she hears a familiar voice—Joanne Moyer, the boarding-house proprietress, calling her name. Lily turns to face her.

On the one hand, Lily can't help but feel a moment of sympathy for Joanne, who looks weary and bedraggled. Then, too, Lily realizes, Luther had run away without any thought of taking Joanne with him. On the other hand, Lily has to ask: "Why are you still here?" She has to have enough cash on hand to leave.

Joanne smiles ruefully. "It's more dangerous to travel out of here on foot or horse than it is to stay right now. But as soon as I can get to Kinship, I'm taking the train—" She shakes her head. "Anyway. I was going to come find you; then I saw you here—Look, not many woulda done what you did. Maybe not even Daniel. So I thought you ought to know that I didn't give that candy box to him. When he came in, he demanded to know what I knew about Eula. I stuck to the story—that she'd run off with a miner. That's what Luther told me to say if Daniel ever came by asking questions."

"And did you think to ask him why he'd expect Daniel to do that?"

"I didn't question Luther 'bout that—'bout anything. Anyhow, Daniel didn't just accept that. He said he wanted to search Eula's room. I said sure—by then she'd been gone three weeks and everything was cleared out. The room was already taken up by some other girl, come down here from a little town north of here—anyway. Eula must have had a hidey spot, because Daniel came barreling down the stairs, fit to be tied, carrying that box. And something else."

"What? What else?"

Joanne shakes her head. "I didn't get a good look. But it appeared to be folded-up papers of some sort. And truth be told, I didn't think much of it—until Luther told me what to say about that poor miner set up for Eula's murder."

"Seeing that he was willing to let an innocent boy take the fall was too much for you?"

Joanne frowns. "I know you don't think much of me, but I don't have to tell you this."

"I'm sorry. I'm weary—and I don't feel very well."

"Well, no wonder. Getting in that foul water, that's enough to make anyone sick. You been to Nana for some tea?"

In spite of everything, Lily can't help but laugh. "Please, tell me what you were about to say, about the miner."

"It's true that I accused Eula of taking my jewelry. But that necklace—she never took that. I handed that over to Luther before you came in. He asked me to bring the necklace he'd given me last Christmas—he didn't say why, and I know not to ask too many questions. What she did take were the matching earrings. And I saw a flash of them in the drawer, when he opened it to get out the necklace."

Lily thinks back, recollects the look of shame and surprise on Joanne's face, right after Luther opened that drawer.

"And I've been thinking ever since, just how did he get that jewelry from her? If she was wearin' it, when she supposedly ran off with that boy? And why'd he get so upset that there was a loose diamond in her play-pretty box? Well, the only way he could have gotten it was directly from her. Why would he be spending time with her? Then I got to thinking, well, his men liked her for lots of reasons, but partly because there was talk she was Daniel's niece—sorry—and what if Luther, well . . ." Joanne looks down, her face again burning with shame.

"My God," Lily says, the import hitting her. What if Eula hadn't been consorting with Harvey Grayson? What if she'd been with Luther?

Had Luther brashly brought her out to the Ross farmhouse, where he lived with Elias?

Did Elias know what was going on, look the other way? Or did Luther keep the assignations hidden?

Lily's stomach turns, the weight of this revelation breaking over her, stirring in with everything else. Had Daniel known? Had he known the girl was dead?

She turns, to hurry back toward Ross Mining, to look in that drawer of Luther's.

"Lily?" Joanne calls after her.

But Lily quickens her stride.

Thirty minutes later, Lily is back in Luther's office. It's empty; Ben must have stepped out to take a break.

Quickly, Lily goes to Luther's desk and opens the drawers. In the bottommost one she sees an elaborate diamond necklace and earrings. One of the earrings is missing a tiny diamond.

Then Lily spots something else underneath the jewelry. A telegram. She picks it up. Her hands shake as she reads.

MARVENA

Marvena says, "What'n the world you mean, she just *ran off*?"

Nana stares up at her, sinks back into her chair.

Marvena rubs her hands to her face. She's frightening the woman. She tries again, more gently. "I could see Lily wasn't feeling well in our meeting. We took a break and Tom and I went to talk to some of the men. Rowena told me she'd been in the tent city, looking for me. So I reckoned she was here." Nana had just confirmed Lily had been, but only long enough to grab her bag and notebook, and then she'd taken off.

Nana stares down at her hands. "I offered to make her tea—"

"Oh, for pity's sake!" Marvena snaps. She has no heart for patience after all. "Why did Lily come here? What did she say?"

"She'd been to the tent city, and then to the Ross Mining office. Said she'd found some important things, that she needed to go somewhere to think, that when I saw you to tell you not to do anything until you talk with her."

"Not do anything?"

"Rowena told her about the dynamite. About the last-ditch plan."

Marvena rubs her eyes. So weary. But she needs to figure out where Lily would go.

"I couldn't stop her. She shouldn't be out in these hills alone!" Nana moans. "I don't know where she took off to. . . ."

"I do," Marvena says. "It's where I'd go."

Where Daniel would go, too.

Kinship Tree, twining trunks, spreading boughs over cool water . . .

LILY

Here at last, Lily runs her fingers over the fused trunk of the Kinship Tree. Three trees, sycamore, maple, beech, growing together since they were saplings, their fates intertwined.

She's sweaty, exhausted. She'd driven most of the way, but she didn't want the sheriff's automobile spotted so near Luther and Elias's. So she'd parked a good ways up Kinship Road and hiked the rest of the way, carrying her shotgun.

Now she leans against the tree, sinks down to the ground. She pulls her notebook out of her bag, rereads all of her notes, rereads the article clipping Abe had given her. And the telegram she'd found in Luther's office drawer.

Above her, branches sway in the soft breeze. Light and shadow mingle. The creek rushes before her, spring-water swift. A bird calls; another answers. Resting a hand on the ground, she doesn't twitch at the tickle of an ant trailing over her fingers. She'd spent years teasing Daniel about his belief in signs. But now she searches for anything that Daniel might call a sign, a sign to answer: *What must I do?*

She spots nothing that might be a response.

A bare snap snares Lily's full attention. She grasps her shotgun, slowly slides up to standing. Then she holds herself still again, waiting.

Marvena steps into view.

Lily says, "How'd you find me?"

"This is where I'd go," Marvena says. "Nana told me that you'd found something at Luther's office. That Rowena told you about the dynamite. Lily, you didn't really think I'd do something like that without warning you? Not after all we've—"

Marvena stops, and Lily takes in Marvena's taut face, the anguished twist of her mouth.

"How did you get here so fast?"

"Mule," Marvena says.

In spite of everything, Lily smiles. But then the words gasp out of her: "Oh God."

MARVENA

"Lily, what is it?"

Lily reaches into her bag and pulls out something. She's already, over the past few days, told Marvena everything about the gathering in Luther's office before the explosion. Then she holds her hand out and opens her fist. Earrings sparkle in the sun. Beautiful, dangly earrings. But one of them is missing a tiny diamond.

Marvena sees in her mind's eye the tiny diamond she'd found in Eula's candy box.

"Eula took the earrings from Joanne," Lily says. "But they weren't on her when we found her. They were in Luther's drawer all along, with the necklace." Marvena listens as she recites her conversation with Joanne back at the tent city. "How could Luther get them unless Eula and he, unless they . . ."

Marvena drops to her knees. She stares up at Lily. "I will kill him. If he . . . I will—"

"Listen! Please . . . Joanne said Daniel searched Eula's room, came out with the box, and something else, a paper of some sort. It must have been something that made Daniel understand the possibility of their having had a relationship, that made him confront Luther," Lily says. "He was so tense the week before he died, so distant. But the earrings alone wouldn't entirely convince me that Luther is to blame."

Lily returns the earrings to her pocket and pulls out a paper. "I found this in the drawer under the earrings. It's a telegram. From George Vogel."

Lily's hands tremble, and Marvena stands. She goes over to Lily, puts her arm around her friend's shoulder. "You'll need to read it to me," she says softly.

LILY

For a long moment, Lily can only stare at the words blurring before her. She is grateful for Marvena's light, comforting touch.

She's worked so much out. The telegram gives another piece of the answer about how Daniel died. But there are still so many questions.

"The telegram is from George Vogel to Luther," Lily says. "Sent March 22. And it states: 'Set for March 25. Send your best.' Harvey Grayson must have been Luther's best—to convince Daniel to come to Rossville. To set it up so that Daniel would stop at the hairpin turn."

Lily thinks about her notes: The hay mixed in with the glass, right there by Ada's farm. Her missing farmhand, Rusty. How easy would it be to pay Rusty to drop the hay bale? Wait for Daniel to be shot? Go get Elias? And by now, Rusty is surely long gone, just like Harvey Grayson, whose wife in Kentucky is probably fictitious. With enough cash, it is so easy to disappear in this vast country, start over with a new name, difficult to trace. The broken tree branch—a sniper George Vogel had sent.

"Lily?"

Marvena's voice comes from a great distance. Lily turns, looks at her.

"What now?" Marvena asks.

"I think Daniel found out about Eula and Luther. That he confronted Luther. That Luther was afraid Daniel would kill him sooner or later." She pauses, thinking of Daniel's calculated violence in the boxing ring. His fury in the alleyway and threat to kill her attacker. The clipping Abe had given her. Luther had been right to fear for his life at Daniel's hands. "And I think that somehow Luther used George Vogel to set up Daniel's murder." The words feel like they're coming from outside of her, as if she's hearing them from someone else.

"My God. If what you say is true . . . I'll kill Luther myself."

"No. And I can't arrest him—or Vogel—either. What we've pieced together isn't enough. Of course, I couldn't possibly bring Vogel down even if I had absolute proof. He has too much power. Too many people indebted to him." Too many people like Daniel.

"Then we can do nothing?" Marvena's voice rises so shrilly that a bird startles from the tree. Lily looks up, seeking the bird, but too late. She sees only clear sky above the tree.

Lily faces Marvena. "Above all, George values loyalty. I know Daniel would not have betrayed him. But Luther must have convinced George that he would. It's the only thing that would make George do Luther's bidding." She holds up the telegram. "This gives us a choice."

MARVENA

Marvena turns the words over in her mind, shakes her head. "I don't understand."

Lily steps forward, folds the telegram in half, puts it back in her pocket. She leans against the Kinship Tree, stares down over the bank. Marvena rises, stands beside Lily, gazes too. For a long moment the women's eyes are bound together on the cool, still water below, different memories resting just under the surface for each of them.

"We go to Abe Miller. He said I only had one favor to ask of him, but if we tell him everything we've pieced together, he'll listen. He may or may not know of the plot against Daniel, but he will definitely know this: His boss cannot abide being used and thus made a fool. Or word spreading that he can be duped in any way. So, we let him know Luther was using Vogel, that Daniel would not have betrayed him. And then Vogel will have Luther taken out."

Marvena waits for a victorious rush of joy. Kill the man who'd abused so many for so long, who'd had her daughter and Daniel killed, who'd foolishly reopened the Widowmaker, causing so many more good people to die.

There's no rush of joy.

Only coal hardness reclosing over her heart.

Marvena waits for Lily to say something more. Sees even darker hardness in her eyes.

"Lily? That's what we're going to do," Marvena says. "Isn't it?"

LILY

Lily wants, with all of her being, to nod at Marvena. To simply say, *Yes*.

This is what she's wanted, ever since *Daniel's been found*: simply to find who killed Daniel. Then, vengeance.

And yet . . . there's another choice.

Lily stares beyond Marvena, prays again for one of Daniel's precious signs. *A sign, dear God. Something to let me know how to choose . . .*

She'd come to the Kinship Tree because here had been set in motion the events that brought her and Daniel together. But there is no hawk facing her, no calls or cries or chirps, no movement in the sky, no sign from Daniel.

Lily has to choose on her own.

If she's going to go with the choice that means letting go of vengeance, she has to choose now. Just beyond these quiet, nearly still, deep and lovely woods, miners gather, ready to kill and to die. The forces gathering aren't going to wait for her to mull over her options.

Lily presses her eyes shut. She wants to see Daniel's face, see him, all of him, one more time before she makes her choice.

All she sees, though, are the others: Eula's corpse in the filthy red-flowered blue dress, Alistair draped nearly lifelessly across her arms, Tom's sorrow as he gathers his boy, Martin's unseeing eyes, Fiona collapsing at the news.

Lily opens her eyes and looks at Marvena.

"There's another way. If we let Luther live—"

"What? No! After all he's done—"

"You know why I accepted being sheriff?"

Marvena frowns. "I don't see how this has anything—"

"I wanted to use my role to see what I could find out about Daniel's death. I thought if I found out *who* and *why* I could take my vengeance and find peace. But here's what I've come to see. Luther, men like him, believe that there is only winning and losing. Only victory and loss.

Only having power or kowtowing to it." Lily shudders, from both fever and memory. "I've seen the evil in our community. But there's also my daddy. Your John. Men trying to take care of their families. Trying to help their community. Eventually life gives us all up, Marvena, and death rends us flesh from bone." The strains of "Pearl Bryant," which Lily'd heard being hummed on her first trip to Rossville, drift to her mind. "Eventually, our faded past becomes the twilight tale of just an old ballad that people hum and sing while they sweep a porch. I don't want Daniel's death, Eula's, the others', to be only some ballad about vengeance. We have no choice about death. Maybe we have little choice about how we're recollected. But we have a choice about how we live.

"If we want to really help these people, here, have some hope, we have another choice. We can take vengeance. But vengeance doesn't bring the dead to life. What if instead we let that go? Choose saving our people, our families—what will help the living?"

"How?"

"We put Luther's life in George Vogel's hands. And we tell Luther that he can either give his workers what they want—the right to unionize—and keep his life or I'll give the word and George can have him taken out as easily as he did Daniel."

Lily draws in a great shuddering breath. Though her heart is riddled with doubt, as she knows it will forevermore be, Lily looks at Marvena and says, "We have to choose together. And I choose saving our people."

MARVENA

For a long moment, Marvena stares past the Kinship Tree, at Coal Creek rushing by. Sees herself, twenty-two years in the past, just thirteen, thrashing and fighting for her life, and saved by the younger Daniel. He'd just been a boy, she thinks.

Then she'd had Eula six years later. Maybe Daniel's daughter, maybe not.

And now she's lost both of them. Lost so much. Her beloved John.

All because of the greed and inhumanity of Luther Ross.

Marvena recollects wanting to spit at Daniel for being a Ross. Now she wants to do the same to Lily for suggesting they let go of delivering upon Luther all the vengeance he deserves.

In the distance, Marvena sees a red-shouldered hawk rising from the trees.

Be alert. Carefully consider one's situation.

The hawk changes course, soaring to the east, over Devil's Backbone. All those men who died in the first Widowmaker explosion of 1888. Then again, last fall. Then again, last week.

Finally, Marvena looks back at Lily, meets her eyes. She realizes that Lily has been gazing at her this whole time, waiting. And she sees in Lily's gaze that she was serious. She wants them to be of like mind, whatever they decide.

They could, Marvena realizes, spin away the day talking the rights and wrongs of the choice before them. But she knows that what she really wants has nothing to do with personal vengeance. And yet letting go of that vengeance, what will it cost her heart?

She takes a long, shaky breath and pushes the image of Eula, beautiful Eula, back, back into a box deep in her heart. And then, finally, Marvena nods.

Lily gives a long, slow exhale. Sorrow and relief.

"How is either of us going to get to either Abe Miller or Luther without being shot up?"

"With Ben Russo," Lily says. "It's too risky for me to drive the sheriff's automobile at this point. But his is clearly marked 'Bureau of Mines.' You'll have to spread the word to hold off on any action for a day or so among your men."

"I'll do that," Marvena says.

"Very well. We'll go to Abe Miller. And then we'll go to Luther."

CHAPTER 28

※

LILY AND MARVENA

LILY

Mr. Williams stares from behind the check-in counter at the Kinship Inn as Lily approaches.

"I'm here to see Abe Miller," she says.

Marvena is outside in the automobile with Ben, waiting.

The proprietor's eyebrows lift. "I . . . I . . . think he doesn't want to be disturbed—" Mr. Williams stops, blanches. He turns away from her, suddenly staring at something on the desk behind him.

Lily feels the back of her neck prickle. She turns. Abe Miller stands behind her, too close.

"You have failed utterly in the tasks I put before you, Sheriff Ross," he says. "It is hard to imagine that product will resume flowing smoothly from this area anytime soon."

"Is it my fault that the new entrance to the Widowmaker blew up? Listen. You told me once that if I ever needed your help, I should come here to ask you."

"I meant with ensuring Mr. Vogel's business is undisturbed. Apparently I wasn't clear."

"Perhaps what I need from you will ensure that. You can't know until you hear me out."

Abe's gaze is coldly piercing, but Lily does not flinch or look away. Abe turns, strides though a door just off the lobby. Lily follows him down a service hallway and a flight of stairs, and into a speakeasy. Inside, people—men and women both—rush in panic through a door at the back of the dark room. Abe looks at a man behind the bar, starts to turn, but holds up two fingers, sits down at a table. It's covered with used glasses, overflowing ashtrays. Abe swipes it all crashing to the floor with one sweep of his forearm.

Lily sits down. Those who remain see that she's alone—that this is not a raid—and the melee settles. The barman comes over, puts two glasses of clear liquid before Abe, who pushes one toward Lily.

Abe picks up the glass, holds it up to Lily, a toast. "Here's to the very legal Vogel's Tonic." He swallows the contents in one gulp.

Lily does the same with her glass. It's a shot of Marvena's finest.

And damn if the burn doesn't feel fine going down.

The man leaves a clean ashtray on the table and scurries away. Abe taps out a cigarette. "Talk."

"I'd rather have you read," she says. She pulls the March 22 telegram from her pocket, along with the earrings, puts them before Abe.

He reads the telegram without picking it up, flicks a look at the earrings, then looks back at Lily. The hardness set in his face, the contemptuous coldness of his eyes, make Lily's heart thud so hard she can hear it in her ears.

But she takes a breath, then says, "I thought that a Pinkerton in Luther's employ, a man named Harvey Grayson, was Eula's killer. That Daniel found out somehow and was going after him outside of the channel of law, and that Harvey set him up to kill him. But then I found these items in Luther's drawer." Lily taps the earring with the missing diamond. "There was a small diamond in a box of effects she left behind. It would fit perfectly in this earring. But the earrings weren't on her body. They were in Luther's drawer. I think that Eula and Luther were, all along, really lovers."

A look of distaste crosses Abe's expression.

"I also found this." She points now to the telegram. "So, I think Luther told Mr. Vogel something to make him think Daniel would turn on him. Duped Mr. Vogel into helping him do away with Daniel, knowing that Daniel would be merciless if he found out."

"As he should be," Abe says flatly. He takes a sip of his drink. "Are you really here to accuse my boss of sabotaging Daniel?"

Lily studies him, the bemusement flickering across his face. Suddenly she's back for a moment in that cave, diving in the noxious water, unable to breathe, struggling to break free.

She leans forward so suddenly that Abe jumps. A mild note of surprise flickers on his face. The room goes silent.

"I have seen, firsthand, how your boss deals with people he doesn't like, people he thinks have used or fooled him. Seen how he likes to control. You know I have. You were there in the alley—the first time I met you both. You may not remember, but it looms large in my mind and always will. You were there at the Sinton, when Mr. Vogel pressed Daniel into service. So, yes. Yes, I believe Mr. Vogel was part of Daniel's sabotage, as you put it. But no, I am not here to accuse him. I'm not a fool."

Lily leans back, to take a breath, and in that moment Abe cocks an eyebrow and says, "Good. But you are here for your favor?"

Lily rubs her eyes. "Yes. I want you to telegram him that I have figured out enough to know he was used by Luther to set up Daniel. I don't know exactly how. Perhaps I don't need to. But that I know. And you let him know as well that I know that Daniel was a man who kept his word. He was true to me. He was true to Mr. Vogel. You tell him that anyone who says or thinks otherwise is playing him for a fool. And I know Mr. Vogel does not tolerate being played a fool. That he would not want others to know they could get away with playing him for a fool. What would that do to his business? You tell him that I'm going to confront Luther—not to accuse or bring him in for Eula or Daniel's death, but to ask him to listen to the miners' demands. You tell him that I need some assurance that if Luther does what I want, Luther will be free of Mr. Vogel's wrath, but that if Luther does not, then I want to be assured that Mr. Vogel will not hesitate to exact the cost from Luther that he foolishly exacted from my husband."

Lily stands up. "I will wait one hour for you to send the telegram and receive Mr. Vogel's response. I will be in the automobile marked 'Bureau of Mines,' parked right out front."

With that, Lily walks out of the speakeasy.

MARVENA

Marvena takes in the changing countryside from the front seat of Ben's automobile, the expanse of rolling pasture for dairy and buckwheat farms. Lily is lying down in the backseat, taking advantage of the time for rest that this ride allows.

Earlier this afternoon, Marvena had watched Lily stride into Kinship Inn, then a half hour later come out with Abe Miller and go down the street to the telegraph office. While Lily was inside, Ben had pressed Marvena for the reason of this elaborate detour, but all Marvena would tell him was that it was necessary for negotiating with Luther. Forty minutes later, as they came out, Abe handed Lily a telegram, and then he walked back into Kinship Inn.

And now here they are, near dusk, at the Ross family farm. Ben opens the automobile doors for Lily and Marvena, saying as they step out, "I'm not sure I'm all right with the two of you going in and talking to Luther, just yourselves. I should go in with you."

Lily starts to open the door he'd just shut. "Fine. We'll go back. Let this play out—"

"I'm with her," Marvena says, stepping back toward his automobile.

"Fine, fine!" Ben says. "I'll be outside whatever room you're meeting in."

Inside the house, Luther and several of his men lounge in the parlor. He looks up as they appear in the doorway, grins as if they've been brought there just for his amusement.

"Well, look here," he starts.

"They've come to negotiate further, Mr. Ross," Ben says. "You'll take it seriously."

Luther looks at Lily. "I hope you're here to say you've come to your senses and are willing to do as Daniel would have done in a situation this dire, whatever his personal belief—end all this before we have real bloodshed by supporting my right to run the mines as I choose."

"We've already had real bloodshed—or do you mean it becomes real when it's your or your men's blood that's spilled?" Marvena snaps.

Lily puts her hand on Marvena's arm, quieting her. But she adds, "Don't speak to me of what Daniel would have done. We are here to speak our own minds."

Several of the men snicker at that.

"Say what you have to say then," Luther says.

"No," Marvena says. "Alone."

Luther waggles his eyebrows and the men around him laugh.

Marvena digs her nails into her palms to remind herself not to attack the son of a bitch. She waits for the laughter to fade, then says, "I don't think you want anyone to hear what Lily and I have to say."

Luther scowls. "Fine. But I want their weapons taken."

As Lily passes her revolver to Ben, Elias steps into the room. "Lily? Is it all right if I join you, Miss Whitcomb, and Luther?"

Marvena studies him. The tingling instincts that have served Marvena her whole life creep up now as she looks at Elias, sees the rigid lines around his mouth and the coolness of his eyes, hears the evenness of his voice. She looks at Lily, to see if she senses this, too, but Lily is looking at Elias with a mix of warmth and sorrow.

"It's your home," Lily is saying, "though I don't think you'll want to know—"

"I insist," Elias says. He turns to lead them into the dining room.

LILY

In the dining room, Elias sits in his usual spot, at the head of the table, lighting his pipe. She sees, in his face, that sheltering Luther's men has wearied him.

Then she looks at Luther, his smug, self-assured expression, as he sits lazily in a side chair, pulled back from the table, so he can let his legs sprawl lazily.

Hatred for him starts to distract her, but Lily reminds herself that she does not want more bloodshed, more death, and she knows this is the only way. She looks at Marvena, standing next to her beside the polished dining table. Marvena nods. Lily pulls the earrings out of her pocket and tosses them on the dining table.

"I found these in your office."

"So? They're a gift for Joanne. I just didn't get around to—"

"They go with the necklace Joanne said Eula stole from her. But I've talked with Joanne in the tent city—"

"What?" Luther exclaims.

"She says Eula only took earrings. A small diamond is missing from one. There was a diamond that would fit perfectly in this setting in the box Daniel found in Eula's old room at the boardinghouse. And Joanne's been wondering . . . just how did you get these earrings? The only answer is from Eula, before she died."

"You got my girl pregnant!" Marvena's voice rises dangerously. "You killed her—"

"What? No!" Luther says. "She got pregnant by someone else— Harvey Grayson."

"You went to the extreme of killing Eula and Daniel to protect Harvey Grayson? Why?"

Luther stiffens. "You sound like a crazy woman. Hysterical!"

Lily reaches into her pocket and pulls out the telegram she'd found in Luther's office.

"I found this telegram from George Vogel, sent to you March 22, in your drawer. Along with those earrings." She doesn't have to look at it to recite it. "'Set for March 25. Send your best.' You sent Harvey Grayson to our house on March 24, to get Daniel to head to Rossville on the twenty-fifth. But he never made it."

A snap of something falling against the floor; the sound draws Lily's attention to Elias, who has leaned over to pick up his pipe. When he straightens, his face is rigid, his gaze upon Lily merciless. His hand trembles, though, and he puts the pipe on the table.

Something in that tremble—it hits Lily that Elias is in on Daniel's and Eula's deaths. "Oh God, Elias, no. Why?"

Elias sighs. "I tried to scare you both off after Marvena's visit on the day of Daniel's funeral."

"Shep—" Marvena says.

"And Lily's chickens. It was easier than you might think to find a miner willing to trade knowledge of Marvena's whereabouts for some scrip, and to hire a Pinkerton to take care of the animals."

"What miner?" Marvena cries.

"Don't know. Got a Pinkerton to find one for us. Does it matter?" Luther says.

Lily looks at Marvena, notes in her expression that in spite of all else, yes, it does matter, knowing who to trust.

Elias shakes his head. "I knew Lily would start asking questions after you arrived. She's always been too keen on questioning. First time I met her, she wanted to know the 'why' of amputating her toe, and an explanation of gangrene."

Lily clenches her fists so hard her nails dig into her palms. *How dare he?* As if, somehow, this is all her and Marvena's fault.

Elias looks at Luther. "And you? Why did you keep those items? Particularly the telegram? I told you to destroy it."

"I . . . I thought if we ever need to have something to hold over George—"

"One doesn't hold things over George!" Elias snaps.

For a moment Lily is again in this dining room as a girl just turned seventeen, toes mangled. She hears dear Sophie's voice trembling with the question about who to get to help with the amputation, *Luther or Daniel?*, hears Elias snapping, *Don't ask me to choose!*

Lily blanches as she realizes that he had, indeed, chosen. All these years, he'd chosen his nephew Daniel . . . until finally, now, he'd chosen his other nephew, Luther.

Lily swallows hard as she stuffs the telegram back in her pocket, next to the one she'd received just an hour before from Mr. Vogel. "Oh, Elias. What . . . what have you done?"

"Eula came to me," Luther says. "She wanted rid of the child, money to get out of here. Or else, she said, she'd show Daniel a copy of a map that she found in . . . in . . . Harvey's attaché."

Luther looks down and Lily realizes that he's lying. Eula had found the map in *Luther's* attaché. She fights back a gag as Luther mumbles, "A map of the plans to reopen Mine Number Nine, where I planned to set up Pinkerton security. She threatened to turn it over to some organizers."

Marvena gasps and Lily looks at her. Cold comfort, knowing this.

Joanne had revealed that Daniel searched the room and emerged with the candy box and folded paper. It must have been the map.

"But then she learned she was pregnant," Luther says. "I talked it over with Elias. I wanted to just have him help her get rid of the child, give her some money, but—"

"Harvey's child?" Lily asks.

Luther shakes his head. "Hard to know, but she said it was mine."

Lily blurts out, "Luther, how could you? Knowing Eula might be your niece?"

Luther shrugs. "*Half.* Or not."

There it is, in the cavalier shrug and reply. The same shrug he'd had a few days ago, dismissing his workers as inferior humans, worth only what he could use them for. That's how he'd seen Eula.

Marvena starts to lunge forward, but Lily gives her a hard look, stopping her.

"I knew she'd never stop trying to blackmail Luther. She said if we didn't do as she asked, she'd go to Daniel. I knew the only man who'd take her seriously was Daniel. But I could also see she'd be ashamed to tell him," Elias says. "So we set up the ruse of making it look like she was just running off with a miner. And then we had Harvey bring her here. I gave her drink to numb her. . . ." He pauses, inhales so hard his nostrils flare. His look is defiant. "I must have accidentally made it too strong."

Lily stares at him, as if seeing him for the first time. Elias, a murderer of a young girl? For she knows, from all the work they did together with patients during the influenza pandemic, that he didn't make accidents in dosing. He'd purposefully overdosed Eula. Then she looks at Luther. There is no surprise on his face about this. She tries to swallow, but her throat sticks. For a moment she's back underwater, unable to breathe.

MARVENA

Marvena bolts from her spot. Suddenly she's behind Elias, a knife whipped out of her waistband, and she grabs him by the hair, yanks his head back, and has the knife at his throat.

Luther jumps to his feet. "I will call for my men, and you'll be dead in minutes!"

"Sure, but I'll have sliced his throat by then," Marvena says. "I'll live long enough to watch this bastard bleed out."

"She's right," Elias whispers.

Luther twitches forward.

Lily says, "Don't move from that chair, Luther. I guarantee she can take you with that knife, and I'll swear in a court of law it was in self-defense."

"She'll hang. What jury will believe two hysterical, grieving women over a businessman and doctor?" Luther's voice coils around the room. "And the army will join my men and crush her little uprising anyway."

For a horrid moment, Marvena thinks, *I don't care.*

But she has chosen against vengeance.

As if from a distance, she hears Lily's voice. "Marvena, move the knife away from Elias's throat so that he is comfortable telling us the rest of what happened."

Marvena gives her a long look but lowers her knife. She remains behind Elias, though. "Just remember I'm right here. So don't try anything foolish."

LILY

Elias looks at Lily. "Daniel came here to confront us about the fact Eula was missing. He'd been to the boardinghouse, searched Eula's room, and found a map laying out the reopening of the Widowmaker and the plans for security in case the miners didn't cooperate. Eula had hidden it under a loose floorboard along with her box. He'd realized Eula had gotten the map from Luther, put together the nature of their relationship."

Lily looks at Marvena, sees the grim expression on her face. It is all Marvena can do, she sees, to keep control. Lily isn't sure she'd be able to, if this were Jolene these two men were discussing so cavalierly. She swallows back bitter bile.

"Daniel started beating Luther. I finally stopped him," Elias is saying. "If you'd have seen his face, Lily, you'd know Daniel was capable of killing him. *Wanted* to kill him."

Those faint bruises on Luther's face at Daniel's funeral. The crack in the curio cabinet. Daniel's cold, murderous look at her attacker in the alleyway years ago. Now, staring at the pitiless faces of Daniel's uncle and half brother, Lily understood the depth of his wrath.

"I told him Eula was fine, that I'd treated her and sent her away, and that I'd send for her to come back," Elias says.

"And he believed you?" Lily asks.

"I was like a father to him."

Of course Daniel had believed him. For a moment, Lily gazes around the dining room. Nothing about it has changed in the nine years since she was first here. She puts a hand on the dining table. She stares down at the heavily polished surface.

And she's back, on this table, terrified, but staring into the deep, dark eyes of the man she'd soon learn was Daniel T. Ross, the man she'd quickly fall in love with. And he's leaning forward, and she's asking him something, something about Elias.

Then it comes back to her.

Her question: *Would you trust him?*

Daniel's answer: *With my life.*

Lily forces herself to look back up at Elias.

"So he just left after you told him that?"

"He gave me a week. Left so angry, he forgot the map. I never saw the box. He must have left it in his automobile."

No wonder Daniel had been so distracted the week before his death. She imagines him coming home from that wretched confrontation with his half brother and uncle, stashing Eula's box at the bottom of the drawer in the jailhouse.

"He didn't yet know Eula was dead, but I realized he'd figure it all out sooner or later," Elias says. "Daniel was sharp, but he also could be . . . ruthless. I'd tried to talk him out of a career in boxing, into a career in healing; he was smart and could have been good at it, but there was some element of bloodlust in him. Maybe from his mother?"

"Just because she was Indian?" Lily snaps. "I doubt that."

Elias smiles sadly. "You're right. Daniel and Luther's father, my brother, was a truly cruel man. I think Daniel's boxing was a way to get out his anger toward him. But Daniel was never going to beat down the shadow of their father, Lily. At least Luther did."

Lily looks at Luther, the smug yet scared look on his face. *No*, she thinks. Luther had truly turned into a version of their father. She thinks, then, of Daniel going to visit Widow Gottschalk, and all the other vulnerable people in Bronwyn County. She fights back tears. Daniel had become his own man instead—flawed, tormented, but kind and beautiful.

"Lily, Daniel would have killed Luther and me when he found out about the unfortunate fate of Eula," Elias is saying. "And I knew he would have never stopped looking, would somehow have found out. I needed to stop Daniel before he could figure out what happened to Eula, before he could contact his friend about stopping Luther's work with the new mine. Then what? Luther would have lost his business. He's lost enough. So I made a trip to Cincinnati and called upon George Vogel. I told him Daniel had confessed plans to me to turn himself and George in to the revenue department, that he'd kept condemning records, that he felt guilty over the loss of a young woman—Eula, who was like a daughter to him—to alcohol poisoning."

"And when he asked you *why* you felt compelled to fill him in?" Lily asks.

"I simply said as a retired physician that I was a great believer in Vogel's Tonic, and I'd be sorry to see it go," Elias says. His voice is as flat as his expression. "I said that I was afraid of Daniel's hothead ways, and all the lives he'd ruin if he wasn't stopped.

"And I told Luther to send Grayson—for him to tell Daniel to come to Rossville that morning, that we had information and wanted to talk with him about Eula. Orchestrating Tom to take the fall was not difficult. Mr. Vogel took care of arranging the rest."

"So nice and clean for you both." Marvena's words grind out through her clenched teeth. "No blood on your hands—"

The guard drops a bit from Elias's face. "Oh no, Miss Whitcomb, I do have blood on my hands." His voice trembles. "I . . . I went out there that morning. I felt it was my duty to be there, to make sure that it was done right, that Daniel didn't suffer too long." Tears start down his face. "The sniper's shot hit Daniel in the stomach. Such a wound would be painful, and take a long time, and the sniper took off running. And so I . . . I had to go to Daniel. And finish."

Lily sees Elias as he had been that morning, bringing her the news: *Daniel's been found.* The blood on his jacket. She imagines Elias, standing over Daniel, delivering the second, fatal shot to the chest, imagines him overtaken for a moment, holding Daniel to him the way Tom had held Alistair. Or does she just want to believe Elias had this shred of tenderness, even in the midst of his cruel action?

"You will fry for what you've done!" Marvena cries.

Elias shakes his head. "We will deny that we've said any of this," he says. "The earrings can be explained away."

"But I know that Daniel was shot on the way to Rossville, not from," Lily says.

"Can you prove that?" Luther asks. "Or will it be your word only?"

"Well, there's the telegram you received from Mr. Vogel."

"Are you really willing to take on Vogel? Plenty of men have tried and failed."

"We'll say—"

"Who will believe you? Two hysterical women?" Elias says. "Now, Lily, I know you think I'm a monster right now, but eventually I'm confident you'll understand. I had to take the most expedient action. To save Luther from his brother. To save the company my own brother built. Really, to save Daniel from his own temper. Who knows who he'd have taken down with him if I hadn't stopped him. I didn't have a choice."

No choice? The words startle Lily, ricochet through her being.

Lily hears Marvena gasp quietly beside her and inhales slowly, willing herself to stay upright, to not let the heat of fever and loathing wrest this moment from her.

She says, "Oh, Elias. We always have choices. Daniel told me that, first thing when I met him. And you taught me that, too, Elias, when we worked side by side during the influenza epidemic. Who we tend to first, who we let die while trying to save someone else. How to choose with a firm hand, a steady eye. You had choices. I've chosen, too. You underestimate George Vogel, his ruthlessness, how much he valued Daniel. How much he'd despise being duped and used. And I've received a telegram myself today."

She pulls it out of her pocket, glances at it, and then tosses it to Luther. "Go ahead. Read it out loud. And I think you really ought to keep this one."

Luther picks it up and stares at it for a long moment. And then, voice shaking, he reads out loud: "'Gratitude for your affirmation of D's loyalty. Assuming yours is as strong as his, I am now ever in your debt. I await your command. Please advise.'"

He looks up at Lily. "'I await your command.' What the hell—"

"It means I can send him your name. Elias's name. *Both names.* And he'll *arrange things.* I've no doubt he'll follow through, especially since he knows you kept his March 22 telegram and thought you might be able to hold it over him. Elias is right about that—it was foolish. And George has now lost a loyal man in Daniel. I've met him twice, seen how he operates. Had more conversations with his man Abe Miller than I would ever want. I've no doubt he's capable and willing to have both of you taken out, when you least expect it, just as you tricked him into doing with Daniel. He hates being tricked."

Lily hears soft crying. Marvena. She's lost her daughter to men upon whom she can take no direct vengeance in exchange for the right to organize. In her way, she's given her life for the miners ever much as John Rutherford had.

But Lily can't look at Marvena now or comfort her. If she does, she may lose her will to see this through. So she keeps her gaze steadily on Luther. "You can choose, Luther, to live with the threat of Vogel—anytime I give him the nod—but still, live. And in exchange, give Marvena all she wants."

"I can't. . . . I have managers, too. They'll never agree." He looks away from her.

"I think you'll find a way," Lily says. "You can choose to punish talks of unionization, push aside safety practices, let this community fall into battle, let perhaps hundreds more men get killed, maybe think you're a hero for a little while, triumphing over the evils, as you see it, of organization, but—" She suddenly strides across the room, grabs Luther's face, jerks it up so he has to look at her, has to see she means every word she says. "Just remember that if you don't agree right now to negotiate, Marvena and I will be escorted from here, and I will go to Kinship, and I will meet with Abe Miller, and it will never matter how far you go from here. Somehow, George Vogel will find you after I send the message: 'Luther and Elias Ross.'"

EPILOGUE

※

LILY AND MARVENA

Four Months Later, August 2, 1925

LILY

Mama asks, "Are you sure you're all right to go?"

Lily glances up in the dresser table mirror at Mama. Lily finishes pinning up her hair. "I'll be fine." She turns in the chair. "Besides, how could I miss Marvena's big day?"

Mama allows a rare wide grin. "Not just a big day for her. For the miners, for Bronwyn County." She adds, a mite too enthusiastically, "And on your birthday, at that!"

Twenty-seven. Half a lifetime. Ten years since the day she'd met Daniel.

"Yes," Lily says when Mama clears her throat, nudging for a response.

A flicker of worry erodes Mama's grin, and Lily wishes she could overcome the flatness in her expression and voice just to ease Mama's mind.

After her and Marvena's encounter with Elias and Luther, Lily gave an interview to the Kinship newspaper in which she stated that after investigating she realized that her husband had been killed on the way to Rossville to pick up Tom Whitcomb, so clearly Tom was not Daniel's killer—but that she doesn't know who it could have been. When pressed, she delivered the only cover story she could come up with. *Perhaps Daniel stopped another driver, likely one passing through our county on Kinship Road, for reckless driving, and the other driver then shot him and drove away? It will remain a mystery.*

She'd recalled that such a fate had befallen another county sheriff, several counties away a few years before. Of course, she hadn't questioned the story then, and no one was questioning her similar story now.

Then Lily spent several weeks recuperating from fever, alternately tended to by Mama, Hildy, and even Nana, visiting from Rossville. All agreed that Lily suffered from the same thing that racked Alistair, illness from being in the foul water in the Widowmaker tunnel. Sometimes one or the other of them would say it's so strange . . . too bad . . . that Elias and Luther suddenly left Bronwyn County. Lily has no clues as to where they've gone, but it doesn't matter. She wants nothing to do with either of them, and she knows, as she warned them, that if she gives the word George Vogel will put his network to use and find them.

Before leaving, Elias put the farmhouse and land in Lily's name. This is not something she asked for, and she only learned of it when she received notice of the deed transfer. She's put it up for sale and will donate the money toward building a proper school in Rossville, one not controlled by Wessex or any future company bosses.

Now Lily forces a smile to her face, stands up, says, "I'll be down in a moment."

But being alone brings her no peace. She can't bring herself to tell Mama or the others that nothing physical ails her, that there's simply no tea to cure her restless, fallow heart.

MARVENA

Backstage at the Kinship Opera House, Marvena sits on a stool, counting off on her fingers the points she wants to make.

One: providing safety measures not only keeps the worker population healthy but also ensures loyalty and saves costs in the long run.

Two: providing a fair pay system not based on company scrip—

And then Marvena drops her head to her hands. This is ridiculous. The points she's tried to come up with for her big speech sound so stilted. Even silly.

In the four months since their meeting with Luther and Elias, she's been grouchy and touchy, even though she's gotten all she'd hoped for. The Pinks have left Kinship and the county. After agreeing that the Mine Workers of America could hold a public forum on the merits of unionization, Luther quickly sold Ross Mining to Wessex Corporation at a low price with the written stipulation that Wessex would honor the miners' right to decide for themselves whether or not to unionize.

The men have gone back to work in all but the Widowmaker mine, which Wessex has permanently shut down. Wessex management has spent time listening to what the miners know about these hills, about searching for new coal seams, but safely and without rushing just for profit. And they are sanctioning a vote for the men to decide on whether or not they want to organize a Mine Workers of America local chapter in Rossville. A few men, enjoying the better treatment from Wessex, are backpedaling on pushing for the vote—why have a union, and answer to those strictures, if management offers fair treatment?—but most are for it.

And yet . . . she isn't getting all she'll ever want. She won't get back Eula. Her beautiful, strong-willed Eula. The men who'd orchestrated her death, and then Daniel's, all walk free.

A gentle tug on her skirt makes her look up. There's Frankie, starring up at her. And Tom, Nana, and Jurgis right behind her.

Tears spring to Marvena's eyes. They'd all come to wish her well. She hops off the stool and scoops up Frankie.

Nana looks up at Tom. "I should have brought her tea! Calm her nerves. Chamomile."

At that, Marvena smiles.

Jurgis gives Marvena a long, somber look. "Just speak from your heart, Marvena. Like you did in the cave."

"Will Jolene be there, Mama?" Frankie asks anxiously.

"I hope so," Marvena says. And she hopes Lily will be there. They haven't seen each other since their encounter with Luther and Elias. Their choice, and the pain of what they'd chosen, will forever bond them. Marvena sighs at that thought. She and Lily—Daniel's old lover and best friend, and his wife and love of his life—bound.

In response to the sigh, Frankie says, "I could sing you a song to make you feel better!"

Marvena hugs her. "I'd like that. Which one?"

"How 'bout the one about prayin' at the river?"

Marvena's eyes prick, as she remembers that Frankie had sung it for Lloyd's mourners, so long ago, on the day that Daniel died.

"That would be right lovely," she says. She sits back on the stool, pulls Frankie up to sit on her lap, and holds her beautiful child while she sings, "As I went down in the river to pray . . ."

LILY

"Will Frankie be there?" Jolene asks anxiously, tugging at Lily's skirt as they walk down the street, around the courthouse on the corner, toward the opera house.

"Of course," Lily says.

"Can she sit with us?"

"I don't know."

"Well, can I sit with her?"

"I don't know."

"Are she and her Mama coming with us, after?"

Mama has insisted on a birthday picnic, down by the Kinship Tree and, after that, black raspberry picking on Ada Gottschalk's farm—with the widow Gottschalk's blessing, of course. Mama has sent word that Marvena, Frankie, Tom, Nana, and Jurgis are welcome to join them.

"I don't know!" Lily says. Jolene huddles closer to Hildy.

"We'll see," Hildy says, giving Lily a long look.

Micah wriggles in Lily's arms, and Lily stops mid-stride. She lowers him to the ground. "Can't you walk? Be a big boy like Caleb Junior?"

Micah's face crumples, his mouth turning down as he works up to a wail.

"Come here, Micah!" Mama calls. He runs to his mamaw and she takes his hand. She shakes her head at Lily, then continues down the street, Caleb Jr. on her left, Micah on her right.

"Lily?" Hildy's voice is tenuous. "Are you . . . all right?"

"For God's sake, yes! Could everyone stop asking me that?"

The women and children continue down the road, the excitement of the morning sapped from them. They're all quiet, except for Lily; as other people pass by and smile and nod at her, she returns the gestures—automatic, perfunctory.

Jolene breaks their group's tense quiet: "Look, Mama! You're in the window!"

Everyone else stops to look, so Lily does, too.

There in the bank window is a new poster, already replacing the one advertising this afternoon's forum being led by Marvena.

It's a campaign poster for Lily Ross, Democratic candidate for Bronwyn County Sheriff.

A few weeks before, Fiona Weaver had come calling on Lily and asked if she'd consider running for reelection this coming fall, in her own right in a special election to fill out Daniel's term until the next election in 1926. The notion had stunned Lily at first, but as more callers—men and women—came by or asked her as she slowly returned to work, she finally decided that yes, she would run.

Lily peers at the poster. She puts her fingertips to it. So long ago . . . and yet it also seemed like yesterday . . . she'd stared at another poster here, the one advertising Daniel's boxing match: "The Middleweight Fight of the New Century for the Greater Appalachian Region." He was beautiful to her then . . . everything she'd wanted in life.

Lily swallows hard, clears her throat. "Who made this?"

Hildy points at script at the bottom: "Endorsed by the Committee to Support the Reelection of Lily Ross, Sheriff, Bronwyn County."

"I have a committee?"

"There's a lot of talk about what you did in Rossville."

Mama touches Lily's shoulder. "Look at me, child."

Lily turns, faces Mama.

"These people love you for what you did," Mama says. "If you hadn't brought in the Bureau of Mines, and somehow gotten Luther to open up to unionization talks and make that part of his deal in selling out to Wessex—well. The whole county would have been torn up. I don't think we'd be enjoying a peaceful stroll down Kinship Road."

A knot deep inside starts to loosen. *These people don't know. They can never know.*

As they pass the grocer's, Mr. Douglas is sweeping the front stoop. He calls a greeting.

Hildy mumbles, "I'll catch up. I need to check on an order I placed."

Lily glances up, but Hildy is already over by him, listening and nodding. He's stopped sweeping. The trilling sound of Hildy's laugh seems to delight Mr. Douglas, a widower. His eyes are on Hildy, his face alight. And she is blushing.

Mama elbows Lily. She is smiling as well.

Lily looks at the sign swaying in the gentle breeze: "Douglas Grocers." The sign used to read: "McArthur & Son Grocers." Mama's smile seems to say, *Somehow, child, life goes on.*

"Oh," Lily says, and the knot inside loosens further.

MARVENA

The opera house is stuffy, crowded with some townspeople, but mostly miners from Rossville and throughout the county, come on foot and muleback and driven in trucks by farmers and supporters—however they could get here.

People gathered here will vote overwhelmingly for unionization. That this is a formality doesn't stop the crowd from cheering when a Mine Workers of America official finally stops droning on and asks for Miss Marvena Whitcomb to come on up.

As the crowd cheers, Marvena takes the stage. She smiles, waves, but she's also looking around, looking for Lily. They haven't talked since that afternoon at Elias's house, but her mama has sent word that later Marvena and Tom and Frankie and Alistair and Nana are all welcome to join them for the picnic at the Kinship Tree to celebrate.

Even as the crowd quiets, shuffles, awaits Marvena's speechifying, Marvena remains silent, seeking Lily. How many might not be here if she and Lily had not sacrificed their own desire for vengeance?

She finally spots her. Lily holds her gaze for a long moment. Even at a distance, Marvena can see the sorrow etched around Lily's mouth, her eyes, what it cost to bring them to this moment. She sees that Lily is noting the very same in her own face.

Then Lily offers her a small smile. A little nod. All these months, Marvena's tasted bitterness on the back of her tongue, as if it wells up from her heart. But now, as she sees these faces, the bitterness starts to dissolve.

Marvena looks away then, and the restless crowd falls further silent as she starts: "A wise friend once told me that life gives us all up and death rends us flesh from bone. And haven't we all seen so much of that? Sooner or later, we have no choice about that—we lose fathers and mothers, our husbands and wives. If we're lucky, we'll not live to experience losing our sons . . . and our daughters. We'll lose ourselves. But in the meantime, shouldn't we have some choice about how we live, what we believe about ourselves, about human beings?"

"Yeah!" someone shouts, and voices around him echo the cry.

Loudly, clearly, Marvena says, "Well, you do have a choice!"

LILY

The knot fully loosens, and from somewhere deep inside a fist punches up through Lily's stomach, into her heart.

"Mama," she whispers, "I'm not feeling well. . . . I'll meet you all back at the house."

Lily works her way through the crowd, out of the opera house. She runs around the courthouse corner, toward home. She stops abruptly, seeing Abe Miller standing on her porch, leaning against the rail, smoking a cigarette.

"I'm heading back to Cincinnati. This will be my last trip to Kinship."

Lily stares at him. No one left George's employ without his blessing.

Abe allows a thin smile across his face. "Oh, don't worry about me. I'm still in Mr. Vogel's employ. Just not here. This territory has been released."

This is George's penance to her, for his part in Daniel's death. Moonshiners here in Bronwyn County are free to produce without selling a portion at a discount to George's operation, and she is free to prosecute moonshiners or not, as she sees fit.

"I can do no more," Abe says, "except ask if there's anything you'd like to know?"

Lily studies him, but the smile has already slipped away. There are no clues in his expression. Then it hits her. There's only one thing she wants to know.

"Those article clips. Did Daniel . . . did he . . ."

Abe starts down the porch steps. Lily's heart clenches. Is he really going to walk away without answering her? But then he stops, then turns, looks back at her. "Sometimes newspaper articles get things wrong. Mr. Clausen was severely injured that night in the alleyway after that last fight with Daniel. That is all."

"But . . . then, where are he and his family now?"

Abe smiles thinly. Lifts his hat again. Gives a small shake of his head.

Lily watches him walk away, watches the street long after he's gone.

She sinks to the top porch step as the sobs come suddenly, convulsing her. She hates Daniel for a moment, hates him for ever having returned to George Vogel, hates him for not having found another way to serve his penance, for making the choices he had, for being dead.

But then a memory, from when they first moved into the sheriff's house, comes to her.

"I just found an empty's bird nest on the eave over the back stoop. I need you to help me clean it out," Lily said, as she descended the cellar stairs.

Lily nearly laughed at Daniel's horrified expression. Lily, certainly not! It's a good sign. For a happy home!

Lily saw that he was nearly finished with the cellar shelves, made from fieldstone and wood cleared from Elias's property, for Lily. He'd teased her the past week that this wasn't really their house, that after all the house belonged to the county, that the sheriff only lived here if elected. Yet he'd made the shelves she was so eager to fill with home-canned goods—green beans, corn, tomatoes, mixed vegetables, applesauce. His favorite black raspberry jam.

He stood up too fast, banging his head on the cellar ceiling, bringing dirt and dust down into his thick black hair. He cursed under his breath. Lily laughed after all.

But then the baby turned, kicked. "Ow!" Lily said, and this time Daniel laughed. "The baby wants you to know that an empty bird's nest is a good sign," Daniel said.

"If the birds have moved out?" Lily was incredulous.

"It means the birds are making way for a new family."

"You know, you wrote me in the war that I'd see a hawk come close to me as a sign of you being safe," Lily said. "I kept looking— and never got my sign."

He grinned at her. "Guess I figured you'd know I was fine and I didn't need to send it!"

Lily hears someone coughs and looks up to see a woman with a baby carriage.

"Mrs. Ross? My husband doesn't know," the woman says, "but you've got my vote!"

In spite of everything, Lily smiles. She stands up. "Thank you."

The woman gives a satisfied nod. Lily watches her walk away.

Maybe she's waited long enough for a sign. Maybe, like Mama no longer taking sentimental note of the changed grocer's sign, she needs to find a way to move on.

Lily goes back into her house, to her kitchen, and begins packing up pies that Mama and Hildy and Jolene had made for the picnic. One of them, she sees, is buttermilk. Daniel's favorite.

"Mama, can we go pick black raspberries now?" Jolene asks. "And can we have some with the buttermilk pie?"

Lily, sitting by herself on cloth spread by the Kinship Tree, looks at up at Jolene and Frankie. Both girls are holding pails, looking at her with eager grins.

"Please? Soon it will be dark, and if we don't get them today it'll be another year."

Lily looks back at Jolene, then at Frankie, their expectant faces lifting to hers, waiting.

She smiles. "All right, then. Gather everyone who wants to go. It'll be dusk soon."

Ten or so minutes later, they're all down the lane. Lily thought Mama would have wanted to stay behind, but there she is with everyone else, butts up as they bend over to peer at the black raspberry bushes, right along with the children, yelping when fingertips snag on the thorny stems but calling out in glee about whose pails are filling up the fastest with the berries.

"Pull from just below the berry, now," Mama admonishes everyone. "Don't break the stems, lest you don't want any next year."

Lily smiles. *Mama, always clucking around, mother hen—*

A screech from above catches everyone's attention. They all stop, look up in the dimming sky, even the children.

A red-shouldered hawk circles.

Lily sets her pail down, goes to Micah and Jolene, lets her arms spread like wings around her children—son to her left, daughter to her right. They're restless, but she pulls them close, tight, and they still, watching the hawk with her.

The bird dives, swooping down as if for prey, and Lily sees that the hawk's plummeting toward them. But she lands on a branch of the sycamore tree just across the lane.

The hawk stares down at them, all of them—Mama and Hildy, Marvena and Tom. The children: Alistair and Frankie, Caleb Jr. and Micah and Jolene.

At Lily.

Lily looks at Marvena.

And Marvena gives a slight, quivering smile, then nods.

At last. Daniel has sent his sign. He is, after all, safe somewhere in the great beyond. And she knows that she made the right choice.

Lily stares up at the hawk for a long time.

Suddenly the hawk rises, shaking the branch with her takeoff, and

Lily watches, even after the bird's disappeared, even after her children have broken from her embrace and run back to the bushes with the other, until she feels a tug on her sleeve. It's Marvena.

"Come," she says.

And so Lily goes back to her children and family and friends, back to picking black raspberries.

AUTHOR'S NOTE

Do ideas find authors, or do authors find ideas?

The former concept seems mystical; the latter, pragmatic.

However it works, I'm glad that the concept behind *The Widows* and I found each other.

Early in our younger daughter's freshman year at Ohio University in Athens, Ohio—located in the southeastern Appalachian region of the state—my husband and I were planning on a visit for her birthday. Gwen majored in outdoor education (and currently works as a teaching naturalist) and we knew she'd be keen to get out of her college town and visit nearby hiking areas and state parks.

To the Google search bar! I keyed in something like "places to visit near Athens, Ohio," and somewhere on the results list was a Web site for Vinton County, which abuts Athens County directly to the west. I clicked on the link, and what popped up on the home page at the time was not information about the place but about a person—Maude Collins, who was the sheriff of Vinton County in 1925, indeed, the first female sheriff in Ohio; the next female sheriff in the state would be elected in 1976. When Vinton County Historical Society officials learned that the 1976 female sheriff was to be recognized as the first female sheriff in the state, they set about correcting the mistake. In 2000, Maude was inducted into the Ohio Women's Hall of Fame as Ohio's first female sheriff.

Maude, who had worked for her husband, Sheriff Fletcher Collins, as jail matron, became sheriff when he was, sadly, killed in the line of duty. Maude had to testify in the trial and was packing up herself and her five children to return home to West Virginia to live with her parents when the county commissioners came back and asked her to fill in for her husband. Later, she was elected in her own right and went on to a career in law enforcement.

But what struck me most about Maude was not the novelty of her being a sheriff as a woman—still something of a novelty; as of 2007, women still represented only 11.2 percent of officers in sheriffs' departments[1]—but a photo of her. She was lovely and strong—the kind of woman I would admire in any era. There was something in the mix of tenderness and toughness in her portrait that intrigued me.

I soon found myself thinking the question that haunts all writers and gets them (and their characters) into all sorts of delicious trouble: What if? What if there was a 1920s wife of a sheriff who did *not* know why her husband had been murdered? What if the murder was not straightforward, as it was in Fletcher Collins's case? What if that wife decided to investigate for herself the truth of her husband's death—and soon discovered that his life had its own mysteries?

From there, Lily Ross was born in my imagination. Her personal history, the reasons behind her husband Daniel's murder, and her life going forward are purely from my imagination and in no way reflect the true story, intriguing in its own right, of Maude Collins.

As for the other voice in this novel—Marvena—again, she is born of my imagination. But as I read more and more about the lives of coal miners, I knew that unionization, and the complexities of organizing unions, had to be part of the story. My father, who worked in the tool and die industry post World War II, was a union leader for the Team-

---

1. Lynn Langton, "Women in Law Enforcement, 1987–2008," Bureau of Justice Statistics, June 2010.

sters at the company where he worked until he left to start his own independent shop, so I am steeped as much in a strong pro-union stance as I am in Appalachian folk tradition (more on that in a minute). I was inspired by activist Mary Harris Jones (aka Mother Jones)—again, her true story is intriguing in its own right—to create my version of a female who comes into her own as a labor organizer, albeit on a smaller scale.

The other strong women characters in this novel—Nana, Mama, Ada—are from my imagination as well but also inspired by the women I consider the strongest from my family of origin: my paternal grandmother, Lorrainey (Engle) Hurley; her sister, my great-aunt Cassie (Engle) Lewis; and my father's sisters, my aunt Opal (Hurley) Mann and aunt Mary Alice (Hurley) Lee. All have passed on now, but I think, for example, of how my grandmother made gorgeous quilts and mouthwatering dried-apple stack cake and yet was steely-eyed strong in the face of difficulties, of how my aunt Opal was a strong proponent of education, particularly for females in an era and region that made pursuing education extra difficult for them. All of these women quietly put forth an attitude that mixed encouragement and a no-tolerance view of giving up in such a way that around them I always thought, *Well, I guess I'll just do what I've set out to do, then.*

As for setting the novel in the 1920s, I'm drawn to historical settings for many reasons, a major one being how by looking at lives and attitudes in the past, we can often see, as in a mirror, more clearly than by just looking directly the attitudes and issues of our own times. Nearly a hundred years later, it is both startling and fascinating to see that issues and problems of the past keep coming back, not quite as resolved as we'd like them to be—such as feminism, fair treatment of workers, and more. As a child, I loved the Time-Life books that explored U.S. history decade by decade, and as an adult, I've made a point of collecting them. So of course I pulled *The Jazz Age: The 20s* (Time-Life Books, 1969) off my shelf as a start to researching the era. I was surprised to realize, which I hadn't as a child, that the book, though fascinating, entirely glosses over experiences of people in rural areas— not in the least glitzy, jazzy, or particularly "swell." I'm indebted to many resources, including an extensive review of newspaper articles of the era, such as the *Vinton County Courier,* for getting a glimpse into life at that time in rural Ohio, life that was as complex and nuanced then as it is now.

Another aspect of writing this novel that called me was the setting in the Appalachian portion of Ohio. Ohio is comprised of eighty-eight counties; thirty-two of them on the eastern and southern borders of Pennsylvania, West Virginia, and Kentucky are part of the vast range of the Appalachian region. My family of origin is from deep in the hills and hollers of Appalachia in eastern Kentucky. I'm a first-generation "Buckeye" (the nickname for an Ohioan), and proud of it, but in terms of my background, I've always felt that I stand with one foot firmly on midwestern soil and the other foot on Appalachian soil. In the household of my childhood, I understood that though we were in Ohio, we (certainly my parents) weren't *from* there, and we took fairly frequent trips to "go home," that is, to Morgan County, Kentucky, though my parents hadn't lived there since World War II. They were part of the diaspora that led many Appalachians to migrate north to Ohio and Michigan for industry and factory jobs that promised—and for a long time delivered—greater economic prosperity than the tobacco farming (in my family's case) of the generations before them or, for others, coal mining.

Yet I grew up on traditional Appalachian foods, faith traditions, music, storytelling (my children tease me that I am like my father; I can't resist "spinning a good, long yarn"), and an emphasis on family that was a mix both positive and challenging. In the prosperous suburban neighborhood of my childhood, Appalachians were often pejoratively called briar-hoppers or hillbillies, so though I was proud of my grandmother's crocheted lace and my other grandmother's quilt making, for example, I knew not to make too much of my Appalachian roots outside of the home.

But perhaps an aspect of being Appalachian is being a bit stubborn, and so I couldn't entirely comply with "not making too much of it." In my senior year of high school, I wrote a musical called *Just an Old Ballad,* based on the ballads I'd learned from my maternal grandmother. (I was hopeless at crocheting lace, so I think she was glad to teach me at least the ballads.) One, "Pearl Bryant," is quoted in *The Widows*. A kind theater teacher let me put it on and direct it. Though it wasn't particularly well received by the student population, the good news is that I cast a certain young man I'd taken quite a shine to in the lead role. Reader, I married him. (Albeit several years post high school.)

With Lily's story, I realized, I could, after all, make much of, or at least draw upon, my own Appalachian roots. Appalachia is a huge region; its dialect, customs, geography, and so on vary throughout the region. One can't just write about Ohio's Appalachia as if it's the exact same as Kentucky's or Georgia's, for example. So I have tried to be sensitive to regional differences. Currently, Appalachia is more in the news than it's been in a while and many folks, from outside and inside the region, seem to want to diagnose it as a whole. In this novel—and in future novels and in other writing—I endeavor to respectfully represent the specific region I'm writing about, which means a mix of celebrating its beauty while not glossing over its troubles, while showing the fictional individuals I've created as just that—individuals, not caricatures.

On a lighter note, I admit I had a great time incorporating everything from ballads to soup beans and sorghum while writing about the region. And my father, who began hunting at age four alongside his father, was tickled to be interviewed by his daughter about shotguns, revolvers, and rifles—any errors are mine, not his. He might also have shared a story or two with me—that he would never have owned up to when I was a child—about "just tasting" moonshine and somehow happening to be at a still. . . .

The specific setting of *The Widows*, Bronwyn County, is not one of the real-life counties of Ohio. My fictional Bronwyn County purposefully takes in the western Athens, eastern Vinton, and southern Hocking and Perry counties. This way, I can pull in the gorgeous Hocking Hills region—truly a stunning natural wonderland in our state—the rolling hill farms, and the coal-mining region. However, I try to stay as true as possible to the history and geography of the actual counties.

And what a diverse, fascinating history and geography these counties represent. In their history, as now, one can find sorrow and tragedy and yet hope, beauty, and opportunity. Included in the area is a microregion called Little Cities of Black Diamonds, referring to more than seventy coal-mining communities—some company-owned in their day—that had a heyday from the late nineteenth through the early twentieth centuries. Many of these communities have faded along with the coal industry of the area. Some, albeit smaller versions of their past, remain and I am grateful to the kind people who talked with me in towns such as Murray City, Shawnee, Nelsonville, and Buchtel.

I relied as well on the nonfiction works of other authors to research both the region and the incredibly complex history of coal mining and union organization in our country. These books include in particular: *Little Cities of Black Diamonds,* by Jeffrey T. Darbee and Nancy A. Recchie (Arcadia, 2009); *Coal Miners' Wives: Portraits of Endurance,* by Carol A. B. Giesen (University of Kentucky Press, 1995); *The Blair Mountain War: Battle of the Rednecks,* by G. T. Swain (Woodland Press, 2009; originally published by Mr. Swain in 1927); and *The Battle of Blair Mountain: The Story of America's Largest Labor Uprising,* by Robert Shogan (Basic Books, 2004).

In these notes, I have shared much of what inspired me to create my own characters, story lines, and settings.

What is purely factual, though, in my novel is the Battle for Blair Mountain—an uprising that I firmly believe should be part of our mainstream history education—and the uprisings and disasters that Marvena recites to inspire the coal miners to organize. To this day, New Straitsville's underground coal seams *still* burn—more than 130 years since the fires were set to sabotage the mines in protest of unfair wages and practices.

ACKNOWLEDGMENTS

Behind every story is another story: the writer's journey to create the story that readers, ultimately, hold in their hands—and, hopefully, their hearts. Thankfully, writers never travel alone. This writer humbly acknowledges that on this particular journey I've been accompanied, comforted, encouraged, guided, and even gently nudged by a merry band of fellow travelers.

First, thank you to the three who are always by my side: husband, David, and daughters, Katherine and Gwen. Not only did you read drafts and offer feedback, but also every time I asked, "Can I really do this?" you unhesitatingly answered, "Yes." An extra thank-you to David for accompanying me on research trips—and keeping me out of too much trouble.

On one such research trip, Brian Koscho, Marketing Director of Stuart's Opera House in Nelsonville, Ohio, gave us a tour that informed several key scenes in my variation of the town. Rose Ann Bobo, a volunteer at the Vinton County Historical and Genealogical Society, located in the beautifully restored Alice's House in McArthur, Ohio, provided invaluable assistance with reference materials, photographs, anecdotes, and tirelessly answering my questions or directing me to resources for those answers.

And on another trip, we happened upon the Murray City Train Depot and Coal Mining Museum, in Murray City, Ohio, where Richard Buchanan and Larry Mitchell spent several hours sitting with us by a cozy coal-fired stove, sharing not only the lovingly restored museum but also personal memories and, as my husband later described it, "memories of other people's memories." I am indebted to their generosity and hope I have thoughtfully and respectfully applied their insights into the mining life and the region's history.

As tempting as it is, writers can't just research a topic forever but must eventually start, well, writing.

When I first shared the idea behind this book with my amazing agent, Elisabeth Weed of The Book Group, she told me to trust it and promised she'd help me through the roughest parts of this journey. Thankfully, she kept that promise, and then some, and I am truly and eternally grateful.

I'm also so thankful for my amazing tribe of fellow writers, who are also among my dearest friends. Their thoughtful insights helped shape this novel and bring my cast of Bronwyn County characters to life; imperfections are mine alone: Heather Webber, Katrina Kittle, Kristina McBride, Martha Moody, Erin Flanagan, Jessica Strawser, and Ron Rollins, who gets extra-credit points for helping me create Mr. Abe Miller.

In addition to these great people in my community, I must thank several organizations. In 2014, I was selected as the John E. Nance Writer-in-Residence at the Thurber House (www.thurberhouse.org /nanceresidency) in Columbus, Ohio, based in part on an early opening to *The Widows*. My month-long stay and the residency stipend enabled me to focus solely on writing, writing, writing—and that meant finishing the first draft. In addition, my employer, the Antioch Writers' Workshop at University of Dayton (www.antiochwritersworkshop .com), where I am executive director, generously gave me that month off. In 2016, I was awarded an Ohio Arts Council Individual Excellence Award based in part on a later version of *The Widows*. The award enabled me to again have focused time to complete revisions of the novel. And thank you, too, to the Montgomery County (Ohio) Arts and Cultural District for a 2017 Artist Opportunity Grant that enabled me to create a robust website with extended background information about the time and place of *The Widows*.

I've already mentioned Elisabeth Weed, but believe me, she deserves a second thank-you (and then some) for her incredible insight and patience and for finding the just-right publishing home for this novel. I'm honored to work with her and the team at The Book Group as well as with Tiffany Yates Martin at FoxPrint Editorial. The wise input of these professionals showed me the way to fully realizing the heart of Lily and Marvena's story

The newest addition to my band of fellow travelers on the journey to bring *The Widows* into the world is the superb team at Minotaur Books. I'm honored to work with them and am especially grateful for Catherine Richards, my editor, who helped me deepen the mystery elements of *The Widows* and see a way forward for future projects. I can't help but add that I was nearly giddy when I realized during one of our conversations that we approach books the same way—not just as professionals but as *readers*.

And on the subject of readers: Thank *you*! Thank you for picking up this book, reading it, and entering Lily's and Marvena's world. The magic of creating a story is only complete when a reader experiences it, and you have my sincere gratitude for being part of the magic. I'd love to hear from you, so please do find me on my website, www.jessmontgomery author.com, or on Facebook @JessMontgomeryAuthor.